EARTHWALK

By

Donnajean Barton

DONNAJEAN BARTON

2007 (C) by Donnajean Barton

ISBN: 978-1-4303-2172-9
PUBLISHED BY LULU
www.lulu.com
North Carolina

Printed in the United States of America

Acknowledgments

Family and friends encouraged me to publish this story to show how things can go wrong in the probate of an estate. This necessitated writing a companion novel -- a continuation or second book, Earthwalk Two, as the story didn't occur over night.

Both novels were originally completed about seven years ago. I copyrighted Earthwalk in 2001. Even so, it wasn't until January 2007 when I made a New Year's resolution to publish the two novels. Therefore, thanks go to the continued urging of family and friends and a determination to fulfill the resolution.

I dedicate Earthwalk to the memory of our precious "Doe".

Special recognition goes to my dear sister and best friend Kathleen Payne Tomassi for reading/editing the text twice. Also heart-felt appreciation goes to my niece Sheryl Newland, former talk show host Len Sampson, high school and college classmate Wayne Carr, former newspaper writer Larry Breer, dear friend Sue MacMichael and very close friend Lydia Johnson of the Yakama and Cayuse tribes-- all for their editing and support.

Still, should any errors remain, I take responsibility and apologize and request that the reader pay greater attention to the story. Once I became acquainted with this litigation, I knew I had to write about it. In fact, I do believe I was put on this earth to tell this story. God has granted me many accomplishments in my own earthwalk, but I consider this project to be my greatest.

Finally, I give loving thanks to my husband Earl for assistance in the final formatting of this novel and escorting me to Scotland to study the brogue for one of the characters.

Donnajean Barton

Prologue

This story is about Dorian Barnes "Rock" Carper of Caucasian and Cherokee persuasion. As the only surviving heir, Rock attempts to probate his uncle's sizeable estate.

He is anxious for swift justice so he can move on with his life. However, the kind of justice accorded him became swift in other ways, unexpected ways -- as far reaching as being accused of being D. B. Cooper. Following trial, he is forced to become his own attorney.

Chapter One

Heading down the long stretch of Queen Anne hill, a suburb of Seattle, Washington, Rock Carper hummed to western music coming from the radio of his bright red Firebird 500. In an attempt to adjust the rearview mirror, he spotted a blue Corvette narrowing their distance. It stayed on his tail for a few seconds, until Rock played his brakes. This caused his playboy calendar to fall on the floor. He heard the Corvette's brakes screech, then watched it swerve and pick up speed. The occupant gestured with a stiff finger as he held parallel, then forged ahead.

Rock mused to himself, determined to not let this get the better of him. Although, the incident was certainly emblematic of the antics of some men -- always in a hurry to go. To get. To take. Rock's roots gave him a solid value system. He believed his sense of fairness and honor was as good as anyone.

Besides he had more important matters to think about than this isolated incident. Today Rock was looking forward to the end of a seven year litigation concerning the probate of his uncle's estate. Coming to mind was a phrase his Cherokee mother taught him: *"Gv ge yu a, heh yu,"* [I love you, hey you] phraseology he liked the sounds of when he was on top of the totem pole.

Continuing southward toward the Ballard Bridge, Rock noticed that a silvery frost tinged everything. It was winter, 1990, the season of the Snow Moon. The window was rolled down enough to smell the crisp air and imagine the taste of saltwater from Puget Sound. His tires hummed across the steel grating of the Ballard bridge.

He exhaled a hearty sigh. Today, his new attorney would aid him during a Clamton County Superior Court hearing in recovering the Carper mansion. Rock used to refer to it as his mighty fine tipi. Someday he wanted to convert it into a museum and exhibit artwork from coastal tribes. His attorney had aided him in overcoming former legal obstacles, so there was no reason to believe anything could go wrong with his plans.

Admittedly, he was partial to the mansion because it symbolized family, going back two generations. He recalled fondly, spending much time there with Aunt Nell and Uncle John, who took care of him like a son when his folks traveled out of town, which was often. Nell stuffed him full of snicker-doodles. John scolded her for ruining Rock's dinner.

When he was eighteen, after his dad died, and Rock had finally grown into his size thirteen shoes, Uncle John decided Rock was capable of helping him remodel the basement into two offices, one for each of them. Too, John hired him as boat engineer on the *Lyda*, a large cannery tender, which added great delight and experience to his life.

Rock reached over and turned off the radio so he could better concentrate on his thoughts. The mansion was supposed to be his when Uncle John died in the early 70's. Although, he couldn't take possession until Nell no longer wished to live in the house, or when she died. This was all set out in terms of John's

1967 will. Unfortunately, that will disappeared at John's death in 1972. Rock was about twenty-two when that happened.

Still immersed in thought, he maneuvered to pass a car. When he learned Nell was probating John's estate with an earlier will, a 1952 will, he visited Nell's attorney, Ralph Houston, to tell him about John's '67 will. A logical decision because Houston was also Rock's attorney on other matters. Houston told him it didn't matter how many wills John left behind. That Nell wasn't using a will, since she and John had a community property agreement. This agreement was news to Rock. However, Houston said he'd keep him appraised of any changes. Rock relied on this.

Steering the Firebird with a knee, Rock glanced in the mirror again. The interior of the car wasn't quite high enough and tended to mess his hair. Winter hair, oily like bear grease and thick like that of a hibernating bear, only shiny and black as a raven, like his character -- written in nature. He smoothed back the top, then pushed the sides into a ducktail. A minor adjustment of the mirror caused his eagle feather hanging from it to sway. The feather, a good-luck charm for safe travel, was also a sign of justice, wisdom and power.

He resumed driving with one hand. Still thinking about Nell. After John's death, she said she'd honor John's testamentary wishes at her death. In fact, she did this in drawing up her own will. But, when she died in 1983 of Alzheimer's disease, her relatives brought forth yet another will prepared by Houston, excluding Rock entirely.

It wasn't until after Nell's death that Rock hired a Seattle attorney to investigate. The attorney discovered court records, showing that Nell and attorney Houston cunningly misused the community property agreement as a means to transfer John's separate property, intended for Rock, into her name. Then Nell repudiated the agreement. Now that was weird. "*Why repudiate an agreement that Houston said overruled any will? Why repudiate an agreement that was supposed to automatically convert separate property to community? Why repudiate it?*" Rock creased his brow. He didn't know. That's why he hired attorneys. All he knew for certain was that Nell and Houston ended up using a will – the wrong will. It wasn't the '67 will that Rock told Houston about.

After braking to a stop at an intersection, he poured a mug of coffee from his thermos. He sat there inhaling the earthy aroma, then slowly sipped, while wondering how a sweet, plump, jolly, religious person like Nell could be so deceptive? Better yet, how could he have been so taken in by her? And by her relatives? They were the Bensons -- leaching parasites who stole what was meant to be his birthright.

Finally, the light turned green enabling him to ease forward onto Dravus Street and up the steep hillside of the Magnolia district. There was still a ways to go in reaching his destination. He recalled that Nell never took the Carper mansion out of John's name before her death. It was inconceivable why she did this, taking only part of John's separate property rather than all of it. It didn't make sense. Especially, since Nell and Houston were perfectly aware of what they were doing during the probate of John's estate. Maybe guilt stopped her from taking all of John's separate assets.

His thoughts would have to come out at the hearing today. Rock swallowed more coffee. Nell and Houston caused a legal nightmare and years of delay. Their actions put him through the judicial mill with attorneys, hearings, depositions, one trial and an appeal. To an outsider this may appear as if he had experience in legal matters. Far from it. He was a client who turned his affairs over to attorneys, paid them well and expected honest representation.

Trusting Nell was another matter. Were she alive now, he wouldn't trust her facing him with his eyes wide open, even if she did leave the Carper mansion deed in John's name. And, his grudge against Houston hadn't eased his feelings either. Houston was an old fart, still working and lying about his involvement in the Carper estates to protect his conniving legal ass.

The case was confusing. Rock didn't know why he had to go through more litigation, since the Carper mansion was in John's sole name and Rock was John's only survivor, an issue Rock emphasized repeatedly to his attorney. The attorney told him not to worry. After today, it would all be behind him.

If his dad were here, things would be different. Being an educated Caucasian businessman married to Leucojum, a Cherokee woman, gave him insight and he would have kept all parties in line. Well that wasn't possible now.

Rock recalled his dad's dying words as being particularly influenced by Leucojum. The words raced through his head: *"You're as rustic as winter, as gullible as an autumn leaf in a strong wind and as compassionate as summer. All three will get you into trouble."* At the time, Rock, being admittedly stubborn, simply couldn't agree. Now, he wondered, but was still convinced of one thing -- he might not be educated like attorneys, but he considered himself streetwise.

He smiled, drained the last of his coffee and set the mug in a holder on the dashboard. Reaching under his coat, he felt for his small good-luck pin fastened to his suit lapel, making certain it was secure. The pin depicted the American flag, a symbol of truth and honor, virtues important to him. Finally, he accelerated up the hill and turned right to Sheryl's house. Ironic. Sheryl, his estranged wife, would be one of his witnesses today.

*   *   *

Rock parked in the driveway, shoved the playboy calendar under the passenger seat, then turned to stare at Sheryl's brick tudor with a 'SOLD' sign on the lawn. The sign put finality to them having lived there for some eighteen years, until they separated. Now, she was in the process of returning to rural Quamas on Chenowah Island, a 20-mile-long stretch of land and one of the largest of a chain of islands lodged between Puget Sound and the Straits of Juan de Fuca. He was born and raised in Quamas not too far from the Carper mansion. And Quamas was where his mom and Sheryl's folks still lived.

"Tally-ho." She waved and came running from the porch.

This was the first time he had seen her in months. She was picturesque in her navy suit and flowing auburn hair. Stepping out to open her door, his breath blew out in wisp-like spirits in the cold air. "Slow up or you'll slip."

Rock spoke in a low voice, in his usual slow manner. A fall could set her off which, heaven forbid, he didn't need right now. His on-going litigation had put her into unpredictable moods. Sheryl didn't share his passion for justice. Divorce was about the only subject they agreed on, having stepped off the same wavelength year's ago. He emitted a grin and walked around to open the passenger door. "Thanks for coming with me, Sheryl."

"Ye caught me in a weak moment laddie." Her blue eyes focused on him, while speaking in a self-stylized corruption of Irish from her father and Scottish from her mum.

7

"Sheryl, you've lived in America long enough . . ." He stopped himself, finding it unwise to criticize. She got further along in classes at the University of Washington than he did, and probably would have graduated had English not been so difficult. She could pronounce 'h' words some of the time, but there were numerous expressions and words she especially clung to such as oot for out, doon for down, a'boot for about, bluidy for bloody and 'ave for have. He was used to it. And, more immediate, he wanted a congenial relationship, especially since he might need her as a witness today.

She put one foot in the car, then gripped the door frame in hesitation. "If my folks hadnae moved from Glasgow to Quamas, ye and I never would o' met and fallen in love doon in the warehouse o' Uncle John's fish cannery."

This set Rock's mind into a flashback.

*   *   *

Rock's mind returned to the time he first set eyes on Sheryl. Rumors circulated that she was new in town and needed work to defray college expenses in the fall. He asked Uncle John to hire her as a stapler in the Carper Cannery warehouse, a standup job.

Arriving home from a salmon run one day, Rock loitered at the warehouse entrance, near Sheryl's workstation and struck a conversation with a man, who happened by. It was only for the purpose of attracting Sheryl's attention, while pretending he didn't know she existed.

A local town drunk, on the wagon because he had a wife and two daughters to support, was her assistant. Uncle John probably put the man with Sheryl to straighten out his ways. Her reputation was straight-laced, no nonsense, yet witty, innocent and sincere.

The assistant would open a new box and slide it over the long arm of the stapler. Once that box hit the stapler, Sheryl pressed on a lever with her right foot and the machine spit staples like a machine gun until she released the pressure. She could move a box through the machine quickly. All the while, she talked to her assistant and stole glances at Rock.

Meanwhile, Rock found her impressive -- small nose, dimpled chin, auburn hair draped halfway down her back, freckles and a svelte figure that protruded in the right places. She was a sight to remember, because at first sight he stepped backwards and fell off the pier into Squawk Bay. Nothing quite like attracting Sheryl's attention and everyone along with her. It wasn't that she was wearing tight work clothes. Nothing could have hidden her assets. Admittedly, he was a horny teen back then.

Rock would have given anything to take the town drunk's place. He also thought Uncle John was nuts for that arrangement. Sheryl was enough to drive the drunk to drink.

When he found out from Uncle John that Sheryl was his age, he believed this was the girl for him. Several times, he asked her out; attend a movie. Her rejections were diplomatic and didn't deter him, because her stares told him she was as fascinated with him as he in her. Recalling with fondness one particular morning on his way to the *Lyda* for a trip to Point Roberts, he stopped at her machine and asked for a date upon his return. She accepted.

That night, after meeting her folks, they drove in the family car. They took in a movie, then went straight home. No holding hands. No kissing.

However, the suspense of courtship etiquette was gut wrenching.

Eventually, Rock was able to afford a two-door, navy Ford with white sidewalls. Rather small, but affordable. His summer job provided enough money to make a sizeable down payment and small monthly installments.

One rainy evening, Rock hurried into dress slacks, casual shirt and western boots. He splashed on cologne, grabbed his keys and headed for Sheryl's to show off his new car. They drove all over the Island.

When the rain lifted, they went for a walk down some narrow path and commented on the view. Leaves shone clean under bright moonlight. A mist rolled in from the sea. He remembered standing behind, admiring her auburn hair pinned off her neck. Her pink dress was elasticized at the shoulders; flared at the hem. Even her sandals were pink. He decided to focus on the scenery before he fell over the hillside.

Another evening, they visited Uncle John's warehouse. That time of year the warehouse was warm and dry. One-pound tins of canned salmon, taken hot from the steam-pressure cookers in the afternoon, would be stacked on cooling racks. It took overnight for the heat to dissipate, providing warmth. He had a key. He even parked the Ford inside. No one would know they were there.

In retrospect, he drove down the gravel road toward the warehouse. Sheryl took notice. "Why we goin' here?"

"Privacy. We can talk."

Without objecting, she crossed her arms as if wondering what he wanted to talk about.

Once the Ford was inside and the warehouse locked again, Rock remained behind the wheel. Leaving his door open, he rested an arm across the seat behind her head.

She leaned her head back and stared straight ahead. He killed the engine and lights. The warehouse wasn't entirely dark. There were large, rectangular windows located in the north and the northeast walls at the far end. Outdoor lights around the building provided more light. "Do you enjoy stapling boxes?"

"Ay. Better than slimmin' salmon. The work is dry."

They looked in the direction of the staple machine a few feet from Sheryl's side of the car. The rain pelted against the tin roof high above. A strong wind howled spasmodically outside. "It's dry in here." They seemed restless, until Rock got an idea. "Want to staple boxes?"

"Rock. I'm dressed in finery." She laughed, punching him in the arm.

"Come on. Teach me how to staple." Before long the machine was running under one lonely light bulb, and Sheryl was giggling, while guiding Rock's big hands, holding a cardboard box, through the machine. "Hey. Not bad for my first time. Now, let me watch you again."

Sheryl took over as Rock stepped down from the machine platform. "I wish the crew could see you now. Most beautiful stapler in the world." From behind, he placed his hands on her hips. She twisted to face him, then plopped a box over his head, shoved him away and ran for the car. He plopped down in the midst of boxes, laughing. "I'll get you for this."

With those words, she pulled her door closed and locked it, still giggling. She was about to close his door, but he was too quick. He gave her a devilish look, while climbing behind the wheel, which led her to cower into the far corner, cross her arms and pull her legs under into a curled position.

Brushing his hair back with his hands, he whooped, grinned and

9

motioned in his Native sign language by moving a right fist in a small circle on his forehead. Before she could ask, he told her the meaning. "My brain's in a whirl." Sheryl was so fascinated in this. He spent the next half-hour, teaching her hand signs.

"Ay." Sheryl exhaled, excitedly. "We can talk at each other when apart and no one a'boot will know what we're sayin'."

He agreed, reaching over to hold her chin in his direction. They stared into each other's eyes. She smelled of sweet flowers. He ran a thumb down the dimple in her chin, then kissed her. She responded. Her lips were warm. He tried another kiss. And, another. The steering wheel jammed into him when he sought to embrace her. "I don't suppose you could turn around and lean into my arms?"

Without saying a word, she turned around and slowly melted into his arms, like he was a cocoon. Her legs curled on the seat facing the opposite door. Her head was against his forehead. Her breasts were resting on his chest like a basket of fruit, ripe and . . . *"Oh, God, this was love,"* he thought. This had to be love, holding all this so close. He buried his nose in her hair, her neck. Kissed an earlobe, lips and shoulders. His right hand roamed from her hip, up her waist, up an arm and across her back. Right then and there, her acceptance netted him in for life. "Oh, Sheryl. I love you."

"I think I love ye too." She gasped. Her arms tightened around his neck.

"I intend to marry you, if you'll have me." Rock was under a spell he didn't want to shake. He embraced her again.

"What a'boot college?"

She was more important to him than college. But, he'd follow her anywhere. "We can still go to college. We'll be engaged. I'll try to join a fraternity near your sorority. My legacy is to join a fraternity like my dad and uncle. Maybe you could join a sorority up there on Greek Row."

"A serious commitment, yer suggestin'."

"Yes. I want you to be mine forever. Be my friend for all seasons. Do you have these same feelings for me?"

Sheryl pulled his head down to meet hers. "Ay. I do."

*　*　*

The sweet scent of Sheryl standing between him and the Firebird unwrapped the memory of how their relationship began.

Sighing, he lingered with the passenger door open. Their love became an addiction. Plunged a magic arrow through his heart and, eventually resulted in an elopement, ending two years of college for him. This upset the Carpers who had wanted family marriages to take place in the Carper mansion, and . . .

She interrupted his contemplation. "On second thought I would o' been better off no meetin' any o' ye Carpers."

This remark snapped him to attention. "Sheryl, get in." He gestured and gnashed teeth at her.

"Oh well. Tis water under the Aurora Bridge." She wrinkled her small nose, pursed her lips and threw him a platonic kiss, then gathered her woolly coat around shapely hips and legs to buckle in. "And, ye gave me a fine son. But, ye know I'm close ta my folks. I feel more comfort bein' with them than with most Americans. So I keep my brogue."

How could he blame her? He came across as two different people

10

because of his cultural upbringing. Around those he loved and those who accepted him, he was himself. Native American. He preferred 'Amerindian'. In the presence of strangers, or Caucasians, he was like them.

Rock nodded and shut the door. He strode around to his side thinking of Sheryl's situation. She was an only child and never cut the apron strings. Now that they were separated and their son was in the Army, the strings to her parents were even shorter. It was only natural for her to keep the brogue.

By the time he clamped his seat belt, Sheryl carried his thought in another direction. "I've lived 'ere long enough ta know the attorneys could 'o picked a better month than January ta ferry over ta Quamas fer courtroom busyness."

"I don't need any more delays." He lingered a moment to study her. Her presence was indicative of a mood. A dab of cosmetics meant she woke up on the right side of the bed. Well, the makeup was on. She smelled honey sweet, another good sign. The attire was dressy, yet conservative, meaning business. "I see a stunning lady this morning."

She smiled. "Ay, navy colors. Same as ye. I figured ye'd be wearin' yer usual court clothes."

"Fancy threads right down to the polished oxfords." Rock switched on the radio in hopes of discouraging Sheryl from talking too much, and made a U-turn to head for the ferry terminal.

"I see ye still 'ave an eagle's feather hangin' from yer mirror."

"Won't see me without it. Brings safe travel, you know."

"Oot and away with ye. Yer needin' the luck o' the Irish, the way this litigation is hangin' on."

"This is the last time I set foot in the Clamton County Courthouse. After today, you can push ahead with the divorce and we'll move on with our lives." He knew the only reason Sheryl delayed divorce action was because Rock's attorney Nelson Anders believed the divorce wouldn't give a good impression and felt it best to wait until the conclusion of the hearing.

Sheryl turned off the radio and loosened her seat belt to twist in his direction. "Taday yer litigation is over? Accordin' ta whom?"

"Nelson Anders."

"Efter seven years o' fightin' over yer Uncle John's estate, I 'ope so. What are ye goin' fer taday?" She moved her blue purse to the floor beside her matching heels.

"A hearing to enter new evidence." He explained the details.

"I remember now. Do ye know yet if I'll have ta testify?"

"No. At least you're available if needed."

"Who else is comin'?"

"You'll meet two witnesses and a document specialist, who will verify my new evidence." Stopping for a red light, Rock adjusted the visor to shade his eyes from the morning sun.

"Ay, then ye can probate under the right will."

"That's about it, aside from Anders revealing misconduct by my aunt and her attorney Houston." Rock focused on the road as he talked.

"Oou. Anders is goin' ta expose Ralph Houston? One attorney exposin' another attorney? Get on with ye."

"Afraid so." Rock inched along in slow moving traffic. "Anders has no choice. He said if I can prove my new evidence showing fraud was committed in the original probate of John's estate, then I can reopen probate and proceed under the right will."

"Well, exposin' yer aunt, God rest her soul, I can see, but Houston? An old-time Quamas attorney? Ye're dreamin' dearie. If yer attorney has the nerve ta expose Houston, it'll restore my faith in the legal profession. Is 'e comin'?"

"I'm sure he is." Rock glanced in the rearview and flicked the hand signal to turn into the terminal.

"T'would be odd if 'e dinnae come. I cannae imagine Anders exposin' Houston behind his back."

There was no doubt in Rock's mind. Anders would have to step on some legal toes.

* * *

Inside the upper deck of the *Palouse* ferry, in the coffee bar, Rock stretched and smoothed his hair with a hand stroke. He peered out the window. Mount Rainier to the south and the Olympics to the west were beautifully visible above a haze of ground fog, the hue of old pewter.

After draping their coats over a bench and giving Sheryl money for their breakfast, Rock listened to the pistons purr. He recalled a time when the whistle got stuck and blew for ten minutes until someone stuffed a jacket in the horn.

He preferred taking the ferry rather than driving the clogged freeway, a choice available to him since a small part of Chenowah Island was connected to the mainland of Clamton County.

"Ye want jelly tots?"

"Maple bar. Coffee."

While she stood in line, he found a table and looked around. Passengers were either procuring food in a cafeteria line or eating at a table. He wasn't interested in the conversations going on about him, but nodded at a few friendly faces. Horns blared in the background. Breakfast aromas permeated the room.

After Sheryl returned with their tray of food, they ate in silence. Rock shared a section of the *Post-Intelligencer* newspaper, which happened to be on the table.

Finally Sheryl rumpled the paper closed. "I'm finished. Tell me. Who's the judge taday?"

"Don't know yet. It can't be Judge Randell. He's retired." Rock drank the last of his coffee and set his cup in the saucer.

"Good. Ye walked oot on him at the 1984 trial. Remember?" Sheryl stacked her dishes on the tray alongside Rock's.

"Yeah, not too smart. But, I didn't like losing. And, I wouldn't have lost if Ralph Houston had told the judge the truth."

"I know. I couldnae believe it when Houston lied in court."

Rock found it hard to believe too. He trusted Houston because he was his attorney on other matters at the time. "That lying fart caused my delay. His denial caused me to lose. Judge Randell wouldn't let me reopen Uncle John's probate for any reason." The thought of it began to rile Rock.

"Judge Randell believed an attorney over ye. Well, ye're bent on gettin' justice. At least ye have the appellate court behind ye with yer new evidence. Maybe taday ye'll get justice. If there's justice fer a mixed breed."

Rock rose and collected their coats, sloughing off Sheryl's last comment.

He believed the facts of his case overruled any racial issue, except for Sheryl. Sometimes, he wondered why she loved him. As soon as they married she tried to bury the Cherokee in him. "Come on. Put your coat on and let's head for the car. We're almost there."

*   *   *

The *Palouse* ferry went as far north as British Columbia. But, Rock and Sheryl disembarked near Arrow Head Point, located on the north end of Chenowah Island. As they inched forward in the lineup of cars, Rock watched the swooping seagulls; always a fascination. They were smart beggars, screeching for a handout. Some were perched on pilings out of the reach of slapping waves and seaweed.

When given the signal, Rock headed over the ramp and onto the road, passing a boardwalk of art galleries, shops, a café and pub. It wouldn't be long until they were in Quamas. He drove through timber country, then passed the Tribal House, flanked by totem poles and a large sign, which proclaimed this to be the Chenowah Indian Reservation, where old ceremonies were carried on and council fires still lit.

Beyond this were a picturesque vineyard and spacious farmlands, fringed in Scotch broom and streams. Higher hills in the distance were dotted with modern homes. When the season was ripe, those fields would bloom with cabbage, cauliflower and alfalfa. While in junior high school, his dad had him working at odd jobs in fields like these. Rock didn't particularly care for any of it. He wanted to work in the cannery.

Rock snaked around a bend in the road. His dad said better work would come with age. He said Rock would change jobs often in his lifetime. *"That's the way it is in today's society."*

Then in the late '60's just before high school graduation, he wanted to join some branch of the armed service, because his dad, Jack, had died and Rock needed to get away.

Rock swerved to miss a chuckhole in the road, then thought about the time when he read where the US Marines had landed on the shores of the Dominican Republic, as fighting persisted between rebels and the Dominican army. But, because of social unrest and riots on the home front against Vietnam and our troops fighting the wars of others, and Lyndon B. Johnson's handling of the war, the Carper men, who saw enough killing, were against it. He felt badly not being able to fight for his country. The Carper elders told him to help the elderly. Again, they placed pressure on him that he was the only Carper to carry on the legacy.

Yet, before that, it just occurred to him, whenever they noticed he was becoming interested in some of the Quamas girls, they'd ship him off to visit some coastal tribe to learn about totem pole crafts. Or, they'd send him to Tahlequah, Oklahoma square dab in his Cherokee country. It was the second largest tribe in America, where he visited his Cherokee uncle's family . . . an uncle who taught him much about his heritage. Sometimes he thought his folks were hoping he'd find a Native bride as his dad did. Oh, he found interests in the girls there too, but wasn't ready to settle down.

His Cherokee uncle taught him all about engines, which eventually prepared him for becoming boat engineer on the *Lyda*. That he enjoyed doing.

13

Of course, he first learned to work in the cannery pitching salmon onto a conveyor belt, a messy, sweaty job.

His right hand fiddled with radio stations, running through a noisy bundle of rock, rap and violin glissandos. Because of receiving more static than music, he clicked it off and stole a quick glance at Sheryl. "Where are your rings? Remember, we can't let the opposition think we aren't getting along."

She held up her right hand and then proceeded to switch them to the left.

Rock watched, recalling how the Carpers liked her and thought their marriage would bring many Carper offspring. However, it wasn't in their destiny. They lost their first born in the delivery room. The doctor sent them home in a saddened state.

Then Sheryl had miscarriages before their son's birth. Raising him and taking care of other children as a nanny was the best she could do. That was her philanthropy along with the Christmas stockings for Headstart and the annual Heart Drive. Rock defended her to the family. None of the Carpers were a very prolific bunch bringing kids into the world. So, they shouldn't be expected to make up for the inabilities of other family members.

"How do ye like bein' a Ballard bachelor since our separation an' all?" Sheryl pulled down the overhead mirror, then braced herself as Rock swerved around a bend in the road. His playboy calendar slid forward. "What's this? Got sex on yer mind, ye 'ave."

Rock grabbed it away and stuffed it under his seat. "I'm lonely, if you must know." Being around Sheryl, he noticed the loneliness even more. Their breakup left him drained, unfulfilled and heartbroken. Her physical presence didn't help matters. "Just don't start on me. I'm not knocking ass at the moment. I sure as hell want to, but my litigation has me tied in knots." Rock scoffed. His peripheral vision took in Sheryl, who suddenly stopped dabbing powder over the freckles on her face.

"Yer disgustin'." Then she chuckled and finished powdering. "Well, tis none of my business. I donnae mean ta heckle ye, but yer money is wasted on attorneys so they can throw parties and buy yachts." She smudged a dab of powder below each eyebrow.

He chuckled a little too as he drove past towering Douglas firs and other trees native to the area. The trees with bare branches reminded him of deer antlers and of the set he had hanging in his room at his mom's house. Above the trees, he noticed rays of sunlight filtering through the fog. He related to the fog in a way. At least, that's how he felt upon first rising in the morning. Sometimes, it took either the sun or a lot of coffee for him to rise and shine.

Rock needed to focus on Sheryl's comments. She wanted to know about his apartment. "I'm crammed into a one bedroom, one bath unit. Rather plain. Furnishings are synchronized with low rent. The telephone cord is long. Allows me to drag the phone all over the apartment. And, Ballard isn't a bad neighborhood. Apartment living is okay. I'll adjust. Don't worry about me."

"I donnae worry a'boot ye per se. It's yer litigation and the money it's costin'." She gestured, waving a little brush in the air.

"Careful with that." Rock held up a hand in self-defense.

"Just my mascara. Anyway, justice is fer the rich. Yer damn case has been hard on us. Payin' $25,000 ta Anders fer one appeal. Now, that ticked me." With a little finger, she ran lipstick to the corners of a forced smile.

"Well, we won." He looked out the window at the black and white dairy cows in a field. "Let's forget the past." She was starting to grate on his nerves.

"Get on with ye. That's what attorneys do. Rake up the past."

"That part can't be helped."

"And, they screw it over." She was working into a fuss, talking faster, the closer they came to the courthouse. "Attorneys are a bunch of pickaninnies. Pick, pick, pick."

"Sheryl, we're almost there." He flicked a hand at the neon-lit community of motels, restaurants, service stations and stores.

"Even though I've lived 'ere a while, I consider this ta be yer town, where ye grew up. Hasnae changed much. Do ye miss it?"

"Not really. The people have changed. My friends from the past moved away to better opportunities than fishing, farming and small-time merchandising." It used to be a community where everyone knew each other and the names of their pets.

Nearing the Clamton County Courthouse, Rock expressed a request. "Look, if you take the stand, just tell the truth. That's all we've got going for us. My new evidence and the truth." He reached under the seat for his antacid bottle, flipped the lid with a thumb and put a bunch of tablets in his suit jacket pocket.

"Ye needna worry a'boot me tellin' the truth. My guide is Keats who wrote that beauty is truth and truth beauty. He said this is all ye need ta know on earth. And, Mark Twain said if ye tell the truth ye donnae 'ave ta remember what ye said."

"Let's hope our judge has read Keats and Twain." Rock laughed. He also thought of his mom Leucojum's words, told to him while growing to adulthood: *"Be an arrow with feathers. An arrow with feathers flies straight."* Finally, he could see the courthouse ahead, just off Main Street -- an uninspiring square, two-story building with Doric columns and wide marble steps.

Chapter Two

After Rock angled his Firebird into a parking spot located behind the courthouse, he and Sheryl walked through the back entrance. Rock was anxious to see his other witnesses and a rewarding outcome to today's hearing.

"Good morning, Mr. Carper." A tall, pudgy man with some official capacity greeted Rock in the lobby. "We're running behind schedule. All the attorneys are in private chambers, conferring with a judge. You wait here."

"Thank you." Rock smiled politely. For some reason, Cherokee words he learned from his mom crept into mind. *Wado. Galieliga*, meaning "thank you" or "I'm grateful". He also learned a little of the Chenowah language used by his former friends in Quamas. But, like him, they had assimilated into the larger community and communicated mostly in English.

He and Sheryl roamed in the lobby when his witnesses approached. Rock, fighting an edgy feeling, nodded at them. He looked at his turquoise watch: 10:15. "The hearing was supposed to start at ten. My document specialist hasn't arrived. Something is wrong. Oh, pardon me, this is my wife Sheryl. Sheryl these are my witnesses. Jasper Fulbright, a Quamas attorney, and his secretary Mrs. Willard."

Jasper was extremely fit for fifty. His hair was brown except for grayish sideburns. Nice even teeth, friendly eyes, red-cheeked. His voice and handshake were solid. Mrs. Willard, rather matronly, with crinkle lines around her eyes, spoke softly.

Rock glanced at Sheryl. "They are the ones who discovered my new evidence. Because of their discovery, I won my appeal."

While Sheryl exchanged pleasantries, Rock spotted his attorney Nelson Anders entering the area in front of the other attorneys. Nelson headed straight for Rock's group: "Everyone is to go home except Rock."

Rock looked down at him. Anders, about fifty-five years, gave the impression of an Ivy Leaguer in an expensive gray pinstripe. His brown hair was well oiled. He had a handsome face with sharp eyes. It was an awkward moment. So unexpected.

Rock shifted his eyes to the vein-marbled floor, while holding his coat in crossed arms. Of course, he'd never met Anders in a courthouse before. Their communication had always been in Anders' office or by phone. Anders told him appeals attorneys usually don't perform in a courtroom. They do behind-the-scene research. But, Anders expressed an interest in acting as a trial attorney, since he had such a strong feeling for this case. From their contacts, Rock knew Anders was smooth and resented being challenged, although at this moment Rock couldn't help himself. "Is this a joke?"

"No joke." Anders walked toward the stairs, then spoke over a shoulder. "The judge wants to consider your new evidence in his own way."

"What in the hell is his way?"

If Anders knew, he wasn't talking. Rock shrugged at his witnesses and spoke loudly to Anders' backside. "I paid hard-earned money for this day. My wife came with me so she stays." He took Sheryl's arm, while climbing the winding stairs and wondering about this change in plans. It was so sudden, he forgot to ask Anders who the judge would be.

* * *

Sheryl draped her coat over a front-row bench inside Courtroom Two. Rock gave her his coat and looked around. The room hadn't changed: florescent lighting, volumes of mustard-brown law books lining high shelves flanking two walls. He sat alongside Sheryl and watched a female docket clerk move into a raised cubicle to the left front of the room. The witness box abutted the judge's bench to the right, near the American flag. A court reporter was setting up her equipment in a well between the judge's bench and the witness box. Also, there were two mahogany counsel tables up front for the attorneys.

His eyes landed on Anders, who opened his briefcase on the table to the right. It gnawed at him that Anders wasn't offering any explanation. Rock knew Anders was one of the most highly-respected attorneys in Seattle. His talk was impressive. Used fancy words like bequeath, inadvertently, notwithstanding and other expressions that convinced Rock he had one sharp attorney.

Hoping for answers, Rock stepped forward. "What are we here for if there isn't going to be an evidence hearing?"

Anders opened his briefcase. "Now calm down. We're still having a hearing." He turned to nod hello to Sheryl, as he arranged papers in little piles. Ginger Haley, another attorney from Anders' law firm, moved in to assist him.

Haley, a skinny flat-chested, five-foot-two lady with Pekinese eyes and pushed in nose, was a little younger than Rock's forty years. She shed her floor-length coat, revealing a maxi-length skirt, fuzzy sweater, neck scarf and loafers, and carried on as if oblivious to this conversation. Rock really didn't expect anything from Haley because he didn't know her well. He didn't even know why she was here.

"I thought this was the final hearing." Rock raised his voice. Stomach acid oozed into his throat. "I was counting on an evidentiary hearing. To enter and prove my new evidence so I can probate John's estate under the right will. We can't do it without my witnesses. Maybe I'm missing something here. How can this be the last hearing when you let my witnesses go?"

Anders ignored Rock's questions, which only increased his curiosity and apprehension. He shifted his weight. Waiting.

Sheryl caught Rock's attention and motioned with the flicker of an index finger for him to return to her, which he did. "Who's this comin'?"

Rock had no idea. She was walking in their direction.

* * *

Puzzled, Rock watched a heavyset, middle-aged lady thread her way across the courtroom carpeting toward Anders. After draping her coat alongside the Carpers, she and Anders greeted each other with familiarity. She was dressed in a pleated skirt, blouse, blazer, dark nylons and patent-leather flats.

Ginger Haley swung around to introduce the lady. "She's a member of our team. Does detective work. We felt she should be here, because there's strength in numbers."

17

Rock tried to smile. Internally, he had to agree with this philosophy, comparable to his belief that many poles make for a stronger tipi. While Anders, Haley and the detective busied themselves with court matters, he whispered to Sheryl. "If they're playing the numbers game, why in hell did they let my witnesses go?" He crossed one leg over the other.

"Ay, and what's it goin' ta cost ye fer this little number's game?" She shielded her whispers as Rock was doing. "What grunt work 'as the detective done fer ye? These lasses hardly look professional enough ta make a difference. I say, that frizzy hairdo on the detective back fired and Ginger's 'air 'as the Biblical look."

"What bothers me is that I didn't hire or request them." Rock sighed. "Sorry, you had to come for this. I apologize."

"They must o' gotten up a wee bit early ta get 'ere."

"Or they came yesterday. Or they took the freeway." As a client, he wanted answers without causing problems, but a commotion at the courtroom entrance drew Rock's attention.

*   *   *

A loud, guttural noise penetrated the low hum of activity from those already in the courtroom. Rock recognized the strange irritating utterance as coming from one particular person. He twisted on the bench to be sure. "Geez. Here comes my opposition, Marvin Benson."

Sheryl quickly glanced, then turned to Rock. "I'm rememberin' when 'e used ta be dashin'."

"He's sagging now." Rock watched with agitation and less envy of a man who used to be big chested, slim-hipped and tall until age set in. He was somewhere in his sixties. Marvin moved in with an arthritic limp wearing a camelhair blazer, white shirt, tie and gray pants. His hair and mustache were white. Everything about him was big. Big feet, hands, eyes, lips. His cough.

As soon as their eyes met, Rock cocked his head acknowledging recognition, nothing more. His insides crawled for doing that much. In retrospect, he hardly knew the Bensons until several years before Nell died in '83. It was like they clambered out of the woodwork. From the very beginning, Marvin was a braggart, jamming it down Rock's throat of how intelligent he was, being a college graduate and wrestling champion. Rock was remembering that Marvin possessed a devious nature. Grabbed hold of everything life had to offer, legal or not, and he was in thick as gravy with old man Houston.

Marvin returned a shrewd smile before turning away. Rock knew there was no love lost in their glances. He remembered several family gatherings where Marvin wouldn't remain in the same room with him. It was irritating how this big moose managed to become the executor of Nell's will, enabling him to represent Nell's estate in this litigation.

*   *   *

Marvin rested on a bench across the aisle, as did his petite wife Beatrice, about ten years younger. She was Nell's niece and major beneficiary to Nell's will. This meant that whatever Nell inherited from John Carper would go to Beatrice. Thus, Marvin, who came into the family as a second husband to

Beatrice, benefited too.

Beatrice put a hand to her coffee-colored hair, pushing loose strands into a bun. Rock found her very plain and very quiet -- a mealy-mouse shadow of a person who took orders from Marvin.

Having Sheryl's attention, Rock used a hand gesture for possessing many ponies, to convey that the Bensons were looking plush on John's money.

"Yer inheritance. They learned their tricks from Nell."

This must be true. Rock recalled a deposition session. Marvin admitted Houston prepared him a power of attorney to manage Nell's affairs and set up separate bank accounts for he and Beatrice. Then he got Nell to change her will, which excluded Rock when she had Alzheimer's disease. Houston probably did this to hide his misconduct in probating John's estate, but it wasn't going to work if Rock had his way. "Where's Houston?" Rock looked about the room.

* * *

As more people moved into Courtroom Two, Rock's curiosity as to the whereabouts of old Ralph Houston, caused him to rise, walk over to the counsel table and approach Anders. "Is Houston coming?"

"No, we don't need him today." Anders spoke nonchalantly.

"Are you going to reveal him for fraud and lying?"

"I'll handle it."

Rock rested his knuckles on the table and leaned forward. "What about my document specialist? Is he coming?"

"We don't need him either."

Returning to the seat, Rock exhaled in frustration. His day was disintegrating. He spoke at Anders' back. "Have Sheryl and I got time to leave the room for five minutes?"

Anders checked his watch. "Sure, go ahead."

* * *

In the hallway outside Courtroom Two. "Rock, there's people oot 'ere. Keep yer voice doon." She motioned with her fingers, like she was flicking a crumb off her thumb, meaning he should tone down his deep voice.

"Okay." He stopped pacing and stood before her, resorting to his Native sign language, meaning: "I just don't understand how Anders knew Houston and my document specialist wouldn't be needed at this hearing?"

Sheryl answered in hand signs: "Things arenae lookin' good. Have ye ever met yer document expert?"

"No. I was hoping to meet him today. Anders hired him." Rock moved out of someone's way, as more people crowded into the hallway for a court session across the way. Then, he resumed talking in sign language: "I can't pry anything out of Anders. And, I don't know what to do." His jaw felt so taut, it ached -- a warning of an oncoming storm.

Sheryl worked her fingers: "Now listen. There's nothin' ye can do. Ye 'ave ta put trust in yer attorney, that 'e knows what 'e's doin' on yer behalf."

Rock guided her back to the courtroom. What could go wrong next?

* * *

Struggling to remain calm, Rock watched beams of sunlight stream into the courtroom from high windows. The fog had lifted. Because of his mood, the room had taken on a prison-like atmosphere, out of touch with his world.

Sheryl spoke in a hushed tone. "Marvin's attorney Fred Adams Jr. just poked his face in 'ere."

Rock recognized the tall, one-by-twelve-timbered frame, the red hair and the most extraordinary Adam's apple in Clamton captivity. Adams Jr. was from the Houston, Adams and Adams law firm. His dad, Adams, Sr. was deceased now, but a powerful influence in getting Houston started as an attorney. Also, Adams, Sr. was the attorney who prepared documents for the Carper brothers, John and Jack, establishing a Carper legacy, leaving assets to surviving heirs. Nell signed one of the documents, acknowledging that the mansion and cannery business were Jack and John's separate property.

Adams, Jr., younger than Rock, was dressed like he'd moved up in the world: a light tan suit, spit-shined shoes. Adams Jr. walked military erect over to Marvin. They gripped hands. Since their firm represented Rock and Leucojum on legal matters in the past, Rock figured that Adams, Jr. and Houston probably would have been Rock's attorneys were it not for Houston's misconduct in Uncle John's probate.

Adams' blue eyes lit on Rock, penetrating like an arrow. Feeling betrayed, Rock turned away.

*　　*　　*

Suddenly, Sheryl poked Rock in the ribs with a stiff finger, then moved two fingers up to her eyes. "Looky. A new face."

Again Rock followed her fingers to spot a small wiry man, neatly attired and under middle age, who paused at the courtroom entrance with a briefcase as though waiting for a band to play "*Hail To the Chief.*" His wispy goatee and kinky blond hair made him aloof. He stretched his neck, as if searching. Adams Jr. flagged him. Rock spoke in Anders' direction. "Who's that?"

Anders rose from the counsel table, pushed in his chair and turned to Rock. "That's Leland Perkins, a trial attorney from California. He set up practice in Tacoma some time ago."

"So, why is he here?"

"You might say, he's an imported legal gun for their side." Anders inclined his head in Marvin's direction.

Rock stirred around on the bench. "Why wasn't I informed?"

"Just happened." Anders walked away.

"Ye mean, ye dinnae know a'boot this?" Sheryl shielded her mouth to keep the question private.

"You heard Anders. Just happened." Rock echoed at Anders' back, gritting his teeth. "Leland Perkins is now co-attorney with Adams and Houston. Geeeezes. Marvin's got three attorneys. I can't stand much more and the damn hearing hasn't even started." Rock complained to Sheryl, not caring who heard.

"There's more chiefs than Injuns in this bluidy place." Sheryl laced her fingers nervously.

Rock ignored her use of Injuns and bluidy. She was following true to form, especially knowing he hated the word Injun. And he was the only Native American in sight. Rather than lock tempers with Sheryl, he let it pass to watch

Leland Perkins talking to Marvin. "I wonder what they're talking about?"

"We havenae way o' knowin' what yer opposition is sayin', thinkin' or doin'." She adjusted her skirt and crossed one leg over the other.

"Yeah, I know, unless it comes out face-to-face or in court papers." Rock leaned forward putting his elbows on his knees.

Sheryl lamented. "If ye're thinkin' this is the last hearin', ye're askin' fer a miracle."

"Sheryl, you never did understand my case, let alone me."

"That's 'cause you deny reality." She peered over at him.

"You're pushing me." Rock glanced up at the judge's bench. He wished this proceeding would start before an argument developed. "Listen. You do your part and testify today, if you're needed. If I win anything, you take half." He knew that's what she was hanging in for. Behind the scenes, Sheryl only cared about her needs, which didn't include him. Over the years, their relationship changed. He learned that being a Carper was her status symbol in the community and outweighed any affection toward him. Rock hated farce and social hypocrisies. "Let's just be friends. Okay?"

"Right. But, Rock, I cannae stand seein' people walk over ye. Somethin's goin' on 'ere that donnae smell good. If things donnae go right, I'm losing oot on my half." She inhaled, counting to ten.

"Hell. What am I going to do? I'm not an attorney. I don't know how things are done in court." He glanced her way. "And neither do you." There was more on his mind. She was such a faultfinder, for too many winters. Always trying to change him. For that reason, he was glad to be living apart, in unguarded peace.

Sheryl raised her hands as though exasperated with the entire mess. Finally, Anders returned to the counsel table and sat down without giving Rock a sideways glance. Since Rock's stomach was progressing from neutral to corrosive, he slipped an antacid in his mouth. He hated to admit that Sheryl was usually right when things didn't smell right. Marvin and Beatrice wouldn't hire another attorney at this late stage, unless something was amiss. A nagging unease told him he was about to find out.

* * *

Rock patted his good luck pin, the American flag, as activities in Courtroom Two were interrupted. The bailiff's heavy voice echoed off the mahogany paneling. "Please rise for the Honorable Judge Ray A. Randell."

"Oh. Hell. Randell is the judge." Rock's eyes followed the black-robed figure walking briskly past the American flag. "What is going on? My attorney should have been on top of this. Judge Randell is the one who ruled against me last time." Seeing him again was like pouring salt on open wounds.

Judge Randell's eyes roamed over his small audience, now standing to pay their respects. The Bensons, the Carpers, the attorneys and a detective. Then his eyes stopped on Rock.

He couldn't remember the judge ever looking at him like this. It was like facing Whiteman's God a second time. A queasy feeling settled inside. There could only be one possible reason. That incident at the 1984 trial. Randell was giving his oral opinion at the time. Rock could remember his words. *I believe Houston. That visit between Rock and Houston never took place.*

To those words, Rock wanted to explain: *"The visit took place. Houston's lying. I visited Houston's office and told him John left a later will. Houston said it didn't matter because Nell was using a community property agreement. Houston caused my delay in acting sooner."* He yelled these words inside his head as he left the courtroom in 1984, before Judge Randell was finished talking. He didn't shout the words, because he already testified as much.

"Please be seated." Judge Randell lowered himself into a black leather chair behind the bench and reached for something. It was a pouch from which he removed Benjamin Franklin-style glasses. He made great ceremony, wiping the lenses with a small cloth and donned them over a beakish nose.

"Someone had prior notice that Randell was presiding. The glasses preceded him. My attorney must have been asleep. We shouldn't be in front of this judge." Rock hunched forward over his knees. Tweed carpeting. Putrid green. He fumbled around in his pocket for another antacid. The judge could sear him over a flaming fire if he wanted.

Moving the gavel off to the side, Judge Randell proceeded. "Good morning ladies, gentlemen, Mr. Perkins, Mr. Anders. For the record, it's eleven a. m., Monday, January 15, 1990. We are gathered here to address Rock's petition to probate his uncle's estate based on new evidence."

At least that introduction was a relief. Rock believed Judge Randell couldn't be pleased over this, because Randell rejected the same new evidence last year, forcing Rock to hire Anders to appeal his decision. The appellate court issued a mandate, a written order, overruling Judge Randell. The mandate gave specific instructions for the superior court to address the misconduct in the probate of John's estate. This was why Rock made it clear to Anders to request a different judge. Whenever they discussed who the judge might be, Anders said he didn't know; that Judge Randell was retired. Not to worry.

There's an saying. *"No matter the height of a person, if he's honest, he stands tall."* Recalling this, Rock stared at Anders, not standing so tall now. Rock wondered how the judge could address his new evidence when Anders dismissed his witnesses. And his document expert and Houston weren't here.

*   *   *

So here, all assembled in the courtroom, the parties quietly waited. Anders stood, secured the middle button of his suit jacket and walked to the lectern. He spoke in a tenor voice. "Good morning, Your Honor. As Mr. Carper's attorney I submit these papers of which you are well acquainted in support of our petition." He approached the bench.

Judge Randell slightly raised his elderly, yet short stocky frame and reached across the bench to receive the papers. He shifted his glasses up and down his high forehead and glanced, hard-ass stern, at the papers. The saltiness of time was evident in facial crease lines as he spoke. "Since Mr. Perkins doesn't object, I will allow them in." Grumpily, he handed the papers to the docket clerk and settled back in his chair, as Anders returned to the counsel table.

Rock hoped that maybe by now Judge Randell knew it was Houston who lied at the '84 trial. If not it would soon be revealed in the papers Anders just handed him. This point was important to his laches defense. Laches was one of those fancy legal words Anders used. Anders explained that laches was a technical term, referring to Rock's delay in acting sooner. Laches must be overcome in order to reopen the probate of John's estate, which meant exposing

Houston for causing Rock's delay.

Perkins stood alongside his counsel table. Rock noticed he wore a tie the color of a dead primrose. "Your Honor, we have a report from our new document expert which we will enter with your permission. It shows a differing opinion on Rock's new evidence."

"Granted."

"Correction, Your Honor." Anders rose. "Their expert found absolutely nothing against our new evidence. Furthermore, Your Honor, I must convey that Ralph Houston and Nell Carper were not above misconduct in the original probate of John Carper's estate. They caused Rock's delay in acting sooner."

At last. Anders stuck to his plan, finally exposing Houston and Nell. Rock relaxed a little, watching Perkins back down like he was no match for Anders. The courtroom took on an icy silence. Judge Randell glared stonily over the rims of his bifocals at Anders.

"Oou." Sheryl let out her habitual expression when things were beyond belief. "The judge's face donnae look happy." She crossed her arms. "Who said silence is golden?"

Anders stiffened and returned to the lectern. "Your Honor, we ask that you grant our motion for a new trial."

"For chrissake, that's the last thing I want and he knows it." Rock wiped a broad hand down his face and turned to Sheryl. Thoughts of helplessness needled his insides. His stomach muscles tighten.

Sheryl squeezed his arm in sympathy. She used hand signs and murmured quietly. "Cool yer head feathers, laddie."

Making matters worse, Perkins stood and requested an evidence hearing. Rock believed this was what Anders should have asked for. Not his opposition.

"Gentlemen." Judge Randell stretched his frame higher in his chair. "The appellate court remanded this case back here for a hearing to consider Rock Carper's new evidence so that he may probate his uncle's estate under another will. I agree, after thoroughly going over the pleadings, reports and records. However, due to the serious nature implicated by Rock's new evidence, I am going to rule for a new trial to consider all the evidence now before the court as requested by Mr. Anders. I will sign an order to that effect. That will be all."

People stood to honor Judge Randell's exit. Disappointment welled in Rock. He wanted to shout above the noises of chatter, paper shuffling and briefcases clicking. Instead, he struggled for self-control. He rushed toward Anders. "I appreciate what you did for me, exposing Houston and Nell, but why ask for a new trial? I've been through one trial already. You know I can't afford starting over again. A simple hearing is what the appellate court ordered, which was supposed to be today." When Anders didn't respond, Rock knotted his fists. "I don't like surprises being dumped on me. You didn't keep me informed."

Anders cut him off. "I'm returning to Seattle for other commitments. We'll talk another day on how to best proceed." Anders left on the run.

Shock coursed through Rock's veins, while watching Ginger Haley and the detective chasing behind Anders. Rock's head buzzed. Anders was being an asshole, having never treated him like this before. Up until now they had a good client/attorney relationship. This sudden change of heart didn't figure.

Sheryl walked over and handed Rock his coat. Exhaling through clenched teeth, Rock felt betrayed by his own attorney, the one person he trusted the most. "Shiiiiit. I've got to get out of this inferno."

Chapter Three

In the courthouse parking lot, Rock started the car, gripped the wheel and raced the engine. His only thought for now was to leave. His peripheral vision took in the sight of his opposition and the attorneys heading in another direction. "I want nothing to do with any of them. However, I'd like to drive this Firebird right up their collective ass."

"Come ta yer senses, dearie. Ye're stuck with 'em so long as ye 'old onta the litigation. Ye're just feelin' spit upon by them, partly 'cause o' their high and mighty attitudes, which doesnae include acceptance o' a hybrid. Screw 'em."

"They make me feel like I came from prairie roots. Almost as if being White is a sign of what is right, of being American." It was bothersome to be looking from the outside in. "My ancestors were here before theirs."

Sheryl remained silent as he headed onto the arterial and cruised aimlessly around Quamas streets. Nothing made sense.

"These damn attorneys are tryin' ta bankrupt ye."

"Well my creek is damn well running dry. I've given Anders $25,000. With what I've given attorneys before him, I've actually spent nearly $30,000 bucks on this damn litigation. Today's hearing was supposed to be the end of it."

"Enough. Let's visit my folks?"

"You're joking. I don't need relatives right now." Feeling raw, Rock screeched the Firebird around a corner.

"We could motor over to yer mum's."

"How can you possibly think of visiting at a time like this? Anders let me down. I don't know what I'm going to do."

"Let it be fer awhile. The answer is oot there."

"Oh sure. Answers grow on trees. Life doesn't work that way, Sheryl. Get real. I've just been screwed and I didn't enjoy it."

"Why donnae ye get real? Ye give money ta attorneys like a zillion pussy buds poppin' open on the willow branch." Her face contorted into a frown. "I donnae know what's a'foot here, but it's ta Anders' advantage ta 'ave a new trial. More money. He's goin' ta drain the well dry."

Rock drove with one hand on the wheel and rubbed his neck with the other. Sheryl's reasoning made sense, as usual. And, he knew he was in for a tongue lashing from her whether or not she made sense.

"The attorneys seen ye as a ball o' determination fer justice and money ta burn. They saw ye as a bitch in heat and they stuck it ta ye."

He reached over to grasp her shoulder. "Sheryl. Don't talk like me."

She yanked away, determine to continue. "Ye've no heard the last o' their tricks. Ye'll see. And, this will be the last time an attorney attempts ta discredit another in a Clamton County Courtroom in this litigation. I'm warnin' ye these attorneys will skin ye and set ye oot ta dry. Fer all the hurtache ye cause me, I wish yer mum 'ad stayed a virgin."

"Damn, don't nag woman. We have the same concerns. I'm sure there's a

24

perfectly sensible explanation." He reached under the seat for his bottle of antacids and flipped open the lid. It was empty. What a day.

While turning down another street to nowhere, his stomach burned. He hit the steering wheel with a fist. "I can't work full time in the jewelry business and check up on my attorney." A jaywalker caused him to stop in the middle of the block. That was enough for him to mellow out. He finally eased forward, thinking of what he should do. Until today, Anders always had a way of telling him to hang in, trust. So maybe he should.

"She hasnae been feelin' well." Sheryl changed the subject.

"Huh? Oh, mom. If I take you over there, you two will be arguing within the hour."

"Only 'cause I took away 'er only son."

This was unfortunate, but true. His mom Leucojum gradually developed a protective, possessive nature. Especially, when she saw this possessiveness in Rock's actions toward Sheryl. Leucojum became jealous. This was one reason why, when the day came for their son to join the Army, Rock defended his son's choice. *"If he wants to join, he can."* It was a big step in Rock learning to let go.

"Drop me off at my folks' place and ye go see yer mum."

"Okay. But only for an hour or so. My boss thinks I'm in court for the day. I thought that was the plan. I thought this whole affair would be over once and for all." Rock hugged the main road, then backtracked passed the ferry landing to Sheryl's folks' place. Deeply concerned, he admitted he couldn't create answers for the actions of others. Without answers, he couldn't find solutions. Result. One big headache.

* * *

Rock entered through the back entrance of his mom's house. Leucojum's mournful humming carried him through the kitchen to the dining room. He found her huddled in her favorite oak rocker in front of the small oil furnace. She was stirring soup in a mug. Upon instant inspection, the plastic sheets he tacked up last Thanksgiving were still draped across the entry separating the dining and living rooms. This way she didn't have to heat the entire house to stay warm in the winter.

A self-sufficient widow since Jack died in 1967, she managed to live comfortably on a small pension. But, at seventy-three years of age, she considered herself beyond packing logs in from the garage to the beachrock fireplace. And, she forbid Rock from stacking a supply of logs by the fireplace for fear of bringing bugs into the house.

Usually, her day began with lighting a kindling fire in a small wood stove in the kitchen, then dressed in her bedroom not far from the oil furnace, tied an apron around her waist to keep newsprint off her cotton dress, slipped on a wool cardigan, braided her hair, then ate toast, jam and tea for breakfast, followed by a tooth scrubbing with baking soda.

The remainder of the day was filled, reading newspapers and visiting with drop-in church friends. Over tea, the friends had to listen to the same stories of what a fine Brave Rock was. Rock shuddered over this.

She welcomed magazine salesmen and Adventists, not of her faith, in the door because they sat down and talked. She enjoyed that. Some of her visitors weren't exactly friends. One time she let in an insurance salesman who suckered her out of a $700 check for a policy she didn't need. Fortunately, Rock found out in time to cancel the check.

During the warmer, windy months, she hung her wash on the outdoor clothesline after wringing them through an old wringer washing machine. Only in the dead of winter did she use the modern washer/dryer Rock and Sheryl bought for her. She was grateful, but complained: *"Modern contraptions make me lazy like you young folks."*

"Rocky, my son. What a nice surprise." With a hand more bronze than Rock's, Leucojum grasped the blanket draped over her frail shoulders, while she reached with the other to set the mug on the round oak dining table. Then, she clapped her hands, smiled and reached for him. "What's the occasion?" Her voice was weak. She shook the sleeve of his suit with a shaky hand and kept smiling. A glint of gold in an eyetooth graced her smile.

He bent over to kiss a sunken cheek. Mentholated vapor rub, a salve to cure colds, permeated the air. She used it as night cream on her face too; claimed it kept her skin soft. Leucojum appeared frail today. For the most part, she was a stoic woman. Her hair was mostly gray. Her dark eyes were almost lost in folds.

"Short visit, mom. I'm in town on business." He wouldn't mention the real reason for being in town. No use in upsetting her over the hearing and his divorce. Leucojum would hate Sheryl even more over the divorce, only because she'd figure it would cause him pain.

"Where's Sheryl?" She glanced around him through wire-rimmed glasses, while smoothing loose hairs into her braid.

"With her folks."

"Just as well. Sheryl's different." Leucojum rested back and twisted her veined hands in a calico-print apron that matched the kitchen curtains.

"Come on mom, let's get along." Rock straddled a cushioned dining room chair. His last visit was at Christmas. He and Sheryl took her out to dinner. Looking around, he noticed nothing had been rearranged. Crocheted snowflakes were fastened to the arms and backs of an old stuffed chair and matching sofa.

The *Cherokee Advocate*, the tribal newspaper, was on the dining table along with the *Quamas Daily* and the *Chenowah Quarterly*. She had plenty of candles, a flashlight and kerosene lamps on the table in case the lights failed. There were picture hangings over papered walls and knickknacks setting on ledges above the dark wood paneling. The indoor totem poles, tucked in the corners, were Rock's cedar carvings.

Rock's totems made personal statements rather than historical statements. He mated physical shapes and his aesthetic ideals. Traditionally, the carver used heraldic emblems relative to his own tribe, denoting wealth. Rock learned this primarily from coastal tribes, including the Haida people of Queen Charlotte Islands, whose totems were from twenty to sixty feet tall. Rock's indoor totems were not much taller than six feet, solely to emit a love for the craft.

The Chenowahs in Quamas weren't much into carving totems. Although, a few Chenowahs used cedar for making shovelnose canoes and bark for clothing and quivers [tube-shaped bags for holding arrows, suspended from a shoulder strap], old crafts that all but faded into museums. The lives of the Chenowahs, as with the Carpers, led them to hunting and fishing. They lived around an abundance of salmon and deer for which east-of-the-mountain tribes considered them rich.

The Eastern Washington tribes made annual trips in the fall to a festival in Quamas, While trading their cured deer, bear hides and perfumes from ferns in exchange for dried salmon, clams, seaweed salt and whale oil, the Natives celebrated in a variety of ways, depending on their age, interest and skill. The ways included ball-and-stick and tug-of-war games, dancing, gambling, wrestling events and eating barbecued salmon. The Bearclaw Bow and Arrow Society sponsored the bow and arrow games.

The society required high standards. At festival time, only blunt arrows were used. Arrowheads were saved for hunting. And, no drinking was allowed, because on one occasion a Brave was shot in the head accidentally. It was reported in the *Quamas Daily* that the Brave and another Brave were practicing for the event, while drinking. One held a basket on his head. The other aimed and missed, slicing through the other's face, fortunately missing major blood vessels. The injured party survived minus an eye.

All that aside, Rock's dad and uncle bought salmon from the Chenowahs as well as from Caucasian fishermen. Their cannery prospered because of this arrangement. The Strait of Juan de Fuca was so loaded that one could practically walk across the backs of salmon. He recalled his dad say that one year the local canneries couldn't keep up with all the salmon caught in fish traps. Thousands of salmon had to be dumped overboard because they spoiled. Measures were taken to limit catches after that.

"She's too different from us Carpers." Leucojum's jaw was set at a stubborn angle, tottering in the rocker, determined to have her say, grinding on a tiring subject.

Rock stopped his daydreaming. "You're forgetting our differences."

Leucojum shook her head in disagreement. "I wish all the foreigners would go back where they came from."

Rock shuddered, hearing this complaint repeatedly. This was one of those visits where she was on a high horse, probably from having too much time to think. There was no use telling her America is a melting pot of foreigners. "You're forgetting. You taught me if we live in peace with creatures of the forest, the water and the sky, we can live in peace with each other." Smiling, he reached over to gently squeeze her arm.

"Guess I'm getting senile. Memories come and go." She reached in an apron pocket for a kerchief and covered her mouth to cough.

"No problem."

She stopped rocking and wagged a knotted finger at him – a sudden burst of strength. "You mustn't forget your heritage. I know. Sheryl would wish you would. But, don't." Her eyes looked stern and emphatic. Then she sneezed and coughed into the kerchief.

"Not to worry." Rock laughed it off. "I wish you'd let me do something for your cold."

"Nothing you can do. There's a pot of water on the heater. Steam is good." She held a hand on her chest.

"Is that pain back?" He recalled the last cold nearly put her in the hospital.

"Oh shush. What hurts is Sheryl interfering with my dreams that one day you would graduate from college and become a famous artist of totems. She destroyed those dreams."

"I became a good artist anyway. Made good money. Equal to anyone."

Leucojum swept an arm through the air toward his artwork. "You've neglected your talent and turned down orders. There's still an unfinished totem in the garage I want you to finish."

Rock rested his head on folded arms over the back of the chair. After Uncle John had sold the cannery, he moved his stuff into Leucojum's garage. With so many other things going on in his life, he let his talent slide. "You're right on all counts." He wasn't about to argue with her on any subject, so he let her rattle on while his thoughts lingered on his craft.

An interest in totems started in boy scouts. He made several small ones, no taller than a foot each. They were very crude since he used rustic slate tools. Leucojum wouldn't let him throw away these little totems. Making small totems was time-consuming and frustrating. His inexperience taught him patience and gave him an admiration of the ancient ways. But, as he grew in size and strength, and by the age of fifteen, and his experience with tools in scouting broadened, his dad let him work in a large room in the cannery warehouse. He used his dad's electric chain saw, grinder and sander as well as hand tools such as vices, rotary drills, chisels, mallets. From a catalog, they ordered adzes – gouge-type cutters, other gouges and rasps. Anything accessible through a catalog to make the job easier was fine with his dad.

His shop included a drawing table for creating templates for wings, eyes, ears, bodies of frogs, birds, fish, et cetera. For a six-foot totem, his dad bought him a cedar log and two-inch-thick boards for wings and fish, and the same for the totem base.

One evening, Leucojum came down to his shop. When she saw all the electric tools, she crowed, angrily. *"These aren't toys."*

"I'm teaching him to take it slow and easy." His dad's support was appreciated even if Leucojum was concerned about safety. His dad was good with electric tools, having made her several Bentwood boxes. He let Rock decorate them with figures of birds, animals, sea and mythical creatures.

Expenditure-wise, Rock only ruined one totem by cutting off too much. This taught him to check his work more frequently. And, his work, especially the two in front of the house, drew community admiration, enough to begin selling his work.

He didn't charge much, not until he felt good enough. Before his dad died in 1967, he was getting more than the going rate of $200 a foot, with a two-year backlog from Canadian customers. Man he made money. Rumor had it that a half-breed shouldn't be allowed to make so much money. After Aunt Nell died and all these inheritance problems surfaced, Rock squandered his money paying attorneys to sort out things.

Leucojum sighed wearily and coughed again, breaking into his trance. Rock reached over to put a hand on hers. "Are you okay? Can I get you medicine?"

"No. I'll fix lemon tea with whiskey at bedtime; best cure."

Rock imagined her swirling in a little honey and listening to the kitchen radio before retiring. The TV set he gave her remained off most of the time.

"You go take care of business." She motioned him away with a parting message: "No one is successful in his earthwalk until he has acquired his song."

"I know, through a dream. You haven't reminded me in a long while." Rock passed it off, knowing that some people go through life not receiving their special song. Some receive it late in life. Leucojum taught him this along with her songs, myths, dreams and all that she considered important in life.

Since his separation from Sheryl, only work and paying attorneys entered his mind at bedtime -- neither produced his dream. Now his dream was to retrieve the Carper legacy. It wasn't for material things that this dream hounded him, but rather he felt it was what the Carper men wanted and expected of him.

Finally, he promised to see Leucojum next weekend, and left, relieved she didn't pump him about his business. When she recently learned about Nell and Houston's dishonesty, she hated them with a passion, causing her to shy away from many folks, except for the Fulbrights. Thinking of the Fulbrights, Rock decided he'd stop by Jasper Fulbright's office before retrieving Sheryl. Maybe Jasper, one of his witnesses sent away from court today, might know what is going on.

*   *   *

"No wonder you don't have the middle-age spread. There are too many steps leading to your ivory tower." Walking through the door into the Fulbright Law Firm, Rock broke the silence, having just climbed multiple flights of stairs. Jasper Fulbright and his secretary, Mrs. Willard greeted him with chuckles. It had been about five years since Rock last came here. He recalled it was at his mom's request, concerning her will.

Jasper was stirring sugar into his coffee. "Rock. I'm partial to this old brick building. It's a family inheritance, you know."

"Even so. I suggest you install an elevator. So elderly folks like mom can reach you."

"Ho no. I've got that covered. "I meet the elderly and the handicapped at the courthouse, when necessary. Glad you stopped in. I'm curious. What's going on over there?" He nodded his head toward the courthouse.

"I was hoping you'd know." Rock raised his brow. "You're in the thicket of the legal forest in this town. I thought you might have heard some talk since you left court this morning."

"Nothing. Want coffee?"

"Yes. Black."

Jasper fussed with coffee fixings, after instructing Mrs. Willard to hold his calls. He handed a mug to Rock. "Follow me."

Rock followed and sat in a chair in front of Jasper's desk. While Jasper was moving into his chair, Rock noticed the back wall contained framed documents. Probably a certificate of law, a license to practice and the like. He wasn't close enough for detail. While inhaling the aroma of coffee, Rock tried to remain unruffled, even though he was still very irritated over the morning's hearing. "I thought today would be the end of the case." He waded through his explanation of devastating events.

Jasper remained silent like a psychiatrist with a client on the couch. He listened intently.

"What I tell you may seem small. My attorney Anders didn't inform me that Judge Randell would be coming out of retirement today. Hell, Randell hates me. Worst of all, Anders asked for a new trial, when the appellate court specified a hearing. And, Randell granted the trial. Then Anders butts out of court without any explanations to me. All I see in the future is legal maneuvering and mounting costs. What's going on?" Rock held out his hands in desperation.

"I sympathize with you, but I imagine Judge Randell came out of retirement specifically for today's hearing, because he knows the case better than any of our other judges." Jasper held his mug in both hands near his chest.

"So that's why. Still, Anders had no right to withhold this information from me."

Jasper nodded. "Yes. Well, I don't know about that."

Rock rubbed his forehead, thinking, "*Does this guy know more than he's telling me?*"

"Do you suppose I can get the court to reverse the decision on a new trial?"

"No. Judge Randell isn't going to step back in court and change his mind. If he said he's going to sign an order for a new trial, he will and that's final."

"But I don't understand why Anders asked for it in the first place." Rock leaned back in his chair to avoid the bright glare of the afternoon sun coming in through the window behind Jasper.

"Probably would have happened even if Anders didn't ask." Jasper fingered through his brown hair and sighed in a tone of fellowship. "Since Randell is retired, a new judge will be assigned to your case. It's easier for a new person to start from scratch."

Rock shrugged his shoulders. "But, not easier for me." The explanation made sense, but so unfair to him financially. There was a brief pause. "Judges in Quamas must be smart enough to read the record, admit the new evidence through a hearing, then make a decision. It's faster."

"Who knows. As far as what Anders has up his sleeve, you ask him. But, don't worry, I'll still be a good witness for you. No one can change that." Jasper readjusted papers on his desk.

They discussed divorce. Jasper favored he and Sheryl delaying the divorce. Unwinding his legs, Rock prepared to leave. The conversation offered few answers. If Jasper knew more, he wasn't saying. But, he was right about one thing. Talk to Anders. Rock drained his coffee, shook Jasper's hand and left.

Chapter Four

Rock drank cranberry juice in his apartment kitchen, while thinking what a long day this had been. Disappointments of the hearing, his attorney's idiotic attitude, the judge's decision for a new trial and his separate visits with Jasper Fulbright and Leucojum emotionally drained him.

Foremost on his mind, however, was Sheryl's reaction on the ferry when he relayed Jasper's belief that she shouldn't file for divorce until after the new trial. That news set bitterly and she wouldn't promise to wait. She'd only talk about moving back to Quamas to be closer to her folks. This didn't bother him. They were getting along. Sheryl was free to do as she pleased, especially because their decision to divorce was mutually accepted. But, she was still such a beautiful lady . . .

The ringing of the phone on the counter broke his reverie. He set the glass down and stepped across the linoleum to answer. "Hello?"

"Mr. Carper." The voice was unfamiliar and formal. The caller identified himself, also saying he was a member of the Quamas Hospital. "I'm sorry to tell you your mother passed on about an hour ago."

"No." His heart pounded in his throat. "I saw her this afternoon." Rock lumbered into the living room, simultaneously dragging the cord behind, and then slumped down on the sofa. "What happened?"

"A neighbor found her collapsed on the front porch by the mailbox. Must have happened after you left. He brought Leucojum indoors. She wouldn't let us do anything for her. Said it was in the Great Spirit's hands. And, we had a time getting your phone number. I'm so sorry for not reaching you sooner."

"It couldn't be helped." He slammed the armrest with a fist at the unfortunate turn of events. "Most of the time, I was on the ferry returning to Seattle." Rock exhaled with a deep sigh, realizing Leucojum didn't have his number since he moved. She didn't use the phone much and he always phoned her. So, it was Sheryl's number they must have phoned, then Sheryl would have given them his. Yet, neither were home. "I'll head back to Quamas tonight and take care of everything."

After discussing arrangements, he sat in silence, bewildered, his fingers clinging to the phone until an irritating noise reminded him to put down the receiver.

Then the phone rang again. It was the neighbor who found Leucojum, a Chenowah Native friend, Woodstalk, so named after the trees. Rock pictured him hampering along the road with bundles of willow switches, which would be used to weave baskets to eke out a living. He originally came from Noo-wha-ah Bayview ancestors who were slaves to a northern tribe until they escaped and came to live among the Chenowah Indians.

"Klahowya." Rock was surprised he remembered the word for 'hello'.

"No need to talk wawa. I'm no chee chako to Quamas."

Racking his brain, Rock recalled that '*wawa*' meant Native jargon and '*chee chako*' meant newcomer.

Woodstalk filled him in with more details. Once that was over, Rock rubbed his forehead and explained. "Most of her relatives in Oklahoma are gone, other than my two cousins." He saw no sense in bringing them clear out here. "She wanted to be buried next to my Dad Jack and all the other Carpers, so I'll give her a regular burial."

"If there's anything I can do. Maybe we could put a feather prayer stick on her grave for a safe journey. And, you and all her friends can come to my place for a potluck after the funeral."

"Thanks, Woodstalk. She'd like that. So would I."

"Buck up Rock. Losing both parents like you did is tough. Leucojum didn't want to be a drain on you. She didn't want to linger like your dad."

"No. Not a drain. I loved my dad and didn't want to lose him when he was ready to go. I would have done no less for mom."

"That's the point, Rock. We hang on because of our feelings rather than their feelings. Leucojum said the doctor taught you how to give Jack shots everyday his last year."

"Yes. She hated needles." His head throbbed, remembering it was the only way to lower his dad's blood pressure.

"Sure and she didn't want that for herself."

"I'm hearing you." Rock thanked him again for his condolences and hung up. But, he still kicked himself for not recognizing how ill Leucojum really was. The signs were there. Watery eyes. Raspy cough. Her parting words: *"Remember, no one is successful in his earthwalk until he has acquired his song."* She was saying goodbye, but too sick to explain the intent behind her words. And, he was too engrossed in legal problems to ask. Guilt traipsed over him like a dark cloud no matter what Woodstalk said.

"Ah mom. Why? I could have at least been there with you. Held your hand that last hour. You being so far from home. So far from Tahlequah, Oklahoma." He spoke out as if she were there. At times like this, being rational wasn't in his grasp. Before returning to Quamas tonight, he'd just have to let himself go, let the memories in and let guilt work its course. That's what Leucojum said when his dad died.

Rock put the phone on the floor. Leucojum did her best to raise him in two cultures. Their relationship always focused on this. He smiled sadly, recalling how she'd sent him on summer vacations to other villages up the coast to learn Native American ways. She even sent him to her hometown near the Trail of Tears, where her only brother taught him more about his heritage.

While living these experiences, he felt they were overwhelming, because ways of doing and thinking varied from tribe to tribe. But this didn't matter to Leucojum, who loved listening to his adventures. In fact, they'd sit in the kitchen for hours exchanging Native experiences over plates of rabbit stew, fry bread and angel cake pudding with a wild maraschino taste. She'd toss back her head and laugh, exposing a touch of gold in an eyetooth. It was that way with her brother. That same touch of gold. That's why one day Rock had the dentist add gold to an eyetooth. A means of identity with them.

His early days were the best. He enjoyed a stream of village life, primarily associating with Indian playmates and school buddies until Leucojum read something about government policy encouraging assimilation. When she arrived in Quamas there were about eighty Whites and two thousand Natives. Time reversed those numbers. Many Natives were driven off their lands and some into the logging industry on the mainland. But, it was a time to put aside all bitterness for this reversal.

Talk of assimilation gave her an idea. Take him out of Indian Scouting and put him into Whiteman's Scouting. To mingle the ways of both cultures. Leucojum felt such an exposure would instill strong values of truth and honor taught in both cultures. It did all of that. It was a turning point in his life, forcing a greater association with Caucasians. Unsettling at first, he adapted well.

A recent letter from Leucojum laid on the end table. He picked it up now and reread her words: *"Be patient and you will finally win, for a soft tongue can break hard bones."* Tears coursed down his cheeks. He searched for meaning. Did she try to tell him his survivability depended on his Nativeness? He didn't know. But, it was wrong of him not to confide in her about his litigation today. Down deep, she really cared about the litigation and wanted to testify for him at the earlier trial with Judge Randell presiding, but the doctor said no. The strain could be a strain on her heart.

He tried to recall the lovely song Leucojum used to sing. "Gv ge yu a, heh yu." [I'll love you, hey you] under the brilliant starry sky, while the ageless moon glows." This was all he could utter, being out of sorts with the Native tongue.

Opening a drawer in the end table, Rock stowed away Leucojum's letter and turned off the light. Just for a while, to get ahold of all this, he'd stretch out on the sofa. Shock and loneliness invaded his existence. Heavy hearted, he covered his face with a pillow and howled in the dark. In his mind, he could hear a flute sounding like a lone wolf above the voices of drums. Eerie music from the mists of time.

Chapter Five

Mona Bradley stepped forward and hugged the chest-high counter, while whispering to the ticket Lady. "I don't care where you seat me, so long as I'm next to that handsome dude. He's standing several people behind me."

The ticket lady's eyes made a double take on the deliverer of the request.

Mona fluttered her eyes and smiled. "Maybe my request is too ridiculous. Forget I asked."

"No. Not ridiculous at all. I occasionally get such requests. Nothing ventured, nothing gained."

"My sentiments exactly. Then would you please arrange it?" Mona flipped back her long blonde curls.

"Hmmm. Several people back." The ticket agent's eyes appeared to be focusing on the man in question. "Are you referring to that tall chief in dark clothing?"

"Yes, yes. That's the one. Dressed in black wearing an aqua-colored tie and turquoise tie clasp. He's holding a briefcase and raincoat."

"You want a ticket to thunder mountain." The agent laughed conspiratorially, moving her fingers down the seating chart. "I'll do what I can." She slid a seat assignment across the counter.

"Thanks." Mona took her ticket and eventually disappeared down a ramp and into the plane, searching for her seat. Ah. A window seat. Damn. In the excitement, she forgot to tell the ticket agent she didn't want a window seat. She didn't even want to know she was on an airplane. The rapid beating of her heart was unnerving. If she sat for a few minutes, the beating would subside. She must be composed. Just because she was adventuresome in some ways, she didn't have to be a chicken in other respects.

Leaning back in the seat, she thought of her little sister, Gena. Gena resented the role of little sister, being born only minutes after Mona. Gena was capable of managing her own affairs, but had let life slip by since her husband's disappearance nearly four years ago. His small plane carrying two passengers was last seen heading over the Siskiyou Mountains. There wasn't even a ray of hope at the end of a month-long search.

It was time Gena moved on. If Mona could prod things along, she would. Even to the point of picking out a man she approved of. This might be just the man for Gena, if he's not married. His muscular build, facial features, hair and skin were surprisingly a lot like Gena's missing husband.

*　*　*

Waiting in the ticket line, impatiently shifting his weight, Rock checked his watch. Friday afternoon, January 26, 1990. At least now he could put behind this work-related trip and put energy into solving his personal problems. Talking with Anders was imminent. Somehow, they had to get on the same pathway.

Situated among the hub of people was a shapely blonde moving to the head of the line. She was staring at him, until their eyes met. She quickly turned away and disappeared.

Before long, Rock worked his way down the narrow pathway among other passengers. When he found his aisle seat, he spotted the blonde he saw standing in line. She was sitting next to the window. What a coincidence. He nodded and busied himself, stashing a few belongings in the overhead. Then he hiked his pant legs to sit beside her.

The blonde was well-packaged with turquoise eyes, oval face, a Streisand nose. She was rolling a paperback novel in her hands.

Rock settled back and shut his eyes a moment thinking of some R and R for the weekend, when the blonde bumped his elbow. Opening his eyes, he noticed the lady exchanging her street shoes for pink slippers. The shoes went into her tote. Next, she excused herself and rose upward.

"You needn't move." Her voice was cheerful.

Nevertheless, Rock jumped into the aisle. He believed she had plans of stepping over his knees. Women's lib. Women wearing pants and stepping over a man's knees. She had the long legs for the feat, no argument there. He watched her stuff a coat and tote in the overhead.

Then the lady turned her head toward him, about to say something when another passenger bumped into her, knocking her off balance and into Rock.

"Ooooh. Ooooh dear."

"Oooooof." His lips met with blonde hair. His arms cradled a mass of movement. This unexpected event was rather likeable, except the location of his hands became a concern. Fortunately, he caught her by the heels of his hands. Ten fingers were pointing outward like riled feathers.

"Oooh. How awkward." She squirmed.

"You always drop in on gentlemen this way?" He chuckled and moved her tense body away. The other passenger apologized and moved passed them.

"I'm sooo sorry." Her face reddened. She adjusted her clothes and returned to her seat.

Once she was settled, he sat, loosened his tie and released the top shirt button. Other passengers moved along. A lady with two children carrying balloons edged by, one whining; the other smiling. Compartment doors opened and closed. Clicking noises and chatter filled the area.

Movement by the window roiled again. Rock decided it wise to keep an eye open and an ear tuned. The blonde was rummaging around in her purse. Their eyes met as she rose. Figuring she was on another mission, he moved into the aisle. No point in pressing his luck. "Want something in the overhead?"

"My tote." Her tone was formal.

Rock smiled. "I can handle this better if you remain seated."

"I'm afraid you're right." She sat down. When Rock handed her the tote, she unzipped it. "Thanks." She smiled demurely and held up a pack of gum. She gave him the tote and nodded at the overhead.

He grinned and returned the bag to the overhead.

"I won't disturb you any more." She patted his upholstered seat cushion.

"It wasn't all your fault, but, well, you're a bit flighty."

"I know. Good thing I'm not sitting in the cockpit. Want a stick of gum?"

Rock settled into his seat. "Thanks, don't mind if I do." He unwrapped the gum, rolled it into his mouth and chewed as the big jet pushed away from the gate. They taxied jauntily to the end of the runway and lumbered into Dallas' sunny skies.

Following safety instructions from a stewardess, a cheerful disembodied voice welcomed them. The voice announced their final destination to Seattle.

Things settled. For how long was anyone's guess. The lady was leafing through her book. Rock stuffed the gum wrapper in the ashtray and rubbed his chin in contemplation.

*   *   *

"I'm Mona Bradley." She offered a hand.

Gold-ringed bracelets jingled as he shook her hand. It was smooth and warm. "Pleasure. I'm Rock."

"Who?"

"Rock."

"Brock?"

"No, Rock. R-o-c-k," he spelled. "Rock Carper."

Mona grinned. "Anyone with the name Rock has got to be interesting."

"Yeah? Anyone who wears pink slippers on a plane has got to be interesting."

"I like my pink slippers." Mona slightly lifted a foot.

Rock chuckled. "Look like dust mops." He cleared his throat. "Pardon me. Dusters."

"They're comfortable. That's what counts."

He stared at the slippers and inwardly admired her feet. Actually, he admired all of her.

"My dusters, as you say, are new. Bought them today in a little shop near the Fairmont Hotel, along with my necklace." She pulled the necklace out from under the neckline of her blouse. "See."

Rock whistled. "Nice. I'll bet you paid handsomely for the necklace."

"Yes." She nodded.

They whiled away the time and continued to converse. Mona inquired, "Were you in Dallas on business?"

"Ummm hmmm. Jewelry business for Turquoise Wholesalers. We buy original-designed new and used jewelry and other artwork from Native American tribes in places like Colorado, Utah, Arizona, Texas and Wyoming for a variety of markets: retail jewelers, museums, private showings, trade shows, specialty stores."

"Your ring, tie clasp and bracelets are Native designs, aren't they?"

"Yep." Rock moved his right hand over for her inspection. "Zuni mosaic inlays. This bracelet is a watch."

"I see that. Fabulous, and your ring?"

He moved his right hand closer. She touched the polished stones and large diamond set in a gold band. It was his wedding ring from Sheryl. Only for court did he wear it on the wedding-ring finger of the left hand.

"Your jewelry is set in gold. I thought only silver was used in Native jewelry."

"Not necessarily. Zuni craftsmen can set clusters and inlays of turquoise, coral, jet and shell in either silver or gold."

"I read where turquoise brings success in love and money."

Rock chuckled. "There's money. Love? That's a new one." He finally withdrew his hand.

"I notice your hands are scarred." Her eyes revealed a concerned curiosity.

"From carving totem poles. A hazard of the craft."

Satisfied, she moved on. " If you tell me where your store is, I'll come in and buy from you."

"We're located on the second floor above the Old Union Bookstore in an antiquated brick building. An area on First Avenue south. Near Pioneer Square. I don't own the store. My boss does. We are strictly wholesalers, operating out of three rooms. A small office, a display room and a big room for storage."

"Oh."

He detected disappointment in her voice. "Watch for ads in the newspapers. Anytime you see advertisements on Native American jewelry, it is more than likely from us." A brief pause ensued as he questioned himself and her motives. Was he missing an opportunity here? He intended to find out. "So, tell me about yourself. Are you on a pleasure or a business trip?"

"Business. Just completed a weeklong writing assignment in Dallas. I'm a freelance travel writer with an absolute fear of flying."

"How so?"

"Ever since a hole blew open in the fuselage of that 747 airliner southwest of Hawaii, I've had this fear. I was scheduled for the flight; but missed it, fortunately. But, it has caused me nightmares. Imagine being one of the passengers sucked out of a jetliner to your death 20,000 feet below?"

"So that explains your fumbling."

"Afraid so. I get so nervous. Etiquette and common sense get lost. My philosophy in flying is to keep busy. Talking helps immensely to forget my fears, too. I hope you enjoy talking."

"I'll talk, as long as you remain calm." He raised one eyebrow at her, obviously appealing to her better sense.

"I'll try." She laughed. "I'm glad you understand."

"Tell me more about your work."

"I'm primarily a liaison between the travel industry and the public, focusing on road, rail, boat and plane travel. So, I'm not up in the air all the time. And, only recent plane accidents have contributed to my fear. You know the saying: the ignorant fear nothing; the initiated fear something. Actually, I want to keep my feet on the ground and write books."

"About what?"

"Something involving law and order, courtroom drama." Mona retrieved the pocketbook novel.

This caught Rock's interest. "You may find my case interesting. I've been brain-deep in a court case for seven years. An estate affair. I don't mind talking about it, especially since I won my appeal." This seemed to be an ideal way of getting to know her better.

"Even so, seven years is a long time. Draining."

"Yep, a budget buster. I no sooner find an interested, energetic attorney to represent me, then something goes wrong and I have to hire another. Haven't figured out why yet. However, a fine attorney is representing me now. He won my appeal concerning an earlier trial, a trial that didn't turn out right."

"I read where relatives and attorneys come out of the woodwork when someone dies."

"Parasites."

"Parasites?"

"Attorneys. At least some."

Mona laughed. "Sounds like you've been bit."

"Where I can't scratch." Rock was delighted in her interest and gave her a condensed version of his litigation. By the time the refreshment cart rolled by, they were on quite friendly terms. He ordered a Martini. Mona ordered a Greyhound. These were placed on small tables lowered from the back of the seats in front of them.

Rock was about to talk, when the plane captain identified himself and spoke to the passengers. "Ladies and gentlemen. We're about to experience some turbulence. Please heed the seat-belt signs overhead. Buckle up until further notice. There's no cause for alarm; merely a precaution. Hang onto your beverages and all stewardesses return to your stations. Thank you."

"Oooh; oh no." Mona pinned her forehead to the windowpane. "The clouds look dark and threatening."

Rock fastened his belt, then took her drink so she could fumble around and fasten hers. A liquor shower on him wasn't in his itinerary. She fumbled and fastened. It was just in time. The plane dropped in a down draft. It wasn't bad.

Nevertheless, Mona braced against the seat and grabbed the armrests. Other passengers were doing the same. No serious mishaps were evident. "This is what pilots refer to as CAT or clear air turbulence. Don't worry. Stop looking out the window."

She nodded, saying nothing, finally lowering the window shade.

"Here, drink this." He gave her his Martini, keeping her Greyhound.

Mona clasped the Martini with both hands and gulped. Her eyes were round.

"Hey, easy on that stuff. Strong power water. Take little sips." He noticed her hands tremble. She was like a frightened bird. "Isn't there a word, a phobia, that describes a person's fear of flying?"

"It's my fear of heights. Acrophobia, better known as scared shitless."

"I guess that's the word. Your description fits well." Rock laughed. "I know how you feel. I used to be a commercial pilot, flying corporate jets for a charter company. I finally quit after losing too many pilot friends in plane accidents. I figured my time was next. But, these big commercial planes are generally safe."

"Keep talking; talking helps. Believe me."

And so talking they did to keep Mona's mind off the flight. Then Rock made a suggestion. "Since you finished my Martini, I'll finish your Greyhound." He drank up. "Not very strong. What in the heck is this?" His expression soured.

"Unsweetened grapefruit juice and vodka. Please, let me buy you another Martini."

He noticed the seat-belt signs were off before glancing down at her. He contemplated. The alcohol content of two martinis was his limit, so it really wouldn't hurt to have another drink. Although accepting her offer might mean drinking another of her Greyhounds. And, he disliked accepting a drink from a lady. "No."

"I insist." Mona rang for a stewardess.

"Only if you drink a Greyhound and I pay."

"Weeelll, okay." One more Martini and one more Greyhound." Mona ordered from the stewardess.

By the time they finished their drinks, Rock detected the aroma of food. "I see flight attendants down the aisle with a food cart. Ready to eat?"

"Not yet. If you'll excuse me, I'd like to freshen up first." Mona stood.

Rock grinned. "Need help?"

Their eyes met. "You trying to be handy again?" She smiled.

"I mean, getting there." Chuckling, he moved into the aisle.

She laughed. "If you hear a commotion, send help."

He sighed, while watching pink dusters and swaying hips traipse down the aisle. What an interesting sight. Looking down at his turquoise, he thought, at the very least, the stone did bring excitement into one's life. His boss Atsidi insisted he dress like this. Good for business. Boss was right.

*   *   *

Mona returned from the washroom without mishap. Finally the food wagon stopped alongside Rock. A flight attendant set dinners with boneless chicken breasts in front of them.

"Where are you headed?" Rock talked as they ate.

"Seattle. Lake City area."

"Ah, northeast end."

"Yes. However, I'm not heading for home tonight. I'm staying with a few friends. They will be at the airport to meet me. We have plans for the weekend. You?" She ate a forkful of carrots.

"Ballard. With the Swedes and the Norwegians." Rock enunciated the words in a makeshift Scandinavian accent.

"Oh, not too far from me."

Rock buttered his roll. "I sometimes do business in Lake City, Kenmore, Bothell. Usually eat in a German restaurant, Shigley's Restaurant. Ever been there?"

"Oh, yes." She swallowed. "I enjoy the place, especially when they have an accordionist play and sing to the diners. Meals become parties." She took a bite of chicken with gravy and stuffing. "Emmm. Good. This isn't bad for airline food. Guess I was hungry."

"Good food, good company." He watched her bite into the chicken.

"Would you like one of my breasts? I have two."

Rock cleared his throat. "Eeer. Sooo. I've noo-ticed." A slow smile appeared as he talked. "And a foot in your mouth."

She held a napkin to her mouth, trying to swallow. "And too much Martini. Please, that's not what I mean. I meant . . ." Her hands gesticulated excitedly. "Oh. What's the use? I give up." She laughed.

Their exchanges tumbled into howls until Rock noticed nearby passengers were straining to enjoy their fun. We'd better tone down." He was pleased it happened. He needed a little craziness. He'd been uptight for too long. And, this was a much-needed change of pace in his hectic life, his litigation, his divorce. She made him want to talk, relax and laugh. It relieved some of the hurt over the loss of Leucojum.

"So where are you in your court case?"

"Near the end, hopefully. I face a new trial to enter my new evidence, which is referred to as the Leucojum documents. Leucojum is my mother's name." His throat constricted and he closed his eyes, wishing he hadn't said the name. One minute he was fine. The next minute he was in remorse as memories surrounding her unexpected death were sad. And, out of respect, one shouldn't mention the name of a deceased loved one for one year following death. He had to convince himself this was an old-fashioned belief because Leucojum was an important part of his litigation. Her name would be mentioned many times before year's end.

"Leu-co-jum. Please. I'm not laughing. A beautiful name. Takes me by surprise. "Where did the name 'Leucojum' come from?"

"A Native name taken from Mother Nature, meaning "snowflake". She came from the Cherokees in Oklahoma. My dad, Caucasian. I'm Amerindian, a mixed-breed." Rock placed a flat right hand upwards, the little finger nearest his chest and moved the hand one foot to the left, then back and one foot to the right. "I'm Caucasian and Cherokee."

"Is that sign language?"

"Yes. Native American sign language. Some folks refer to it as gesture speech. I learned it in Indian Scouting, and used it to communicate with my dad who became hard of hearing years before his death."

"You are amazing. But, how did your folks find each other, coming from two states so far apart?"

"Dad was visiting in Oklahoma sometime around 1947, after the war. He met mom in a gift shop. He took her dancing. They two-stepped all night, and fell in love." Rock crossed his wrists over his chest, indicating love.

"The Cherokee are beautiful people."

"Mom was beautiful. She married dad and moved to Quamas, where I was born and raised. Mixed marriages are common among the Cherokee."

"That explains your nice coloring. Look at me. Paleface." She held a hand alongside his.

"And beautiful eyes a shade of turquoise." He found her engaging.

Mona responded shyly. "You don't sound Native American."

The remark caused him to snort. He and his Indian friends used to joke about living in the White tribe. Like Whites, they lived in houses and watched the same insects fly up to summer's song. They heard the same murmur of wind in the pines.

"Are we supposed to sound different? We breathe. We bleed. We love." He held her eyes with his momentarily to emphasize what was important to him. She appeared to listen intently. "Just because we have different languages, cultures and histories, we still have the same needs. This is 1990. Get real. I was educated and raised in the same environment as you. I am Cherokee by blood; White by conditioning." He felt he was becoming too serious and decided to make light of his comments. "I'm surrounded by White eyes."

"But, you've been amply exposed to your heritage, I presume."

Rock pointed to his heart. "It's in here. A chest full. I pull my beliefs out occasionally. What would you like? A cigar-store Indian? A Hollywood Indian? Or the real me?"

Mona seemed fascinated. "Oh, I want to know about the real you. So, you must phone me after your trial, or before, if anything new comes up. I want to know how this litigation turns out. I just might write a novel about you."

"Me." He stopped eating to think about this. He was a part of Seattle's Native American population, one percent. Tribal Indians had long ago been forced out to distant suburbs. Famous Natives listed in an almanac didn't include Indians. And, this pretty lady wanted to write about him? "Me?"

"You and your litigation. From what you've described, I see a most unusual probate case. Atypical."

"You're buffaloing me." Judging by her eyes, she wasn't. He liked the idea. "I'd be delighted to phone you about it. You'll have to allow me a month or two. My schedule is tight." He knew he needed time to gather information for her. And there was a trial for which to prepare. After some silence, Rock broke into her thoughts. "Married?"

"Divorced." She hesitated. "And, you?"

"Separated with plans for divorce in the near future. Are you committed to anyone?"

Her mouth curled into a grin without showing teeth, averting his eyes.

"I know. None of my damn business." Rock cocked his head to one side. Nevertheless, he pressed for an answer, wanting to know more about this lady. There was no denying her charisma. A little flighty perhaps. Nevertheless, he thought she was one he'd like to get to know. He was no longer beholding to Sheryl. Living alone, well, he sought female companionship whenever he could. But, why this one? He closed his eyes. Her perfume. It had to be her perfume. Yes, her perfume was playing tricks on his emotions. It riled romance and urges that Sheryl had a way of suppressing.

"There's someone I date. He's tallish, emmm, about your height, nice looking, fun to be with. We spend time in museums and enjoy the opera. He's elderly and . . ."

"Elderly." Rock interrupted, guffawing. "Goooood Lord. The guy sounds like a museum piece." He raised an eyebrow. "I can't picture a good-looking lady like you robbing the grave." He figured she had to be in her early thirties.

"You, my dear man, know how to flatter." She laughed, taking it in good stride. Before she could say another word, the plane executed a rough landing, causing her to brace her feet and stiffen.

Rock dared to place a hand over hers, finding it soft. "We're okay." Her hand trembled, so he released his hold, not wanting to add to her discomfort. After the plane taxied up to the Seattle terminal and stopped, everyone moved into a frenzy of activity. Mona busied herself recovering a few belongings on the floor. He insisted on assisting with the overhead. "You aren't going to wear those dusters off the plane, are you?"

"No. Give me the heels." She laughed and changed the subject. "We should exchange phone numbers."

Rock felt enlightened by this. Someone writing about his case, especially if he recovered his inheritance and the Carper mansion. What an ending that would be. Rock pulled a card from his pocket. "Here. My business card."

"Good idea." She put his card between her teeth and opened her purse to locate a card for him. They studied each other's cards. "Oh, your name is Dorian Barnes Carper. I like it."

"Thanks, but to all my friends and you, I'm Rock." He winked, smiling. "We'll keep in touch. I like your idea about the novel." He had more than a novel on his mind.

Chapter Six

While swimming the length of the community clubhouse pool with her twin, Mona noticed the chlorine was strong, a smarting effect to her eyes. As much as she swam, it was something she didn't like. But, the water was warm on her skin. The noise from kids and parents echoed off the domed ceiling. She sliced the water with her arms and fluttered her feet close together to move around other swimmers. And, she thought about her plans for writing a novel on Rock's litigation. It was a unique case. Drawn out. Problems with attorneys and relatives.

For her to write his story, it would take a team effort. The team: Rock, Gena and herself. Unfortunately, Mona was the only one to look at it like this, since Rock and Gena had not yet met. But, that would have to change.

While moving around swimmers, Mona continued to the end of the Olympic-size pool. Her thoughts turned to Gena stopping short of becoming an attorney when her husband, Shumway, and two passengers in his float plane disappeared somewhere in the Siskiyou Mountains. Gena had been dragging through life ever since, filling in her days working as a court reporter in Seattle. Since this happened four years ago, it wasn't likely that Shumway was alive. Marriage and family were important to Gena. At age thirty-two, she needed to move on. Surely, there would be no harm in sending Gena in Rock's direction, at least to get his story. If it didn't lead to anything, there would be no harm.

Mona was really too busy this month with travel assignments anyway. The twins had done this ploy before in their past but nothing on a grand scale.

And, Mona had already told Gena about her flight from Dallas, how scared she was, meeting Rock, his stunning Native American jewelry, their spontaneity and interesting details of his litigation. She hoisted herself onto the pool edge and shook her hair from side to side. It was time to put her plan into motion. She flagged Gena's attention.

Gena nodded and side stroked toward her. "What?"

"I need advice." Mona adjusted the bottom rim of her one-piece suit.

Gena squeezed water from her braid. "You're bent on writing that book aren't you?"

"You know I need your help. I need your analytical mind and your knowledge."

"Working at the superior court doesn't qualify me for anything special."

"You're more than qualified for what I have in mind." Mona didn't expect this to be easy.

"Remember, I'm not an attorney."

"So? I'm only making a simple request."

Gena sank into the water. "Very well. What can I do?"

"Advise me. I need to learn more about the Carper estates. Tell me how I go about it?"

Gena jumped up onto the pool ledge and moved her feet in circles. "Read everything on file at the Clamton County Courthouse. You can phone the clerk's office and order the filings. If you want everything. Hmmmm. Let's see. Trial transcript, affidavits, depositions, exhibits, motions. It might cost you a pretty penny because you're looking at seven years of paperwork at fifty cents a page for copying. That doesn't include mailing costs."

"Without spending much." Mona kicked at the water.

"An alternative. Drive there. Sit in the clerk's office and read each page. That could take a week, longer if you take handwritten notes. Less if you dictate into a recorder."

"I said without spending much. Your suggestion would take a week. What I save in copying, I'd spend for food and lodging." Mona shoved Gena into the pool, creating splashes.

Gena tried to grab Mona's left foot on the way down, but missed. She surfaced, giggling and shook water from her ears. "The expense is deductible, if you do the book. What did you do with the money from last year's garage sale?"

"In the bank earning interest."

"There you are. Case solved." Gena splashed away and twirled. "My suggestion. Go to the Clamton Clerk's Office and just read, get the feel of the case, give it a little more time." She paused. "Or phone Rock. Ask him to provide copies."

"I like your last suggestion. That would be simpler." She'd get Gena to do this when the time was ripe.

*   *   *

Once Rock's feet were firmly planted on Seattle soil, he became upset all over again, concerning the recent hearing and the difficulty he was having reaching Anders. Today, he was determined to talk to Anders. Pacing the kitchen, he phoned the law firm, knowing Anders was a morning person. He wanted an answer as to the reason for a new trial when a hearing was all that was necessary.

Ginger Haley intercepted. "Anders is out of the office. Perhaps I can help you?"

"I need to know why he asked for a new trial, when he knew I was in hopes of a hearing."

"Listen." She was abrupt. "Judge Randell's order for a new trial is not much different from having another hearing. He followed directions from the appellate court to consider all evidence of record. It's not as if we're starting from scratch."

"So, the trial won't cost more?" Waiting for her answer, he stared out the kitchen window, noticing a cloudy day.

"You'll have to talk to Anders."

"When will he be available?"

"Well, I don't know."

The conversation with Haley was hopeless. He decided she could help him in another way. "Then, could you tell me how to get ahold of Uncle John's papers before the new trial? Marvin Benson has control of all papers of an estate I'm trying to probate." He tried to be polite.

"I'll make arrangements through Perkins, or Adams."

"No, I can do it. Really, let me assist in research and discovery, to hold down my legal expenses. Let me help."

"No. You don't do anything without your attorney." Haley snapped in a shrill voice. "Wait a minute. I'll phone you back."

Rock hung up and waited, drumming his fingers on the counter. Within minutes she phoned.

"We're set. Be at Perkins' office in Tacoma at nine Thursday morning."

"Okay. Thanks." He phoned Sheryl, inviting her to come, otherwise she'd be furious.

* * *

Before bedtime, Gena sat up to the home-office desk and stared at the phone. A twinge of doubt gnawed at her, knowing she was about to pose as Mona. How could she have let Mona talk her into this madness. Switching places was something they hadn't done for quite some time. Well, this was a favor for the sake of the novel. Rock meant nothing to her personally. She shoved all thoughts aside, picked up the receiver and dialed. Rock answered, identifying himself. His voice had a deep sonorous quality. It seemed to draw her into the receiver.

"H'lo. This is Mona Bradley." Gena cleared away a lump in her throat for the deception. "Just touching base with you. I'm still interested in writing about your litigation."

"Oh, yes. The travel writer with a fear of flying. How are you?"

Gena thought he sounded most receptive. "Fine. I hope I'm not calling at a bad time."

"Not at all. I just returned from the senior citizen's center."

"Oh?"

"Yes. I volunteer time at a senior citizen's center. And, you caught me on the way down to the basement to do a little carving on a totem pole. That can wait. I'm delighted to hear from you. Sooo. You really are serious about planting your feet on the ground and writing that book, huh?"

"Of course. Nothing ventured, nothing gained." Gena remembered Mona telling her that the ticket lady at the Dallas airport made this clever remark, not realizing its appropriateness until now. She laughed, playing with the phone cord.

"Well, I like your thinking, but my case is hanging in limbo at the moment. I'm not sure you'd find it interesting."

"We can decide that later. Meanwhile, I'd like to know more about the Carpers. I have my recorder set to roll. Do I have your permission to record this conversation?"

"Sure. I trust you. Where do you want me to begin?"

"I'll ask questions I know you can answer quickly." She pushed the start button, located the first question from her legal pad and leaned back in a slat-back chair. "When did the Carpers step foot on Quamas soil?"

"Actually, it began in the early 1900's with my grandparents Erin and Mary Carper and their sons John and Jack. They traded in the country air of a large cattle ranch in central Oregon for a new future in the cannery business and the smell of fish and saltwater in Quamas, Washington."

"The small village on the west side of Chenowah Island? Travel brochures describe it as a gray, misty, windy land made brilliant by wavy whitecaps flashing off the waters of Puget Sound and the Straight of Juan de Fuca." Mona had provided this information to her.

"Hey. That's the place."

"So, eventually, John married Nell, the aunt and uncle in your litigation? And, they had no children?"

"Right to both questions."

As the questioning progressed, Gena found him most congenial and not the least bit suspicious. She was grateful Mona had provided sufficient background information. "And Jack married Leucojum, who became your folks?"

"Yes. They had me late in life."

"A little after thought?" She giggled, hoping he didn't mind a little teasing.

"No. A big one. Like ten pounds. Mom had a rough time. The doctor told her things got a little rocky for a while. They nicknamed me Rocky. I switched to Rock in middle school."

"I wondered how you got the name. Okay. Go on." She wrote his name in large capital letters on the legal pad for no particular reason. A form of doodling.

"After the move to Quamas, the Carpers lived in temporary housing while building the mansion."

Something clicked against the phone on his end. She thought he was drinking something.

"The Carper Cannery was located downhill from the mansion. We had a small fleet of fishing boats, mostly gill-netters and cannery tenders."

"What were the Carper men like?" Mona had told her Rock was Cherokee from his mother's side.

"Tall, husky, broad shouldered. They were fair-skinned with brown hair. Irish descent. The Carper men were educated in business affairs. Occasionally, they used the Carper mansion and the cannery as collateral for bank loans to expand their business. They established this practice in a trust agreement."

Gena opened a lower side drawer to the desk to use as a footrest. She flipped off her shoes and adjusted her jeans. "Explain the trust agreement."

"The agreement was hatched by Uncle John and my Dad Jack years before I was born. After Mary died and Erin retired, John and Jack, by this time married, signed the trust agreement. It established a Carper legacy, leaving assets to surviving heirs. Nell signed this agreement, acknowledging that the mansion and cannery business were Jack and John's separate property."

Gena scribbled the words trust agreement and separate property on the legal pad as important. "When were you born?"

"I was born in 1950."

This put him at forty years old. His voice sounded mature and so appealing. Ideas of meeting him surfaced. Yes. It might be fun to meet him. No harm. She would be doing it for Mona's book. "So, when did John write a new will?"

"Several months after dad died. 1967. The will gave me the mansion after Nell no longer wanted to live there."

"How did John and Nell originally take possession?"

"They just nested in shortly before Erin passed away. They never left. Then years later, dad died. John sold the business and used the money to invest in business loans, still honoring the trust agreement. Early in May of '72 on their vacation there was a car accident putting John and Nell in a hospital. John died of a heart attack days later."

"What about Nell?"

"She survived but didn't submit John's 1967 will to probate. Instead, she led me to believe she would honor John's wishes at her death. I knew she executed her own will to this effect. Too, she hired a Quamas attorney, Ralph Houston, to handle John's estate with a community property agreement. So I didn't pursue the house."

"Stop. I though John's property was separate." She drew a big circle around the word separate on the legal pad with a question and two exclamation marks.

"It was. This community thing was a total surprise I didn't know existed until Nell's attorney told me. But it was recorded so I figured it was legitimate."

"Hmmm. I would think the trust agreement would make a difference." Gena was certain, but she wasn't an attorney and wouldn't offer legal advice.

"My attorney Anders thinks so. The trust agreement is part of my new evidence."

Gena was relieved that his attorney was aware. She recorded his answers to a few additional questions. "This is helpful Rock." The information was interesting, maybe useful to Mona. However, this was only a surface scratch, leading to the most important question. "Do you suppose you could provide me with copies of your documents? At least some transcript to save me time. Then I won't have to travel to the courthouse in Quamas."

"Sure. I'll bring my copies. When would you like to meet?"

Gena established a meeting, thanked him, hung up and clicked off the recorder. So far so good.

Chapter Seven

Rock and Sheryl arrived at Perkins' fourth-floor office in Tacoma at nine sharp. This was a prearranged visit to go through some boxes of Uncle John's papers, under the control of his opposition. The receptionist asked them to wait, then quietly made a phone call. Rock devoted his time to pacing over the lobby's earthy-colored carpeting. Then, he stopped to gaze at the scenic view of the Sound. Finally, he sat to read the *Tacoma News Tribune*. Sheryl flipped through *Fortune* and *National Geographic*. After forty-five minutes, Rock was about to explode.

The receptionist started to talk when in flew Ginger Haley, red-faced, wind-blown hair and narrowed eyes. She marched across the carpeting to Rock. Her long coat hung open, cloak-like.

Rock thought she looked like a leech ready to suck blood. His. He spoke first. "What are you doing here?" He was cordial, trying to hide his surprise.

"The receptionist phoned me. You're not supposed to be here without me." Her voice was stern.

"Well, I'm not talking to anyone. Merely waiting to go through some boxes. A job my attorney should have done long before today." Having just insulted her and Anders, he uncrossed his knees and sat at attention, not knowing what to do next.

The receptionist approached, telling them to follow her into a backroom before Haley had a chance to comment. Once the boxes were set up on one end of a thirty-foot, wood-grained malachite conference table, Haley left, after devoting a total of fifteen minutes at the law offices. Rock and Sheryl were now under the watchful supervision of one of Perkins' associates.

* * *

Inviting Sheryl to sleep in his bed while he slept on the sofa was the only sensible thing to do, knowing it would take two days to go through all the boxes in Perkins' possession. Sheryl agreed. The morning following the second day, they hurriedly ate breakfast, then cleared the sofa of blankets.

"Thanks fer lettin' me stay the night in yer flat, Rock. But, I think I'll be headin' back ta my folks' place in Quamas now. We're lookin' ta find me a house." Sheryl stood by the door.

"Hold on Sheryl. Something isn't right." Rock pushed aside two toss pillows on the sofa to sit and sift through the xeroxed copies he amassed at the end of two days spent at Perkins' office. "Sonofabitch. Perkins obviously went through our pile and removed what he didn't want me to have."

"What's missin'?" She raised her brow while removing her coat and settling down next to him.

Rock rattled the papers in his hands. "Several. The most important was that 1984 letter Houston wrote to Marvin, showing the value of Nell's estate as more than $500,000." Rock remembered when he discovered the letter in a folder in one of the five boxes; he showed it to Sheryl. She wanted to pocket the letter, xerox it themselves at some establishment outside the law firm and return the letter to the box on the second day, but Rock wouldn't let her. Honesty was something he didn't mess around with in the legal system. Even though it was one of the highest virtues to Native Americans, he suddenly wished he hadn't been so damn honest that day.

"Oou, begora. That letter was important 'cause we know Uncle John's estate ta Nell was worth that much in 1972 when John died. It must be worth more than five million now 'cause o' stock splits and such."

"The letter also proved that Marvin and Houston misrepresented to the Clamton Court in '84 that Nell's estate was worth a piddling $165,000."

Her eyes widened. "Let's bang oot a letter o' complaint ta Haley. Ye dictate ta me. I'll type it in the computer and we'll both sign it." Sheryl moved over to the computer, sat on the stool and proceeded to start a new document.

"Good idea." He was pleased because she was a good letter writer. She always said it was a way to put records and events in order, like a paper trail. Rock paced the carpeting, holding his arms in the thinking position, one arm under an elbow; a finger to his lips. "Address the letter to Anders and Haley."

Sheryl typed, then waited.

The ticking of the Carper antique wall clock penetrated the silence. "Damn it, Sheryl, I'm so riled. I can't think. My brain's in a whirl." Rock moved a right fist in a small circle on his forehead as he continued pacing. Finally, he touched two fingers to his forehead, forcing himself to think. "Ahhh, say something about Perkins purposely withholding documents. Point out there were only five boxes provided to us, all Nell's papers. Ask, 'Where are Uncle John's papers?'" Rock dug around in the end table drawer for an envelope and stamp.

She did as instructed, then printed several copies. Rock inserted carbon between the copies. They each signed at the bottom. "I'll post this on my journey home. We'll get ta the bottom o' this. Ye can bet yer shamrock we will."

"Whoa. You're getting ahead of yourself." He addressed the envelope and licked the stamp, while Sheryl slipped into her coat. Again Rock reminded her, "If I win anything from this case, you get half."

She took the stamped envelope and tucked the letter inside. "Thanks. I'm countin' on it. That's why I'm helpin'."

Rock was satisfied. At least they weren't arguing.

*　　*　　*

Following the end of the workday and an hour of volunteer work at the senior citizen's center, Rock welcomed relaxation in his apartment. He loosened his cuffs, rolled his sleeves and sat at the small kitchen table to eat a boxed take-out Chinese meal, while sorting through the mail. One pile was junk mail to be thrown away. Bills were put in another pile. Any correspondence from Anders, he opened immediately, because he was hoping for an answer to his question on the location of his uncle's documents.

Instead, he read the unexpected. Anders' brief letter arrived with a bill for Haley's fifteen-minute appearance at Perkins' office.

After pushing plates out of the way, he went for the phone on the counter, returned to the table and dialed Sheryl in Quamas.

"'Eeeello?"

"Anders wants $150 for Haley's fifteen-minute appearance."

"Get away."

"Hell. I didn't ask her to be there that day. What an outrage." He gritted his teeth. Down deep he wanted to pull a few tail feathers. "And, that's not all."

"What else is 'e wantin'?"

"Wants another $25,000 upfront to handle the upcoming trial. He announced his hourly rate rising to $190. Shhiiit. He knows I'm strapped." Rock reached for his antacids on the counter and moved into the living room dragging the phone cord.

"Rock, efter seven years with attorneys, I'm no surprised they're drummin' up expenses. Ye should drop yer madness?"

"No. I want justice and I'm going to get it." Rock popped two antacids in his mouth, while flipping on the television with his remote control and slumping down on the sofa.

"What's that racket? The telly?"

"A Charles Bronson rerun."

"Too bad ye cannae solve yer problems like Bronson, or Rob Roy." She cackled.

"At this stage, I'm not going to seek a new attorney."

"Rock, ye havenae alternative other than ta talk ta Anders. Do it and let me know."

"Sheryl, I'll keep trying." He hung up deciding it was bad enough just thinking about the cost of a new trial, let alone search for a new attorney. Anders was in hiding. Haley wouldn't let him do anything on his own. Perkins was withholding documents. Rock's misery was finally replaced, watching Bronson solve problems underhandedly.

Chapter Eight

"I feel skullduggery coming on." Gena said to Mona in the Jacuzzi at their swim club.

"I came to that conclusion from what Rock told me on the plane. Behind the formalities there exists a facade with facile operators. I hoped you would become interested. Rock didn't learn until after Nell died in 1983, that she probated John's estate under a mysterious 1952 will."

"I thought you or someone said that a community property agreement replaced any will." Gena liked the water bubbling around her chin.

"That's what attorney Houston told Rock. But, that's not what actually happened. Houston and Nell used John and Nell's community property agreement to transfer John's separate property into her name. Then Houston had Nell repudiate the agreement. Then they probated John's estate with a '52 will."

"Weird. They used a will after all. Did you say they transferred John's separate property? With or without court permission?"

"Without court permission."

"That's impossible. Illegal." Gena was adamant.

"Ho boy. Well, that's what happened. And, ironically, Nell never took the Carper mansion deed out of John's sole name."

"She didn't add her name? Or transfer the deed in her sole name after John's death?"

"No. She left the deed as is, or as was. Now the plot thickens. Nell Carper left behind a niece, Beatrice, who's married to Marvin Benson. They moved into the mansion a year before Nell died, and reorganized her affairs and intention of honoring the Carper legacy."

"How?"

"With a power of attorney for Marvin, prepared by attorney Houston. This entailed drafting a new will for Nell, excluding Rock entirely and favoring themselves, at a time when Nell was suffering with Alzheimer's disease."

Gena hoisted onto the ledge. She played the water with her feet.

Mona followed Gena. "First, after Nell's passing, Beatrice, Marvin and Houston stepped in to further alter the Carper Legacy. Public records show they transferred the mansion from John's name to Nell's estate and sold the mansion. All without court permission, striping away what rightfully belonged to Rock."

"I detest conniving relatives." Gena splashed back into the water and floated on her back with outstretched arms. "This heat feels so soothing."

"Rock said since Nell's demise, the mansion has changed ownership four times to families outside of the Carper name."

"Yet, the mansion still remains in the separate name of John Carper?"

"Right."

"No wonder the mansion has changed ownership four times. I suspect no owner can claim a clear and free title so long as Rock Carper and his descendants remain alive."

"That's the picture I have." Mona became curious as the two talked a while longer. "What's this thing called justice? Gimme a quick, easy answer."

"Hmmm. Okay, an impartial adjustment of conflicting claims. You just got a dictionary definition. Now, let's go home."

"Impartial adjustment." Mona recited it over several times, traipsing through little puddles of water while trailing Gena to the showers. "Impartial is the most powerful word in your definition."

"And, it will be the most difficult for Rock to get around I'm afraid, knowing how justice works today."

*   *   *

During a coffee break at Turquoise Wholesalers, Rock straddled a stool in front of an old rolltop desk his boss shared with him in a small office. He admired his boss, Atsidi Shaw, an educated Navajo. Atsidi was off to the southwest on a buying trip, dealing with the Navajos and the Pueblos of Zuni, Pojoaque, Santa Clara, Tesuque, the Utes of Colorado and the Taos of New Mexico. He did most of the buying until his wife of forty-odd years died several years ago. After her death, Atsidi lost a spark of interest in traveling and gradually began training Rock for the task.

Rock wished he were on assignment instead of here stewing over Anders' demand for more money. Bent on facing the inevitable, he grabbed the desk phone and dialed Anders' office. While waiting, his eyes scanned the wall above the desk. The pine-paneled room was lit by natural light filtering through a tall narrow window that faced First Avenue south. The light highlighted a large map of the southwest located above the desk. It depicted cliff dwellings and village outlines of prehistoric missions of Spanish priests and crumbling adobe forts of the cavalry.

Finally a receptionist took Rock's request for Anders, then put him on hold with classical music. He no sooner pushed back his stool when Anders came to the phone. Rock wasn't one to waste time on formalities. "I don't know how I can afford your demands, two attorneys, a detective and a new trial, unless you'll accept $200 a month. That's the best I can do."

"Have you considered remortgaging your house?"

"I don't have a house." Rock pleaded above the piercing siren passing the window below the building. "My wife owned the Magnolia house we were living in many years before we separated. That was her separate property. She sold it and is in the process of buying a house in Quamas."

"How about your mother's house in Quamas? Since she passed away, you could deed that house to me as security."

"She left that house to my son, since I was supposed to get the Carper mansion after Nell died." His irritation deepened. He penciled totem pole motifs on a scratch pad. Obviously, Anders had been checking on his assets.

"Fine. If you can't afford me, you find another attorney."

"Thanks a helluva lot Anders." Rock bared down on the pencil, breaking the lead. "I've trusted you. I've appreciated your help and I've always paid you on time. I paid $25,000 for appellate work. I can't believe all that money is gone. You know my word's good. I'll pay $200 a month. More, when possible. I can't start all over with a new attorney." Opening a pocketknife from his pocket, Rock made a weak attempt to sharpen the pencil.

"Rock, $200 a month won't work when my rate is now $190 an hour. The $25,000 was only for the appeal. You owe me for back pay since the appeal. Tell you what, Haley, can take over. If she needs help, I'll poke into the matter. She doesn't cost as much and she knows the case. Besides, I'm always around. I'll be there at the trial. But you have to figure a way to get another $25,000."

Rock hung up feeling desperate. At one time Anders was good. No question. But lately, Anders hadn't been treating him right. Yet, the idea of hiring another attorney had to be worse than putting up with Anders' demands. There had to be a solution. But what? Rock threw the pencil across the desk and cleaned up the shavings.

Without a solution, he devoted the next half-hour to lifting weights stored in a cupboard at one end of the office. Frequent workouts relieved tension, especially when business was slow.

*   *   *

With effort, many phone calls and Anders' connections, Rock executed a payment solution in record time.

While preparing dinner, Rock phoned Sheryl. "I did it."

"What ye talkin' a'boot? What's that noise?"

"I'm pan-frying steak." He lowered the heat and clicked on the fan. "I raised the money to pay Anders by contacting our son in the Army. He understood the situation and deeded the Leucojum house, minus the contents, over to me. Then Anders helped me secure a $30,000 mortgage."

"Get oot. Ye gave Anders $30,000? Are ye daft maun?"

"No, I only gave $12,500 to his firm for continued representation through the new trial. I'll give him the balance later." Rock turned the T-bone and added dashes of salt and cayenne. The sizzling sound of spattering grease and the aroma tantalized his hunger.

"Only $12,500." Sheryl's groan grated in his ear.

He moved over to the counter and sliced a beefsteak tomato onto a plate.

"Ye put yer leavin's in trust o' a beggar. Anders is a toady ta the bone. Ye could o' dished out a wee bit at a time. Had ye no thought o' that?"

"Sheryl, I am dishing out a wee bit as you put it. Giving Anders $12,500 upfront will make him work harder." Rock felt confident Anders now had no excuse to do anything other than forge ahead. Therefore nothing Sheryl said could dampen his spirits. It only mattered that she be aware of what he did since it involved their son. He couldn't expect her to understand.

"And where is our son goin' ta store the contents?"

"The contents in the Leucojum house can stay for now. I still stay there when I visit. I hired a man to mow the lawn. So, I have to check on him. Anyway, we can always rent a storage place, if need be."

"Where ye gettin' the 'we', laddie?"

"All right, I will handle things, because our son isn't the least bit interested in the Carper legacy. Obviously, you aren't either."

Rock hung up believing he did the right thing. If he'd hired another attorney, it would have cost a lot more. How did his dad's saying go? A fish in the net is worth two in the sea.

Chapter Nine

"I'm weary listening to the recorder and transcribing information from Rock's case." Mona entered the kitchen, finding Gena staring out the window. "I see Rock mailed me documentary information for my novel. But there's more to come so we still have to meet." She paused and waited for a response. "Watching the rain won't make it go away."

Gena turned around and smiled; then slid in behind the trestle table on the chaparral bench, a new addition to Mona's kitchen. "I spoke with him by phone."

Mona adjusted the bow in her hair and leaned against the counter. "I hope you didn't give away anything." Having Rock learn about Gena was the last thing she wanted at the moment.

"No. He thought he was talking to you."

"What'd he say?" Mona narrowed her eyes.

"Suggested dinner at Shigley's Restaurant. He has more paperwork for you."

"You'll have to go for me." Mona vocalized enthusiasm, sensing Gena would comply.

"Hey. Don't pull rank. Just because you were born a few minutes before me doesn't mean I'm your slave. I may be the afterthought in this family and I don't mind faking your voice over the phone. That comes naturally. But, I've changed my mind. No dates in your place."

"Please, Gena. Just this once. You need to know what he looks like just in case."

"In case what?"

"Well, you two work near Pioneer Square. You on one side; he on the other."

"See. Already you've got me in trouble." Gena fiddled with the small tray of seasonings on the table.

Mona straightened her posture. The rain had stopped and the sun beamed in through the barren trees and curtained corner window. "Until you meet him, stay out of the art galleries, boutiques, antique stores and especially jewelry shops."

"Ha. I'm supposed to get out in the world. Get a life so long as I don't wander away from the courthouse. A court reporter's job requires too much sitting as it is." She snickered and leaned away from the table. "He might wander into the courthouse, you know."

"Doubtful. He's too busy with legal matters in Quamas. Besides. I need your help in writing this novel." Mona scratched her head, realizing that Gena had become a tough sell since her husband disappeared. The only way to get her dating again would be to trick her.

"So, where does dating fit in?" Gena pushed away the tray and crossed her arms on the table.

"We need to know his beliefs, feelings, grudges, perceptions, conflicts with others. You know. The kind of information I can't procure from court records. Information we couldn't get if Rock knew you were married."

"Right. And, you're single. So, you go."

"I'm too busy traveling at the moment. And, I'm compiling information from Rock's documents. Besides, with your legal background and experience, you'd know the kind of questions to ask him better than me. Reading our collection of books on courtroom drama doesn't necessarily prepare me."

She watched Gena wrinkle her face in defiance, then relax. "He does have an interesting case. For example, the attorney Ralph Houston, who probated Rock's uncle's estate, definitely testified that Rock never approached him about probate matters. The attorney who cross-examined Houston was his partner Adams, who is representing Aunt Nell's relatives. That troubles me."

"Hum." Gena moved over to the coffeepot and poured a mugful. "Want some?"

"Please." Mona sat up to the table.

Gena brought the coffees. "Smacks of a conflict of interest."

"Kinda hits me that way." Mona felt a twinge of excitement, having gotten this reaction. If she talked enough, Gena would become hopelessly involved before she realized.

"Well, based on what I've gathered from you and Rock, picture this in your mind. Houston is intertwined in the probate of the aunt and uncle's estates. Since the niece, Beatrice, inherited from Aunt Nell, who inherited from Uncle John through possible misconduct by Houston, who is represented by his partner, both of who have represented Marvin and Rock, and Rock's Mom Leucojum and . . ." She interrupted herself, laughing and shook her head. "It's an imbroglio."

Almost spilling her coffee, Mona giggled. "A what?" She watched Gena drumming her long, tapered fingers on the table, appearing intent and serious.

"An imbroglio. Confusing. Definitely too cozy and too controlling against Rock."

"You see. You hold so much in that pretty blonde head." Mona placed a hand over Gena's fingers, squeezing them in fondness and admiration. "When you talk about something that interests you, you blossom."

"I'm brainy and bashful." Gena sighed and blew loose strands of hair from her face.

"You're downbeat because of Shumway's disappearance. The time has come to climb out of your shell."

"Don't forget. Your travel makes you more outgoing. You know how to use your good looks to best advantage. I don't. What if Rock recognizes this? I don't see how we can pull this off. Me pretending to be you."

"Rock talks nonstop about his litigation. So long as you keep him on track, there's no problem. Journalism requires the ability to amass information regardless of personal feelings."

"Maybe so, but one has to think of the consequences of our actions too."

"I care. It's not as if we're sending a herd of buffalo through his path."

Going against her better judgment, Gena relented.

Chapter Ten

"How can Anders poke into my case if he's out of reach?" Rock raved to Ginger Haley over the phone, while pacing the apartment hallway. His clothes and hair were damp, since he bucked wind and rain running from his car to the mailbox after work. Anders' letter announced he was going on a seven-month sabbatical. In this weather? The news was shattering. Rock felt as limp as seaweed.

"Calm down. I can always reach him. By the way, I attended a short hearing before a commissioner at the Clamton Courthouse to take care of a few details before the upcoming trial."

"Like what?" The hearing was a total surprise.

"Like requesting a tracing of assets Nell inherited from John's estate, since the two estates are consolidated. And I asked for paperwork missing from the five boxes you and Sheryl went through at Perkins' office."

Rock could hardly be upset over this. "Good."

"Not really. At the same hearing, Adams Jr. and Perkins filed a motion requesting that Marvin be released from overseeing Nell's estate. Come to my office tomorrow afternoon and we'll discuss it."

"Can't we discuss it now?" He didn't particularly enjoy fighting car bumpers and red intersection lights unnecessarily just to reach Anders' building. And, he begrudged their highrise view of Seattle's waterfront, plush carpeting, tree-size plants and an impressive art collection his fees likely helped purchase.

"No. I haven't time. Too involved. We need to discuss settlement."

"Settlement?"

"Settlement."

He hung up, determined that there wasn't much Haley could say to him that would cause him to settle.

*   *   *

The following afternoon, Rock bent over to rest his hands on the back of a client chair in front of Ginger Haley's desk. "Why do you want me to settle when I've got everything going in my favor?"

"The Nell estate is out of money." While swiveling away from her computer, located to the left of her desk, she gestured open-handedly. "Take a seat."

Rock held his stance. "Out of money, my ass. My opposition Marvin and Beatrice are using my inheritance to defeat me. They haven't paid a damn dime out of their own pockets. No, they drain both estates, while I burn my red hide spending my own money. Now, you tell me they're out of money. They aren't out of money. You know Marvin sucked funds from Nell when she had Alzheimer's."

He gripped his fingers into the chair padding. "I know there are records proving as much. Uncle John's estate is worth over five million." He gave her a second to cogitate his points. "When do I get to see records from Uncle John's estate? Marvin's attorney Perkins only let me see five boxes of records, mostly Nell's papers. You said there were more than five. And, when do I get a copy of the letter Perkins removed from those boxes? That letter supports what I'm saying." His eyebrows creased, as he tried to get her to admit he was right.

"You've seen all you're going to see from your opposition." Her gray eyes narrowed to cat-like slits.

His eyes fixed on her. He waited for more, but nothing came. Finally, he let go of the chair and stretched upward out of frustration. Not being able to see papers from an estate he was trying to probate didn't make sense. Judge Randell consolidated the John and Nell Carper estates before the 1984 trial. Anders said this meant that one estate couldn't be considered without consideration of the other. Her answer made his stomach burn. "Why aren't I going to see more?"

"Because in the short hearing I attended while you were out of town, the commissioner turned down our motion, which requested a tracing of funds from John's estate to Nell's estate." She drummed her fingers on the desk as if she had better things to do with her time.

"How convenient." Rock held his lips in a thin line. He figured she might as well have thrown hot tar over him. To keep from exploding, he took a few steps toward the picture window. Skyscrapers dominated the street scene below. An overcast day had settled over the Emerald City, livened by neon signs.

Rock sometimes wondered what he was doing living in Seattle, a city dominated by rolling hills, tall buildings and acres of concrete. The people in those cars down there had no idea what he was going through in this high-rise zoo. If only his antacids weren't in the car. He raised a fist over one hip and glared at Haley.

She smiled. "You can be pleased about one thing. The commissioner turned down Perkins' request to excuse Marvin as the executor of Nell's estate."

If she was placating him, it wasn't working. He nodded. "That's my point. The commissioner knows they aren't broke."

"Rock, face it. The estates are drained." Haley opened a desk drawer and pulled out a two-page list. "Here. One of Marvin's attorneys prepared this showing expenses to the Nell estate."

Rock walked over to take and scan the list, finding nothing convincing. "The estates were drained through misconduct by my opposition. I want that to come out loud and clear." He set the list on the desk and returned to the window.

"My, my. I see you've brought in a barrel of stubbornness." She slammed the drawer shut.

Rock swung around and reapproached her desk. He leaned on knuckled fists to the left of a pile of papers. In the process, he knocked over a fake flower arrangement on the right. "You know Marvin sold the stocks and bonds Nell illegally inherited from John and placed them in accounts in his and Beatrice's names seven months before Nell died. Then Marvin transferred the mansion from John's estate to Nell's estate and used that money for legal fees. That's stealing, in my book."

She returned the fake flowers to the vase, crossed her arms and leaned away, all but ignoring him.

"You haven't left behind your stubbornness either." He stared, wishing he could read her mind. There had to be a reason for this sudden change. And it wasn't because the Nell estate was out of money. "Remember, I have a lien on the Carper mansion. If the estates are drained, so be it. But, I'm entitled to the house."

As if Rock placed one too many requests on her, she pounded a skinny fist on the desk. "Well I'm not about to be caught in the middle of some worthless vendetta."

Rock didn't think he said anything out of line. "This isn't a vendetta. I want justice. I'm not being unreasonable. Thanks to Anders' fine appellate work, the appellate court remanded this case back to the superior court to unravel the misconduct. I hired you folks to help me probate my uncle's estate under the right will. You accepted. I've paid you plenty upfront. What changed your mind?"

"I don't care for trial work." She shouted. She raised her petite frame to pace behind her desk like it was a safety zone. "I'd rather do research for appeals. See this pile of papers on my desk?" She stopped and slapped the papers. Her straight dark hair fell forward splaying her shoulders. "I can earn more money from these than from you." ·

This was a horrible remark, leaving Rock emotionally drained. No case could be more important than his, money or no money. He feared that his opposition had gotten to her. "Obviously, you damn attorneys are more interested in money than justice. You'd better discuss this with Anders. Tell him to finish the job."

She pointed to the door. "Go home. Think about settlement. Phone me in three days."

Rock huffed. Somehow, he had to reach Anders to straighten out this matter.

Chapter Eleven

Rock thought about his visit with Ginger Haley. He concluded his only choice was to seek help from his bachelor friend, Efrem Abernethy, the one attorney he trusted. Even if his specialty was handling maritime cases, he could offer advice, and he owed Rock a favor.

Sitting on the stool in front of the old rolltop desk at work, Rock picked up the phone and dialed Efrem's office. A receptionist with a pleasant voice put him on hold. While waiting, he remembered their first meeting years ago when they were freshmen attending the University of Washington. Efrem was standing in line ahead of him at the Common's coffee shop in Raitt Hall. They killed time talking about the Huskies football games. Eventually they attended many football and basketball games together. Their friendship was solid.

Efrem came from a Maryland family. His dad and brother were attorneys and the mother was deceased. Efrem graduated from the University of Washington law school summa cum laude. Secretly, Rock reckoned if he had been smart enough to complete his college studies, he would have graduated summa cum last-a, because of chasing Sheryl all the time. Too, writing papers and memory work for tests weren't his forte.

Anyway, Efrem loved the northwest and never left. Not one to talk about it, Efrem slipped once in mentioning a special woman in his life. There was reluctance to explain further. Out of respect, Rock never asked.

"Hey, buddy, how are you? Things going okay?" In answering the phone, Efrem spoke in a jocular voice.

Rock pictured him as a big, hulking man with a sense of humor. "Have you got a minute? I need to explain. Bring you up to date." He toyed with his empty coffee mug, moving it in circles on the desk.

"You betcha. Shoot away on the works. I've got two minutes."

"Actually, give me ten." Rock laughed and explained the latest. "I've been shoved into an abyss. Ginger Haley kicked me out. In so many words, she hates trial work and wants me to settle. I don't know why she took this case. I want Anders back on the case. He's the one I hired in the first place. Aren't attorneys supposed to represent the client's interests?"

"Yes. Are you going to settle?"

The question hit a nerve and Rock thumped a fist on the desk. "Hell no. I want the Carper mansion."

"Gotcha. Let me phone Haley and navigate things. And stop by the house one of these nights."

"Will do. Thanks Efrem." Relieved, Rock hung up, knowing things would go better. Efrem was always good for his word.

* * *

A bummer day. Not much going on, Rock thought as he braked the

Firebird and slowed into a parking spot in front of his apartment complex. Smoggy breeze. The smell of exhaust fumes. The sun was all haze. It was the third day. The day to phone Ginger Haley and tell her settlement was out of the picture. This weighed heavily in Rock's mind, knowing this decision wasn't what she wanted to hear. Turning off the ignition, he grabbed the keys and climbed out. The mail van pulled in behind. He ambled over and smiled. "Any mail for Rock Carper?"

The mailman handed him a letter. Oh, oh. From Haley. There was no mistake. It was from Anders' law firm with Ginger Haley's name above the logo. Odd she'd be writing to him when her instructions were for him to phone. What little correspondence he received from Anders was a push for more money. But he didn't believe he was in the arrears, so this couldn't be the reason.

Rock braced against the car and planted his feet slightly apart on the grassy side of the parking strip directly under the Japanese red maples. He knew he was procrastinating. A joy for mystery or the unexpected wasn't exactly a part of his emotional makeup. Yet, why was he thinking negatively? Just because so many things had been adverse in his litigation, didn't mean this was. Whatever was contained inside could just as easily be positive.

"What the heck." He slit open the envelope with his small pocketknife. In a matter of minutes, his breathing became labored as his eyes moved down the typewritten page:

"I spoke with Efrem Abernethy on the phone yesterday and understand you wanted him to relay your position on settlement. Efrem told me you are determined to fight this out to the end.

I respect your position, and fully understand the basis for it. I wish you the best of luck at trial.

However, given your belief that you cannot communicate with me because I am a woman, which was also relayed to me by Efrem, our firm will be unable to represent you any longer. I therefore am enclosing our Notice of Intent to Withdraw.

I have thought a lot about your apparent inability to comfortably communicate with me and about the effect that has on our firm's continued representation of you in this action since my conversation with Mr. Efrem Abernethy yesterday.

As you know, I was to have been responsible for preparing this case for trial. That process will involve close contact with you, and whoever does it must know that they have the client's complete confidence, and that the client is comfortable communicating with the lawyer. I cannot effectively represent any client who does not feel that he or she can communicate with me.

Communicating through intermediaries, or preparing for trial in a communication vacuum, is unworkable. I refuse to practice law that way, and I cannot effectively represent a client under those circumstances. Therefore, I must withdraw.

I have spoken to my partners about having a male attorney in the office work up the case to accommodate your perceived inability to communicate with me because I am a woman. My male partners consider me as their equal. They rejected such an arrangement. None of us want to perpetuate or accommodate a client relationship that by its very nature implies that all of the attorneys in this office are not equal professionals. Because I cannot effectively represent you in this case, the entire firm must withdraw.

Your new attorney will have three months to prepare the case. We will coordinate with new counsel, I will sit down and bring him up to speed on the issues in the case.

Please read this letter carefully. We are withdrawing because we can no longer effectively represent you now that you don't believe you can effectively communicate with me. We are not withdrawing because you do not wish to settle the case. Our decision to withdraw is not negotiable, and is not contingent on other factors."

Rock found the letter outrageous. In anger, his fingers curled menacingly into the page. He looked up into the hazy sky, feeling bitterness. This was a cop out. Attorneys never write the real reasons. Nevertheless, Haley's accusation of him not liking women cut deeply. Why, he liked women. But, reflecting on it, he didn't look at Haley as a woman. She was an attorney for chrissake.

His dad taught him that one shouldn't love those he worked with business-wise, and he didn't have to argue with them either. His only argument with Haley was in trying to reason logically. And, he had lost track of the times he pleaded with her to let him speak to Anders, the attorney he hired in the first place. Nothing prejudicial about that.

He reread the letter. The realization of what this meant, losing Anders, was sinking in, making his muscles tense. There was no indication that Anders knew about this letter. Rock hadn't figured Anders as the kind of man that would hide behind a woman's skirt. Or was he?

Turning around, Rock kicked the front tire, summarizing through expletives, what Anders' law firm had done to him. Enhanced its bankability and bled him of nearly $50,000 for an appeal, a few hearings, phone calls, a private detective and letter writing. Now this. Everything was going fine until that hearing in Quamas. Anders was the one to ask the judge for a new trial. After that, Anders took a sabbatical and passed him off on Haley, an attorney who hates trial work. "Shiiiit." His words escaped into a sharp gust of wind against his face.

While fumbling the letter, he read the last line. It mentioned an enclosure. He spread the envelope open with tense fingers. It was a bill. They wanted another $6,000. An ache in his stomach shot upward into his chest and arms. The sensation was paralyzing. He wanted to shred the papers in his hands. "Screw 'em. They'll never see another dime from me." He gazed upward talking to everything and nothing.

Walking through the gate and up the walk toward the apartment, Rock forced himself to think. Leucojum would tell him to keep a level head. To talk to the source of his troubles. He must talk to somebody. Anders was conveniently out of reach. Talking to Haley was out. Maybe Efrem would have some ideas. Efrem asked him to stop by some evening. Yes. Rock would make arrangements. There was no future hanging on to these attorneys.

*   *   *

Rock pushed the buzzer to Efrem Abernethy's house set in the steep east side of Queen Anne Hill. He listened to the chimes, blew into his chilled hands and shifted his weight. Waiting. Hoping. Efrem might have an idea or two finding a new attorney. If only he could be his attorney. It was really odd that they were friends. Efrem knew he disliked attorneys in general and still welcomed their friendship.

The porch light flipped on and the solid oak door swung open. "Hey, little buddy. Swim ashore." Efrem stepped back and gestured for him to enter.

Rock stepped inside. "Little buddy, hehehe. We're the same if you'd take off your Stetson."

Efrem's eyes were deep set with bushy eyebrows, a prominent nose, blue eyes and a faint scar in the middle of his chin. He brought his arms and fists into a sparing position and jabbed Rock on the shoulder, chuckling deeply. "Follow."

Rock followed, stepping down about six steps of the split-level. He removed his coat while walking along the slate-floor hallway. "Hmmm. See you've added a new painting to your collection." He stopped for a closer inspection: an acrylic collage of a mermaid, a mariner, water, sandy beach.

"Represents sobriety, false hopes and misguided assumptions. That mother hummer was a steal."

"If you say so." Rock was impressed. Other than having a fancy for women, this was one thing they had in common: a love for art, even if their artistic interests veered in separate directions.

Once in the den, Efrem pointed to a beanbag. "Plant your feet over there."

Instead, Rock walked across an Oriental rug to a window and stared into the night. Stars flickered in the sky. The rhododendrons flanking the patio were full of buds. He turned and looked about. "The room seems different. Still decorated with lumpy furniture and tomes on poetry, architecture, ships."

"I changed the wall color to a pale yellow."

"Yeah. Like the sun's shining in." Rock nodded agreeably.

"Well kiddo. I'm sorry over your latest news. Let's talk. Fill me in on any changes." He slapped his large hands together.

"Big changes." Rock folded his coat in half and set it on a barstool, then plopped into a beanbag. His knees were darn near level with his chin. "You're looking at a man who can't communicate with women." He paused.

"That'll be the day. Excluding Sheryl, of course."

Rock nodded. "Ginger Haley said you relayed that information to her, minus the Sheryl part. Why would you say that?"

Efrem's bottom teeth met his upper lip as he moved sideways to the bar. His eyes widened. "Nonononono. Haley's got that wrong." He removed two bottles of beer from a small fridge. "All I asked was that you be allowed to speak with Anders, wherever he is. I told her Anders is the one you want handling the case. Maybe she misconstrued my meaning. Are you with me?" He opened the beers, making a fssst sound and handed one to Rock.

"Yeah. Well. She and the male attorneys in the law firm can't represent a client who can't communicate with her. And, she refuses to practice law through intermediaries. You being one of them." Rock set his beer on the glass-inserted coffee table, making a clank. Feeling hot, he loosened his tie and unbuttoned the top of his shirt. "She wants to be rid of me. There's no other reason."

Efrem shook his head, sank down into another beanbag across the room, stretched out his long legs and crossed them at the ankles. "I'll phone her tomorrow and straighten out this mess. You can count on it." He swayed his western boots from side to side.

"Hell no. Forget it." Rock shook his head. "Their decision to withdraw isn't negotiable. Plus, I gave it considerable thought on the way over here. I should have dropped them for not communicating with me." He raised his bottle in the air and mouthed "cheers".

There was a brief pause while they gulped. The contrast of Efrem's clothes compared to his neatly furnished home never ceased to amaze Rock. If anyone knew how to relax outside a courtroom, it was Efrem. "Geez, I wish a judge could see you in your off-court hours in those jeans and ragged sweatshirt. Tacky, man. And that cockeyed hat. What's your problem? Going bald?" Rock laughed.

"Hell no. I love my hat." He lifted the hat to show off his brown hair, then lowered it again. "Now, let's take it from the top."

"Okay." Rock guzzled more beer, while still eyeing the hat.

Efrem grinned. "Forget the hat. We've been through this scenario before. My hat is the least of your worries. Now listen. If you're bent on pursuing this monkey, you need to think about a new attorney." He took a swig of beer.

"Hell yes, a new attorney." Rock clicked his nails against the bottle, while studying Efrem as the best attorney for him.

"Don't look to me." He held up a palm. "I'm swamped in maritime cases."

"And you don't do probate work. I know." Rock leaned back and looked up at the recessed lighting. He frowned in disappointment. Hiring a stranger was frightening. "Well. Hell. Since you're too busy for me, where do I start?"

"I suggest you contact Jasper Fulbright. If he can't help you, he can recommend someone. You need a Quamas attorney. Attorneys there do better in the Clamton County Court system than do outsiders. And, they don't charge as much as city attorneys. Are you with me?" He took another pull on his beer.

"Yeah." Rock struggled to sit up straighter. "What you're saying makes sense." He stared across the room and milled this over in his head. The more he pondered Efrem's suggestion, the more it grew on him. "Jasper is a damn good attorney and he's a witness to my new evidence. First thing Monday morning, I'll phone Jasper."

Rock commiserated a while longer. "Now, how do I get out of this damn bag." Rock finally rolled over onto his knees to rise and adjust his pants. "You've got to get rid of these bags, man. We've been conversing between our knees."

"Fat chance. Not until they disintegrate." Laughing, Efrem followed Rock to the door.

"Thanks again for helping." Rock held out a hand.

Efrem grabbed his hand and pulled him into a backslapping hug. "Look buddy. Ninety percent of what we worry about never happens. I'm not saying anything new. Quit worrying."

Rock left feeling better.

Chapter Twelve

Gena beamed when Mona entered the kitchen, as she had things to discuss before bedtime. "I delved into records at the courthouse during my work break today. If I'm going to gather information for your novel on Rock's case, we'd better know about his character."

"Ummmmmm." Mona was attired in her pajamas. She yawned and stretched her arms wide. "I've pegged Rock as having good character."

"That's because you enjoyed his company on the airplane. He took your mind off your fear of flying. You judged character by companionship and conversation. There's more to a person."

"I suppose you're right. I was judging Rock from the eyes of a travel writer. That's why I need your courtroom experience. Well, talk away. Tell me what you've learned."

"Relax. Rock has a clean record."

Mona clapped her hands together. "Hot damn. I'm a good judge of character."

Gena frowned. "Your intuition might get us into trouble someday. You must stop taking chances. Anyway, his opposition, Marvin Benson, isn't a good character. He has had some offbeat experiences." Gena reached for her notebook on the counter.

"What'd Marvin do?"

Sliding on the bench in the corner nook, Gena read from her notes. "Marvin owned a paint company before retirement. Back in the early-to-mid '80's, he was taken to court numerous times for not paying company bills. Even got a judgment against himself."

"Really?" Mona's eyebrows arched. She opened a cupboard. "Want some cocoa? I'll fix."

"Sure." Gena sensed Mona's delight in her interest. Because of out-of-town assignments, Mona really did need her help. Also, Mona's writing experiences weren't exactly akin to legal matters, although she was learning. "All the suits are settled now, but this could prove interesting in Rock's upcoming trial. Then again, maybe not." Gena shrugged.

Mona mixed milk from the fridge into mugs with the cocoa, and added a touch of vanilla. "I get the picture." After zapping their cocoa in the microwave, Mona shuffled over to the table. "Here's yours." Mona sat. "Does this mean you'll date Rock in my place? We're identical, if you'd let your hair down. He'd never know the difference."

Gena slid her notes to the center of the table. Rock and his case were fascinating, yet for some reason she felt hesitant. Mona met him first and she was such a flirt. It was difficult to determine what effect their first meeting on the airplane might have on future meetings. Maybe, if she played hard to get, Mona would provide more information. She sipped the cocoa and swallowed.

"I'm awkward on blind dates. Are you sure you don't want to phone and talk to Rock? You could cancel the date for another time when you're free." She pointed to the phone on the counter, and proceeded to leave the kitchen, while pretending to be bored.

"Gena, come back here and discuss this. I'm booked solid with travel assignments. Please." Mona's voice was pleading.

Gena stopped and put a hand on her hip. "This isn't another of your schemes to get me dating again, is it? I'm not sure a man in my life is wise right now." Gena looked sternly at Mona.

"Stop." Mona waved a hand. "All along, we've been using the wrong word. Dating. Consider it a business meeting. Believe me. He isn't your type." She talked fast. "He's married. So, you see, we need only concentrate on the story that's in him. Okay?"

"Aaaah, so that's why you aren't postponing things. He's married. That's different. Okay, I feel better about impersonating you." Gena figured if Rock was happily married, their meeting would be strictly business. Dating a married man who wasn't serious about his marriage didn't exactly appeal to her, remembering her best friend falling in love with a married man. After he got what he wanted, he left for someone else. The friend, so full of life and talent with big curious eyes and winning laugh, who couldn't take rejection, committed suicide. Gena wasn't going to let this happen to her. Besides, she was still licking her own wounds over a disappearing husband.

"Oh thank you." Mona puckered her lips and blew an air kiss in Gena's direction.

Gena returned to the bench. "Okay, so what's the agenda?"

"Meet Rock and get copies of the latest depositions and affidavits. Even with unanswered questions on my mind, I am looking forward to writing a book on this case. Oh, did you find time to put a new ribbon in the typewriter?"

"Yes. It's ready to go, hon."

"Good. Think I'll type for an hour. Must be the sugar in the cocoa that wired me awake."

Gena only nodded. Their conversation put an entirely different perspective on things and eased her mind. She decided to have another cup of cocoa before crawling into bed.

"Oh, by the way, I finished reading our latest purchase, *The Gavel Cracked*. You can read it now."

"Great. I'll start it tonight." This would take her thoughts off the uncertainty of meeting Rock.

Chapter Thirteen

Rock had just returned to Turquoise Wholesalers from a jewelry meeting at the Burke museum. His wall calendar showed two reminders: Phone Jasper. Date with Mona. He picked up the phone and dialed Jasper's office, then stared out the window. April showers dripped off the tall green trees onto pedestrians and umbrellas below. Mrs. Willard answered and said she'd fetch Jasper.

"Rock. Jasper here. What can I do for you?"

He explained the situation, while trying not to sound too anxious. "What it all boils down to, I need an attorney. Since you know me and my case, I was hoping you'd be my attorney."

"Well." He paused as though taken by surprise. "I suppose that can be arranged. You must realize, if I become your attorney, then I can't be your witness. Which do you prefer?"

"I can't have both?" Rock gazed at the space between buildings across the street. A tugboat pulled a heavy barge. A stream of fresh air gusted into the musty office.

"No. That's stretching the rules."

"If you can't be both attorney and witness, why is it that Houston is a witness and his partner Adams is an attorney for Marvin Benson, especially when Houston is involved in the probate of both Carper estates?"

"Oh, I'm not saying it's illegal. I personally frown on the practice. Rather sticky."

Rock returned to the desk. "Damn. This puts me up a creek. An attorney in Quamas is what I need."

"I can help by being your witness on the discovery of your new evidence. You need me for that more than you need me as an attorney. Believe me."

"Oh, I believe you. I don't want to foul that up."

"Tell you what. I'll find an attorney in town here."

Rock's heart quickened, while reaching for a pencil and paper on the desk in preparation for taking a note. "Yeah? Who?"

"His name is Joseph Scott. I'm told he's well-seasoned in estate matters. I haven't used his services so I can't speak from direct experience, you understand? But I haven't heard anything bad about him."

"Yes, I understand."

"Tell you what, I'll give him a jingle, explain the situation and have him phone you tonight about nine, one way or the other."

"Thanks. I appreciate your help." After giving his apartment phone number, he hung up, feeling relieved. He hummed quietly, while closing the office, convinced that things do have a way of working out. Now he could rush home, shower, shave and change before meeting Mona at Shigley's.

* * *

Gena arrived at Shigley's Restaurant apprehensive about meeting Rock for the first time. Could she pull it off, posing as Mona? She brushed back her hair and walked over to a table in plain view. This would enable him to recognize her first. The table was nicely set with a candle and fresh flowers. Second thoughts nagged. Why did she let herself get involved? It was nerve racking. Even though they'd visited over the phone several times, it was like a blind date with someone she'd never met.

Removing a small case from her purse, she opened it and checked her makeup. Recently, she had her blonde eyebrows, her eyeliner and her lips tattooed in more vivid shades by a cosmetologist because of her swimming. Only on rare occasions did she feel it necessary to apply a liquid powder and rouge. This was one of those times.

Then she put the case away and smoothed the hem of a new ivory knit dress over crossed knees. The dress felt good, belted at the waist, flared at the hem. A pearl necklace decorated the neckline. She rarely wore earrings. Now, all there was to concentrate on was business. Mona's business. All so Mona could write a novel.

The sound of an accordion came from the background. It drew her attention to the moment. No sooner had Gena slipped out of her coat, when Rock appeared in front of the cash register, tall, stocky through the chest and shoulders. His black clothing and turquoise jewelry were eye-catching. Mona said he worked for Turquoise Wholesalers, a Seattle firm that dealt in Native American jewelry. In any event, she thought this guy glowed above the surroundings.

Gena drew in a deep breath, blew at loose strands of hair about her face, wishing she had used more hair spray, and acknowledged his wave. He walked slightly bowlegged, yet with noble bearing toward the table and settled in a captain's chair next to her. His raven eyes darted about the room like a scout taking in the environment. When things seemed safe, he focused on her.

He cleared his throat. "Good to see you again, Mona." His voice was deep. He talked slowly.

"H'lo." Gena hoped the quivering in her voice wasn't obvious, suddenly realizing he thought she was Mona. Maybe now she could relax. That would not be easy as he was more than expected. A princely mystique about him.

"Sorry I'm running a little late. My life hasn't been my own. Legal problems, you know."

When he rose to hang his leather jacket around the back of the chair, she noticed his silver belt buckle with a gold eagle etched in the middle. She cleared her throat. "I understand. Legal matters are so involved. And attorneys can be quite nebulous. Statutes and cases are anything but black and white." The words rolled off her tongue, without thinking.

Rock centered his attention on her again, but said nothing.

Gena felt she should clarify her comment. "Well. So I've been told." She clenched her hands under the table, while cautioning herself to be careful.

They talked a while about the weather, his work, his case, and this restaurant, when finally a costumed accordionist swayed by the table. He sang and played a lively folk tune. Rock smiled and moved his entire body in rhythm as though he loved music. After the accordion player moved away, a dark-haired waitress approached. She recommended the pot roast.

"Sounds good to me." Gena smiled at Rock. "You'll love it, if you're a meat-and-potatoes man."

"I am. You like beer?" Rock raised his eyebrows at her.

"Fine."

"Bring two steins, please." He slapped his hands together. "Well. Here we are meeting again. First off I must apologize. Our dinner will have to be cut short. I can't miss a phone call from a prospective attorney."

"Oh?" His cordiality was pleasing, but his news was disappointing, because already she felt caught up in a delightful experience. So much so that the surroundings escaped her. She nearly forgot where she was. It wasn't just discussing his case, but thoroughly enjoying Rock's company. She wondered what he thought of her. He couldn't think much of her, or Mona, to be giving escape excuses so soon.

"Will you let me make it up to you another time?"

The question was a relief. "Yes." She smiled.

When the beer arrived, he raised his stein. "A toast to a future best-selling author of justice. Or injustice."

Gena laughed and clicked his stein. "I can't go wrong with such confidence. Here's hoping you receive the justice you seek." They drank and conversed like long-lost friends until the dinners arrived.

During dinner, Gena asked many questions to distract his meeting with Mona on the plane. The past told her that dear Mona was good at forgetting key points. "Did you bring your documents for me to read?"

"Yep. In my car. I'll transfer them to your car before leaving. Hope the paperwork will make sense to you. Keep in mind, I'm still living my litigation. It's not over by any means. I find it interesting that you want to write a novel about my case."

"Right. This could be a slow process. And, until I read everything, I won't know how to use the documents." Without realizing, Gena rested her left hand on the table.

Unexpectedly, Rock placed a hand on top of hers. "You look fantastic."

Gena sensed a flirtatious ring in his voice. His hand was rough, warm and powerful. The move was confusing if he was married. He was not wearing a wedding ring, but that was no indication. She felt slightly embarrassed and decided to change the subject, while pulling away her hand. "So, what's the scuttlebutt about losing your attorneys?"

Rock removed his hand too and offered a recap of Ginger Haley and Nelson Anders. And he discussed his conversation with Jasper. His turquoise watch reflected light as he talked. "Yes indeed. I'm searching for a new attorney."

While eating a chunk of potato, she listened and watched the corners of his eyes and lips curve into a smile. There was an attractive fierceness about him. His hair was sleeked back. His face creased slightly on each side of a square chin. His movements were deliberate as if planned. A thought crossed her mind. His wife was lucky to have him. Gena had none.

"I may have one."

"One what?" Paying attention around this unique person became increasingly difficult. He was entirely different from anyone she'd ever met. A tray of food could have hit the floor and Gena doubted she'd hear. His eyes were so focused with his words, his thoughts. He was extremely handsome. Yet there was naivety.

"A new attorney." He sprinkled pepper over his vegetables.

After dinner, Gena strolled to the parking lot with Rock at her side. The walkway was lined in spring flowers. The evening sky was clear. An evergreen hedge blocked the area from the traffic on Lake City Way. He put a hand on her shoulder. "You open your trunk and I'll fetch the documents you want."

Gena walked over to her Camaro, unlocked the lid and held it open. As he transferred documents from his trunk to her trunk, she inhaled his spicy aftershave. It awakened something inside her. She accidentally dropped her keys. "Oh, how clumsy of me."

Rock retrieved the keys with a grin. "No alibis. You aren't flying in a plane."

During an attempt to remain steady, Gena held out a hand for the keys. While he slammed the lid and brushed his hands, she recalled privately not having been in a plane for four years. Not since her husband, Shumway, disappeared in his floatplane. Mona predicted he'd never return. Gena still had some hope he might reappear. But, in all that time, she hadn't looked sideways at a man. She unlocked the car door.

Rock opened the door for her. "These documents are enough for starters. For your reading enjoyment, my lady."

She hesitated a moment, with the door ajar, to thank him.

He gently caressed one of her hands in his. "Sorry I can't stay longer. I'm flattered you agreed to have dinner with me." He paused, as if studying her. "I'm looking forward to our next meeting."

"Until then." Gena moved in behind the wheel. Rock eased the door shut. She lowered the window to visit a few minutes longer. Finally, she waved and drove away with thoughts of his friendliness. He seemed outgoing and trusting. Since he was married, Gena scolded herself for being ruffled by his aftershave and his hand contacts. Next time, she wouldn't react this way. It was imperative to think strictly business. Even though she studied his every move, and liked what she saw, she mustn't allow any man to touch her feelings in a way she couldn't control.

*   *   *

Back in his apartment, Rock cleaned dishes left since breakfast. His meeting with Mona was very much on his mind. "Yeah." She was worth a second meeting and many more he hoped. "Yah hoh hi yi." He hummed softly, trying to anticipate the next meeting that might lead to something, when the phone rang. He dried his hands sloppily on a T-towel, then rushed to answer. "Hello. Rock Carper speaking."

"Yo. Mr. Carper. This is Joseph Scott calling from Quamas. Jasper Fulbright said you need an attorney."

"Yes. Yes. Mr. Scott." He liked the sound of the man's voice. Commanding and direct.

Before long, Scott fired solid questions. A good sign. Indicative that Scott knew legal jargon pertaining to estate probates, including the Revised Code of Washington 11.20.070, a statute for lost wills.

In the excitement, Rock realized he was sitting in the dark, except for the kitchen light around the corner. He reached to turn on the table lamp.

Finally, Scott gave him his address. "Meet me at my office around ten

Saturday morning. Bring your boxes of documents."

"Whoa. Let me grab a pen and pad here." He opened the drawer in the end table and scribbled the address repeated by Scott. "Okey Dokey. See you then."

Rock leaned back, elated. He could hear an airplane rumble overhead, when the phone rang again. "Hello?"

"I'm comin' ta Seattle tomorrow. A shoppin' trip. Let's meet. I have some o' yer personal belongin's ta deliver." Sheryl sounded chipper, since moving to Quamas.

"Fine. I'll pick you up in front of Nordstrom's after work." That was Sheryl's favorite place to shop for apparel. "You can help me retrieve my documents from the offices of Anders and Haley."

"Why?"

He relayed the latest news about his new attorney. "I'm not a loose screw ready to be screwed by some damn attorney. I'll explain more when I see you."

"Ta ta, then."

Rock listened to the phone go dead. He was in high spirits. Everything was falling into place. He was regaining control of his life. And, the best part of the day, aside from Scott, was meeting with Mona, a lovely distraction. Seeing her again was a shot in the arm. Especially tonight. It wasn't going to be easy concentrating on the novel she was writing about him while he was around her.

After switching off the lamp, he headed down the hallway. "I'll love you under the brilliant starry sky, while the ageless moon glows, "Gv ge yu a, heh yu." It seemed ages since he sang Leucojum's song. The rest of it was rooted deep in his brain. He was trying to grasp his Native tongue. And, each time more words were returning to him. Since Sheryl discouraged the Nativeness in him, it was a wonder that much came out. But, that was Sheryl. Talked incessantly too. Not Mona. She kept him busy talking. Granted. It was for the novel. But, unsaid words and sidelong glances told him there would be more than what met his eye tonight.

He stripped his clothes and stepped under the hot shower water. For some unexplainable reason, being with Mona tonight made him feel more connected to his Native heritage. Something he couldn't hide to save his soul anyway, but this was different. "Gv ge yu a, heh yu."

* * *

After rubbing lotion over her face and hands, Gena snuggled under the covers and rested for a time on the edge of sleep, while trying to pass off the meeting with Rock at Shigley's as purely business and that her part in it was for a good cause. Still, her mind wandered beyond business.

She liked his masculine demeanor. He was tall and husky. The dark clothing with his jet black hair, eye-catching. His walk was almost bowlegged. The touch of his hand, warm and rough. His presence towered as he placed an arm across the roof of her car, giving a close feeling. And, they had such a grand time kibitzing that by the end of the evening they were like old friends.

But, he stirred feelings she tried to bury over the last four years, since her husband Shumway disappeared. That's when she moved in with Mona and returned to her maiden name of Bradley as Mona did after her divorce. Thus far, Gena and Mona were the only ones in Seattle who knew about Gena's past.

She fluffed the pillow under her head and stared into darkness. Streetlights filtered through the sides of the drapes. The neighborhood was quiet. Mona was on an assignment. Only Gena's thoughts were difficult to muffle.

Now and again she liked to recall the old memories. Shumway used to take her to Cashmere's Apple Days, an October festival, staged at Pioneer Village and Museum, dressed in pioneer attire. One year, her aunt won the apple pie contest. There were all kinds of apple treats to feast on, too. Shumway entered the cowboy poets contest. A neighbor man played the fiddle as Shumway read. Later, she and Shumway held hands on a nature hike.

She tried to think of her husband further, but memories were gradually fading, along with interest in his memorabilia in the trunk at the foot of the bed. All that really remained was their Wenatchee farm, Skywalk Ranch, which she leased out to a family. They grew apples, peas, corn, zucchini, beans and okra.

Gena clutched at the covers, perhaps in guilt. Maybe she gave up on Shumway too soon. While they dated, he said his folks were dead. Then, after their marriage, she learned his folks had been alcoholics, that they abandoned him and that his grandmother, who belonged to the Klamath tribe in Oregon, raised him.

At the age of sixteen, Shumway and another Indian friend, determined to do well on their own, hitchhiked to Washington and ended in Wenatchee doing farm work. Come Autumn, the Indian friend moved on, but Shumway stayed. The farmer took a liking to him and had him invest his savings in the stock market. Shumway did very well, so well that he made a down payment on acreage with the farmer as a co-signer.

After rolling over and adjusting a strap of her nightgown, she recalled the time she stayed with her aunt in Wenatchee during a summer break from the University of Washington. She picked apples in Shumway's orchard. By summer's end they were married.

The fact that she was a Reformist Jew didn't matter. He liked the Jewish philosophy of tolerance toward others. The live and let live philosophy. Perhaps this was why, when news came that she was accepted into law school, he insisted she go. In turn, he expected her tolerance when he went in some other direction to do his thing.

At first, in preparing for his last plane trip, he expressed an interest in photography. Gena murmured in her mind Shumway talking about wanting to capture the hundreds of ducks, geese and swans in the Klamath Basin. He said that in the winter bald eagles roosted on the lakeshores. And sandhill cranes danced in the marshes filling the air with warbling music. But, everything changed after learning about the death of his grandmother. That's when he insisted going on a vision quest to seek enlightenment.

"Enlightenment won't bring your grandma back." Gena struggled under the covers as their conversation surfaced. She knew Natives on reservations had problems, but Shumway wasn't raised on a reservation.

The Klamath tribe was landless. That is, following the federal government's decision to terminate tribes across the country by forcing them to assimilate into the dominate culture, the majority of tribal members relented and voted to withdraw from their tribe and receive assets from their land. In 1961, each member who withdrew received over $44,000 each.

At first, Shumway's family didn't withdraw. They were holding onto Richard Nixon's 1960 presidential campaign speech, wherein he emphasized abiding respect for Native American values and their undeniable right to preserve their traditional heritage.

Nixon said: *"Our overriding aim, as I see it, should not be to separate the Indians from the richness of their past or force them into some preconceived mold of human behavior . . . . Every conceivable effort will be made to shape our actions and our policies in full harmony with the deepest aspirations of the Indian citizenry."*

Gena sighed. So much for campaign promises. She recollected Shumway telling her that his folks gave up on Nixon's promise after losing their jobs in the lumber industry. Without jobs, they could no longer pay the new property taxes and basic utility bills. The loss of federally-sponsored social, educational and health services and facilities were disastrous to their health and welfare. Deep down, Shumway said, they felt like outcasts in the national Indian community. What federal money they received quickly evaporated in paying medical bills and drinking and gambling debts.

Shumway also said his grandma had his shares kept in a corporate trust until 1975, at which time he received approximately $150,000. At first, he treated the money as dirty. It didn't make up for a destroyed family, a destroyed tribe. Months later he used most of the money to buy new farm equipment. Eventually, he built a small house on the property for his grandma. Then, having her die set him off kilter again.

A loud moan escaped her lips. Hindsight was clearer now. Gena was too busy to recognize his dark depression. At the time, she tried to pin him down to explain his moodiness, but he didn't want to talk. Now, it seemed evident that Shumway had been struggling internally, searching for a new identity.

Pulling a pillow over her head didn't help much in shutting out the memories of her former negative thoughts that Shumway may have skipped out, following some vision that meant little to her at the time. Yet, his disappearance caused her to quit law school and help in the search.

Tonight she didn't know what to think about Shumway. He left her financially stable, but having him back was more preferable to her lonely existence. Yet, each day the past year she found herself letting go.

Her Jewish mother once explained: *"When one assimilates from one culture to another, he must adapt to survive. Each person faced with this experiences a different world and adapts in his own way, in his own time. Some people can adapt. Those who can't often develop maladaptive behaviors to cope or return to their original culture. One thing for sure, adapting is a continuous challenge."*

This brought her thoughts to Rock. Raised differently in American society, he too was undergoing some sort of adapting. At least he was willing to talk about it. The more she learned, the greater the intrigue to his character.

And, as Rock's case became more interesting, the more she learned. Mona was right. He loved to talk about his legal experiences with attorneys, not always favorably. Yet, his knack for wisecracking about aspects of it showed he had balance.

Gena covered her ears with her hands, trying to muffle these thoughts. This meeting couldn't mean anything. She's married. Mona met him first. Mona's divorced and therefore available. And, Rock's married. So why even think like this? Besides it was important to stay immersed in her existence. Not very exciting, but safe and comfortable.

At least Mona would be pleased with the information realized from tonight's meeting. That's what mattered. Rock didn't reveal much about his mom, Leucojum, saying some days he could talk about her. Other days, he couldn't. Because of Shumway losing his grandma, the only real mother he knew, Gena was better prepared for these feelings.

So Gena questioned Rock about those in his legal life. She rolled over in bed again and recalled Rock's description of Ginger Haley as a petite whippersnapper with a spitfire temper. Nelson Anders was Mr. Establishment, who hid behind his women workers and passed it off as strength in numbers. In reality, Haley and the detective were gophers.

Rock described Ralph Houston as an old geezer, who couldn't recognize truth to save his ass. Marvin and Beatrice Benson were shady connivers. Leland Perkins was a prissy attorney from California. Redheaded Fred Adams, Jr. was quiet and slippery. At one point during dinner, Rock referred to Marvin, Perkins and Adams as the tricky trio. *"They're as thick as sticky rice."* Gena chuckled when sleep finally took hold.

Chapter Fourteen

Rock and Sheryl recovered his two boxes of documents from the receptionist at Anders' law firm. Then they boarded the elevator and Rock pushed the down button. He kept stepping to the back until finally he was crammed in one corner, as more and more men in tailored suits crowded into the area. Most were carrying briefcases. Several were talking in legal lingo. They had to be attorneys. The building was a hive of law firms.

Sheryl broke into his concentration of soft syrupy music piped in from speakers. "I was told there are more attorneys workin' in this 'ere buildin' than there are in all o' Japan."

Rock didn't give a hoot what was going on in Japan, let alone hearing about some isolated bit of information outside the parameters of Seattle proper, at least at this moment. Even so, he couldn't resist venting his feelings. "That's one too many. Someone should feed every sonofabitching attorney in the building to the sharks."

He looked up at the lighted panel of numbers above the door, feeling many eyes scanning him from head to toe. He was unconcerned about locking muscles with any of them, should that matter. He was bigger. All through school, he was big enough to command respect from his classmates. No one tangled much with him. These men appeared too refined to fight back physically anyway. And, Rock knew muscle was no match to attorneys trained to fight verbally. Yet, making them squirm was more in line with his intent.

Following some groans, like a few attorneys had been in this predicament before, all talking stopped. It was golden silence, except for the whine of the moving car and soft music. Sheryl, still clutching one of his boxes, moved away and shrank into the back corner opposite him. The others herded forward, like an indistinguishable glob with dark shoes aimed for a collective interest: the door.

Rock had ample space around him. While entertaining his isolation, he noticed the elevator wasn't new, smelled dusty, but the ride was smooth. The ceiling mirror reflected hairstyles for those with hair. Funny, money can't buy everything. Bald-headed attorneys fit in there somewhere, he thought.

Although not visible to him, Rock knew that at least ten sets of eyes were fixated on the crack in the door when not looking up at the decreasing floor numbers. Their heads went up and down like puppets. The elevator stopped. The door opened. The occupants squeezed out and off in all directions.

"The blood suckers are on a mission." Rock looked at Sheryl, as the door closed. He was intoxicated with power.

Sheryl stepped forward. "Rock, now look what ye've done. We're the only ones continuin' doon the lift. Ye created an explosive situation. Oh, Lordie, I could just imagine a pile o' bodies and documents all over. I donnae like attorneys any better than ye, maun, but ye mustnae orchestrate yer feelings again 'em when there's no escape hatch. Not in my presence. I could o' got my feet trampled. Aside from that, those attorneys looked the models o' decency. Ye bloke, shovin' yer muscle over 'em."

"Enough. I don't need a lesson on elevator manners."

"Nae. But, I know ye dinnae mean that crude remark. Why did ye say it?"

Rock's grin erupted into hearty laughter. "Hell, it feels good to see them squirm." He continued to laugh. This elevator trip did more for him than a month's supply of antacids.

Sheryl shook her head. "They werenae squirmin'. They were paralyzed."

"Not too paralyzed to squeeze out of here like one foul fart. Internally, they were squirming."

"Ye could o' been more humane, maun."

"Wrong. It made my day." No attorney had cowered from him before. Witnessing this was like an injection of power water. Nothing anyone said could change his mind. "You're too late Sheryl. What's done is done. Don't rob me of a few minutes of enjoyment. I'm sure I'll never get the chance to repeat it. Yeah, it felt good. Sometimes the wrong thing is the right thing."

"Sure, and what if a bobby is waitin' fer ye doon in the lobby? One o' the attorneys is sure ta complain."

That remark sobered him in a hurry. "Good point. Let's get off on the second floor and take the stairs to the parking garage."

"Oou. There ye go. And us with all these documents and me in heels."

"Stay behind me. We'll go slow." He was still chuckling. As a rule while growing up, Rock was taught to respect power figures. And, to speak only when spoken to. For some reason, he broke away from custom today and didn't care why.

Chapter Fifteen

Rock slowed his Firebird for a flock of bobwhite quail to scurry off the road, bordering the edge of Quamas. He hummed enthusiastically, eager to meet his new attorney.

Entering town, he looked around for Scott's office. Scott said it was a simple one-story structure like most of the squat buildings on his block. There weren't many tall buildings in town. Jasper Fulbright's old relic was one. And there were a few others, including the courthouse, jail and hospital.

Since it was Saturday, parking in front of Scott's office, away from the busy part of town, was no problem. Rock stepped into the street to stretch his muscles. Robins chirped. A light blue sky and sunshine shone through the overhead mesh of foliage, casting lacy shadows below.

Even though Scott conveyed an interest in representing him, a sense of apprehension fell over Rock. What if Scott was merely doing this as a personal favor to Jasper Fulbright and really didn't care about representing him? He walked to the entrance to Scott's firm. The door was open. He held back and knocked.

A voice hollered. "Yo."

"Rock Carper here." He waited a minute. "My trunk's open. I can bring in my documents, if that meets with your approval?" He kept it formal since this was their first meeting.

"Sure. Bring them on back."

Joseph Scott appeared, standing in the doorway of an office from within. Rock estimated Scott as a man approaching sixty. He was stocky with a thick neck supporting a round face, framed by an odd-shaped head, chiseled nearly round, but oversized and bald.

Rock set the box on the floor in front of a rectangular desk and straightened up to shake Scott's proffered hand.

"Get yourself comfortable Mr. Carper." Scott motioned with one of his freckled arms.

"Call me Rock." He finally settled in a brown leather sofa near the back wall. Old law journals on a shelf decorated the room.

"Okay Rock. Would you like coffee before we start?"

"Thanks. No. I got coffee logged on the ferry." He sat and crossed one leg over the other.

Scott sat behind his desk and fussed with a legal pad, a pen and his coffee. "I want to get down to the nuts and bolts of this case in a hurry, since I'm the new kid on the block." He rubbed his hands together. "So, I suggest you give me the appellate remand and Judge Randell's order for the new trial."

Rock was amazed because right off the bat Scott was taking over. It was that simple. Scott, another Caucasian, was his attorney. He was analytical; knowledgeable. Suddenly Rock verbalized a thought. "I don't want Judge

Randell involved in the trial." Rock spoke adamantly.

"No need to worry about that. He's retired from the bench."

"Yeah, I've heard that one before." Rock snickered. "Randell has a way of worming his way out of the woodwork whenever I'm in court."

"Mr. Carper. I mean Rock. Judge Randell isn't returning for any reason. Don't know who we'll get." Scott picked up his pen and began tapping it against his front teeth. It was a bit irritating.

Rock sighed in relief and handed over the requested documents. He watched Scott leaf through them quickly.

"Good. Now, how have you organized your documents so I can find things?" He leaned forward over the desk. "For example, where are the depositions and affidavits of your witnesses?"

"In the back there. All labeled as such. Depositions. Affidavits. Witnesses in alphabetical order."

"Very nice. Neatly organized. I shouldn't have trouble finding anything." He eased back in his chair, making a tipi of his fingers. "If I do I'll phone you before nine a. m. or after nine p. m. on any given day. The trial will have to be postponed. I'll file a motion for continuance and notify you of that."

"Do you think the court will grant a continuance?"

"Has to. The court will know it'll take me a beat or two to catch up. Now, I charge $100 an hour in civil cases such as yours."

"What kind of a retainer do you have in mind?" Rock sat back in the sofa, dreading the answer since Anders had nearly drained him.

Scott's chair squeaked as he moved around. "I need a $2,000 retainer to start. For trial work, I charge $1,000 a day. I'll try to keep the trial down to three days, as I understand your financial situation. Does this meet with your approval?"

"Yes sir." Rock felt the fees were reasonable compared to fees Seattle attorneys charged. "Mr. Scott. There are a few issues about this case that concern me." Rock explained Houston's misconduct. "He's a liaholic. This has to come out at the new trial just in case my late defense, laches, comes up. You know, my reason for not acting sooner in this case."

Scott nodded in understanding.

"Also, I have a lien on the Carper mansion. That house was always Uncle John's separate property intended for me after my aunt's death. The title report is on file in the auditor's office." He cleared his throat, moved his documents to a corner of the desk and continued.

"My aunt did some weird things in probating Uncle John's estate, as you'll find out, but she never removed ownership to the Carper mansion from my uncle's name, not even before her death. I want that house. Built by my grandparents. A family thing."

"See what I can do, Mr. Carper."

"Don't suppose you'd be more specific? You must understand that's my inheritance. It's my right to retrieve the Carper legacy." Rock moved off the sofa in readiness to leave. He dug in a pocket for his keys.

Scott stood and stretched. "Hey, I'm a dynamic figure in the courtroom. If old Houston did anything wrong, I'll expose him."

Rock visualized an attorney with a passionate need to dominate the proceedings. The over-all nature in which Scott spoke, his confidence, his friendliness and his quick grasp of the case fit like a well-worn moccasin. If first impressions can be relied upon, this man was ready to charge.

On the way out of the office, Scott stopped him. "Wait." He scribbled on paper. "Here's my private phone number for special clients. Use it in emergencies."

"Thanks." Rock received the paper with a broad grin. They shook hands. At last, he hired someone he could count on. A world of woes floated from his shoulders.

*   *   *

Rock knelt down on the grassy knoll of the Quamas Cemetery to place flowers over Leucojum's grave. He reached out spreading his fingers in the empty air, wanting to touch her frail hand just one more time. To feel warmth instead of the small, cold marbled nameplate. She didn't give him time to say goodbye. He wanted to tell her it wasn't her fault if he didn't quite measure up to her standards. It was her idea to assimilate. It became an idea that he lived, but never quite accepted.

He held back the pain of reality. His voice cracked, speaking under his breath, sensing hushed sounds of faraway drums -- a faint chant that rides the fog. "Ah, Snowflake, whose ancestors floated across the land from the Trail of Tears. You gave your heart to a Caucasian and from then on you also tried to assimilate into another environment. Why? So you could earn a little plot of land in this graveyard? Evidence of your existence on this earth? Because that's where you are, dressed in your finest clothes. Alongside your dearly beloved and all the other deceased Carpers."

Rock swallowed hard. "Somehow, you and I never quite belonged, especially after dad died." Pulling a kerchief from his coat pocket, he blew his nose. It couldn't matter what graveyard she was in. She was oriented toward spiritual influences in wind and water. And, Rock believed she carried with her a universal harmony of her village. By now, Leucojum's spirit had passed the portal of the tomb and floated beyond the stars. In joining her ancestors, the Great Spirit had embraced her.

The wind blew his hair just like the day of her funeral. A small group attended the simple graveside service. They stood in a circle holding hands. Out of respect, Sheryl dressed in widow's weeds. Northeasterly winds had whipped over them. Rain pummeled on their umbrellas. The minister, who spoke of her as the loveable lady she was, mentioned the fulfillment of dreams.

As a long-standing member of a local Indian church, she was their wisdom keeper. In her quiet way, she chanted in excitement when many of her dreams and the dreams of others came true.

Rock thought at the time that she certainly kept him on his toes. But, away from her, he grew lax. Couldn't fulfill all the dreams she had for him. One moment she wanted him to be an artist. Another time it was an inventor. Why is it that mothers cast their dreams off on their offspring? He recalled her parting words that no one is successful in his earthwalk until he has acquired his song. This saying wasn't new to him. It was the way she said it. The timing. He wouldn't rest until he understood her meaning.

Answers would not come from the cold ground. Rock rose off his knees and brushed away a little debris, still deep in reverie. From the time he was five years old, his dad and uncle told him his station in life, that his song was to carry on the Carper legacy. To carry on where they left off. Even Grandpapa Carper told him this. So he believe this was his song. Leucojum wasn't so sure.

He looked out, seeing the Sound in the distance. The wind caused him to pull the collar of his overcoat closer, while thinking of both men as being his dads. The three of them had such good times fishing together. It wasn't so odd that even if he was more like Leucojum and could never be like these men, he wanted to measure up to their expectations, at least in carrying on the family legacy as they had done for their folks.

A persistent gust of cold salt air stung his face. He sucked in the smell of the land and took one last look down the hill. We live and we die. Only sky and the seasons endure. Leucojum's pass through life was gone. Flesh to ashes to dust, like a swirling eddy.

The mysteries of the All Mighty fell upon him. The wind whipped his coat and pants as he looked skyward. "Oh Great Spirit. What kind of life is this? That you take away the things I cherish." He hated death. No more voice and laughter. No shape. No smile. No consoling hand. He gripped the kerchief in his fingers. "Gv ge yu a, I love you Snowflake."

As he walked away, his bones and heart weighed heavy. At least there was some resolve in his mind that there were no courthouses and big city skyscrapers in the great beyond. Leucojum refused to venture very far away from Quamas for that reason. Rock understood. At times, Seattle's skyscrapers smothered him, forcing him to walk near Puget Sound to inhale nature even if some of it seemed artificial. The southwest, especially the spacious areas of Arizona, gave him a sense of freedom.

Oh God, he needed the southwest and Indian country. But, his boss, Atsidi, didn't have any jewelry-buying trips planned specifically for him in the near future.

Sighing, another thought passed through Rock to keep working on the unfinished totem pole as Leucojum wanted. She would have also wanted him to continue his volunteer work with senior citizens, although with the litigation, this was becoming increasingly difficult. But, he'd try.

Chapter Sixteen

Rock carried the phone to the sofa, leaned back against the pillows and crossed his moccasined feet on the coffee table. After a busy day at Turquoise Wholesalers, he realized it had been months since Leucojum's demise. Her absence still weighed on him. No doubt, he'd remember her for the rest of his life, but it was time to move on. She wouldn't want him brooding like this. And, he couldn't delay his promise to deliver more documents to Mona.

While dialing her number, he decided to keep the conversation light. "Mona, Rock here. I'd like to deliver more documents to you. Perhaps next Saturday. I know you'd like to become better acquainted with my case. I have the day free and I could bring you up to speed for your novel, if you like." He could hear music in the background.

"I'd like that fine. Wear jogging clothes."

This was unexpected. Yet, he welcomed the idea. He wasn't getting any exercise in his small flat. A brisk walk in the fresh air sounded ideal, although jogging wasn't something he ordinarily did. "Jogging clothes? What's up?"

"My routine. I jog on the Burke Gilman trail Saturdays. Join me. I'd like to bring my tape recorder along, if you don't mind."

"Hey, no problem." Rock rose, and packing the phone with him, wandered in circles. "See you at ten." He walked back to the end table for pen and pad. "Give me directions to your house."

"I live a stones throw from the lake." She gave the address.

"See you then." Rock lowered the receiver. "Hmmm." For someone who didn't like surprises, this one grew on him faster than pulling silk hairs off an ear of corn.

* * *

Gena knocked some magazines off a corner of an end table in the front room. She righted them, then stretched upward and gazed beyond the bay window. There was little daylight left, so she turned on a lamp. Inviting Rock over next Saturday had interrupted her workout and put her deep in thought. She must pretend to be Mona again as there was no alternative with Mona out of town.

Before leaving, Mona conveyed to her that Rock's story would better evolve in less formal settings. So jogging was perfect. Pretending to be Mona surely wouldn't hurt, as this wouldn't go on forever. It wasn't a date. Rock was married.

She scooted down on the carpet to begin sit-ups to classical music. Twenty more to go. Swimming at the community swim club with Rock would have been more suitable to her. Yet, the club regulars knew her and Mona. They knew about their heart-shaped tattoos with the initials located slightly above the front line of their bathing suits. If Rock saw a G on her instead of an M, he'd ask questions. Keeping their identities a secret was becoming a challenge. *"Mona and her crazy ideas for getting a story."*

After the sit-ups, a craving for a cinnamon roll nagged her. She could smell the cinnamon and taste the raisins. Instead, she sat cross-legged and looked around for a distraction from food. Yikes. There were signs of twins on the far wall: a framed studio picture taken ten years ago. For now, she decided to check out the entire house and put away things that showed telltale signs of twins in readiness for Rock's next visit. A visit she looked forward to.

*   *   *

Following dinner, Rock stretched out on the sofa and opened a letter from Joseph Scott, a man with a cool breath and a firm handshake. The letter indicated that Marvin's attorney, Leland Perkins, wanted to take further deposition testimony from two of Rock's witnesses. This meant more questions of attorney Jasper Fulbright and his secretary, Mrs. Willard, as well as from Rock and Sheryl.

The news didn't set well. He tossed the letter aside and tried to reason the logic of this situation on the way to the fridge for an apple. Ginger Haley told him the Nell Carper estate was broke. Yet, Scott's letter suggested Marvin and his attorneys wanted to drum up expenses as if they robbed the Indian Nation. At this rate, they could financially drain him. He didn't want to be operating in a dry hole.

After a few bites of apple, Rock grabbed the phone and returned to the sofa to dial Scott's private number. He answered on the third ring.

"Mr. Scott. Rock here."

"Yes Rock, what can I do for you?"

"I just received your letter. I don't mean to tell you your business, but what the hell is going on? I don't want to support all this foolishness. Marvin's bunch had since 1985 to do this. Can't you do something? My witnesses have already reported their findings, in one form or another, at least once, if not more. I've given hundreds of pages of deposition testimony, all on record, which is more than anyone else in this bloody mess can say." Rock sounded pleading because he didn't want to roil the waters.

"Okay, sit tight."

"Sit tight? Mr. Scott. Every time the opposition requests depositions, I have to fork out more money."

"I'll request a short hearing. See if we can limit discovery." Scott sounded sympathetic.

"Much appreciated. You want me there?"

"No. I can handle it."

"If there's anything I can do or provide, please let me know. I'd like to move matters along as quickly as possible." He wanted desperately to help, but Scott passed off all his offers.

*   *   *

Early Friday evening, Rock pushed against the wind-whipped rain and into his apartment. He set groceries on the kitchen counter, draped his wet jacket over the back of a chair and smoothed his hair, when the phone rang. After quickly drying his wet hands on his pants, he answered, pleased to hear Scott's voice. "I'm reporting results of the hearing. Further deposition testimony is limited to one hour from you and two hours from each of your two witnesses, Jasper Fulbright and Mrs. Willard."

"What about Sheryl?"

"No further deposition testimony is required of Sheryl. However, she is expected to testify at the upcoming trial."

Rock stared out the kitchen window. Sheets of rain splashed against the pane. "I can't guarantee much more than her presence, Mr. Scott. She hates this litigation, especially because of the events in my case. When you meet her, you'll understand."

"Why do you say that?"

"Because Sheryl was not only a witness in my last trial, but she witnessed the trial. And, she saw what Anders pulled on me at the last hearing and knows how he dumped me. Since then, she's had no use for the legal system in any form."

"That's it?"

"You want more? Well, she dislikes the way attorneys interrogate witnesses. Sheryl believes attorneys lord over their power in the courtroom, belittling witnesses to the advantage of their own clients. She says the judicial system relies on the John and Jane Q public to fear its members and what they can do to laymen. And, their way of cross-questioning is to intimidate witnesses to trip them." The word cross-examination would have been a more appropriate word than cross-questioning, but Rock's stumbling over 'ex' words was embarrassing; therefore he tried to avoid them. "Sheryl believes that truth can come out under less harsh circumstances."

"Hmmm."

"And she dislikes my making plans for her without her being in on it."

Scott sighed. "I can understand that. My wife would feel the same way. All the same, if she refuses to testify at the new trial, Perkins will subpoena her."

Rock began unpacking the groceries, setting canned goods on the counter with one hand. "Oh. Geeezus, that would really tick her off. Why can't you read her testimony from the 1984 trial transcript? She hasn't anything more to add. Why repeat what's already been said, done and paid for?" He tried not to sound argumentative, an exercise in futility with Anders and Haley.

"Well, we'll cross that bridge when it gets closer to trial."

"When is the trial?"

"I won't ask for a court date until after the discovery process."

The conversation ended with Rock feeling uneasy. The hearing Scott reported on only served to shorten the deposition times and excuse Sheryl. Big deal. The last thing he needed was history repeating itself.

He looked at his watch. There was time to change into dry clothes, pick up a pizza and wheel over to Efrem's house.

* * *

"Ever feel like your life is on a merry-go-round?" Rock sat in a beanbag visiting with Efrem while drinking beer in his den. They were devouring pizza piled with extra cheese, green and black olives, green pepper strips and sausage.

Efrem chewed, holding a wedge over a napkin. "You betcha, Rock. Life is a merry-go-round. You have no patent on problems."

"I'd like to bottle mine and sink the bottle. Nearly everyday feels like Friday the thirteenth." Rock took another bite.

"All right. All right. You found a new attorney. So relax. Take a vacation." Efrem shifted around in his beanbag.

Rock's raven eyes narrow to slits. "Vacation. You've lost your sails. I've got a trial coming up."

"Uh-huh. There's time." Efrem shook his head and licked his fingers. He wasn't wearing a hat this time. Rock could see his bushy eyebrows move up and down.

"What's a vacation without a good woman to share it with? A vacation with Sheryl is out of the question. Besides, she's busy decorating her new house, since she moved back to Quamas." His napkin slid onto the Oriental rug.

"Oh, hohoho. Come on. You've got lady friends. Don't kid me." He swallowed a mouthful of beer.

Efrem's laugh was infectious enough to bring a grin across Rock's face. He grabbed his napkin. "What gave you that idea? I've been too damn busy supporting attorneys so they can afford vacations and sabbaticals." Still, thoughts of Mona surfaced. "As a matter of fact I have met a lady. Very attractive."

"Well, tell me about her." Efrem's eyes gleamed.

Rock gestured with his hands, indicating a shapely lady. "Nice-looking, blonde hair. Divorced. She's a travel writer. Afraid of flying. High strung. Very interesting." He explained the plane trip. "I wouldn't mind nesting her."

"Don't drag anchor, man." Efrem reached across the coffee table for another pizza wedge. "You think there's a chance?"

"Ahhh." Rock shrugged. "We've gone to dinner. But . . ."

"But what?"

"Oh, I don't know. My case makes me moody. And, she's more interested in my litigation for a novel she's writing." He took a swig of beer and swallowed. "When we first met, she said she was interested in someone. So, this novel and me may not go beyond a writer's interest. I get mixed signals from her. We're going jogging tomorrow." Rock shrugged. "Ahh. A writer's interest. That's all there is. Anything else is a wishful vision."

"Oh Rock. Get it through your thick skull. All is fair in the three els: life, love and litigation. Seriously." Efrem stomped a booted foot on the floor.

"Yeah. Like that mother-hummer painting of yours in the hallway. A mariner. A mermaid. False hopes. Misguided assumptions. A real steal?"

"Leave my mermaid out of this. Don't let your lady's interest in someone else stop you. Give her something to compare. Just because you're in litigation doesn't mean you stop breathing. Romance her."

Rock gulped a mouthful of pizza. After swallowing, he fired back. "What would you know about romance? That fireplace over there hasn't been used in years. Clean as new."

"Hell. I don't need a fireplace to enjoy life." He howled in laughter, slapping a knee and shaking a finger at Rock. "Experience love like those bubbles in your beer."

Rock held the bottle to the light and watched the bubbles chasing each other up to the top. He chuckled lazily, while wishing answers to all his problems were contained therein, all within his grasp, under his control. "Acknowledged, daddy-o." No question, his gut yearned for a challenging activity.

Efrem raised his beer in the air. "Okay buddy. Tomorrow. Now finish that pizza."

Reaching for the last piece, Rock laughed. "I'll try."

"Try what?"

"The last of the pizza. What else?" He hesitated in taking a bite, as he tried to stop laughing.

Efrem's infectious laugh filled the room again. "You shithead. Don't play dumb."

Rock muffled a chuckle, admitting he didn't need a vacation to pursue Mona. No question, he was interested in her. But, could he fall in love again? Did it matter?

Chapter Seventeen

Saturday morning, Rock held tightly onto his load of documents as he pushed Mona's doorbell with a finger, then stood back to glance out behind him where the Firebird was parked. The street was wide and curbless. A spectacular profusion of morning light reflected off Lake Washington. And, there was a wide path between the lake and the porch. This must be the trail where Mona jogs. Having someone write a book about him was turning into an adventure full of surprises. The sounds of a door unlocking drew his attention.

"Oh, let me help with those." She motioned for him to enter, while taking some of his pile and walking backwards through the entryway.

"Thanks." He liked seeing her dressed informally. Her faded blue jogging clothes practically matched his.

"Follow me." Pivoting, she led him down the hallway past a spacious living area to reach an office beyond the kitchen.

He noticed her hair was attractively banded in one thick braid down the back, quite unlike the first time he met her on the plane and at Shigley's. As they moved along, a colorful display of wall hangings, knickknacks and art objects, which gave the house an interesting cosmopolitan touch, caught his attention.

"Well, obviously you travel." He figured she purchased these items while on her travel-writing assignments, but she didn't respond to his comment and he let it pass, because there was so much to see and appreciate. Wherever he looked, there was a clever division of space with screens, fluffy rugs and several tall artificial plants with flat green leaves. "Are you a decorator too?"

"You josh. Hit and miss decorator is more accurate." She cleared a spot on the desk for his documents.

It was a large room with a narrow bed against one wall; a trunk at the foot. He saw file cabinets, book shelves with records and cassettes, a desk of organized clutter, a typewriter. "Everything is neat. I'm a casually tidy person. And, what's this? A collection of Native American basketry." He exhaled into a whistle through his teeth.

She grinned. "I knew that would grab your attention."

Rock admired the baskets in geometric designs in black, red and ecru, depicting snakes, trees and birds. Some exhibited a fine braided rim around the top edges. "I don't recognize the designs as being from any tribe around here. Coastal tribes used to make plain baskets for gathering and carrying clams. At least the ones I've seen."

"You're right. The collection came from my mother, who bought them from the Thompson River tribe a long time ago. Clan members from Canada came down to Sumas to sell their baskets. Mom happened to be there one day. Over the years, she built up the collection through commissions." She pushed her sleeves up to the elbows. "I understand that today few of the women weave these baskets in the traditional manner."

Rock walked over to pick up a basket. "It's coiled."

"Yes. A thick core of split cedar root wrapped around a thinner root. The designs are called false embroidery, meaning the designs are only on the outside. The outer part of the design is overlapped with cherry bark. Sometimes, maidenhair fern stems or bear grass are used."

He listened to her interesting history surrounding the collection. "Very nice." Rock returned the basket to the shelf, still admiring her collection of various sizes and shapes, until his eyes settled on three flat, tray-like baskets hanging vertically down one wall. The handles had leather straps, facilitating the vertical draping. "Same tribe?"

"Yes. Those are very rare. And, nicer than anything you'll see in museums around here."

"Why are they rare, besides being old?"

"The starfish and butterfly designs are rare because of the difficulty in creating them. Much more difficult than the geometric designs."

"Besides raising a beautiful daughter, your mother reveals fine taste."

"Why how nice of you." She seemed genuinely surprised at the compliment. Even blushed.

"Just being honest. Leucojum would say we never wait to say something beautiful to make another person's day nicer." He smiled. "I like your braid too." His eyes moved to her feet. "So, now you're in blue dusters?"

"Oh, I have an assortment of colors." Ember faced, she reached under the desk for jogging shoes.

Rock inclined his head and watched with admiration. Scents of stock, sweet william and lilacs scented the room, making it easy to remind himself life is more than depositions, attorneys, wills and trials. Efrem's voice crept into his brain that life could be an interesting circuit of human interactions. Nothing could be more evident in the presence of this attractive lady, putting him in the swing for the unexpected.

*   *   *

With Rock's permission, she carried a recorder in hand as they talked and jogged along the Burke Gilman Trail. At first, he considered the recorder as an intrusion, like two is company, three is a crowd requiring some mental adjustment. In any event, they laughed and inhaled the Lake Washington air. Swallows skirted low overhead and seagulls flew about. He could see the lake in between houses lining the shore.

"Oh, hey, I wanted you to see this."

Following the direction of her pointing, he saw a totem pole, about six feet tall with three crests. Rock moved out of the way of a passing inline skater before commenting. "The top one, with outstretched wings, is called the thunderbird, a mythical whale-eater." Outstretched wings, curled appendages on the top of the head and the upper beak shaped like a hawk's beak, enabled him to identify it. "The others are obvious. A bear. A salmon."

"I should have expected you'd know about the thunderbird."

"I don't proclaim to know all crests. Those crests belong to the Pacific Coast tribes. I carve too, you know."

"I remember you were working on one when I phoned you."

"Um hmm. I'd like to show you someday." They continued on the path, until blackberry vines caught his attention. "Ever pick the berries?"

"Me and everyone else. We eat out of hand."

They walked over to the berry bushes. "Ah. Just to see these bring memories. In my childhood, Leucojum and I gathered wild berries for Paul Bunyan pies. Big. Ummm. I can hear her now: 'The first berries of the season will put summer in your step.' And, we dug in the earth for wild onions, wild carrots that tasted sweet and tiger bulbs that tasted like potato. Let's see. We gathered herbs, lamb's quarter and other greens. Leucojum believed wild foods made the best food and medicine. That there's something in the earth to cure everything, apart from . . ." He paused temporally, amused by his own thought. "Apart from dishonesty in mankind."

Her laughter and an elbow in the ribs pleased him over the dishonesty part. "Seriously, Leucojum believed that touching the earth and its bounty were like finding new beginnings."

"How interesting, although I'm not sure I understand."

"It's like sensing a pulse that tranquilizes the mind, freeing it from problems." At this moment, Rock actually did feel free of problems. "But, you can't find many herbs and roots anymore, unless you go into the wilderness."

"I wished I could have met Leucojum."

"I do too. She'd like you right away because of your braid. Makes you look Native."

"Aw, I'm too fair skinned to pass as a Native of any kind."

Rock shook his head. "No no. There's more than one tribe around the country with blond, blue-eyed Indians."

"Really?"

"Yes. But, more importantly, Leucojum would like you because you approve of us and try to understand what you don't understand about us." A finger of wind lifted her hair like offshoots of corn silk. "Inviting me here on this trail is a new beginning."

She smiled.

They resumed talking about general things, when she stopped. "The path forks here. We can go down there to Matthew's Beach or continue on the main path."

The landscape dipped sharply with a gravel pathway leading downward. He saw trees, low growth shrubs and ferns, the beach, playground and small basketball court. "No. Let's stick with the main trail."

"Okay." In the process of pivoting, she slipped and started to fall, with one arm reaching for him.

In the process, she squealed. He grabbed an arm, pulling her toward him. "Whoa babe. Careful."

Through a moment's hesitation, they stared into each other's eyes, before Rock righted her balance and released his hold.

She panted breathlessly. "Thank you."

"You welcome." He guided her into taking a slight lead as they continued on the main path, enjoying the unusually warm day, becoming better acquainted. So much so that Rock forgot about the recorder. What's more, she kept the conversation light. No pressures, until the unexpected question came.

"What does your wife think about your litigation?"

"Trying to ruin my day?" A whiff of wind sent a shower of leaves cascading over them.

"Sorry. I don't beat around the bush."

"My wife hates it. That's why we're ending our marriage." He wasn't about to offer personal reasons.

With widened eyes, her jogging pace slowed.

"I told you about our divorce plans during our first meeting on the plane." He was surprised she hadn't remembered this discussion.

"Oh. Of course. Guess I forgot." After jogging in silence a while, another question came. "How's your separation progressing?"

"We'll never live together again. My marriage is definitely over with absolutely no chance of reconciliation. I believe in marriage, but she kicked me out." He stopped to sit on a log, while motioning for her to do the same. "My wife Sheryl and legal advice suggested it unwise to end our marriage until after the law suit. That way it appears she's behind me. She's behind me anyway, but is against the way the legal system works. And the divorce is what we both want. I will say, even though the marriage didn't last, she and I are still friends."

Through the tree branches, tassels of sunlight ribboned down on her face. She looked angelic, like a painting of a Native maiden, but her eyes showed concern. He picked up a twig and drew a motif in the dirt. It gave him time to pause and think whenever he was puzzled. Her reaction to his situation disturbed him.

"Are your drawing some kind of Native mask?"

"Not just any mask. A Cherokee booger. They used such a mask to make fun of their enemies and ward off evil." Finally, Rock looked at her. "Not to change the subject, but I assure you, I don't use people."

He waited for a reaction. She turned her head toward the small boats, motoring noisily across the lake.

"Oh, I won't deny my coming here was to bring documents for your book." He paused and tried to formulate his thoughts carefully, not wanting to offend her. "But I wouldn't be here if I wasn't interested in you too." He felt better, having gotten this out in the open. She said nothing, while staring outward. "If that borders on dishonesty, I am guilty. You can send me back to my tribe." Her eyes flicked in his direction, then straight ahead.

Passing clouds blurred the sun temporarily. Two sparrows flew low, then faded like dots in the sky. "We had some good laughs on the plane. The pleasure of your company was enjoyable. It meant something to me. I think my presence meant something to you." Teasingly, he gently tossed pieces of twig in her direction. "You, a travel writer being afraid of flying."

She finally smiled and leaned her arms forward over her knees.

"Don't ask me why, but there was something about you at Shigley's I liked. I didn't see it on the plane. Maybe it was your quick grasp of legal matters, your attentiveness, your willingness to read everything." He noticed a surprised look on her face. "Anyway, my marriage is over." Her demeanor remained affable.

"Kaput? I mean 'over'?"

"Yes." He reached over, putting a hand on the back of her neck. "I was hoping you might need rescuing from that museum piece you date. In any event, I want to be friends. *Unali.*"

"*Unali?*"

"Yes. Friends." He wanted a lot more, but for now, her friendship was terribly important to him. He wasn't one to need a large circle of friends. Those he had didn't relieve the loneliness, the yearning he carried around in the pit of his stomach. "You writing about my case gives us a common ground on which to be friends. Agreed?" He held out a hand, palm up.

"Agreed."

"Unali," that's what I want to call you. Do you mind?"

"Different, but I don't mind." She shrugged her shoulders.

He relaxed when she placed a hand on his. It wasn't much, a pat of reassurance, encouraging enough. They sat quietly for a moment as other joggers passed. "What about you Unali? What's in your future?"

She fidgeted. "I'll settle down someday. Marriage and a family maybe. Come on. Let's jog back to the house. I'm hungry."

Rock brushed aside a few pinecones, rubbed out the booger mask with a foot, then ran after her. He was in no hurry. Admiring the view was more to his liking. The view was this Unali, sleek, round and long-legged. Her movements were supple and strong. Finally, he caught up. "I'm glad you invited me here. You and these surroundings are clearing cobwebs from my head." Unali was as appealing as Sheryl, but Rock had been bitten once thinking the attraction was love at first sight. Today, he was confident that a relationship had been established. That's all that mattered for now.

* * *

Gena set a corn dog on the placemat in front of Rock, who was sitting on the chaparral bench at one end of the trestle table in the kitchen. That's where she usually sat when Mona was home. Before sitting down in Mona's chair, she made several trips between the counter and the table to place their malts, bowls of fresh strawberries and the tape recorder between them. Fingers of sunshine streaming in through the window made his hair appear blue-black to her.

"Haven't you had enough taping for one day?" He kidded, munching his corn dog.

"Not yet." Her head brushed against an ivy-planter hanging, as she joined him. Her appetite had waned, thinking about Rock's marital status and realizing Mona had tricked her. Yet, she couldn't very well hold a grudge against Mona for deceit. Their folks, in the business as private investigators before retirement, taught them to be schemers.

After pushing these thoughts aside, Gena flipped back her braid and clicked on the recorder. "I'm puzzled by your litigation. The facts are these." She itemized the facts with her fingers. "Your uncle passed away in 1972. His probate was finalized in 1974. Your aunt died in 1983. And, you're trying to probate your uncle's estate in 1990. How can this be? Usually, once probate of an estate is finalized, that's the end of it. Explain."

Rock swallowed. "We'd be here all day if I told you everything here and now." He wiped his mouth with a napkin. "In a nutshell. I found copies of my uncle's later will and other papers with a letter. The letter defined his testamentary intent. In it he said he left his important documents in his safe deposit box, a box to which only my Aunt Nell had access. That evidence convinced the appellate court that my aunt possibly committed fraud probating with an earlier will. This enabled me to reopen probate to prove the fraud and then follow the terms of the right will."

"You're saying there's no time restriction on reprobate or even time of probate when fraud was committed against John's estate?" Gena held a strawberry to her mouth, waiting for his answer.

"That's how I understood it from my former attorney Nelson Anders. Right. Aren't you going to eat your lunch?"

"Guess I'm not very hungry." Rock's answer to reopening John's estate was important information for Mona's book, but Gena was still thinking about his marital status too. His availability, or unavailability. Her unavailability. His charisma. Admittedly, his charisma affected her. Finally, she ate the strawberry and then bit into the corn dog, not wanting him to notice a trembling hand.

"Your hand wouldn't shake if you'd eat more, Unali."

Gena grinned, trying to smooth over her momentary loss of control. "Sorry. I don't know what's wrong with me today."

"Want to call it a day?"

"No. Really." She felt it was best to keep going. Rock was behaving gentlemanly. It was just her nerves acting up. "I have another question. You were John's only surviving blood relative. So, why didn't he give you a copy of the right will to begin with, since he favored you?"

"That would have changed everything, if he had. John did let me read his papers. I should have made copies. Maybe, he thought I did. But, he named both Aunt Nell and me as co-egg-u-tors."

"That's co-executors." She prompted him.

He lowered his head embarrassed. "Please understand. Some of us Natives have trouble pronouncing words with 'ex'. It took me years to halfway master the word 'exhibit'."

"I'm sorry. I didn't mean to assist you; to cause embarrassment."

"It's okay. Anyway, John trusted her. So did I. But, in the end, the original will disappeared." Rock finished off the malt and set down the glass. "You writing a book about this will raise public consciousness and maybe effect some changes. It might prevent others from making my mistakes."

"Yes, I see. Otherwise, what happened to you could happen over and over again to others." She bit into another strawberry.

"Ummm hmmm. I understand it does happen to others. But I hope their attorneys aren't like Nell's attorney, Ralph Houston. Maybe that's why I keep losing attorneys. When they learn of his misconduct, they drop out rather than reveal him. My new trial will unmask both Houston and Aunt Nell."

Gena beamed with interest. "I hope so. Some great attorneys in our nation have gone down in history for misconduct."

Rock finished his malt and reached over to squeeze her shoulder. "Thanks for patronizing me."

"I'm not. I believe you're right." Her voice was serious. "I do wish there was a foolproof way for a testator to pass on his estate."

"There's one legend that after the death of a chief, his prospective heirs appoint his leading nephew to become the new chief, who takes the old chief's name. And the raising of a totem pole crowns the event. Too bad Uncle John wasn't a chief, me being the only nephew." He winked at her as he pushed away from the table.

"Oh, that is so interesting. I love it when you talk about your beliefs and myths. I feel it's the real you speaking."

Rock stared at her a moment. "You Caucasians confuse me. Most don't care. You have a way of bringing it out of me."

"I do?" This pleased her, because she didn't think it mattered that much to him.

"Yes. Remember, I've lived the Whiteman's ways too."

"Rock. You should live the way you want to live. Not the way someone else dictates."

"Suppose you're right. Up until now, I've tried to live to please others. You're telling me to live to please myself."

Gena watched him shake his head, as if he were puzzled by this conversation. For the first time, she actually forgot about their separate problems and spoke from the heart. "Yes. We have to be a little selfish and be ourselves. Otherwise, we can't be happy."

"Mona, you don't know how important that is to me." He smiled at her.

She looked down at her corn dog and wondered if she had stepped across some imaginary line beyond a friendship. A line she wasn't ready to cross. A true identity she couldn't reveal, and adjusting to a new name that wasn't her. "I like the name Unali."

"Unali then." Rock folded his napkin and placed it on the table. "Thanks for the delicious meal." He looked at his watch and whistled. "Two o'clock. Let's call it a day. I need to check on one of my seniors, an old friend of the family. He's alone and can hardly see anymore. He's back in his own home and has a cook come in to prepare his meals."

"Is he a Native American?"

"No. At first he didn't remember who I am. That's because he had patches over his eyes when I ran into him. Eye surgery, you know. The patches are off, but he still can't see very well. What I am doesn't matter. Friendship is what counts. And, he's an Indian sympathizer and from Oklahoma. That makes us kin in a way." Rock rose. "I've got to make sure he's okay."

"Yes. Well, I guess we should call it a day, being that it's so late." The names Mona and Unali echoed in her head as she escorted Rock to the front door and out to the porch. While waving goodbye, a vision surfaced. She was standing before a judge. Her head hung low. An imaginary judge pounded his mallet on the bench. "Gena Bradley is an impostor."

After Rock left, Gena piled their dishes together, set them in the sink and broke a dish in the process. His cologne still lingered in the kitchen. She was shaken over her deception, because suddenly Rock mattered to her.

Chapter Eighteen

Saturday evening before nine o'clock, Rock sat at the kitchen table. With pencil in hand, he doodled on paper, while waiting for Scott to return his call. The phone was on the floor by his chair.

He jotted down notes as a means of recapping the latest events. A court date had been set for August. That was good. The depositions of he and his witnesses were completed. Perkins became ill. That wasn't so good, meaning more delay. And, Scott's letter was an upsetting notice: Marvin hired a new expert witness, a Florida ink expert.

The ringing of the phone caused him to jerk his pencil across the page. He reached down to answer. "Hello?"

"Yo. Got your message. What's the problem?"

"Hell. My legal affairs are fading with the buffalo."

"What's wrong?"

"After the taking of depositions from Jasper Fulbright, Mrs. Willard and me, you said discovery was complete. "We did that. So, what's with this Florida ink specialist? I thought Perkins was ill. What was he doing in Florida, beside stirring up trouble and expenses?" Rock exhaled in exasperation.

"Oh. Well, he's recovering. He found this expert. Don't know how he heard of him. I forgot to mail the report to you sooner. There's nothing damaging to your new evidence. But, to save the opposition money, I thought it best if they just file the Florida expert's written report."

"Yes, of course. But, what'd Perkins do? Fly to Florida?"

"No, he hired the Florida expert to fly to Seattle, then took him to Perkins' Tacoma office."

Rock held his temper. His emotional compass told him to hang in there. After all, he didn't want to lose Scott.

Again he reminded Scott of his financial circumstances. In turn, Scott informed him they would have to attend another deposition session. Marvin's document expert, Ben Anderson, was to be further questioned at Perkins' office. There was nothing Rock could do, other than promise to attend, which didn't particularly thrill him.

* * *

Rock headed his Firebird south on I-5 from Ballard to his office at Turquoise Wholesalers. His eagle feather swayed from the mirror, reminding him of a recent date with Unali. She wanted to know about the feather and more on his background. He remembered them driving to Snohomish to browse through bookstores.

He followed her through one store after another. When a book felt right, her eyes gleamed. Suddenly she'd become very quiet. Then, he recalled her saying, *"Yeah. I want this."*

Rock found it absorbing that a travel writer collected used books on courtroom drama, especially while he was living it. She admitted to being an avid accumulator of legal books and novels containing courtroom drama, and handed him two books to hold. It didn't take long for him to get into the swing of her interests. While she bent over novels on the floor, he read titles aloud from shelves above.

Thinking of this now brought a smile to his face and anticipation of future meetings. He took the James Street exit and headed toward Pioneer Square, still recalling things such as Unali being curious about Sheryl's attitude against the judicial system. He gave her the same explanation that he gave to Joseph Scott, including that being a witness is punishing. Being a litigant was equally punishing, Rock was learning.

While pulling into a parking spot near work, Rock felt good about his meetings with Unali. Her interest in his litigation and their dates elevated their friendship to a new level.

*   *   *

"Thanks Unali." Rock put an arm around her waist and escorted her across the front yard. "I must rave over the meal you treated me to in that cabaret this evening." The place was an unusual cubbyhole in Ballard with tables for two in discreet nooks. The menu was bistro influenced. They ate grilled salmon, baked potato, eggplant and spinach salad served with vinaigrette dressing and grated Parmesan cheese.

"My pleasure."

Rock admired her braid draped over the left shoulder. She looked lovely in a simple dress, belted around the middle, which highlighted the fullness of her breasts. "Stay out here with me for a while before I leave." The grass felt soft under his shoes. Dusk was moving in. Unali lingered like she was studying him. It made him curious. "What's on your mind?"

"I'm sorry. You caught me staring."

"Ummm hmmm. In the act of looking me over, what have you decided? Am I prime, preferred, pickled or plain?" He chuckled not believing any of these described him. Wild and unsettled were more appropriate, because of the Native stirrings struggling to surface. Drumbeats and Indian flutes echoed in his soul, like his ancestors were alive inside him.

"Oh. Prime." She laughed and sat down on the bottom porch step.

"Why thank you." Rock bowed slightly, then sat beside her. He elbowed her and pointed to the flowerbed of tall purple trumpet flowers next to the house. "Look."

"Oh, hummingbirds. Did you know there's a myth that these little birds are resurrected warriors brought back to earth to fight battles in the sky?"

"Ummmm. Interesting, coming from you." Rock appreciated any connection with nature. Even small things -- the coos of pigeons, the song of a rooster at dawn, little hummingbirds in a garden. All of nature added to his life, reminders of wildness and fine wine. Yet, her words sent him off on another vein. "I need those little hummers to fight my battles down here, not in the sky."

She giggled and further explained. "Your beliefs have an influence on me. I found a book on myths in a second-hand store too. I've been reading a lot about Indians and listening to Indian philosophy on library tapes. I believe these help to understand where you're coming from."

"I'm flattered, although I wished you had taken me along." Rock began singing very softly. The area was quiet and tranquil.

"Sounds like the makings of a Native American song, Cherokee perhaps. Where did you learn to sing with such elegance, such vibrato?" She scooted up one step above him.

"Yes, Cherokee. Started singing on my dad's knee." Rock moved up to her step.

"You didn't take lessons?" Her voice sounded edgy, moving up to the next step, again above Rock.

"No, dad and mom taught me to sing." Rock shifted to her step. A slight breeze off the lake felt good. "My folks would probably turn over in their graves if they knew I also love bluegrass and mountain music. On second thought, mom would definitely turn over. She was partial to Native American music."

"I can't carry a tune." Unali shifted up another step.

Laughing quietly, he figured she must be running out of questions. There were no more steps. What will she do next? "My folks taught me much about life through song." He whispered, finally rising full height, clasping her hands in his, and raising her to face him. "Mom encouraged me to believe that no one is successful in his earthwalk until acquiring his song. She left me thinking that I still need to work on mine."

"Really? Tell me how you'll acquire this song?"

"Through a dream." He gazed across the lake. Darkness was closing in and house lights flickered off the lake.

"I don't understand. How can this dream make one successful?"

"It helps him recognize his power and skills. Until then, he doesn't know he possesses them."

"Are Native American music and mountain music alike?"

"As different as night and day. Although, both are at the base of many American folk songs." He thought a moment for a better description. "My music, or tribal music, is sensuous, a glimmer in the eye of a riddle, an anomaly. Not war songs, but songs of prayer to the Great Spirit. The idea comes from many tribes and has its origins in nature and mythology. What some folks refer to as the supernatural."

"Tell me how all this works?"

Her hands were warm and rigid in his and she appeared nervous by their nearness. "Usually through an encounter with a sensation, a dream or a vision." He smiled. "I prefer a dream. You see, I remember Leucojum sending me into the woods on a vision quest when I was a kid."

"Vision quest." The words flew from her almost in anger.

"Yes. A mission so to speak. Why are you upset?"

She turned away from him. "Aaah. Well I knew someone who went on a vision quest and never returned."

"That's odd. Maybe something dreadful happened. I was supposed to stay for several days without food or water, or until I communicated with a spirit. In the middle of the first night, my vision told me to go home before temptation took over to devour cattail roots. So, I did. Leucojum asked why. I told her my stomach was craving food. Leucojum said it was the Whiteman in me."

Appearing to have calmed down, Unali raised her head and joined in with his laughter. "You were a little devil."

"Yeah. Well, I was thirsty and hungry." He reached to hold her hand. A vibration seem to shoot through, like the string of a bow quivering from the release of an arrow. "May I demonstrate?"

"Please do."

He waited a moment for a car in the area to pass. Then, his palms cradled her face. She stared at him. "Close your eyes." He raised her chin slowly and stroked her eyelids with his thumbs until she held them closed. Her skin was smooth and radiant like a laurel leaf. "You are sweeter than the flowers."

In the distance, he heard sprinklers watering grass and dogs barking. These sounds were no match to the beating of his heart. They were standing so close. He felt her warmth. Inhaled her sweet scent. Her lips were inviting. Her face, trusting. So trusting that he could do no more than kiss her forehead. Finally, he stepped back while releasing her.

Unali blinked her eyes and smiled. "That was a nice demonstration."

Her remark drew out his thoughts. "You'll never know how much our meetings mean to me. I enjoy being with you. I'd like us to have many future times together."

"I'd like that too."

He hoped for this answer.

Chapter Nineteen

"Gena, I'm home." Mona hollered from the front entrance. She arrived home late from a travel assignment.

"Yes." Gena, mesmerized by the faint murmur of wind against the house, sat at the trestle table in the dark and thought about a vision quest. Rock's explanation indicated the quest had nothing to do with a person's intentional disappearance. That he'd never disappear without letting loved ones know. He wouldn't even go hunting or fishing without family knowing his whereabouts. *"You always leave a plan and you always stick to the plan."* That's what Rock told her. And, that if he'd experienced a vision quest, it would be a time for celebration with loved ones.

A small corner of her mind now held this major difference between her missing husband, Shumway, and Rock. Shumway didn't stick to his plan and the search party couldn't find him, his friends and the plane for that reason.

Mona stirred in the background. But, Gena felt enveloped in Rock's mysticism, while watching the dim moonlight through the curtained window. His virile presence during the demonstration still shook her foundation, as if the warm, delicate touch of his fingers and lips were with her now. His nearness felt so good. And his song was touching. She couldn't decipher all the words. Actually, it wasn't words so much as sounds that twined in melody.

Tree limbs scratched the windowpanes like a nudge on the shoulder. What would Mona think of her for feeling like this? The scratching snapped her back to reality. Gena decided to try a plan that would force out Mona's personal feelings for Rock, that is if she had any, and what her actual plans were.

Mona switched on the light. "Oh, oh. Should I turn the light off? By the look on your face, something must be wrong."

"You can leave on the light. We have to talk."

"Okay. Give me a minute." Mona left the room.

Gena played solitaire while reasoning things on her mind.

Mona returned in pink slippers and robe. "Hey, I arrived in Seattle before the stores closed and ordered a new computer. Our writing will go much faster now."

"Our writing?" Gena released a sarcastic grin. She pushed the deck of cards to the center of the table.

Mona bubbled with enthusiasm, while appearing to ignore Gena's mood. "How are things going with Rock? Isn't he neat?"

"Very. So much so, I'm flummoxed. You and your schemes." Gena moved away from the table to lean one arm against the counter. The other hand on her hip. "You go out in the world, put on those pink slippers so you can get attention on planes, flirt with men and bring one home to me. I didn't ask you to do that, you know." She stopped to breathe.

Mona fired back defensively and flung herself into a chair. "I don't flirt.

Well, not exactly. I survive. I have to engage people in conversations to forget my fear of flying." She crossed her feet under the chair and stared downward.

Gena pressed further. "Forget that sorrowful look. Won't work." She was going about this haphazardly. Anger never solved problems. There had to be another way. "I can think of less problems for you, and me, if you found more women to talk too."

"I guess so, but it wouldn't be as much fun. At least now I recognize my problem. The need to overcome my fear gives me uncanny nerve. I butt into the lives of others."

"In more ways than one, I might add."

Mona rolled up her sleeves, went to the cupboard for a mug and poured coffee. "Ah, sis. You have a right to a life too. And, you're not finding it buried in a courtroom. What cataclysmic event happened to cause all this? Did Rock do something I'm about to regret?"

"You may have put me, supposedly you, in the middle of a messy triangle, neglecting to tell me he's getting divorced. I should have stopped this project as soon as I found out. But, no. I just kept trudging on for the sake of your novel, kept filling in for you while you traipsed about the country."

"Oh, don't pay attention to the divorce bit. Divorces do fall through. Until the dotted line is signed, he's married." Mona returned to the table.

"So." Gena chuckled sarcastically. "You're suggesting I get a life with a married man?"

"No. If he tries anything, just remind him he's married. Meanwhile, we'll get his story." Mona paused, as if thinking. "At least it gets you back in circulation. Besides, you need practice."

"Practice with a married man or a married man separated with divorce intentions? You care to retract that remark?" Gena couldn't believe she heard right. She forgot her original plan for a moment and spoke from the heart. "Under this skin you think I'm dead. Well I'm not. Dormant at times, but not dead. I've got blue blood in my veins."

"Okay. Forget I said you need practice. But, if you have blood in your veins, for God's sake get a life, Gena. Shumway isn't coming back. We both know it."

"I know." She stared at Mona. "But, I don't know. He could still be alive. Oh, Mona. I do want marriage and a family. I'm not getting any younger. But one doesn't go looking for this in a married man." After some silence, Gena pleaded. "Let's concentrate on you for a moment. Why don't you take those classes to overcome your fear of flying? They're free."

"Oh, all right, let up. I promise I'll look into it. If I do, will you take the classes with me?"

"No."

"You have a fear of heights and planes, too."

"I'm too busy right now. Thanks to you."

"Oh boy. Do as I say, not as I do, huh?" Mona sipped coffee.

"Something along those lines." Gena pushed back the cuticles of her fingernails. Finally, she returned to the present and her meetings with Rock. "There's no way for me to remember all that happens each time and I can't tape everything. We're losing control of this situation. I'm exhausted racking my brain for quick alibis when I slip. Rock isn't the kind of person who uses people. Anyone can see that. A huge sense of guilt is seeping into my soul, I swear. Half the time I don't think he's aware I have the recorder on." She looked at Mona. "He's a bona-fide hunk of humanity, of flesh and tenderness."

Gena went to the sink for a glass of cold water, then turned to Mona. "God should strike me dead. I feel like a complete heel. We're using him for a novel. He's genuine and sincere. Are we? Think on it." She returned to the table and plopped down.

"Gena, there's more to this than what you're saying. Right?"

"You'd better believe it. He's falling for whom he believes is Mona. I can sense it as sure as I am of you ogling at me." Gena flung her hands in the air and twisted on the bench. "Wanna know what I really feel like? Like a member of the Ralph Houston clan or, or the Houston imbroglio. A sneak."

Mona swallowed more coffee. "You feel like a sneak against Rock. And, against me. That's it, isn't it? Hot damn. You're falling for him."

"Well something happened to me I don't understand." This situation was becoming confusing, even to Gena, who fell silent, not wanting to hurt Mona. How could she get it across to Mona that Rock's true interest was focusing on her, Gena? That it grew after meeting her at Shigley's. That she actually knew Rock better than Mona. If he really divorced his wife like he says, that could change things. It could prompt her to change things in her life too. She returned back to her original plan for this conversation. "Mona, are you interested in Rock, the novel, or both?"

"Okay. Truth time. I went after Rock for you, not me. The bottom-line. I believe his divorce is eminent. You could get a quiet divorce. Like that." Mona clicked her fingers together. "You wouldn't even have to tell Rock. The only one holding you up is you. All I care is that you have a good time in life." She played with her empty cup. "I have listened to some of what's on the recorder. You two are doing a lot of panting. Your words are garbled."

"We were jogging."

"Do you enjoy being around him?"

"Yes." Gena snapped out the answer. "There's something about him: exciting, aristocratic, trusting, naïve, sometimes austere and incredibly serious. He has an interesting philosophy. There's a restless Native vitality there that can't be denied. The more I'm around him, the more I see this."

"Well, I admit Rock isn't the noble savage we've seen portrayed in movies, television and books on the Wild West. As a matter of fact, he seemed more Whiteman than Native American when I met him on the plane."

"Yes, but around me his Nativeness is coming out more all the time. It's as if he can't suppress it any longer. He has admitted to being lost between two cultures. He calls it running in the woods. All a part of his charisma that draws me in like a magnet." Her voice trailed off softly. "Remember, he's still a man."

"That's good for my book." Mona became exuberant.

"Oh really." Suddenly, Gena fired up again, "This all started out as a favor to you and the novel and a friendship. Now? I just don't know." She paused. "Okay, yes, I'm attracted to him. But, how can I get romantically involved with Rock, Mona? Divorces take time, sometimes too much time. And, look what happened to my roommate falling in love with a married man who dumped her after he got what he wanted. I don't want this to happen to me. And you should have thought of that."

"At least you're thinking about it." Mona walked over and hugged Gena. "We both have a lot to think about. Meanwhile, let's swap names?"

Gena sighed. "Seems like this is what twins do best. I'll be you a while longer."

"All settled then. I'm the writer, nothing more. You'll have to answer all phone calls, posing as me. Of course, I'll return my own messages." Mona raised her eyebrows. "Clear? A while longer."

"Clear. What are you going to do with his documents?" Gena nodded her head toward the office.

"I'm going to the office and read the latest stack of papers." Mona left the room.

Gena felt relief, but how much was still difficult to pin down. It was like trying to reel in a kite on a blustery day. At least for now, she didn't feel guilty of stealing Mona's territory, should this relationship come to that. But, how could she let it come to that?

She resumed playing solitaire, recalling herself agreeing with Rock of wanting those next times together. But, this didn't mean either one was going to fall deeply in love. Rock's divorce was dragging on due to the litigation. So, there wasn't any immediacy in pursuing her divorce for a while. And, her divorce attorney had ordered fliers for a second time to send to police departments in the Klamath Falls and other neighboring areas, just in case someone fitting Shumway's description was wandering around down there under another name.

Mona yelled down the hall. "Check the front door and be sure the porch light is on."

"I will." Gena left the kitchen and went to the front door. As she opened it for a quick breath of lake air, moths fluttered around her and the light fixture. That's what she felt like. The proverbial moth attracted to the light bulb. Finally, she locked up. A little voice warned if she fluttered in too close, she might get burned.

Chapter Twenty

While waiting for Scott to return his call Friday before dinner, Rock tried to convince himself for the umpteenth time that things would work out. In the bedroom, he removed his work shirt, as he felt sweaty from nerves and the heat of a seventy-degree day. He milled over the recent deposition meeting with Marvin's document expert Ben Anderson. It was a drawn out event, but Anderson was inconclusive. Scott said there was nothing to worry about. But there was. Rock's financial situation.

Then the phone rang. He rushed down the hall to the kitchen. "Yeah, Rock here."

"Got your message. I thought it would be a good idea if I file a pretrial motion with the court. The motion is a request, enabling us to enter all prior records already in evidence. This can be used as testimony to save trial time and costs for all parties."

"Whatever you think best." Rock's weak response was due to a slight quandary. "I thought this was the plan all along. The appellate court ordered it. So did Judge Randell. What does your plan mean?" He opened a cupboard door to scan several cans of vegetables. He finally grabbed dill beans for his dinner.

"Basically, it means that witnesses living near this area will be called to court. I'm wondering about your out-of-state witness, Darnell Eberling, a fraternity brother."

"Yeah, Eberling. He lives in Houston, Texas. What about him?" Rock opened the can with a hand-cranked can opener on the counter and poured the contents into a pan. He ate several beans in the process.

"We'll enter his '84 trial testimony by reading his transcript into the record, saving you the expense of bringing him here. That will save you a bundle of greenbacks, if agreeable with you?"

Feeling thirsty, Rock returned to the refrigerator for cranberry juice. Not much juice was left. He drained it straight from the bottle. "Hell, yes. I'm agreeable. Do you need my other fraternity brother, George Arnold? He lives in Bellingham."

"He'll have to come to court. Can you get ahold of the third fraternity brother, Laurence Radford?"

"No chance." Rock put the empty juice jug in the garbage under the sink. "Laurence would have been my best witness, but died of cancer." Leaning with his back to the counter, he crossed his feet. "Another good witness is Henry Stoner, a banker in Quamas and longtime friend to Uncle John. He signed as a witness on John's will. We definitely need him."

"No. He's a no show."

"Whatdaya mean?"

"He's going to be out of town. He told me so. But, no problem. We'll enter his testimony from the '84 trial transcript. This is agreeable with Perkins."

It dawned on Rock that the attorneys had already discussed these matters.

Maybe this is the way they do things here. "And, what about having the postmaster come? Remember that the large mailing envelope containing my new evidence didn't have sufficient postage. The postmaster can testify that the letter would have been mailed anyway. That was the practice in the '70's."

"Oh, I don't think that's necessary."

"I do. It wouldn't cost much." He turned around and wiped toast crumbs off the counter into the sink.

"No. The judge will know that's common knowledge. There's an evidence rule governing common knowledge, whether or not I ask the judge to notice."

"Okay. If you're sure." Who was Rock to argue? He didn't know about evidence rules. "And, don't forget to contact my document specialist. Nail down his fee." Rock paused to stifle a burp. "Maybe I should contact him?" He returned to the fridge, searching for the last chunk of ham to heat with the beans.

"No, I'll take care of contacting him and discussing his fee." Scott cleared his throat. "I need to talk with him anyway."

He could hear Scott talking to someone over his intercom. Scott returned. "Okay, I'm back. What were you saying?"

"Well, sounds like you have things under control. I appreciate you leaving no stone unturned. All is in writing."

After hanging up, and encouraged by Scott's ideas, Rock added chunks of a scrubbed potato to the pot and set it on the burner. Then he phoned Efrem, Sheryl and Unali to inform them about the latest and that the three-day trial was now reset for October.

During dinner, Rock made plans to work on his totem pole in the apartment basement. It kept his mind busy. The work required concentration.

While working, somehow he felt close to guiding spirits. Needing that now, he rose and headed for the basement.

Chapter Twenty-One

"Whew. Let's slow the pace. My dinner hasn't settled." A week later, Rock huffed, jogging with Unali on their favorite trail near her house. He grabbed her around the neck to slow their pace.

"Okay. Okay." She laughed. "Careful. I've got this recorder on." They slowed their pace. "Tell me, how did you discover your new evidence?"

"Leucojum decided to change her will prepared by Jasper Fulbright's dad, Cod."

"Funny name, Cod."

With one hand, Rock used the towel around his neck to blot moisture from his forehead. "Yeah. He was an enterprising man. Not only was he an attorney, but Cod owned a fish cannery not far from the Carper cannery. Ran a gift shop in town too. Our families were close. These men belonged to the Mason's lodge. After dad died, Cod hired Leucojum to manage the gift shop."

"How nice."

"We thought so." Rock paused to let an inline skater pass. "Anyway, Leucojum asked me to phone him about her will. By then, Cod was deceased. But, Jasper checked their files and discovered they had mom's will for years, but their records contained a notation that they had mailed her the will several years back." Rock grabbed a blade of long green grass and resumed walking again with his arm around Unali's neck. She placed an arm around his waist.

"Leucojum checked a lockbox in a backroom closet where she kept important papers and discovered Jasper was right. She asked me to take the envelope to Jasper to update her will." He grabbed another blade of grass along the path with his free hand.

"And?" She blew hair from her eyes.

"And Mrs. Willard opened the large envelope. Contained inside were Leucojum's will and another envelope. Then Jasper came from his office and opened the inner envelope. I emphasize, both envelopes were sealed. Jasper found Uncle John's important papers, including a copy of his last will, in the inner envelope."

"So, that's why you refer to them as the Leucojum documents." Unali asked other questions, which kept him busy talking, until he reached over to turn off the recorder.

"Enough legal talk, my lady." He noticed her neck and face showed blotchy signs of nervousness. "Does my nearness bother you? Your face is red."

She raised her hands in an attempt to cover her face. "Why doesn't your face turn red by my nearness?"

Rock looked up at the last light of day. "Ooooh. You're in trouble now. I'm going to get you for that." He raised his arms high, formed his hands into bear claws and lunged.

"Rock. Stop it." Unali took off running.

Her giggling made it easy for Rock to catch her. Oh, how he wanted to kiss her. Instead, he made light of the incident. "You're turning into a tease."

Her eyes twinkled. "I have fun with you."

They walked and held hands, until she asked another question. "If those envelopes were sealed and Jasper and his secretary testified to such in their depositions, what have you got to worry about?"

"Nothing, I guess." So why did he feel uncertain?

*　　*　　*

Because of needing to phone Scott, Rock sped home during an afternoon work break and parked in the street in front of the apartment. A hint of fall colors from the maples graced the area. Strolling toward the entrance, he noticed his shadow was shorter.

The heat of late summer seeped through tree branches. It felt relaxing. It freed his mind to concentrate on questions to ask Scott. After gathering his mail, he entered the apartment, set the mail on the kitchen counter and dialed Scott's private number.

After formalities, Rock got to the point of phoning. "I understand there are some essential requirements in my proving a lost or destroyed will. What precisely are they?"

"Right. Finding a copy of a will isn't proof that it's the last will your Uncle John intended to be honored. That's why your new evidence, the Leucojum documents, are so important in meeting these requirements."

"How does it work?" Rock grabbed his mail and moved to the sofa.

"The Leucojum documents, authenticated by your document expert, prove the existence of your uncle's last will at death. Not the day before. This is important. And, your documents prove the original of the lost will was in the safe deposit box to which Nell had access. And they prove your aunt misrepresented John's estate."

"Any other requirements?"

"You need to prove will contents through two disinterested witnesses."

"I have three." Rock slid deeper into the sofa. He liked Scott's explanations.

"And, you need to address the reason for your lengthy delay. Laches."

"Yeah, I know laches means delay. Caused by Houston. No problem there. Proof is in the record."

"So relax. We've got everything necessary to forge ahead. Except . . ."

"What?" Rock sat up, not liking Scott's tone.

"Did you receive a copy of Perkins' most recent letter to me?"

"I haven't opened my mail yet. Just a moment." Rock cradled the receiver between his ear and shoulder and quickly found the letter, which he ripped open and read:

"We will show conclusively that Rock's new evidence, the Leucojum documents, could only have been produced at a much later time, by someone with access to a thermofax and a xerox-type photocopy machine, as well as an Underwood typewriter with pica type, just like that used by John Carper, if indeed not the same typewriter."

Words came slow to Rock, suddenly realizing Scott was still on the line. "What's the meaning of this last-minute outrage?"

"Yo. I thought you should read it." He remained upbeat.

"Oh shit." Rock dragged the phone cord, as he paced around. He raised his voice. "The letter mentions someone. Doesn't say who. If they are implying it was me, there's no way they can prove I had all that equipment because I had none of it." This news was like a shot of acid that set his stomach on fire. "Implying doesn't make fact."

"Well, hang on now. You're right. They have no hard evidence."

"There's no evidence, period, unless they created something. Where's their proof?"

"None that I'm aware of. They're just throwing out guesses."

Rock heard Scott yawn with little more enthusiasm than a dead elk. "Those documents were produced by Uncle John. My document specialist confirmed this finding in his report."

"Oh, by the way." Scott perked up again. "I'm glad you brought up your expert. He sent me a bill. Wants his $2,000 fee upfront for his court appearance. You'll pay it through me."

Rock hung up with a new problem. If he paid Woods, there won't be enough to pay Scott unless he was willing to accept monthly payments. His only resolve was to stretch out on the sofa. The ticking of the Carper antique clock agitated his nerves. Agonizing over Perkins' preposterous accusation put pressure in his head. The Leucojum documents were discovered in 1985. Marvin had five years to do something about it. But, no, he waits and hires Perkins who creates delays, additional costs and bullshit. Repeated obstacles in his pursuit for justice. Through a quick hearing to probate his uncle's estate and get on with his life were so simple at first; but not now.

He searched around for his antacids. The bottle was empty. It was too late anyway. Deciding this obviously wasn't one of his better days to sit on a high tree branch to enjoy the view, he ran to the bathroom and vomited. Sleep finally overtook him and his woes, with no solutions.

About an hour later, the ringing of the phone woke him. Scott relayed the news that the opposition was willing to settle out of court. "You have two days to think it over."

Rock groaned. He knew he was slow to make decisions. Two days didn't seem nearly enough.

Chapter Twenty-Two

On an August Saturday evening, under what is called a Thunder Moon, Rock and Unali walked into Shigley's. Following her blonde hair and light perfume made him feel like bear fat melting under the hot grip of the sun.

He assisted in removing her lightweight jacket. "You look especially delicious tonight. Blue is becoming on you."

"Why, thank you for noticing." She smoothed her dress and scooted across the seat in a corner booth. Her face blushed a bit.

Rock moved in alongside. A waitress brought them menus and water in goblets, then lighted the candle, centered on the table.

With his permission, Unali set the recorder on the table between them. "So Perkins made an outrageous accusation and a settlement offer?"

"You'll never guess what the offer entailed. Scott phoned me about it." Rock guided the conversation, watching her play with a single rope of pearls around her neck.

"I thought they were out of money?"

"They're only admitting to having six etched silver napkin rings and $160,000." He chuckled, sounding cynical. "They are willing to give me the napkin rings." Competing with the accordion music caused him to speak louder.

"Ohhhhhhhh no! Why so generous?" She laughed, while turning slightly to better face him.

"And, they are willing to divide the $160,00 among Marvin, Beatrice and me. That's about $53,000 to me."

"Pretty nice carrot."

"There's a catch." He paused. "Only after all costs are paid."

"What are the costs?" Her eyes widened.

"Hell. I haven't the slightest. That's the odd part. Those crazies want me to sign an agreement before they reveal undetermined costs. That's like asking me to sign a blank check. They're full of riddles that gnaw. My opposition wants it all their way. So Scott told them no." He fiddled with a fork, tapping it on the table. "Go figure that one."

"You can't figure until you know the expenses."

"Right." He inhaled deeply. "Soooo, the trial is still on." Rock opened the menu. "Of course, my document specialist's testimony is important too. Scott received another report from him. He sent everyone a memo to show his testimonial input."

"And, what is that?" Unali checked the recorder.

"I'll give you a copy for your book. Essentially, the specialist told Scott that my uncle's last will doesn't fit the classical case of a foundling will." Rock talked slightly above the din in the busy restaurant.

"What's a foundling will?"

"An original will that mysteriously appears. Nobody knew anything about it before, or couldn't find it, and is commonly linked with forgery. My uncle's will doesn't fit in this category, because there are several related documents brass-stapled together."

"And, from the copies I have, I noticed your uncle signed each page 'JFC 5/9/72' and attached them to his original cover letter before mailing them to his attorney."

"You catch on fast."

"I try." She smiled. "Your uncle's will isn't strange in appearance either. The language is formal, legal language and fairly complex. I mean, not the type of language used by laymen. I'll bet your expert noticed."

"Matter of fact, he did. He told Scott that the witnesses to John's will are solid citizens. With foundling wills, the witnesses are usually bums, or drinking buddies. Speaking of drinking, would you like a beer with your meal?" Rock scanned the menu.

"Sure, if you won't think me a bum." She punched him lightly below the shoulder.

"Never." He chuckled. "What are you ordering?" Rock noticed the menu held a good variety, as a waitress approached.

"Ummmmm. The veal dinner a la carte."

Rock looked at the waitress. "Make that two veal dinners, one a la Carte, and beer for two." The waitress wrote down their orders and left with their menus. Rock stretched his legs forward under the table, accidentally resting a leg against Unali's leg.

"Ooooh." Her voice reached an unrecognized falsetto sound.

He inched away. "If I remember right, you had no problems attempting to step over my knees on the plane." One eyebrow arched, teasingly.

"Will you ever forget that?"

"No." He shook his head, grinning. "Actually, I enjoyed it." They kidded around until the waitress brought their beers.

Then Unali raised her stein. "A toast to the success of your trial."

"And, to our friendship." They clicked glasses. "Turn that damn recorder off." He wanted to enjoy the meal and their evening without further discussion of his case.

*   *   *

A hot shower took some of the soreness out of Rock's arms, shoulders and back, after having hollowed out some areas on his totem pole. Now he crawled under the bed covers and thought a while before dropping off to sleep.

If only he could concentrate on Unali rather than the litigation. Both had his emotions working like a vibrating bow. Cherishing the idea of him having that effect on Unali, he chuckled, while fantasizing their meetings to come, when the phone rang.

The ringing hadn't registered as anything beyond a dream. He rolled over wishing he had an adverse effect on Perkins, like a constant ringing in Perkins' ears. The phone rang again. This time Rock became fully awake. He reached for the extension on the nightstand. "Hello?" He noticed the clock read eleven.

The caller spit out his wrath. "If you don't settle, I'll impeach you by deposition. I'm going to show how impossible it was for Nell to go to the bank and destroy the will. Nobody is going to give you the silverware or anything."

"Mr. Perkins?" Rock flipped off the bed covers with his feet.

"Yes." His tone was not cordial. "Even tonight's phone call will cost you. Have no doubt about it. I'll beat you in court. I'll make the discovery of documents so unbelievable that the court will not accept them. There are many ways to do this."

Rock sat up, turned on the lamp and held the phone at a slight distance. There was no mistake. This wasn't a dream. It was Leland Perkins: live and livid, acting like a crazy man.

Perkins' anger picked up speed. "If Nell went to the bank and got the '67 will and put a match to it, it was all right as she didn't want to be left without anything." Slam.

"Hello. Mr. Perkins." There was no answer; only a dial tone. Rock couldn't understand this behavior. Nevertheless, he was now wide-awake, greatly irritated enough to immediately phone Scott at home.

"Yoooo?" Scott didn't sound awake and eager for a powwow.

"Your God should have thrown away the mold before he made that sonofabitch Perkins." For the most part, Rock believed that his Great Spirit and God were the same. But at this point, he figured there had to be two creators. No way would the Great Spirit create a man like Perkins.

"Rock. What's wrong? Do you know what time this is?"

"He just phoned me with threats." Ignoring Scott's yawning indifference and the time, Rock flopped back on the pillow and explained.

"Well Perkins was out of line. A scare tactic. Ignore him. Go back to bed."

Rock slammed the phone. Shit. Ignore Perkins? He hadn't fully recovered from Perkins' former upset. Either Rock was overreacting or Perkins was using evil magic on him. He chose the later. Yes, Perkins possessed *skee-nah*, an evil spirit.

Chapter Twenty-Three

Rock found himself branching into another activity. Swimming. Unali convinced him they needed a diversion. She said a diversion was necessary, because when she saw him upset, she got upset. She convinced him a good swim would settle them down. They went to an Everett club.

He was uncertain just how much unwinding he could do, while watching her dive into the pool from the edge. Her one-piece blue swimsuit was designed for respectability: high in front. It made her curvaceous figure and long legs all the more alluring.

"Let's race." She hollered at him and shoved off.

Rock followed with interest. Before long he was chasing her and caught hold of a foot.

She splashed, sputtered and fought the water, like a king salmon. "What are you doing?"

"No contests. I don't try to best women in contests. Good way to ruin a friendship." He was thinking of his legal hassles with Ginger Haley.

"You challenged me to a race on the Burke Gilman Trail."

"I'll never do it again. Promise." He let go of her.

"Then we'll swim side-by-side. How many laps?"

"Put me in for ten." He stroked up alongside her.

She raised an eyebrow. "Ten it is, if I last that long."

"Doesn't matter. I'll quit when you do." The ten laps were sufficient for Rock. And, it didn't take much coaxing from Unali to lure him into the Jacuzzi.

"Ahhhh. If the great chiefs could enjoy such luxury." Rock felt his body melting slowly down through a cloud of steam into the hot bubbling water.

"You haven't done this before?" She sat on the edge.

"A first." He began singing in a gruff kidding manner, his eyebrows lowered. His arms stretched out expressively. He urged Unali to join him. She rolled over the edge and slid down nearby.

"A tribal love song?" She spoke above the background noises echoing off the walls.

"Yes. Sometimes my songs are thoughts driven by joy or sorrow." At one brief moment their eyes met, like their souls and spirits touched. He finished singing, then submerged under the water briefly and finally surfaced, Rock flipped back his hair, quietly staring at Unali. "I've worked up an appetite." Judging by the expression on her face, he believed she took the comment wrong. Lunging away to the opposite edge, Rock quickly corrected himself. "For food."

"Ooooh. Me too."

They headed for the showers.

* * *

After enjoying hamburgers at Dick's in Lake City, they drove back to Mona's place. Gena stood with her back against the front door. Her arms were around Rock's neck. She felt his lips against hers. So far, she had pushed her own problems in the background, because Rock was still married with no divorce in sight. But, his advances and her acceptance of them were complicating matters.

In the shadows, she watched the glint in his eyes. A desire. Guilt crept over her. "I think we're heading for trouble here."

"Let's not talk about it."

"But . . ."

"Not tonight. I'm drained with worry over my case. Most troublesome are all the delays in my court date. Perkins' threats and accusations hurt. I just want to enjoy this wonderful moment with you."

After several more kisses, he slowly released her, moved slightly bowlegged down the steps to his car and disappeared up the hill into the darkness like a lone wolf.

She lingered a while on the porch. Instead of a moon, she imagined seeing moonbeams. And flickering lights from houses across the lake shone on the water. There was a faint clean smelling breeze in the air. Sitting on the top step, she hugged her knees and tried to capture the evening.

Being with Rock, no matter the occasion, was splendid although tonight there were times when he was overly focused on the litigation. She chuckled at his reference to his documents as "*talking papers*". A twinge of jealousy nagged her. But, she rationalized how silly it was to be competing with an inanimate thing. Surely Rock wouldn't let the case dominate his life.

With closed eyes, Gena inhaled his spicy aroma on her clothes. That and a trace of chlorine placed her back at the swim club. She loved the way he pulled himself out of the pool. So strong. A heave of his arms and he was out and standing on the edge. Water beaded and drizzled down his bronze skin, as he flipped back his hair and combed it with his fingers. He had such nice broad shoulders, hairy chest and legs, glistening biceps, firm thighs, tight derriere revealed by a clinging swimsuit. Their eyes focused on each other through the steam in the Jacuzzi. Rock's eyes were untamed and wolfish, holding her, licking her desires. In the process of getting to know him, she was learning to think like him, especially since he was calling her Unali.

Even now, sitting on the porch, his electricity rumbled through her brain. A breeze on her face carried his songs. He said music portrays the movement of leaves. Flying birds. The flutter of hearts. His singing pulsated in genuine and ennobling sounds and words: a slurring of his voice from one tone to another. At times he sounded almost war-like. Sometimes, it was a little savage and primitive to express his feelings, rather than to entertain her. He said he was singing southern-drum, the Oklahoma singing style, a low pitch. Gena sighed. Everything about him was delightfully surreal. And very male.

This kind of excitement hadn't happened to her before, even with her missing husband. Yet, the fact remained. She was still married to Shumway. What if he wasn't killed in a plane crash? Or, maybe he was lost somewhere with amnesia as her attorney thinks, even if the police said amnesia cases are rare. There had been incidences in the news where an amnesia victim recovered and eventually returned home.

Experts say amnesia is shrouded in mystery and the least understood affliction of all the neurological sciences. Shumway could have suffered a physically or emotionally overwhelming event such as a plane crash that blocked out all memory of the event and everything leading to it, including his identity. He could have created a new identity.

Gena decided it could only be death or amnesia to explain Shumway's disappearance, because their marriage had been a happy one. For certain, life hadn't been the same since he left. And, as yet, her attorney hadn't made any progress with the fliers he sent to Klamath Falls. He wanted more time. She agreed. To comply with the attorney's wishes seemed necessary out of respect for Shumway. And, she believed there was time because of the delay in Rock's divorce.

She looked up into the dark sky and sighed. Life had an elusive meaning. Things happened beyond her control. In college, she was taught to organize, organize, organize. This was somewhat of a misnomer now. One can't organize a life one can't control. Events and the unexpected controlled her. Moving in with Mona had eased her loss of Shumway; his absence. Floundering through life had become her pattern.

And, now Rock was in her life, changing it, taking her in new directions. It was frustrating and exhilarating. But for her own needs, she should get on with a divorce. It was either that or wait another three years to see if Shumway returned. She could have told Rock about it tonight, had he felt like talking. Well, she didn't see any harm in waiting a while longer. But, the kissing had to stop. Probably.

Chapter Twenty-Four

During a work break, Rock sat on an office stool with his back bent, leaning on an elbow against the rolltop desk. A quick glance at the window indicated the weather was changing. Light drops of rain made the tree leaves quiver. He realized there was little time to appreciate the petal spill of Indian summer.

By October, Scott had to postpone trial until after Thanksgiving, due to conflicts in scheduling for a court date. This didn't much settle Rock's stomach. The doctor said he'd end up with ulcers if he didn't quit worrying. Meanwhile, through arrangements with his boss Atsidi, Rock sold most of his turquoise jewelry and replaced his gold watch for a silver one. He kept his gold ring. Every extra dollar saved from his paychecks went to Scott, but it wasn't enough to meet all his debts.

He spent the morning doing paperwork, while waiting for a jewelry shipment to arrive. Sit and wait. That's what he was doing. Working out with his weights, stored in the nearby cupboard to kill time, wasn't appealing. Besides, his muscles were sore from working on the totem pole. Yet, it was the one pet project that settled his nerves when apart from Unali.

Rock opened a desk drawer to remove a jar, uncapped it and rubbed cream into his battered hands. His mind shifted to his litigation and the leaders in the judicial system. He worried about the meaning of justice. Finally, he picked up the phone and called Scott. "I'm strapped for money." He lined up several pieces of turquoise jewelry that happened to be on the desk.

"Don't worry." Scott sounded spirited. "We can use your document expert's written report, as if he were present and testifying. His report is part of your pretrial motion anyway. I'll file the motion shortly. Trial is set for November 26th."

"Terrific." Elation flowed into exhilaration, as the brief conversation ended. Rock added a tiny cross to the calendar, marking November 26 as the first day of trial.

* * *

"Hope you don't mind eating dinner in the Ballard Bar." Rock sat at the mahogany counter with Unali.

"Why should I?" She motioned for his assistance in removing her jacket.

He hung the jacket over the back of her barstool. "Not formal like Shigley's. This place has good food and lots of atmosphere." He folded his hands on the counter and looked around. Western music came from corner speakers.

The tables were packed with couples. "This place is the last refuge in a mean world." They put their heads together to study the menu. "You seem calmer. Not the ding dong I met on the plane."

She laughed. "You don't miss much. Having my feet on the ground makes a difference. Besides, I'm more comfortable being around you now."

"Ah. A fearless woman when she has her feet on the ground." Rock hung his leather jacket over the back of his high-back stool. "And you think you're safe around me?" He chuckled and held up two fingers to the waitress. "Two beers and two corn-beef sandwiches." The waitress nodded.

"No, that's not what I meant." She flushed, while putting a napkin to her mouth. "Heavens, I didn't intend to insult your masculinity. I said comfortable. Don't embarrass me." She twisted her braid with a hand.

"Why? I'm growing used to a red face on you." He spoke almost in a whisper because there were others moving up to the counter, practically shoulder to shoulder. "And, judging by your eyes, you have something in mind."

"No. Not really." She appeared to be eyeing the meringue pie a waitress was cutting into across the narrow aisle.

"Get a load of that painting. Pretty nice mural, huh?" Rock was referring to a western scene with a cowboy on a bucking horse, taking up the length of the wall just above the waitress.

The picture extended from eye level to the ceiling. "I used to have my own Indian pony. He was about thirteen hands high. When I was a young buck, my pony and I were caught in a snowstorm overnight. From the event, I quickly learned that by taking care of him, he'd take care of me. Named him Gitchee, which means 'great'." Rock remembered Dad Jack warning him that Gitchee was unpredictably wild from mistreatment by former owners. But, Gitchee never mistreated he and Leucojum.

Unali raised her eyebrows. "Accounts for your bowlegs?"

Rock squinted his hard, indomitable eyes at her with a lopsided grin. "Ahhhh. You're looking?" He held her chin in his direction, like he was waiting for an answer.

"Well, er, ah." Unali laughed it off and tried to brush away his hands, unable to mask her apparent frustration. She returned her focus on the mural. "It's a beautiful painting."

"Some famous Seattle artist painted it."

She nodded. Her eyes studied it for a while. Then she changed the subject. "Oh, I remember a question I wanted to ask you. The initials. What does your document expert say about your uncle's initials on your new evidence, which you refer to as the Leucojum documents?" Unali swung her stool toward him with the tape recorder running.

"He concluded that the initials are genuine, fluent, consistent one with the other. This is a fundamental test of forensic handwriting analysis." Their orders were placed in front of them.

"Did he say anything about the size of your uncle's initials?"

"Nothing significant. Marvin said there weren't any egg-ternal samples." Rock shook his head, negatively. "I'm sorry."

"That's okay. I know you mean 'external'."

"Yeah, no samples of Uncle John's kicking around to compare." Rock drank a mouthful of beer, appreciating that she never made fun of him for his inability to enunciate many words beginning with the infernal 'ex'.

"Sounds as though you and Scott have everything under control." She bit into one of the small sandwich triangles.

He grinned and cocked his head. "Better damn well have." Acting with confidence offered no assurances. And, as the trial neared, his fantasies with Unali were transferring into nightmares over Perkins' scare tactics. He'd wake up in sweat and anger.

"Well. I must admit I've never before taken so many antacids. I didn't even have stomach trouble until these legal bastards came into my life. Here, take my pickle."

Unali complied. "I think you're hooked on antacids. How did you ever pick up the habit?"

Rock opened his sandwich to add a light sprinkling of pepper. "I think it was the power of suggestion from TV ads. The ads described my condition brought on by legal hassles." He wondered if antacids did him any good. In any event, he closed the sandwich and took a hefty bite.

"Well. Calm down Rock. Threats and warnings from attorneys mean nothing without proof and ethics." She sounded consoling, while sipping beer. "Everyone gets jitters before trial."

"How would you know?" As he talked around his food, he thought she gulped, when the waitress interrupted to ask if everything was all right with the food. "Yes. Fine." He raised his beer to emphasize praise.

"Er, so I've been told. Besides, it stands to reason. Haven't you ever been in a stage play? The actors are nervous before curtain time. Once things start, you'll calm down."

He shook his head doubtfully. "I don't know. Legal matters tend to put me on edge. I get uptight. Can't relax." They lingered over their beers. No one rushed them as they enjoyed their last evening before trial.

At the conclusion of the evening, Unali dropped him off in front of his apartment. Pitch darkness had set in like a blanket covering the earth. Lights from the apartment and street provided lighting. He walked around to her side of the car to visit a while. She wished him good luck. "Keep two thumbs up. And, remember justice is the impartial adjustment of conflicting claims."

"I hope you're right. The courtroom isn't my happy hunting ground." He looked down at his boots. He was standing in fallen maple leaves, which had curled, making a crunching noise. "I wish you could come along. You have a calming influence."

"I'll be with you in spirit."

"I'm going to miss you. Won't see you for a week, eating up my vacation time on legal matters. I thank the Great Spirit that my boss is behind me. And my senior friend, the old guy who had eye surgery, is behind me."

"So am I."

"Thanks."

"Rock, what do they call you in your tribe?"

"Visiting Warrior."

She chuckled a little, but her demeanor hinted displeasure in his answer. He bent down to kiss her good night.

She moved her head for a kiss on the cheek.

"Don't look so worried. We're all visitors on this earth. I'm on my earthwalk. Good night."

"Good night."

Rock slid his hands in his pockets, while watching her leave. Shunning his kiss was puzzling, but her kind words would linger.

Chapter Twenty-Five

While watering the ivy planter in the kitchen, Gena thought how difficult it was to make conversation with Rock. Oh, how many times it crossed her mind lately. That it wasn't easy faking travel assignments. To tell him about her problems was out of the question with his up-coming trial. He had enough on his mind. And, she found it challenging to avoid talking too technically about legal matters.

Admittedly, Gena missed the love of a man, but she tried to   not encourage love talk with Rock due to their unique situation. The only safe ground was to keep Rock talking about himself and his litigation, and offering him legal encouragement.

As she placed the watering can on the trestle table, she looked down into the questioning face of Mona, who sat snacking on chocolate-frosted brownies before bedtime. Mona was munching like she didn't have a care in the world. Mona swallowed and spoke first. "He'll be fine. The brains of justice are controlling things now."

"Oh, sis, that's what worries me." Gena joined Mona. "Just because justice is offered in good faith doesn't mean it's practiced in good faith. And, just because Rock is made of muscle, leather and turquoise, doesn't mean he's streetwise in the courtroom."

"Isn't he? There was a trial in '84."

"A two-day trial doesn't give anyone experience. His view of the world is limited to what he learned in Quamas. He's a beginner in this. Justice isn't what he thinks it is. Justice. A pretty nebulous term. There are ways to get around the laws."

"What do you think will happen?" Mona picked brownie crumbs off her pink robe and ate them.

"There are many fine attorneys and judges. But it's anyone's guess what will go on in a courtroom, especially in a small town where justice isn't as sophisticated as in Seattle and Tacoma. Rock is dealing with men like Marvin and Perkins who think men like Rock should take any bone they offer as a peace offering, be it silver napkin rings."

"That was a miserly offering." Mona slid the brownie pan and a pink napkin over toward Gena.

"And, Perkins is a big city defense attorney. I've seen defense attorneys manipulate evidence and witnesses with a bag of tricks. They demonize their opponents. I pray this doesn't happen to Rock." Gena halfheartedly knifed out a square onto the napkin.

"But, you said the courtroom is a search for truth." Mona licked her fingers after another gooey bite.

"Only the naive believe that. The courtroom is the most unlikely place in this country where there's a search for the truth." Gena chewed on the brownie with closed eyes. "Oh, this is deeeeelicious."

"But Gena, we live in a civilized society today. I mean, even judicial language is easier to understand than years ago."

"I know." There were times like these when Gena wished she were ignorant of goings-on in the courtroom. Swallowing, she concluded her worries didn't mean the worst for Rock. He had an attorney.

"Eat another one."

"No. I need an antacid tablet." Her stomach was upset. She moved to a cupboard. "We simply have to know things will come out right for Rock." She paused. "Do we have any antacid?"

"No antacid. Milk works just as well."

Gena fixed herself a glass of milk.

"Are you okay?"

"It's just that we don't fully understand where Rock's coming from. Sure, we've read most of his talking leaves. We have taped conversations. But, there's more to him that's hidden.

"What's hidden?" Mona's eyes lit up.

"Primarily, Rock has experienced success, independence and acceptance in the wider world. It's the vagaries, the whims of that world that could trip him. You see, he has a different philosophy. For the life of me, I can't pin it down, except that in spite of what I've just said, he's been taught to be subordinate, and I don't know how this will affect his behavior in the courtroom." Gena gulped her milk.

Rock's tribal name, Visiting Warrior, lingered. His explanation was logical in that his contacts with the Cherokees were visits. What if that was all he could ever be to her? A visiting warrior on some vision quest, seeking enlightenment like Shumway? If she professed her love for Rock she might get hurt again, like walking the high wire. She could fall either way.

"You love him, don't you?"

Gena walked over to the counter and set the empty glass down with her back to Mona. "I realize I'm involved in more than gathering information for your book."

Mona laughed. "Now you sound like an attorney, giving me an indirect answer."

Gena turned to face Mona. "More importantly, I detest anyone being taken advantage of. Rock has a good heart and head, but some attorneys know how to get around goodness. You can bet your last dollar, attorneys never go to trial unprepared." She shuddered at the thought.

"Besides Rock being a subordinate in society, he's a subordinate litigant who has to rely on the whims of his attorney Scott, whom I know nothing about. As far as being a subordinate, even hardened criminals, the tough and strong of any race are subordinate to the whipping post. If Scott flubs up, Rock's going to get hurt. Scott takes his money and runs. See what I'm getting at?"

"Yes. But, what about the judge?"

"Depends on who the judge is. He'll be influenced by his race, his upbringing, his conditioning, his education. That's why I prefer jury trials."

Mona licked her lips free of crumbs. "I'm not sure I follow you."

Gena returned to sit and face Mona. "If a judge doesn't know Rock's beliefs and thinking, how can he judge him?"

"I doubt any judge knows much about those who face him."

"Oh, yes. Mentally, a judge puts people in categories. Rock is one you can't categorize. Not even by a judge."

"Do you think Rock might panic?"

"No. As a rule, having been taught primitive ways of survival in the outdoors, Rock isn't the type to panic. However, primitives can act impulsively."

Mona laughed. "Primitives? You make him sound ape-ish."

Gena grinned and shook her head. "No. Not that primitive. Think modern. When modern primitives are lost in the woods, they stay put and get ahold of themselves. Get their bearing." She sighed, still trying to get her point across. "Rock fits in between."

"You're saying his impulsiveness won't work in the courtroom."

"Right. Could work against Rock. Remember in his '84 transcript, he walked out in the middle of a court session, highly insulting to the judge at that time."

"Well, surely Rock has learned his lesson."

"Maybe. But, Rock's also a dreamer. Dreamers build beliefs from misty ideas." Gena could tell by Mona's puzzled expression that she was mystified. "Look out the window; what do you see?"

Mona turned her eyes toward the window and the outdoors. "Night. Darkness."

"To Rock darkness is tangible; a blanket that covers the earth."

"That's impossible. Darkness is not tangible. I can't hold it in my hand."

"See. You judged him by your belief."

"Ooooh. Wow. That's interesting . . ."

"And, frightening if Rock gets the wrong judge." Gena's stomach was still upset. Yet there was nothing to go on other than an unsubstantiated hunch. Finally, she decided to push it aside. What could possibly go wrong in a civil trial in the small fishing village in Quamas, Washington?

*   *   *

"Is Sheryl testifying at trial?" Scott asked Rock over the phone late Saturday, before the scheduled trial on Monday. "Because I have a letter on my desk from Perkins. He will subpoena her."

"She's not happy about the idea, but she will testify." While standing near the kitchen counter, Rock held the phone in his left hand and used the right to towel dry his hair. He had stepped out of the shower minutes before and barely had time to don his bathrobe and moccasins. "Did you file my pretrial motion, Mr. Scott?"

"Eleven days ago."

"Well, there you are. That motion includes all her testimony from the '84 trial transcript. Her position hasn't changed. How many times do those muckers want her to repeat the same damn testimony?"

"Now calm down Rock. We're expecting her anyway."

"Calm down. Hell." He knew Perkins would try to discredit Sheryl.

If Scott was shocked by Rock's informal talk, he wasn't letting on. "Your motion also includes what I titled 'Trial Memorandum of Dorian Barnes Rock Carper'. You should have received all this in the mail. We'll use all prior records and address Nell and Houston's fraud during the '72 to '74 period of John's probate as directed by the appellate remand."

This news about Houston's fraud calmed Rock. "Good." Searching through a small pile of unopened mail on the counter, Rock found the information Scott was referring to. "Anything else I should know about?"

"No. That's it."

Rock could hear Scott tapping his teeth. "Perkins is behaving himself?" Waiting for Scott to answer, Rock slid a hand into his bathrobe pocket and felt a small bottle. He pulled it out. It was a prescription bottle, containing pills to calm his nerves. He clutched it tightly. He should take these pills to the trial with him. They certainly helped to calm him down after losing the first trial in this litigation. He quit taking them because his doctor told him they were habit forming and mind altering, but for short periods it would be okay as long as he didn't take more than half a pill at any one time.

Scott broke into his concentration. "As far as I know Perkins is behaving."

"See you Monday then. Rock hung up and ambled into the bedroom, where he tossed the bottle and robe on the dresser. He would pack these in his suitcase tomorrow. While turning off the light and settling into bed, Rock wanted to believe the long-awaited trial would erase seven years of legal delays.

Chapter Twenty-Six

They were sitting on the front bench to the left in Courtroom Two of the Clamton County Courthouse. Sheryl brought along coffee in styrofoam cups for herself and Rock. Her blue eyes shone from an oval face. Dimples surfaced on each cheek when she smiled. Returning the smile, he noticed her wedding rings glinted on the left hand. When she reached over to adjust the Windsor knot in his tie, he noticed her hairdo, pampered up in back. Curls on top. "What did you do to your hair?"

"Like?" She patted a hand gently to the back. "I 'ad it styled." She turned slightly. "A Gibson style."

This was for the best, he rationalized privately. Seeing her with her long auburn hair worn down only brought on the incessant memories of their early days. Of his amorous advances, gently grabbing her by the hair, bending her backward and caressing her until . . . He stopped himself. "Damn."

"What?"

"Nothing." Sheryl was predictably unpredictable, he reflected. Trying to keep her happy for long seemed impossible. Several years after they were married, they almost split up. To appease her, he deeded the Magnolia house into her name. Yet, it was he who kept the house in good condition, even added a new roof, two roofs before they separated for good.

To focus on their bad times, their arguments and mood swings made it easier to accept the breakup. But, now, in her presence, he wasn't seeing the same person, causing him to remember the good times. He scolded himself. Those good memories were best forgotten. "You look beautiful. I just never pictured you in anything other than hair hanging down."

"Unpicture yer image. I donnae need ta please ye anymore."

"Geezeee, what a witch." Not wishing to attack her remark, he smiled, while checking his watch. Thirty minutes past one o'clock. Time for trial. He gulped the last of his coffee. "Come on, finish yours so I can stash the cups out of sight." As Sheryl did so, a loud cough, identifiable as belonging to Marvin Benson, erupted from the back of the room.

That wasn't all Marvin was doing. He lumbered in with several helpers, who moved along the right-hand wall. They hauled in three-by-four-foot white poster boards and stacked them against the wall. The face of each board replicated each document of Rock's new evidence. "I wonder why they're displaying my documents?" Rock felt concern while talking softly to Sheryl.

"Ask yer new attorney."

Rock looked for Scott. "He's coming up the aisle." As soon as Scott approached, Rock introduced him to Sheryl. Scott set his briefcase on the counsel table directly in front of them, then moved to shake Sheryl's hand. He smiled broadly and nodded his baldhead.

"Good mornin', Mr. Scott. Would ye be havin' a nip o' Britain in ye with all yer freckles?"

Scott, unbuttoning his blazer, rolled his eyes and chuckled. "A nip, yes."

Rock anxiously directed Scott's attention to Marvin's display.

Scott stroked his smoothly-shaven chin. "Impressive. Expensive. Gives 'em strength. Nothing surprises me anymore." He opened his briefcase and spread papers and legal books across the counsel table. "We'll deal with it when we have to."

"Marvin has strength in numbers, too." Rock tapped Sheryl on the arm, a motion for her to glance at the gaggle of Benson relatives. "Uncle John would roll over in the grave, if he knew the Bensons were in the middle of this mess."

"Lookin' ultra vogue. Especially Marvin and Beatrice. Probably with money that should o' been yers. Well, 'tis best the dead donnae know where go their bequests and bequeaths."

Disgusted, Rock turned away. He knew they used John's money to feather their nest, buy a Mercedes and live high on the horizon. In order to remain calm, he took several deep breaths and exhaled slowly. Other activity in the area soon distracted him. A docket clerk in a short, tight skirt planted herself to the left of where the judge would sit. Her attractive legs were now hidden. And, a court reporter in a long skirt stationed herself behind a stenographic machine immediately below the judge's bench.

Rock watched Perkins drag an easel to the front. Marvin brought along one of his posters to prop on the easel. The two men stood back as if checking the correct placement of the display.

The poster was an enlargement of Uncle John's May cover letter. It was the letter written to Jasper Fulbright's father Cod, before leaving town on the trip that led to his death. Rock's dad's name, Jack, was in there. This letter was part of Rock's new evidence. He read silently:

May 9, 1972

Cod J. Fulbright, Attorney at Law
Box 275
Quamas, Washington

Dear Cod:

In response to your advice, attached, dated and initialed in ink, are true and correct copies, which are exact duplicates of the originals now in my safe deposit box at the bank here in Quamas.

As we previously discussed, most of the U.S. Savings Bonds, my stocks, several savings accounts and securities as well as the property that the Carper Cannery is situated on -- all relate directly to the attached Trust Agreement of April 25, 1942, between Jack and myself. This Trust Agreement has never been canceled or changed in any way; it is still honored and valid. I have always held the above-mentioned assets as separate and personal property and they do pass completely in their entirety by my Last will and Testament of August 18, 1967 and my second Codicil of May 8, 1972, to Dorian Barnes Carper as his Legacy and birthright.

Along the lines of my concern, a friend only just mentioned a service which is provided by Peoples National Bank, where important papers can be deposited for safe keeping. I will discuss this friend's suggestion with you as soon as Nell and I return from our Reno trip, in about two weeks.

Leucojum has several things that she would like you to take care of. I will make arrangements to bring her along when I next meet with you, until then you might include these papers along with hers.

In closing, I greatly appreciate your alertness and your advice. You are indeed my very good friend.

Fraternally,

John F. Carper

Trying to figure out this display as any advantage to Marvin was a puzzle. If anything, it was unfavorable. Rock would have to wait and see.

As Rock propped an elbow on the back of the bench, his mind roamed. If only his dad hadn't died before John, he wouldn't be here now. While scanning through the May letter again, he knew its reasonableness would be obvious when all facts were in.

The room grew quiet as Houston's redheaded partner, Fred Adams Jr. slipped into place alongside Perkins. The two whispered. Finally, Adams looked beyond Perkins' shoulder. He gave Rock an expressionless stare.

*　　*　　*

The bailiff walked in. "Please rise for the Honorable Judge Robert Dodson."

Rock rose, rubbing fingers over his lapel pin of the American flag. He thanked the Great Spirit that it wasn't Judge Randell. Scott was more honest than Anders about this. Nevertheless, Rock stared at Dodson, a husky, stern-faced man. The sixty-ish-looking man held an air, like a great rain cloud and he owned every drop.

The judge adjusted his black robe to sit, dipped his head of wavy brown hair to don dark-rimmed glasses, then peered out. "You may be seated. Good afternoon. Mr. Scott, Mr. Perkins, I presume you are ready to proceed in the matter of the Carper estates." He appeared to make a quick survey of his audience. Rock did too. There were basically three tribes: members of justice, the Bensons and their relatives and the Carpers.

The attorneys presented opening statements. In this civil case Rock believed the burden of producing evidence was primarily up to the opposition. He already produced his evidence, including his document expert's written report through his pretrial motion. Of course, Rock expected Scott to bring attention to his expert's report and his new evidence, the Leucojum documents.

After Scott finished his brief opening remarks, he squatted low near Sheryl and requested she fetch Rock's witness, attorney Jasper Fulbright. He gave her instructions to Fulbright's old brick building around the corner. "He's waiting in his office."

"Why me? I donnae remember what 'e looks like."

"He's in the only office on the top floor. Ask anyone."

While appearing not too pleased in Rock's estimation, Sheryl stood and adjusted her skirt. He watched her walk down the aisle, mumbling. He knew she didn't want to miss anything. He didn't like it either and wondered why Scott would send her. After all, it was Scott's idea she be present.

*　　*　　*

Jasper Fulbright took the witness stand and, given the opportunity, wasted no time recalling Rock bringing him a large sealed envelope in 1985 to update Leucojum's will.

Jasper: "My secretary, Mrs. Willard, opened the outer envelope finding Leucojum's will prepared by my Dad, Cod Fulbright. There was also a smaller sealed envelope in the bigger envelope. Mrs. Willard called me from my office. I opened this inner envelope."

This testimony greatly pleased Rock.

Scott summarized Jasper's discovery in the inner envelope as consisting of copies of John's originals: "A 1942 trust agreement between John and Jack Carper, John's 1967 will, two 1972 codicils and an agreement as to status of community property."

Then Scott waved the community property document for emphasis, explaining it as John and Nell's repudiation of their 1971 community property agreement, executed before John's fatal trip. Rock knew this was important to show that Nell had no business repudiating an agreement after John's death, when they had already done this before John died.

Scott: "Another point Your Honor. John initialed and dated each page of these documents before mailing them to Cod Fulbright. Attached to these documents is John's May cover letter." Scott pointed to the enlargement propped up on the easel. "It states, 'Dear Cod: In response to your advice, then Fraternally, John. At this point, I am simply showing the court the gentlemen had a conversation someplace and talked about the '67 will."

Rock chuckled quietly, listening to Scott take advantage of Marvin's poster.

Perkins stood: "Objection."

Judge Dodson loomed forward: "Sustained."

Scott shrugged his shoulders and returned to Jasper: "Explain the relationship between Cod Fulbright and John Carper."

There wasn't time for Rock to justify any logic for the objection and the judge's sustaining, because Jasper proceeded into a lengthy dissertation on the historical background of the Fulbright Carper relationship, highlighting the fine, fine achievements of his own family. Jasper carried on in such detail that Rock figured springtime would come and pass, and flowers would go to seed.

Perkins rose: "Hokay. This is speculation. Not relevant. I'm not even sure what question is on the table anymore."

Rock snickered at the way Perkins said the word 'okay'.

Scott looked at Perkins: "John Carper wouldn't have mailed important documents to somebody he didn't know." He switched his eyes to Jasper: "Explain your reaction to the trust agreement."

Jasper: "The trust agreement was structurally, technically sound. I told Rock to tell his lawyer. I knew the Carper Cannery was a partnership between John and Jack from their parents."

Perkins: "Speculation. Jasper lacks knowledge."

Rock gritted his teeth at Perkins' remark.

Jasper sat up straighter: "I'm not speaking to the knowledge of a document, but only to the Carper partnership."

Scott: "I agree Your Honor."

Judge Dodson clasped his hands together: "Sustained."

Rock's head moved from one to the other in trying to decide why the judge would sustain Jasper's personal knowledge of the partnership. A trial was supposed to be built around personal knowledge, rather than hearsay. He wondered if the judge was speaking with a vacant mind.

Jasper: "Rock was genuinely surprised."

Scott walked over to the docket clerk to enter the Leucojum documents as Rock's exhibit, then returned to his chair. Sheryl squeezed Rock's arm. He smiled at her.

Perkins adjusted his jacket and moved forward to begin cross-examination: "Mr. Fulbright, you talked about a social relationship with the Carpers?"

Jasper: "Yes, what you and I talked about before court this morning."

An uneasy feeling came over Rock that Jasper and Perkins fraternized before court. It wasn't right. Or, if it was, it shouldn't be. He observed Perkins enter exhibits into evidence. They were xeroxed copies of the Leucojum documents. The docket clerk accepted the copies as Marvin's exhibits. This confused Rock. It seemed logical that his exhibit was sufficient. Entering copies was an unnecessary duplication. How could both parties lay claim to the same documents?

The docket clerk stamped the xeroxed copies and returned them to Perkins, who walked back to Jasper: "Now, Mr. Fulbright, this is the large envelope Rock gave you in 1985 when he walked into your office. Was this envelope sealed?"

Jasper, looking at a xeroxed copy of an envelope, confirmed that it was. Perkins went through the same procedure with the xeroxed copies of all the other documents in the bigger mailing envelope. Jasper identified each as coming from his law firm.

Perkins: "And this is a copy of a date stamp used on the smaller envelope and on John's May cover letter. The stamp shows Cod received these May 14, 1972. Do you recognize that as a date stamp either you or your father used in 1972?"

Jasper: "It might have been my father's. I didn't use a date stamp. We had a practice which was pretty much separate."

Perkins appeared hyper pacing the carpet, while firing one question after another. He wanted to know if Cod had done any legal work in probating John's estate and Jasper didn't think so. Jasper's answer was okay, but the question made Rock's stomach cringe. It was a dumb question; a flagrant effort to mislead the judge. Everyone here knew it was Ralph Houston who did the legal work for Nell regarding John's probate, not Cod.

Perkins: "Do you think your father would have phoned Nell or her attorney about these documents if he date stamped them the very day John Carper died in Nevada?"

Jasper: "I have no idea what dad was doing that day."

Good for Jasper, thought Rock. This was speculation. He had learned that much about justice. Yet, he knew the court's attention should be drawn to why neither Cod nor Jasper would have reason to know who Nell's attorney was at John's death.

Concerned, Rock leaned toward Scott: "Records show Nell didn't return from Nevada for two months after John's death. Houston filed no notice with the court that he was the attorney of record for nine months. Please bring that to the court's attention."

Scott nodded his round head, talking over his shoulder in response to Rock's request: "I'll clarify that later in the week when Houston takes the stand."

This satisfied Rock: "When's he going to be here?"

Scott: "Oh. Not sure yet."

The judge stifled a yawn and recessed court until nine a. m. on Tuesday. Rock invited Sheryl to join him for pie in town.

*   *   *

"I'm ticked off. Those attorneys are sleepin' tagether, fraternizin' outside of court. Jasper admitted it on the stand."

"Appears so, but Jasper's never given me cause to mistrust him." Rock forked into a wedge of lemon pie, while sitting in a small café a block from the courthouse. The entrance wall was mostly window, framed in boughs of fir, red ribbon and Christmas baubles, with a red neon sign that read *Clare's Kitchen* from the outside. "Scott looked tired and puffy-eyed. Probably up half the night. Perkins doesn't look perky either."

"I donnae think those attorneys should be hobnobbin' ootside o' yer presence."

"They don't hide it. So it must be legal. Well, what else do you think?"

Sheryl, who sat in a booth across from him, turned her attention from watching a young male employee stacking cups, saucers and water glasses in front of the cash register. "Ummm, I'm thinkin' things'll go okay. Too soon ta tell, I say."

"You're right. But entering copies of my documents seems odd. And I hope the judge doesn't conclude that Cod didn't do any legal work for John, simply because he didn't probate John's estate. Hell. None of us know all the legal work Cod did for John, because it never came up until today." The thought that this trial was different crossed his mind. It was like starting out in new territory. Like he didn't know where he was headed. "This trial is starting out different from the '84 trial."

"Includin' sendin' me oot o' the courtroom in front o' everybody ta fetch Jasper. Twas embarrassin'." She ate a forkful of pie and savored it a moment before swallowing. "Donnae Scott 'ave better sense than ta send a lady in 'eels on a 'illy errand up and doon flights o' stairs? I dinnae want ta miss the action. A simple phone call would o' been better, but nae."

"I agree. I don't know why Scott picked on you."

"They're treatin' me as the least important person in the room, that's why."

Rock wiped his mouth with a napkin. "No. There's probably a simple reason. Jasper is my witness. One of us had to go. Scott picked you. Although Scott should have had Jasper there to begin with. Keep in mind this is a small town."

"Ay, a small town, where rumors travel like wildfire. What if the locals find oot we're separated, now that I'm livin' in Quamas?"

"There aren't any friends left here who care. But, just don't volunteer information. Jasper, Scott and your folks are the only ones in Quamas who know. They aren't going to tell anyone. Besides, we aren't divorced, so it's really nobody's business."

As Sheryl simmered down, he changed the subject. "Sheryl, I want you to know I'm seeing someone else."

"What ye meanin'?" Sheryl's eyes widened.

"A lady I met coming home from Dallas. We're dating. Her name is Mona, a travel writer. She's writing a book on my case."

"What fer? There's nothin' particularly interestin' a'boot yer case. Death, wills, probate, crooked attorneys." She emphasized each word, talking with her fork.

"There is when injustices are committed." He swilled coffee to wash down a mouthful of pie. "Interesting. Mona says that justice is the impartial adjustment of conflicting claims."

"Let's 'ope yer bonnie is right. Maybe this new judge'll give ye justice, which is more than the last one gave ye. I heard a rumor that there are two defense attorneys in a case like this. One wears a black robe."

Rock didn't like hearing this rumor. "You can't go by rumors." They ate in silence for a while. "What do you think of Joseph Scott?"

"Love the freckles on him better than on me. God dinnae know when ta quit sprinklin' freckles on the man." She giggled, then became serious. "Wimpy in the 'and shake department, 'e is. Real flabby grip. No enough ta hang onta a live trout. Like his lawyerin', maybe?"

"Sheryl, you can't go by a handshake. Scott just didn't want to hurt your hand, that's all."

"We'll see."

After finishing their pies, Sheryl departed for her house. Rock headed in the opposite direction to stay at the Leucojum house. He felt things went okay today. Otherwise, Scott would have said something.

If only he could calm down and know things would be better than what past experience dictated. It was the unexpected he didn't like. What would tomorrow bring?

Chapter Twenty-Seven

Tuesday morning after Sheryl treated Rock to morning coffee, they went to court. They took their seats in the front row. After Dodson's lackluster trip to the bench, Scott hiked his slacks and squatted on bent knees to approach Sheryl in a whisper. "Would you fetch Mrs. Willard, Jasper's secretary? She's in the same brick building where you went yesterday."

Rock noted Sheryl had one knee crossed over the other. The upper leg bounced lightly, rhythmically. Not exactly a favorable movement. She stared down at her heels, then at Scott. Air slowly escaped through her teeth. Without saying a word, she raised her curvaceous figure and left the room.

Chuckling to himself, Rock pictured her going through the same up-and-down maze as yesterday, perhaps hearing the skirl of pipes, ranting on to herself that this is why they threatened to subpoena her. To use her as an errand girl.

Waiting for Mrs. Willard gave Rock a chance to ask Scott why the attorneys were using xeroxed copies of his new evidence. Scott explained it as a method to lessen unnecessary handling of the Leucojum documents since they were so old and paper-thin. This made sense, much to Rock's delight.

*   *   *

The exaggerated shoulders of Mrs. Willard's jacket reminded Rock of padding on a hockey player. An oddity in fashion. She looked nice, however. Motherly. On direct examination, Scott put her through the same routine as Jasper Fulbright yesterday. This time he handed her Rock's exhibit, the Leucojum documents, to identify, causing Rock to ponder what happened to Scott's prior explanation of the unnecessary handling of old, thin documents.

Mrs. Willard sounded slightly out of breath from rushing to court. She soon identified the large mailing envelope as one used by their law firm years ago for bulk mailing. And, she admitted to have typed the firm's address in the upper corner. Then Scott switched from Rock's exhibits, the Leucojum documents, to Marvin's xeroxed copies of the Leucojum documents: "I'm handing you a copy of a letter. Do you recognize the letter to Leucojum?"

Willard: "Yes. I sent Leucojum the will we had at Leucojum's request, after Cod Fulbright passed on."

Switching exhibits was soon forgotten as Rock was pleased with her testimony. That is until Perkins' cross-examination of her provided a problem to sweat over. Mrs. Willard didn't recognize the date stamp as used by Jasper's firm. Rock didn't expect her to. Riled, he prodded Scott for attention. "Sssst."

Scott turned and leaned an ear in Rock's direction.

"She can't speak about the date stamp. Jasper's law firm didn't hire her until two years after John's death. Ask her. And look in her deposition."

"Oh, the judge isn't going to let me fish the Puget Sound. He'll read the prior record of depositions and testimonies as outlined in your pretrial motion."

Witnessing a different side to Scott set Rock back on the bench. Soon, he popped an antacid pill into his mouth, crunching in exasperation. Why wouldn't Scott appreciate his interference? He leaned forward and studied the carpeting, a putrid green.

Sheryl nudged him to speak in sign. "The prior record doesnae contain her latest deposition. Did Scott file the new depositions?"

Rock returned in sign. "No. He said they weren't needed."

"I beg ta differ. Case in point just happened."

Scott moved forward as Perkins took his seat: "Would you describe the Leucojum documents?"

Willard: "There was a thin onionskin paper wrapped around the large outer mailing envelope. Inside the inner envelope were many small, old-fashioned brass staples securing John Carper's documents to his cover letter."

Rock's stunned reaction to Scott's outburst of fishing the Puget was replaced with relief when Mrs. Willard described the documents as appearing old.

Perkins interrupted: "By the way, Your Honor." He jabbed a pen in the air. "The paperclip, onionskin paper wrap and brass staples have disappeared. We'd appreciate the court's acknowledgment that we recognize this carelessness."

Judge Dodson: "So acknowledged." He removed his black-rimmed glasses: "Now, we'll take a fifteen-minute recess.

Rock released five fingers downward from a balled fist, sign language known to he and Sheryl for 'shit'. Animosity griped him. Finally, he clenched his hands into fists and jetted off the bench to catch Scott, who was already heading toward the exit.

*   *   *

Rock paced the hallway; his stomach in knots, when he suddenly spotted Scott exiting a court office. Rock rushed him. "What happened to the missing evidence?"

"Oh, nothing serious. I think the onion paper covering and clip disappeared in Jasper's office sometime between 1985 and 1990." He headed for the men's room.

Rock followed. "And the staples?" By this time, they stood over wall-mounted urinals.

"The staples were recently removed, thrown away by someone in the clerk's office, after photocopying the documents for microfilming purposes."

"They had no right to destroy evidence before this case is closed. Geez, that onionskin paper was the original of mom's old will, which would tell why she didn't open the envelope she received from Jasper. She thought only her old will was inside."

"Don't worry. You've got enough other things going. You just don't understand our way of doing things in Clamton County. I'll handle this case." Scott zipped his pants and walked out.

Rock followed suit. "Yeah? Well, I hope you'll enter my document specialist's report. Because you can quote him as finding those staples and a large paperclip that made a rust mark and a very definite impression, both on the outside of the envelope and on the other documents in the envelope. He said this

125

is something that would have taken time to occur. That supports Mrs. Willard's testimony."

"Yeah, yeah. I'LL TAKE CARE OF IT."

"Thank you." Rock frowned, not appreciating Scott's cold treatment. Since the opposition Marvin and Perkins had entered the area, Rock and Scott moved away. Scott acted anxious to leave. Rock lagged behind and told himself to ease up. But, it seemed logical for an attorney to let a client offer advice when things aren't right. What a predicament; hiring another touchy attorney.

*   *   *

When called upon, Rock cut a proud path, walking proudly forward past the American flag. He held up his right hand before a silent audience. Only the bailiff's words could be heard: "Do you swear to tell the truth, the whole truth and nothing but the truth?"

"I do." Rock's voice came out loud and clear. The oath reminded him of the Scouting Oath, in keeping with Indian teaching, he recited once a week for many years. *"On my honor I will do my best to do my duty to God and my country. And to obey the Scout law, to help other people at all times, to keep myself physically strong, mentally awake and morally straight."* This coincided with what his folks taught him about treating others the way he wanted to be treated. Without honesty, there was no trust.

Clinging to these thoughts, Rock then walked to the witness box and edged into the chair. Pride masked the tension inside him. For the moment, he focused only on Scott.

Presenting an offer of proof by summarizing a few facts from Rock's '84 trial testimony, Scott reiterated that in the Fall of 1967 while Rock was a student at the University of Washington, his uncle had given him his new will to look over. He had asked Rock to return it during his next trip home. The will appeared to be an original, signed in ink, on legal-size paper. Rock had stored it in the glove compartment of his car for about ten days.

Rock relived the occasion, reminiscing that on a Saturday Uncle John had stopped by the fraternity after a Husky football game. Three of Rock's fraternity brothers were present during John's visit and heard everything.

Scott's voice broke into Rock's daydreaming: "Did you show the 1967 will to anyone?"

Rock: "Yes, to three fraternity brothers and to my fiancée Sheryl, now my wife. I discussed it with them."

Rock's mind flashed back to that day. Sheryl sat in his car and followed his instructions to open the glove compartment to remove the envelope and read the contents. They read it together. He could visualize it now. like it was almost real:

LAST WILL AND TESTAMENT OF JOHN F. CARPER

I, JOHN F. CARPER, of Quamas, Clamton County, State of Washington, of the age of seventy-three years, being of sound and disposing mind and memory and not acting under any duress, menace, fraud, or undue influence of any person, do make, publish and declare this my last will and testament:

FIRST: It is my will and I hereby direct that my co-executors hereinafter named, shall, as soon as convenient and when funds are available for the purpose, pay my funeral expenses and expenses of last illness.

SECOND: I hereby give and bequeath one-half of all joint community property, of whatsoever kind and character to my beloved wife, Nell D. Carper, and do hereby give, devise and bequeath my one-half of said community property, of whatsoever kind and character to my only kin and blood nephew, Dorian Barnes Carper.

THIRD: I hereby give, devise and bequeath the remainder of my property and estate of whatsoever kind and character and wherever situated, real, personal and separate unto my nephew, Dorian Barnes Carper.

FOURTH: I hereby grant that my beloved wife, Nell D. Carper, shall remain living in the 'Carper mansion', for as long as she so desires. The 'Carper mansion' in its entirety, which I hold as separate property, will eventually and exclusively pass to my nephew, Dorian Barnes Carper, to be his separate property.

FIFTH: I preference that my nephew, Dorian Barnes Carper, assist my wife, Nell D. Carper, if she so requests, in the management of her affairs, as well as provide for her additional support, that she may continue her way of life.

SIXTH: I preference that my nephew, Dorian Barnes Carper, shall not act inadvertently and allow my wife, Nell D. Carper, to be put in a retirement home.

SEVENTH: I hereby nominate both my wife, Nell D. Carper, and my nephew, Dorian Barnes Carper, as co-executors of this last will and testament.

EIGHTH: It is my will that my said estate be handled, managed and settled by my co-executors without the intervention of any court whatsoever other than to make proof of this will, to file an inventory and to do such other acts and things as may be required by law.

NINTH: I have considered all persons who may be considered the object of my bounty, including without limitations, every person whom may be related to me by blood or marriage. I make no bequest, devise or provision for any such persons herein EXCEPT those specifically named and provided for herein and herebefore. Any person or persons not mentioned in this will, who make a claim of inheritance through omission of their name, then a provision is made for that such person, by a bequest of one-dollar.

TENTH: I hereby revoke all former wills by me made.

In testimony and witness whereof, I have hereunto set my hand and seal the ___18___ day of ___August___, 1967, A. D.

John F. Carper
John F. Carper

The foregoing instrument, consisting of this and one other typewritten page, was, on the ___18___ day of ___August___, 1967, signed, sealed, published and declared by the said John F. Carper as and for his last will and testament in the presence of us, who, at his request and in his presence and in the presence of each other, have subscribed our names as witnesses thereto.

Russell Fulton	_Henry Stoner_
Russell Fulton	Henry Stoner
Seattle, Wash	Quamas, Wash.

At the time, Sheryl told Rock she had never before read a will and hadn't seen legal-size paper until then. She was full of questions. Rock hoped that Scott would ask her about this on the witness stand.

Finally, Rock's reverie was interrupted to identify the will contents: "Nell was to receive her half of the community property. I was to receive John's half of the community and all his separate property. Nell was to have use of the Carper mansion as long as she lived and I was to see that she was taken care of, never placed in a retirement home." The air in the room was dry. Rock poured a cup of water and sipped between questions.

Scott: "Do you recall visiting Ralph Houston about John's '67 will?"

Rock: "I recall making the visit around 1973 while probate was still open. Houston said Nell was using a community property agreement which replaced any will." Rock remembered that any witnesses, such as Sheryl and his fraternity brothers to John's later will, would have done him no good for this reason.

Scott: "Did you ask Ralph Houston to keep you advised as to anything that developed in the probate?"

Rock: "I asked to be notified if they were going to use a will. He said there was no need because Nell had a community agreement. I asked him to keep me informed. He said he would. He was my attorney on other matters."

Scott: "Did you ever hear from Houston again?"

Rock: "No. I engaged Houston to do legal work in the '70's and was handed over to his partner, Fred Adams Jr." Rock looked down at redheaded Adams Jr. sitting in a three-piece suit beside Perkins. Adams Jr. gave him a look as cold as brushed silver.

Perkins rose: "Objection, no relevance."

Judge Dodson: "What's the relevance, Mr. Scott?"

Scott: "Your Honor, we have a time issue, laches, that's been bandied about. Rock didn't take formal legal steps at an earlier date because of his conversation and relationship with Ralph Houston. So, any dealings he had might have allowed him to think he would hear from Houston if there were any changes in the handling of John's estate. That's relevant."

Judge Dodson: "Sustained."

Rock rubbed his forehead, wondering if the judge sustained his testimony or Scott's summation or both.

Scott continued, while leaning on the lectern: "When did you learn that John's estate was probated with the 1952 will?"

Rock: "One of my attorneys discovered it in the 1980's."

Scott wanted to know what arrangements Rock had made in trying to find the original 1967 will. To this, Rock said he had advertised in the state bar magazine and contacted attorneys, or relatives of deceased attorneys, whose names were on John's and Jack's business papers involving the Carper Cannery.

Scott: "Isn't it true, you discovered two copies of John's will and an April 1972 codicil tucked in an envelope in an old journal that Nell had given you in 1980?"

Rock: "You bet." He described one of John's wills as a two-page legal size typewriter-ribbon copy signed by John and his witnesses. The other was four pages, standard size and thermofaxed. He had absolutely no idea the envelope containing these wills was in the journal at that time because Nell made no mention of it.

Recalling the occasion in 1980, he and Sheryl visited   Nell in the morning when she would be more focused. Nell had asked him to go to the basement office to find three boxes of memorabilia on Dad Jack's old rolltop desk. He did. They were old logbooks from the *Lyda*, the boat Rock had worked on years ago. And, there were old magazines. He wasn't interested in these, but took them to please Nell. Later, they visited Leucojum and Sheryl's folks.

By the time they arrived home in Seattle, both were too tired to care what the boxes contained. Rock put them in his attic and forgot about them. His mind, along with most Washingtonians, were more focused on the eruption of Mount St. Helens.

Scott held up the exhibits: "I can see the marks in the journal where the envelope was located. I see the lines and marks on the envelope that match up. I see mold marks. So these were in your attic for four years?"

Rock: "Yes." He explained that he didn't look through the boxes until a friend at Nell's funeral suggested he go through everything Nell ever gave him to find the will. He knew this information was verifiable through prior depositions of record taken of him, Sheryl and Nell's friend, now deceased.

Scott: "Would you identify the signatures on the will and the April codicil as John's?"

Rock: "Yes, the signatures are his. He had an old-style of writing, ornate. Not many people could write as well as he could."

Scott walked over to the docket clerk and handed her the journal: "Your Honor, I wish to make this an exhibit but, I'm not going to ask Rock questions. Mr. Perkins and I went over this last night. We've decided he can ask the questions and I can proceed from there."

Judge Dodson: "Okay with me." He called for a twenty-minute recess.

Again, Scott disappeared before Rock could reach him and ask why he was skipping direct examination of his discovery in the journal. This put his nerves on edge.

Chapter Twenty-Eight

Following recess, Rock returned to the witness chair. He experienced further astonishment watching Perkins pace with one hand in the other behind his back. The little man had such an irritating, arrogant air about him. He really was an ass. But then, Judge Dodson, appearing refreshed, was coming across no better. He clapped his large hairy hands and looked at Perkins: "Let's cut the head off this thing."

That offbeat remark didn't offer any assurance in Rock's anticipation for fair justice. He swallowed with difficulty. Geeze, they were probably meaning his head.

The arresting scrawny figure of Perkins strode forward with a confident cock-walk: "Hokay." Perkins kicked a foot forward. "Mr. Rock Carper." Perkins kicked the other foot forward. "Explain the escape hatch you designed for an airplane in the event of fire or a crash."

Rock: "There's nothing to it. I designed an escape hatch." Rock saw nothing wrong with this.

Perkins: "Like D. B. Cooper who ditched from a plane?" Perkins emphasized 'Cooper' and 'ditched'.

This jarring question sent vibrations up Rock's spine as well as in his stomach. In fact, his entire body felt like a weed stalk being batted back and forth in a storm. He suddenly recalled reading about D. B. Cooper parachuting out of a plane with large sums of stolen money. Cooper, who was never caught, was nevertheless known in the Pacific Northwest as a notorious skyjacker. Rock was dumbfounded. The question affronted his sense of decency.

How to respond was a bigger question. He didn't know attorneys could legally use such means in a courtroom. No other attorney had destroyed his credibility like this. Perkins was working him over like a wood carver, chiseling his life away.

Everyone looked at him, like wondering why he was stalling on an answer. Rock glanced at Scott, waiting for him to object. Scott remained sitting on his butt, bent over his legal pad like a drooping potted fern, while taking notes. This outrageous remark required notes? In an attempt to rein in his feelings, Rock returned his attention to Perkins: "Well." He paused, fidgeting nervously until his rising temper subsided. "I was a commercial pilot on a corporate jet in the '80's. I flew VIPs around the state, sometimes over water. After that, I designed an escape hatch to use in emergency landings while over the seas."

All eyes were fixed on him. Judge Dodson turned away to slip a lozenge in his mouth. Sheryl's eyes were beady, like fireballs. Marvin and Beatrice and their relatives were all smiles, along with Fred Adams Jr., perhaps knowing they hired the right man to achieve their evil purposes. Stone-faced, Rock glared at redheaded Adams, who quickly busied himself straightening papers; his Adam's apple bobbed nervously.

Perkins: "Now, I am going to take you through the boxes in which you found the journal. I am handing you what has been marked as your uncle's journal, which Nell gave you in 1980 and which you stuffed in your attic for four years before taking a peek at its contents."

Rock hated the way Perkins spoke, making it sound unbelievable, over emphasizing the word "stuffed".

Perkins: "Would you find the spot in the journal where you found the envelope containing copies of John's 1967 will?"

Rock complied, ruffled by Perkins' derogatory tone. Two words were foremost on his mind: focus and concentrate. He tried to keep cool, but he was sweaty, especially his palms.

Perkins: "Now Mr. Carper that envelope is detectable at both ends, isn't it?" Perkins inserted the envelope inside the journal.

Rock: "As you are showing it, yes." He hadn't looked at the journal and contents in years, since these remained stored in the court's files as evidence from the 1984 trial. Maybe Scott hadn't looked at them either. Maybe this was why Scott didn't question him. Maybe.

Perkins turned toward the judge: "No more questions."

Dodson nodded, drowsily and recessed for lunch.

Rock made a beeline for Scott, wanting to know why he skipped direct exam of the journal exhibit and the meaning of the D. B. Cooper incident.

*   *   *

"Does Perkins have any idea how offensive that Cooper accusation was? Is that bullshit legal?" His barometer up, Rock didn't have to elaborate what angered him to Scott, who joined he and Sheryl in front of the courthouse.

"Afraid so. I don't operate that way. Some attorneys do. Attorneys are privileged in judicial proceedings to say what they want in their efforts to secure justice for their clients."

"Secure justice? Hell." Unconvinced, Rock, combing his fingers through his hair, continued. "You could have objected. I was left hanging. Didn't you notice? And why did you skip direct questioning of my journal discovery?"

"To save time. Look, I know the judge." Scott put a firm hand on Rock's arm. "I live next door to Judge Dodson. He isn't going to pay any attention to the D. B. Cooper incident."

This explanation was some solace. Rock paced around on the courthouse landing, trying to calm down. He had no choice. But, it was difficult knowing Perkins wasn't through with him. "Just don't let Perkins make any more of a fool of me than he already has."

Scott nodded in compliance with Rock's request, then disappeared into the courthouse.

Rock and Sheryl went in another direction in search for a restaurant. Although Rock didn't feel much like eating.

*   *   *

In questioning Rock after lunch, Perkins zeroed in on the inquiries Rock made around town in trying to locate the original of John's will.

Rock said he went to state offices in Olympia and got certified copies of documents on the Carper Cannery for names of John's friends or business associates. He hoped for leads.

Perkins: "Where else have you seen your uncle's signature?"

Rock: "On fish ticket orders and papers he signed involving the cannery. I worked for him a couple of summers. He signed my checks." Rock's throat constricted. He had no clue where Perkins' line of questioning was taking him other than in the bushes.

Perkins: "On or about December 11, 1985 you, or your mother, discovered in her lockbox an envelope containing her will and an envelope containing what we call the Leucojum documents. Are you contending these prove that John left a 1967 will and put it in his safety deposit box before he left for Reno?"

Rock: "Yes." He remembered Leucojum stored her lockbox in a closet in a seldom-used room at the back of the house.

Perkins: "And you contend that since those documents weren't found in John and Nell's safe deposit box, that Nell, or somebody working on her behalf must have destroyed them?"

Rock: "I contend that the originals of the Leucojum documents must have been destroyed by Nell, you bet."

Perkins: "Now, do I understand correctly, that when these Leucojum documents were discovered, it was your mother who asked you to make a copy?"

Rock: "Wrong." He leaned forward, intently.

Perkins cut him off: "Let's jump ahead then."

Rock: "No. Let's finish that one." He raised his voice. That's when it dawned on him. Perkins was trying to rile him. Rock could get quite upset especially when someone was trying to confuse him or make him look foolish. But, at this trial in front of Judge Dodson, no asshole attorney was going to accomplish this. Perkins was glaring at him with a savage look, waiting. If anything, Rock was looking at the savage in the room -- Perkins.

Rock: "I went to Jasper's office to ask him to review mom's will. They said they didn't have it, that they mailed it to her a while back. Several days later I returned to mom's house and told her they didn't have it. And, then she searched in her lockbox and found it."

Perkins: "And then you took that envelope down to Jasper's office?"

Rock: "That's right."

Perkins: "No further questions." He took his seat.

Judge Dodson massaged his forehead, then motioned to Scott to proceed.

Rock calmed down, having been given the opportunity to explain. He waited for Scott to move in behind the lectern. Rock decided it was Scott's favorite post, as if any form of exercise was beyond his interest, other than shifting weight from side to side.

Scott: "With regard to the boxes in your attic, when you first received them from your aunt in 1980 and took them home, did it ever occur to you that those boxes of memorabilia might contain any valuable legal documents, or anything pertaining to your uncle's estate?"

Rock: "Absolutely not." He had no reason to believe otherwise, especially since Nell's mind was unpredictable.

Scott nodded, like giving him a thumb's up, then looked at the judge. "That concludes my questioning of this witness, Your Honor."

Judge Dodson: "Very well. Court is dismissed. Mr. Carper, you may leave."

Rock left the stand and walked proudly. He told the truth to the best of his ability. Based on what knowledge he possessed, he knew that any of his testimony favorable to him would be discounted, since he had the most to gain. Any disfavorable testimony, however, would be used against him.

At least now he better understood what Sheryl meant about attorneys abusing witnesses. Perkins abused him badly. In his fears, he wondered if Perkins' abuses would have a more powerful impression on Judge Dodson than Rock's answers.

*   *   *

While exiting the courthouse, Scott told Sheryl she would testify in the morning before waving good-bye.

"At $1,000 a day fer trial, I hope frecklepuss knows what he's doin'." She shivered in the wintry breeze.

"Here, wrap this around your ears." Rock pulled a scarf from his coat pocket. "Let's walk and talk." They worked their way down Main Street and wove in and out of pedestrian traffic. Odors and sights of evergreen decorations, candy canes, roasting peanuts, cinnamon rolls and festive music filled the air. Storefronts were decorated to instill memories. "A season to be jolly." Rock laughed at the irony of the situation before him. His ears were ringing and it wasn't Christmas bells. The trial had his emotions going up and down like a buoy on rough seas. Yet, his desire was to give Scott the benefit of any doubts.

"I'm thinkin' these attorneys are playin' games."

"Oh, I wouldn't go so far as to say that. Perkins, sure, but Scott cooled it." He slowed his walk so Sheryl could keep pace. It felt good to breathe fresh air and stretch the leg muscles. Rock needed to give his soul a feeling of freedom. The outdoors was strengthening and healing. And, for the moment, he wanted to forget the trial, Scott and the opposition.

"Well, what else would ye call it? Ye've been run doon with Perkins plantin' doubts and draggin' yer name in the mud. He's a heartless wonder."

"Sheryl, I do believe you can read my mind." Rock chuckled.

"Referrin' to ye as a designer of an escape hatch fer crooked means was horrid. I maintain the purpose fer cross-examination is ta bring oot the full story and determine the truth, not muck it up. Perkins is doon-right mean with no scruples. Taday, 'e showed a'boot as much compassion fer mankind as a boa constrictor ta a defenseless rabbit. Is this yer impartial justice?"

Rock knew it wasn't. However, there was no point in belaboring today's events. "Settle down. Let's hope things go better tomorrow." Trying to reason out the actions of others was beyond him. Besides, he was feeling weak and hungry. "Hey. Smell that aroma. Clams, potatoes, onions and bacon." The Chowder Grove was across the street. "How hungry are you?"

"I'm no hungry now. My tummy is in one big knot. I 'ave ta testify tamorrow. What will that witness-destroyer Perkins do ta me?"

"Easy woman." Rock took hold of her arm. "Come on, I'll treat you to dinner." While guiding her across the street, he believed things smelled fishy. It wasn't the Chowder Grove.

Chapter Twenty-Nine

Wednesday. Rock sat in the empty courtroom and admired the turquoise designs on his wristwatch. He wondered what this day would bring. The room was a little chilly. Before long, his witnesses would testify. At the '84 trial that took a full day. Sheryl and his fraternity brothers' testimonies were essential to verify the contents of John's will.

Sheryl came down the aisle and sat alongside him. She sighed. No talk. No smile. It wasn't like her to be so quiet. Then she shot up. "Tally-ho."

He grabbed the hem of her coat and held firm. "Whoa. You just got here."

"I've changed my mind, dearie." She tried to pull away.

"Today is your big moment." He wouldn't let go.

"Fer the electric chair, ye're meanin'."

"You'll wow 'em. Come on. You look great." He produced a broad smile, suddenly realizing that down deep, he still felt love for her. A love he couldn't shake loose, define or understand. While stirring uncomfortably, he tried to push aside this feeling. Too many ill feelings resulted to change things now.

"I donnae feel great." Sheryl frowned and sat down. "There's no new info fer me ta add. Why cannae they use my prior testimony?" Her eyebrows creased upward.

Rock held her hand in his; not fully trusting her to stay put. "Scott and Perkins want you here. I want you here. After today, you don't have to come." He talked about other things.

* * *

Before long, Scott stood in front of the lectern to interrogate Sheryl about the will contents: "Did you read John's will in Rock's car in 1967, the same year John made out his will?"

Sheryl: "Ay. Both pages sittin in Rock's car in front o' his fraternity. I dinnae know some o' the legal terminology. I remember askin' Rock what co-executor meant 'cause that was one o' his responsibilities. I dinnae know Rock's real name was Dorian Barnes Carper 'til I read that will."

Rock saw a lady with strong convictions, equal to her temper. Her memory was sharp too. Their marriage seemed doomed many years ago because of her insatiable desire to own everything, her growing disinterest in satisfying his innermost needs and her hatred for this litigation. Yet, she always loved the Carper mansion and Nell had built her expectations to live there someday. The possibility of this not happening after Nell's death had crushed Sheryl.

And, everytime Rock forked over money to attorneys, she'd cry for days. Only a distant friendship could exist between them now. He knew she could prove the will contents. Scott had told him this information, coupled with proof of Nell's and Houston's misconduct would satisfy important requirements required by law.

Sheryl: "I recall the Carper mansion. Rock was ta receive that in the event John died and Nell was through with it. Rock was ta receive John's separate property."

Scott asked a few more questions. Then, finally Scott rested.

Perkins strolled up front for cross-examination. Everything went smoothly until he threw in a complete surprise by asking if she wrote a letter to Nell stating that "You can't choose your relatives, but you can choose your friends and if Nell was a relative you'd choose her, both as a friend and a relative." Perkins stopped pacing, focused on Sheryl, and shouted. "Right?"

She shrugged her shoulders and remained unflappable: "I donnae recall writin' that, but I certainly felt that way o' her."

Rock had no idea either what Perkins was talking about. This wasn't part of the '84 trial. It wasn't part of any discovery proceeding. He watched Perkins wheel around on his heels and pick up a letter Fred Adams Jr. had slid across the counsel table. Perkins handed it to Sheryl.

She took hold of the letter for perusal: "Nae."

Perkins appeared flustered. He pointed to the letter: "Look through to the signature page."

Sheryl: "Why would I write a 'Ta whom it may concairn' letter ta Aunt Nell? That's no the way I'd address her." Sheryl quickly glanced at the letter again. "This letter was written efter she died." She looked up at Judge Dodson, once more expressing her confusion. "This concairns me."

Scott came forward: "This is a new one on me too. Your Honor, before she answers any questions, I want her to read this document."

Judge Dodson moved about in his chair: "I'm concairned, I mean concerned too." He was obviously focused on Sheryl's enunciation. "We'll have a fifteen-minute recess."

Rock rose immediately. He wanted to get to the bottom of Perkins' surprise.

* * *

Rock and Scott shadowed Sheryl to the hallway. The wide corridor hummed with activity. They sat on a long bench against the far wall, one on each side of her, hunched forward with elbows on their knees, peering down at the letter in Sheryl's hands. She sat upright. "See, this was written two months efter Nell died." They proceeded to read the letter quietly:

"There's a saying that you can't choose your relatives, but you can choose your friends. Aunt Nell was one relative I chose both as a friend and a relative. She was positive thinking, looked for the best in others, loved drop-in visitors, the more the merrier, and sparked with energy. What I liked best, she never said an unkind word about anyone."

"Oou, begorraugh. I remember this." They read more:

"Rock, our son and I enjoyed visiting Nell for years. It was the last five years of her life that she was no longer Aunt Nell. By 1976 she was living in the past, believing her folks and Uncle John were still alive."

Rock cleared his throat to explain. "We didn't know she had Alzheimer's Disease. We saw no sign of it until 1976. That was the year Aunt Nell gave me thirteen-cent postage stamps commemorating Chief Crazy Horse. In 1979, I wanted to help her, but Beatrice claimed she was more her aunt than mine, and had the locks changed." They continued reading:

"Because of my work experience at the Carper Cannery, she encouraged me to write a seafood article for a magazine. I didn't feel capable. Nell said nonsense. 'If anyone can do it, you can. I'll ask John to help you. He knows all about the cannery and seafood business.' I said nothing about her offbeat remark."

Scott looked up. "What did you mean by 'offbeat'?"
Sheryl sighed. "John couldnae help me. He'd been dead fer four years."
"Hmmm. See what you mean. Did you write the article?"
 Rock answered. "She did. They paid her $700."
"Well, good for you."
"Ay, I did, with Rock's help 'cause Uncle John wasnae alive." They continued reading.

"In early September 1978, Rock took me to see her. I kissed her on the cheek. She asked if I brought Jack with me. No, I brought Rock with me. She asked, 'Why are you and Rock together?' I said, 'Aunt Nell, I'm married to Rock. Who do you think I am?' 'Why you're Leucojum,' Aunt Nell answered. It took a while to convince her that I was Sheryl. Then she told us, when her mother wasn't watching, she'd sneak over to play with the neighbor kids.
 "Every weekend we stopped by, her niece Beatrice and Marvin were there. We finally quit going on weekends, went on a weekday instead. It wasn't long until Beatrice and Marvin were there weekdays too. And every family picture we gave Nell disappeared. Nell kept asking for pictures. They all disappeared.
 "In 1980 I prepared salmon popovers on the Seattle Today, Channel 5, television show. The day before, I phoned Beatrice to have Aunt Nell watch. That evening Beatrice phoned and talked to Rock, asking about my scheduled TV appearance the next morning, explaining that Nell was sleeping at the moment, but they'd watch. Beatrice took Aunt Nell shopping instead. And, I remember an occasion when Nell asked Rock to tell Ralph Houston, her attorney, to phone him about changing her will. I went with Rock when he relayed the message to Mr. Houston. The meeting took place in his office about 1976 when he was doing some legal work for Rock and his mother, Leucojum. Ralph Houston's comment: 'It's a little too late for that; it's all over town, she's not with it.'"

Sheryl looked up from her reading. "I remember Houston really said, 'It's known all over town, she's nuttier than a fruitcake'. So, Houston and Marvin were up ta no good makin' a new will fer 'er in 1979. In her former will, Rock was favored as Uncle John wanted." Returning to her letter . . .

"And, on another occasion Aunt Nell brought up the subject of a will and her funeral. Rock became upset and said, 'Look Aunt Nell, just be sure Sheryl, mom, our son and me are allowed in the family room.'"

Sheryl explained: "None o' us were allowed in the family room at Uncle John's funeral. Aunt Nell was still in Nevada. The local newspaper dinnae even mention us as John's relatives. Even when Nell died, our names werenae mentioned as relatives in the local paper. That's the kind o' folks Beatrice and Marvin are." Sheryl began to cry.

Rock and Scott fished in their pockets for hankies. She looked at both and picked Rock's.

Scott drew Rock's attention and mumbled something about searching for the bailiff to request an extension for another ten minutes recess time. As soon as Scott was out of sight, Sheryl dropped the letter, jumped up and bolted down the stairs.

Rock was slow to rise, but taking two steps at a time, he soon caught up and pinned her in one corner of the landing. She held his kerchief over her face, still crying, leaning her head against his shoulder. "Sheryl. Get hold of yourself. You can't walk out now."

"Why not? The letter has nothin' ta do with Uncle John's will. It's a trap. Donnae ye see? These bastards arenae searchin' fer relevant facts."

Her eyes were so pleading. Rock patted the top of her head, while taking care not to mess a single hair. "Shhhhh. It's okay." He put his arms around her and held her close. "We'll tell Scott how you feel." Rock looked over his shoulder. Scott appeared at the top of the stairs, watching with hands on hips, his knees locked. "We're coming." Rock led her up the stairs to the water fountain and remained close while she sipped water. Then they returned to the hallway bench and related Sheryl's outlook to Scott.

"Don't worry. I'll see to it that Perkins doesn't pull any more tricks. Now let's finish reading this and return to the courtroom." They continued reading.

"After Aunt Nell died Beatrice and Marvin didn't invite us to the Carper mansion to pick up any of the Carper belongings. Nell didn't realize how manipulated her life had become since 1976. Even so, she remained loving to us. I'll never believe she intentionally left us out of her will. We loved her, and will remember her as a great lady."

Sheryl looked at Scott, her eyes a river of tears again. "We dinnae even get a picture o' Nell. Only in my memory do I see 'er."

Rock put his arm across the back of Sheryl's shoulders. Scott squeezed her trembling right hand. "Are you going to be okay?"

"Ay." She twisted the kerchief in her hands. "I wrote this letter ta one o' Rock's former attorneys efter Nell died. The one who took up minin'."

Scott's eyes broadened. "Mining? An attorney who practiced in this town? Must have been before I came here."

Rock looked over the top of Sheryl's head at Scott. "I've had some odd happenings with attorneys. The miner was my first attorney in this litigation. That was back in 1983. He took a few depositions, then quit to become a full-time miner. He didn't like the legal profession." Rock could hardly blame him.

"Perkins must o' got this letter from the miner's partner." Sheryl sounded feisty.

Rock liked this. Her spirit for a fight was coming out. The best thing he could do now was to support her. "Yeah, the miner's partner is still in business. Isn't this unusual? A conflict of interest for that law firm to be giving out a document meant only for them, especially when the books were closed on that phase of the case?"

Scott looked at it again and shrugged. "But it says 'To whom it may concern'."

Rock was riled. "I don't give a damn. It wasn't filed with this court in any litigation. It wasn't a part of any discovery proceeding. That letter was intended only for a will contest I filed in 1983, but dropped when I found John's documents in the journal."

The three stood to return to court. Rock popped an antacid between his teeth. Judging by the direction things were going, Rock decided he'd better load up on antacid the next time he went to the store. "Why focus on Nell anyway, other than revealing her misconduct in John's probate? This letter doesn't do anything."

"This could be a break for us. It opens the door to undue influence by your opposition."

"Ahhhh. Okay then." This shed new light on the proceedings in Rock's mind as they returned to the courtroom. Sheryl seemed pleased too.

Chapter Thirty

Sheryl resumed her place in the witness box. Even though Perkins threw a surprise letter into the proceedings, Rock felt she could handle it. She had the gutsy fortitude to pull through tough situations.

Perkins continued where he left off, pacing, waving the letter in the air: "Do you remember writing this letter to present to Judge Randell in 1984?"

Sheryl: "Nae. I wrote it at the request o' Rock's attorney, the young one who took up minin'. I still express those same feelin's a'boot Nell taday."

Without asking another question, Perkins moved toward the docket clerk to enter the letter as an exhibit. Before Rock had much time to puzzle over this, Scott stood: "I don't see any relevancy to it, unless there's some impeachment purpose here."

Perkins: "I was just asking what Sheryl thought of Nell." Then, Perkins ignored Scott. "Now, the rest of the letter goes on to describe an event where Nell isn't in touch with reality anymore. Isn't that right?"

Sheryl: "Ay."

Rock chuckled in disgust at the way Perkins shunned Scott and not waiting for the judge to intervene. It was as if the judge didn't matter. It was evident that Perkins was the kind of person who hogged the slop trough and everything therein.

Perkins: "In fact, the letter was in support of Rock's petition to set aside, to contest Nell's 1979 will on the grounds she was mentally incompetent."

Sheryl: "Ay."

Perkins: "And that wasn't successful, as that contest was abandoned by your husband because of Nell's doctor's deposition, stating she was sane?"

Rock didn't have to strain his brain to silently remember the gist of the medical histories on Nell's mental health between 1979 and 1982, which he read after her death. The doctor, who treated her for many years, wrote in his 1978 records that Nell experienced confusion, memory loss and unusual behavior.

But then, Beatrice had Nell switch to a new doctor, Dr. Henderson, later that same year. Dr. Henderson was Beatrice's employer. She worked as his nurse. Dr. Henderson put Nell in a hospital acutely ill with an apparent episode of confusion. And his records showed that Nell got exasperated because her housekeepers whispered and she felt they were whispering about her. By September of 1978 Dr. Henderson reported Nell as semisenile and unable to focus on problems. By the end of '78, he found her more senile and unable to keep a train of thought or explain what was going on at home.

Between 1979 and 1982, Dr. Henderson noted Nell was hallucinating. He wrote that there was a progressive decrease in her mental capacity, which illustrated a progressive organic dementia, or Alzheimer's disease, in an elderly patient.

Even Nell's tax accountant knew about her condition. He filed an amended tax return for her in 1980, for the year 1979 explaining that she was forgetful and failed to inform him of income from Massachusetts Investors, dividends from American Tel and Tel and interest on Series E savings bonds. Her total undeclared income for these was over $18,000.00.

Then, Rock recalled, because of his litigation after Nell's death, Dr. Henderson contradicted his very own medical records in a letter to Ralph Houston. It was a letter written in request by Houston. Dr. Henderson wrote:

"On reviewing my notes, I note that up through the summer of 1980 Nell was independently able to make appropriate judgmental decisions as to her own care and affairs, and could reliably relate to me her feelings and observations as to her health and environmental situations."

Surely, Marvin wouldn't want this contradictory information publicized. Dr. Henderson could be called forth and impeached for lying. Rock's ears tuned back to Perkins, who was again hammering Sheryl: "Your husband abandoned that contest, because Nell's doctor's deposition stated she was sane?"

Sheryl: "Nae, sir. I dinnae get that impression at all."

Rock loved her answers. It was as if she knew what Perkins was going to ask before he asked.

Perkins: "But Rock abandoned his contest against his aunt's will?"

Sheryl: "That had nothin' ta do with Nell's doctor's deposition. Rock abandoned that contest 'cause o' new evidence. Legal advice suggested Rock ferget that contest and proceed with a petition ta probate John's estate."

Perkins walked with his head down like he was searching for another approach: "They were a well-matched couple?"

Sheryl: "Nae. Nell had a way o' upsettin' John. One time efter we spent a day shoppin' in Seattle he drove fer miles oot o' town fergettin' our shoppin' bags in a parkin' garage. We 'ad ta drive back. Nell heckled him ta the point he fergot ta take the wrapper off a stick o' Dentyne gum I gave him. He put the whole thing in 'is mouth."

This answer stopped Perkins' pacing. He appeared dumbfounded. His cheeks puffed out. Snickers came from the Benson family. Rock chortled to himself. Her answer came across as entertaining, but rather foolish unless she was attempting to confuse Perkins, put him off guard. Hard telling with Sheryl. She certainly had a stubborn look on her face as she looked over at Rock, who raised his palms, fingers slightly extended, slowly moved them in and out like a silent, inconspicuous clap. Sheryl would know this meant she was doing great.

Perkins: "Hokay. Other than chewing gum with the wrapper on and forgetting bags, they got along?"

Sheryl refocused on Perkins: "Nae, they werenae gettin' along. They 'ad separate bedrooms fer years."

While staring at the floor, Rock recalled Sheryl having done this to him their last year or so together.

Perkins resumed pacing, while cocking his head, stroking his wispy goatee, appearing to be playing along with Sheryl: "So John chewed gum with a wrapper and forgot some bags, and even though they had separate bedrooms, they never got divorced?"

The room became quiet. Rock wished he knew where Perkins was headed. The small audience watched and listened intently as if they were wondering too.

Sheryl leaned forward, her eyes glared: "That's why they were on their way ta Reno." Harsh whispers of disapproval came from Marvin Benson and his relatives from across the room. Rock nearly choked on his saliva. But, it was true. John and Nell weren't getting along. Leave it to Sheryl to say it.

The advent of her remark caused Perkins to stop pacing: "That's not answering my question. They didn't get divorced." He shouted and stepped closer to her.

Sheryl winced a little: "Nae."

Perkins: "And Nell ran the household." Perkins sounded emphatic.

Sheryl became theatrical: "She ran the show. Took the bull by the horns. Was her own person."

Rock knew Sheryl wasn't about to back down. He had never known her to take any path other than her own.

Perkins beamed, like he had taken her down his path: "Nell was independent, in the sense, when she wanted to do something, by jove, that's what she did?"

With little hesitation, Sheryl smirked down at Perkins and quietly answered: "Puttin' John in a separate bedroom, obviously she got 'er way."

Since he wanted to laugh, Rock looked away and struggled for composure. Perkins couldn't have figured on this answer. He must have expected Sheryl to stick by her letter. And, she would have, except Perkins forced her to expose a side of Nell that Sheryl didn't want to reveal. Truth backfired on Perkins' tactics, because he had no idea ahead of time what her answers would be. Marvin's irritating guttural throaty thrust and murmurs from his relatives penetrated a moment of mumbling from Perkins. Judge Dodson remained emotionless.

Apparently not knowing what more to say, Perkins' face turned pale: "Hokay. No further questions." His voice trailed off.

Judge Dodson removed his dark-rim glasses to rub his eyes and confer with the docket clerk, after excusing Sheryl from the witness stand.

With a red face and flashing eyes, she rushed over to sit by Rock. Scott assured them that she hadn't perjured herself. Sheryl didn't care. "Perkins threatened ta subpoena me fer that garbage? I'll never testify in this damn litigation again. Twas a rigmarole ta discredit me."

Scott overheard and frowned back at her. "Settle down."

"You did great." Rock patted her hand in reassurance. However, he saw no evidentiary value in her testimony beyond will contents, and wondered how it opened the door to misconduct by Marvin and Beatrice.

*   *   *

During the short lull in proceedings, Scott turned to Rock. "We will further address the contents of John's will through your fraternity brother Darnell Eberling. Because Eberling lives out of state and isn't here to testify, his testimony from the 1984 trial record will now be entered."

Rock felt this would be easy. "So, enter it."

"Not that simple. We have to read it in."

"Oh." Rock vaguely remember this was the plan anyway.

"Yeah." Scott scratched his chin. "I'll read Eberling's direct-examination answers. Adams Jr. will ask the questions from the written record. You'll see. Pretend we're actors in a play."

"Okay." Rock watched Scott button his blazer and move into the witness box. Adams Jr. stood military erect in his three-piece suit behind the lectern.

Rock would have preferred the real thing just to be able to see Darnell Eberling again. There were fond memories of them pledging the same fraternity in 1967. But what surfaced at this moment was how opposite they were. Darnell was tall, fair skinned and painfully shy, except where Sheryl was concerned. Rock suspicioned more than once that Darnell had the hots for her. So, Rock kept a watchful eye on Darnell whenever the three were on Uncle John's boat or heading for classes on the University of Washington campus.

Adams Jr. smoothed back his red hair and began reading from the '84 transcript: "How did you meet Dorian Barnes Rock Carper?" This reined in Rock's attention. He kept his eyes away from Adams, so as not to watch his Adam's apple moving like a confused dumbwaiter.

Scott: "While attending the University of Washington. We were fraternity brothers." Scott read Eberling's answer. And, so it went, working in favorable testimony. Rock recalled Eberling being a good witness at the '84 trial because they worked together on the *Lyda* for Uncle John. Eberling was the cook. He knew Uncle John and had seen him at the fraternity house when John gave Rock the will in '67.

Also, Eberling's testimony brought out the day he and Rock ate at the Top Notch Restaurant in the University District, at which time they went over the original ink-signed will together. Being the first will Eberling had seen, it made an impression. He also knew John Carper had substantial wealth and was impressed by the amount of money involved.

Also, Rock recalled Eberling mentioning a provision about a rest home that stuck in his mind because his mother had always kidded him that if she ever got old she didn't want to end up in a rest home. Eberling kiddingly told her back then that that was exactly where she was going.

Scott read Eberling's words with conviction: "Everything was basically going to go to Rock. It was the Carper family and everything that his uncle owned was Rock's. He was obligated to assist his aunt should that be necessary." Rock listened intently to Eberling's words being read, in identifying the two-page carbon copy of John's last will and testament.

Next. Scott and Fred Adams, Jr. traded places to enter Eberling's cross-examination testimony from the 1984 trial record. Rock didn't expect Adams Jr. to read the transcript with enthusiasm, especially since his partner, Houston, and their law firm had a personal interest in the outcome of this trial. Adams Jr. lowered his pencil frame into the witness box and waited for Scott to begin.

The reading revealed rigorous questioning in an attempt to destroy Eberling's credibility, because he didn't quote the will word for word. Rock knew that even he couldn't do this. Still, Eberling's testimony was strong.

Scott returned to the witness box to read Eberling's answers on redirect examination, focusing on a letter Rock wrote to Eberling.

Adams Jr.: "Mr. Eberling, showing you what has been admitted as an exhibit, which is a copy of a letter you sent at Rock Carper's request, this was in response to what?" Adams Jr. read the question, then looked at Scott to read Eberling's answer.

Scott: "Rock phoned me saying he was having problems and asked what I could recall. I told him. He asked me to put it in writing and send it to him."

Rock recalled the letter Eberling wrote back then. His letter mentioned it was John's will he read and the intentions of both John and Nell. Eberling knew they did things together. His letter mentioned being invited over to the Carper mansion. Rock knew this was to discuss a fish order. Uncle John told Eberling he had affection for Rock. When this was read, Adams Jr. objected. Judge Dodson sustained.

Scott stopped reading and looked up: "Your Honor, because Mr. Eberling's letter references the 1967 will we can now enter, as exhibits, the will copies Rock found in the journal in 1984."

Judge Dodson: "You may enter them as exhibits at this time." He received the copies and looked them over before handing them to the docket clerk.

Rock's eyes lit up in elation. One of these exhibits was a two-page legal-size original typewriter carbon-paper copy with typewriter-ribbon and conformed signatures typed in, which was as good as the lost or destroyed original. He hoped Scott would also enter his document expert's authentication of the two-page and four-page copy, both of which were part of Rock's pretrial motion.

Scott poured himself water and sipped, then proceeded with his own comments: "I don't know what we can make of this last little bit. The comment where John Carper told Mr. Eberling he had affection for the boy. The objection is based on the Deadman's Statute. That is an erroneous ruling."

Rock didn't like being called 'boy'. The word 'boy' reminded him of the time he flew two senators to Spokane. After the landing, one senator gave him an order: *"Get my bags, boy."* Rock wasn't a boy. He was a man, but said nothing. How could he when his livelihood depended on the job?

Judge Dodson: "It's really hearsay."

Perkins stood: "Actually that statement by itself doesn't come within the hearsay exception either. So, as far as I can tell, the statement in Eberling's letter says, 'I like the boy.' I don't know that it makes a whole lot of difference in this law suit."

Judge Dodson: "If there's no argument, let it stand. I can't see that it has any significance, the fact that John Carper had affection for Rock Carper. Now, I believe we'll recess for lunch."

Admittedly, things could be better, but on the whole, Rock was satisfied with the way things went concerning Eberling. Any problems could be ironed out later by Scott. And, having testimony read into the record kept Perkins fairly inactive. Rock glanced over at Perkins, who was stroking his goatee. Geez he'd love to grab him by that wispy goatee and drag him around like a bagged deer.

Chapter Thirty-One

It wasn't possible for Rock to visit with his other fraternity brother, George Arnold, who arrived shortly before lunch. Scott ushered him to a private room somewhere in the courthouse. Now that lunch was over, Arnold was sitting up front answering Scott's direct-examination questions to establish his residence, his business as a general contractor and fraternity association.

He pledged the fraternity house in '67 with Rock. Arnold was heavier in '67 than today, but still had fair Norwegian features and spoke firmly in relating the occasion he saw John's will.

Arnold: "I was studying in the fraternity library. Rock brought the will in for me to read. We talked about it." Arnold described the will as legal-size white paper with John's ink signature on the bottom line and that he saw it again in 1972 at his Lynnwood home-office when John visited Rock that day. "My home/ office was a fire burnout when I bought it. We were putting on a new roof. I had two other employees and Rock helping me."

Scott: "Were those the only two times you've ever seen John's will?"

Arnold: "The original, yes."

Scott: "You've seen more than one copy of that 1967 will?"

Arnold: "Two copies. One was two pages legal size, the other was four pages standard size."

Scott: "This two-page, legal-size copy is what you saw at the fraternity in 1967 and your office in 1972?"

Arnold: "Yes."

Scott: "And, here is a copy of the four-page, standard-size will. When did you see a copy of this?"

Arnold: "At the taking of my deposition."

"Ooooh no." Rock felt edgy about this issue of two wills. Rock found two wills in the journal. One was the two-page legal-size will. The other was a four-page thermofaxed copy. Standard-size paper. Only the opposition attorney Adams Jr. would know why he xeroxed copies of the four pages and stapled them together to resemble two legal-size sheets of the will at Arnold's deposition meeting. It caused Arnold nothing but confusion in this case. Well, if Arnold doesn't realize it now, Perkins will destroy him later. Rock hoped the attorneys didn't spend much time on this. Scott finally moved on to will contents, which Arnold adequately described.

The afternoon was moving slowly. Rays of sun splashed in through the high windows of the room. Rock felt sluggish from a big lunch and wanted to nap. Highly unlikely. Soon, Perkins livened things with a puffy ego during cross-examination, digging Arnold for dropping out of college. Rock snickered in disgust. What did this matter have to do in the measure of a man anyway? What mattered was that Arnold had to take over his dad's business, because his dad fell off a roof, which killed him instantly. But, no attorney brought this out.

Perkins: "Rock worked for you for a time?"

Arnold: "Right, until 1974. We separated. I moved away to Bellingham."

Rock couldn't remember working with Arnold much longer after completion of the Lynnwood project in 1972, because he backed into a closet on stilts. One stilt slipped down a laundry shoot. It injured his back and required a reevaluation of his career.

A pilot friend prompted Rock into the flying field, which consumed his time with such avidity, that he passed all test requirements for single engine, twin engine, floatplane and instrument ratings. This launched him into the private chartering business, away from Arnold.

But, Rock soon forgot about flying when Perkins asked Arnold if he knew when John Carper died. Arnold couldn't recall. This was damaging.

Perkins: "Preposterous. Rock was working for you in 1972 and you don't recall? He didn't run and say: "Uncle John died?"

Arnold: "He probably did, but I . . ."

Perkins: "Speak up please."

Arnold: "I said he probably did, but I have no recollection. I just don't remember." Arnold poured himself water.

Perkins: "He didn't come to you and say, George, I was supposed to be the executor of my uncle's estate and they are probating the will and I am not going to be executor of the estate?"

Arnold: "Not that I can remember." He gulped the water.

"Oh, maun." Sheryl turned to Rock to talk in sign. "Perkins is makin' a big mess o' things. Or, George isnae doin' ye much good 'ere. Perkins is rattlin' him."

Rock recalled the day Nell's niece, Beatrice phoned Sheryl about John's demise. Sheryl contacted him at work with the news. Arnold gave him permission to leave work early. Yet, It didn't come as a surprise that Arnold couldn't remember today. This affair wasn't close to him.

Perkins: "According to your deposition, you can only remember two things about the will you read. One was Aunt Nell wasn't to go into a nursing home." Perkins pushed harder.

Arnold: "Yes." He answered sheepishly, like he was trying to be accommodating.

Perkins: "And number two, if anybody contested the will they would get one dollar?"

Arnold: "Correct."

Geez Rock thought. Arnold's memory is shot. A few minutes ago, he told Scott he remembered Rock as co-executor with Nell and Rock was to receive John's separate estate. Scott appeared to be listening, but not reacting.

Perkins pried a finger in one ear like he was intent on reaching an itch: "Is it fair to say you had no specific recollection at the '84 trial of how much property John had or to whom it was supposed to go?" Perkins' questioning was becoming ruthless.

Arnold: "I did not testify to those facts. I said Rock was to receive John's part of the estate."

Perkins: "In your deposition on page twelve you were asked if you had any specific independent recollection back in 1967 of knowing how much property was supposed to go to whom and your answer was no, I don't."

Arnold: "Correct."

Perkins: "No further questions."

Rock nodded favorably to this testimony. Yet, ill feelings toward Perkins were flooding his mind, while knowing that John's will contained absolutely no verbiage on how much property or exact dollar value was to go to whom. And, he knew Arnold testified to more than two things in John's will. Reminding Scott of these concerns met with no apparent interest.

*   *   *

Scott was now glancing over his notes at the lectern in preparing for redirect examination: "When Fred Adams Jr. took your deposition, he handed you a copy of the 1967 will that had been copied onto four pages?"

Arnold: "Yes, to give the appearance of a two-page legal-size will."

Rock groaned over Scott reopening this issue. Why did he have to be the one to bring it up? The issue of two pages versus four pages of John's will. This single maneuver performed by Adams Jr. the day of Arnold's deposition showed Rock how the damn attorney operated. A stapling stunt to confuse the witness and the judge years down the road. How very clever. And Scott had to hone in on it. Hell. At least Arnold's answer put it in prospective, that the pages were stapled to look like two legal pages, the longer paper. Rock stirred around and crossed his knees.

Scott: "I don't want to be putting words in your mouth, but did the four-page copy at your deposition look like the copy of the four-page will on exhibit here, exhibit 9?" Scott raised his head.

Arnold: "Yes, except that the set at my deposition was stapled to look like two pages."

Scott: "Then how many pages did the will have that Rock showed you at the fraternity in 1967?"

Arnold: "Two pages. The last page had an ink signature."

Scott: "Is the same true of what you saw at your job?"

Arnold: "Yes."

Well, this didn't seem so bad unless it opened the door for trouble later. But, while pushing the cuticles back on his nails in a moment of tedium, Rock worried what Perkins would do with Scott's questions to clarify any confusion over the two pages versus the four pages of John's will. That wait wasn't long.

Perkins practically jumped forward: "Hokay. I can't let this one go by. You are saying that Rock showed you an original document that had an ink signature and it was an original?"

Arnold: "Yes."

Perkins: "But in your deposition you said it didn't have an ink signature."

Arnold appeared uncertain.

Perkins: "And, just a couple minutes ago you testified that when John Carper came out to the work site in Lynnwood he was carrying a copy?"

Arnold: "If that's what I testified to, that's not what I meant."

Scott: "Object. I don't recall that testimony at all."

Rock fought off a yawn and waited for Scott to stop the proceedings to clear up this issue, especially since Judge Dodson conveyed his uncertainty too.

Instead, Perkins hammered on: "So, you are saying that on both occasions you saw that two-page original rather than a copy?"

Arnold: "Correct."

Perkins: "But this is not the same as your testimony in the deposition."

Arnold: "Then I was in error on my understanding of the question."

Perkins raised his voice as if lecturing Arnold, reminding him that the day of his deposition Adams Jr. gave ground rules. One was to tell him if and when he didn't understand any questions.

Arnold agreed with this reminder.

Perkins: "As I read your deposition testimony it was crystal clear. It was not an original."

Arnold: "If that is what it says." He backed down and admitted he was confused as to the way the copies had been presented and didn't understand what was going on in that respect.

Perkins pivoted: "Your Honor, I wish to publish the 1984 deposition of George Arnold."

"He's goin' ta impeach him." Sheryl furrowed her eyebrows.

Frustrated from a sense of helplessness, Rock leaned over his knees and rubbed a hand over his eyes. He knew there was nothing in the deposition to impeach Arnold. If anything it only showed that Adams Jr. confused Arnold by flashing a four-page will, stapled together to resemble a two-page will. That's all. But, no way was Perkins going to leave it at that.

Perkins: "Now I am going to show you some of your 1984 trial testimony." Perkins handed him some pages. "Does that refresh your memory as to what your answer was when you were asked at that '84 trial whether it was a two or four-page document or whether it was an original or a copy?"

Arnold: "Yes, it does."

Perkins: "What did you testify to then?"

Arnold: "My testimony was that it was four pages."

Rock sighed under his breath. "Yeah, four pages stapled into two." Rock nudged Scott's chair with an outstretched leg. When this didn't bring results, Rock popped an antacid. His head buzzed. By the look on Arnold's face, his head must have been buzzing too. His posture was slumped down like a beat dog. It was shameful what these attorneys were doing to Arnold.

Finally, Judge Dodson leaned back, while focusing on the attorneys. Sighing, he removed his glasses and toyed with the stems: "Is there anything else that is going to confuse this situation."

Scott laughed: "I don't think I can torture it any further. I have no questions for Mr. Arnold."

"Sonofabitch. My own attorney trying to be cute." It should have been Perkins to state this, not Scott. Either way, they didn't do justice to Arnold.

After his release from the witness stand, Arnold walked over to sit by Rock and Sheryl. "I've been put through the wringer by both attorneys. Which one is yours?" He whispered, kiddingly with sarcasm, not expecting an answer. "They had me so damn confused. Sorry, guess I wasn't much good."

Rock smiled, while trying to hide his hurt. Sheryl patted Arnold on the hand. "Ye did yer best. Just too much time has gone by the wayside."

"Yeah. But, don't invite me to another trial. I don't like the way these attorneys twisted my testimony. Well, I have to leave."

Rock mouthed a "Thank you, buddy" and reached across the front of Sheryl to shake his hand. There wasn't a thing he could do, but talk to Scott.

* * *

Following adjournment, Rock ricocheted on one foot and headed down the courtroom aisle. He wanted to buttonhole Scott in a hurry. He caught Scott heading down the stairs. "Look, I was at George's deposition as well as the '84 trial. It boiled down to this: Arnold saw the two-page will at the fraternity and the Lynnwood job site, because he viewed a handwritten signature and the name John Carper." Scott kept going. Rock tried to explain how Adams Jr. injected confusion stapling a four-page document to resemble a two-page document at Arnold's deposition.

"Well, you heard him. Pretty damn confusing." He talked over a shoulder.

"Arnold admitted his memory isn't good."

"And his getup didn't help matters."

"Getup. What does getup have to do with this?"

"You don't wear jeans and a plaid shirt to court. Gives a wrong impression."

"Hell. In this town? Come on. So, you're telling me Arnold's duds and confusion caused by you attorneys will destroy my proof of will contents?"

"Not necessarily. Proof of will contents is in the judge's discretion. The law is that it isn't necessary that each of two witnesses have direct personal knowledge, nor that proof rest exclusively on their testimony."

"Whew." This was a relief.

Scott stopped. "Rock, I know you expected today to be the last day of trial. But the experts have to present evidence. And proper execution of John's will has yet to be addressed. And, I think it would be a good idea if we make room for Nell's relatives Beatrice and Marvin Benson."

Geez. This was Wednesday, the end of the third day and the trial wasn't over. His expenses were mounting. "Huh, at $1,000 a day, what value are the relatives?"

"We can use them to establish Nell's condition as to her ability to access the safety deposit box before the state inventory. And, I'll try to squeeze in undue influence."

"Ye'd be doin' Rock more good if ye brought oot 'ow Beatrice and Marvin Benson put their greedy straws inta one John Carper estate, like suckin' everythin' oot o' one peachy-keen soda." Sheryl caught up to them.

"Sheryl, what do you think undue influence means?" Rock was ticked over her interruption. And the way this trial was being run, he was confused himself. He barely had time to chew over one problem when another surfaced. And, what Rock thought were problems, Scott didn't. The strain was getting to him. And, now Sheryl interfered.

"Oou. Pardon me." She slowed her gait, acting embarrassed.

Rock ignored her and focused intently on Scott as they approached the lobby. "Okay. I especially like your idea, since Beatrice revealed in her deposition of leaving Nell alone for one week before the state inventory of John's estate." Scott beamed with Rock's reaction. Rock and he shook hands on it. Then, they bid one another a good evening and went their separate ways.

As Rock left the courthouse for his car, he noticed Sheryl was no where in sight. While driving toward town, he thought he probably wouldn't see her again at this trial. She wasn't needed.

He parked and roamed around town a while. This brought him staring at a shapely blonde mannequin in a storefront window. The mannequin was dressed in a slim-fitting silvery gown tied over one shoulder with a red velvet bow. This sight elicited visions of how Unali would look in the dress and how much he missed her. Finally, he jammed his hands in his pockets and walked away.

*   *   *

Back at the Leucojum house, Rock hummed and dusted off a set of deer antlers mounted on an oak plaque before hanging it above the fireplace. Next, he decorated it with red Christmas balls. This would be as close to a tree as he could get this year. And, it was a cheerful way to shut out the day's events.

Then, he sat on the dark-brown velvet couch to consume his sustenance of a roast-beef sandwich and beer purchased at a deli on the way here. The crackling fire provided light and warmth. The rest of the house was dark.

Moisture from the heating logs snapped occasionally, jostling his nerves. He wanted to chuck some of the events of the day into the fire. Arnold's confusion, his clothes, the plaid shirt and jeans, nagged him. What's wrong with plaid shirts and jeans? These were as American as barbecued salmon and apple pie. In his estimation, Arnold's clothes didn't make him any less of a witness. It was the behavior of the attorneys that made them less as men. Those attorneys didn't have balls enough to wear jeans and a plaid shirt. He mentally drafted a plan to approach Scott about Arnold's clothes in the morning.

Wearing down, he removed his clothes and draped them over a chair. He wrestled under blankets on the couch and watched the fire reflect from the red Christmas decorations. The wind whined against the house. Now and again, he heard the back gate bang. He was too weary to care, when finally his mind carried him to a special Christmas present his Uncle John gave him. A present he had to stare at until the spring winds came. This made no sense at all, because he was quite young. John, Jack and Leucojum figured this was a good idea in teaching him patience. *All good things take patience*, they said.

Rock didn't think March would ever arrive so he could open this special present. When the day arrived, Uncle John and his dad Jack took him to the beach. They romped with beachcombers and sandcastle builders. Salty waves licked at their feet and forced them to move. He remembered countless tidepools loaded with exotic water creatures and a ground littered with leafy-strewn logs. Winds whipped overhead. Uncle John told him to open the surprise present. A kite. His first. Running up and down the beach with it made him happy. Even now, he felt the tug of power between the kite and the wind.

Oh how he longed for those days when his dad said a man's word was sealed with a handshake. He pondered the value of Scott's handshake and his word as he yawned, and thought maybe he should take his prescription medicine tomorrow to ensure patience. After all, Scott was trying, wasn't he?

Chapter Thirty-Two

In the courtroom Thursday morning, Rock's mind was in a shambles from a lousy night's sleep, waking up several times so full of doubts that he rose early and took half of a prescription pill. That was probably more than what he should have taken. Sitting on the bench this morning without Sheryl would be difficult to face alone. In depositions, hearings and trials, he'd grown accustomed to her being at his side.

As the lost feeling lingered, in walked Sheryl. An eye opener. She slid on the bench beside him, with two cups of coffee. She looked Scottish in a green tartan suit and ivory-colored blouse that matched her ivory teeth.

Her teeth were that way because, as Sheryl explained, certain minerals were lacking in the water in Scotland. For this reason, she rarely wore white. One day, she asked him if the color of her teeth bothered him. The question irritated. *"Hell no. Why do things have to be white?"* He remembered giving her a quick kiss and laughing wryly. *"The next generation may paint their teeth blue to match their fingernails."*

Receiving a cup of coffee from her, he toasted a good morning, sipped and stared, dumbfounded, since she wasn't needed in court today and could have walked out of his life yesterday, if she wanted.

She reached over with a free hand to pick lint off his lapel. "I decorated my tree this mornin'. It lifted my spirits, 'cause as I piled on more and more baubles, I realized 'ow this added ta the tree's beauty, you know, like strength in numbers."

"Come on, Sheryl. You really think the two of us impart strength?" He guffawed, while rubbing his lapel pin with hopes for better things to come in this house of justice.

"Suppose not. Ye and me used ta be powerful together." She looked away, then back at him. "Then I'm offerin' moral support."

"Thanks." They chatted and drank their coffees. It tasted bitter. "Geezus. This coffee doesn't taste the way I like it. Is this some foreign brand?"

"Ay." She drank hers.

Starring over the rim of his cup, Rock watched her. Since she was drinking, it must be okay. Maybe his taste for coffee was changing since he started taking those prescription pills. A half pill a day shouldn't cause this, but he downed his coffee anyway. "You seem to be holding up well."

"Yesterday efternoon, I was gettin' near the end o' my strength. Are ye holdin' up?" She searched in her bag and soon dabbed perfume behind her ears.

"Hanging in there, growing poorer by the day." He crossed a foot over the other knee.

"I know. The expandin' trial is increasin' yer expenses." Sheryl sympathized with a sweet smile. "I saw Marvin and Houston outside smokin' cigars. They were chummy."

"Two cronies from the legal mob." Rock joked, then noticed Marvin and

Houston filing in to sit with the Benson relatives. Houston was overweight and wrinkled.

Scott rushed in red-cheeked and out of breath. He nodded to Rock and busily arranged legal paraphernalia across the top of the counsel table; his courtroom routine. Rock leaned forward. "Are you going to use all those documents and books?"

"Probably not." He laughed. "Attorneys do this to put on a good show. Looks impressive."

Rock had to admit it was impressive like Scott was armed for a bear hunt. But, it was concerning having papers left there during lunch and sometimes at night. "Aren't you afraid someone will snoop or steal those?"

"Nah. The bailiff keeps an eye on things and locks up during lunch breaks and in the evening."

Satisfied with Scott's answer, Rock checked his watch. There was enough time to inquire about Scott's interrogation procedures used against Arnold yesterday; yet, Rock felt it best to leave it alone. He was learning that attorneys are allowed freedom to say whatever they want to bring out the truth and that the judge was onto underhanded tricks. Rock needed to trust more.

True, yesterday's tactics used by the attorneys brought doubt and confusion. Logic, in the presence of confusion, was difficult for Rock. Nevertheless, today was a new day and he was feeling in control of himself, after having taken extra medication.

*　　*　　*

The court session began as Judge Dodson eased into his chair like a higher form of life. He instructed Perkins to start first.

Perkins rose, but stayed behind his counsel table. He clasped his hands over his stomach and stuck out his goatee: "Sheryl should not be able to testify. Her testimony should not be considered."

Rock and Sheryl looked at each other, flabbergasted. Rather than this, they expected Ralph Houston to take the stand.

"What's Perkins jabberin' a'boot. I already testified." She nervously poked a fingernail between her teeth. They returned their focus to Perkins.

Perkins: "Sheryl is an interested person, even though she was not a beneficiary of John's will." He bellowed from behind his counsel table, his kinky blond hair bouncing: "According to Joseph Scott, Rock and Sheryl have used nearly $100,000 in community funds in Rock's separate property litigation to date."

"That much?" Sheryl nudged Rock.

"Afraid so." He closed his eyes and inhaled.

"Yer sick, I say." Her eyes glared at him while speaking in sign, rubbing her stomach to denote throbbing or a sick feeling.

"Shhh." He didn't need a family squabble. Not here.

Perkins drummed on: "If recovery in a lawsuit is community property, then the wife's testimony is excluded because she has a bias." Through the art of persuasion, Perkins pleaded that the court should not consider Sheryl's testimony at all.

Scott rose: "An inheritance is separate property. That's what we're facing here. Sheryl can testify to things that John said and did regarding the will; things that Rock can't testify about."

The room fell silent for two drumbeats. A thought crossed Rock's mind. Yesterday, neither attorney asked Sheryl questions on anything Uncle John said to her.

Judge Dodson cleared his throat: "Well, I've listened to your arguments gentlemen and agree with Mr. Scott's analysis. I stand on the ruling that Sheryl Carper may testify with respect to conversations with John Carper."

Rock was thrilled with this determination, jumping to the conclusion he won something. At least he felt a lot better.

Sheryl whispered to Scott. "Yesterday, I wasna asked a single question o' conversations I 'ad with John, by either ye or Perkins. Are ye goin' ta put me back on the stand?"

"No. The judge will read your conversations with John in the former record. That's the reason for filing Rock's pretrial motion."

This satisfied Rock and Sheryl, because the pretrial motion included the 1984 trial transcript containing her testimony on conversations with John, important in addressing testamentary intentions as required by law.

*   *   *

It had been about a year since Rock last saw Ralph Houston. Now, here Houston was, stoop-shouldered, appearing all of seventy-plus, walking slowly toward the stand to be sworn in.

This was a day Rock had waited many years for: Houston vowing to tell the truth, while standing in front of the American flag. What a disgusting scene. Rock pondered how Houston could stand up there without any sign of shame, knowing of his former lies at the 1984 trial.

To Rock, any oath is taken as inviolate. An oath must be kept by all. At that very moment, he remembered Leucojum impressing the importance of truth upon him through a story she related when he was a youngster. She said Major General George Custer lied about his intentions for the military, while smoking a pipe with Stone Forehead. Not long afterward, Custer lay dead in the dust of Little Bighorn. The Indians had shot an arrow through the General's testicles for dishonesty. Even now, the story brought pain to Rock's groin. Leucojum scared the daylights out of him with this tale, and further said that to lie was to bring godly wrath down upon one's life.

Finally, Houston raised a shaky, knotty-fingered right hand in front of the bailiff.

Bailiff: "Do you solemnly swear to tell the truth, the whole truth and nothing but the truth?"

Houston's fleshy jowls shook under thinning gray hair with tufts hanging down over the ears: "I do." Then he edged into the witness chair with geriatric slowness, and stared out calmly with toad eyes, assessing everyone, except Rock.

"The old chap's complexion is so ruddy. Looks like 'e has been sippin' too much high-proof tea."

Rock saw a portly man with cheeks and nose as red as a sun-kissed Winesap. Every inch of him was blighted with age. Rock remembered when Houston, a quiet man, was the Carper family attorney. In the 1970's, Houston helped Leucojum with legal problems concerning the sale of a boat she sold after Jack's death. And, in the 1980's, Houston prepared a power of attorney for Rock to manage Leucojum's affairs, even knowing Uncle John, for some reason, never liked Houston.

Before this litigation, Houston was always nice to Rock. So was Houston's executive secretary of the Houston, Adams & Adams Law Firm, originally housed in an old building with high ceilings. Rumor had it that she was the brain of their business. Rock believed it must have been said in jest, because over the years, Houston proved he had a brain. Today, Houston carried fifty some years of legal experience.

Rock leaned toward Sheryl and whispered. "Under Houston's decrepit face is an astute brain." He knew old Houston was loaded with unspent words, enough to fill a dictionary of deception.

Sheryl looked straight ahead, nodding.

The trial proceeded with the same small group of onlookers, including Houston's partner, redheaded Adams Jr., who sat, with an air of confidence, at the counsel table on the right of the judge's bench. Although, he stretched his neck like the collar of his shirt was too tight.

Unlike the past three days with Rock's witnesses, Perkins was gentle with Houston, like a father and son having a cordial chat: "You did legal work in the estate of John Carper?"

Houston sat with his hands clasped over his lap: "Oh yez. From 1972 through '74."

Rock noted that Houston sounded lazy, but knew he was anything but lazy. He unbuttoned his checkered brown and green jacket, revealing a knitted tan vest over his white shirt and brown-print tie. He claimed to have not known John well. Also, he said John left a 1952 will, which he found in the safe deposit box at the Quamas Bank.

Perkins: "What was the will date?"

Houston: "The will was dated May 9th, 196—excuse me. Errrr. The will was dated December 9th, 1952," He shook his head, coughed and waited for the next question.

Rock's heart nearly stopped when Houston hooked himself on May 9th, the date of the 1967 will. Rock and Sheryl smiled at each other, thrilled over this slip. There was no doubt in Rock's mind, Houston had the original 1967 will all these years.

Perkins almost stopped pacing over the slip, then continued, quietly and gently: "It was filed with the Clamton County Clerk on August 31, 1972?"

Houston: "Oh yez, I filed it."

Scott appeared to be taking notes. Rock hoped so. Houston explained that his other partner, Fred Adams Sr., deceased, had prepared the will. Fred Adams Jr appeared pleased at the mention of his father. Perkins moved on asking Houston to identify John and Nell's 1971 recorded community property agreement.

Houston held the document, glanced up and down, then handed it back: "I'm not sure where this was found. It just surfaced at the opening of the deposit box when the state tax commissioner was there, the latter part of July. Nell was present, barely able to ambulate."

Perkins set the document on the defendant's counsel table: "How did you learn of the safe deposit box?"

Houston: "Nell must have told me about it. I wrote letters to banks where she thought they might have accounts."

Ah, Rock thought. At least no one can say Nell didn't know what was going on. She knew about the banks where John conducted business. Houston admitted she had the key and he opened it.

Perkins: "What was in the box?"

Houston: "A sizable number of stock certificates; the 1952 will."

Perkins: "An inventory was made, according to this letter you wrote to an accountant, right?"

Houston: "Right."

Rock's mind was feeling slightly spaced out at times. One minute he was focused and the next minute he was foggy. Inhaling helped him to rationalize that he was okay. His thoughts told him to focus. It was to Houston's advantage to conceal the '67 will that favored Rock. Nell had selected Houston as her probate attorney. So, naturally Houston would use the '52 will. There was money to be had if he brought forth only the 1952 will and even more money if Houston could convince others that the community property agreement included all Carper property. If Nell found out Houston was misusing the property agreement, she wouldn't say anything because it was more money for her too. And if Marvin ever found out, he wouldn't say anything because he was also after John's money.

Oh man. How to prove this was beyond him. Yet, Rock knew Houston's letter to the accountant misrepresented John and Nell's community property agreement as vesting all John's property in Nell as her sole and separate estate. Perkins avoided this verbiage. Surely, Scott would drill him. Instead, recess was called.

*　　*　　*

The Carpers followed Scott to the hallway. "Why isnae Perkins askin' Houston a'boot misrepresentin' the community property agreement in that letter?" Sheryl pressed Scott, who said nothing, and who kept his eyes on the floor. "That Houston letter contradicts what was written in the community property agreement. Remember, the community property agreement vested only the Carper Cannery property to Nell, nothin' else."

Rock was eager to hear Scott's answer.

"Don't worry your pretty little head. I'll pin things down during cross-examination." Then, Scott excused himself to make a quick phone call to his office.

"This is asinine. He's no concentratin' on yer case."

"You don't know." Rock remembered Leucojum's advice to keep his mouth shut, least he speak with ignorance. That's how Scott was treating them. Rock shrugged and headed for the men's room.

Chapter Thirty-Three

Following recess, Perkins posed in front of Houston, who reseated himself in the witness box. Surprisingly, Perkins inquired about him talking to Rock about the community property agreement.

Houston: "I do recall talking with Rock about that community property agreement and that the judge, I believe it was Judge Lord, knew about it. He wouldn't admit the will to probate."

Perkins: "Rock testified that you told him that there was a community property agreement and so the will that was being probated really wouldn't matter?"

Houston brushed back a thin tuft of hair splayed over one ear. "Rock may have interpreted my remarks to mean that, but I don't recall my saying anything about the will not being probated."

"That damn liar." Rock spoke barely above a whisper. "He said no will made a difference."

Sheryl trembled in annoyance. "And, without a thorough interrogation o' Houston's testimony at the '84 trial denyin' this conversation took place, Judge Dodson is goin' ta whittle yer conversation ta a communication problem."

Rock's eyes riveted from Houston to Sheryl. "Better not. That would send my laches defense downhill."

A vein seemed to bulge in Houston's right temple as he shifted in his seat: "There's no question, I had my problems probating the estate."

Perkins: "Problems. How?" He slowly paced like he was working in his daily exercise.

Houston: "Well, in trying to transfer stocks. The stocks were in John's name only and cost of transfers was a problem. We finally decided to repudiate the community property agreement and proceed under the will."

"Yeah, transfers because the stocks were John's separate property, you conniving, thieving son-of-a-bee." Rock seethed, stirring uncomfortably.

"Shush. At least 'e admitted tellin' you the court wouldnae admit the will ta probate."

Perkins continued: "Hokay. These letters indicate you had some question about how to proceed, under the will, or under the community property agreement?"

Houston: "I suppose so."

Rock decided that Houston's poor communication extended to others besides him. What irked Rock was when Houston announced John left no separate property. He figured Scott would disprove this with the Carper house deed, showing the house remained John's separate property through Nell's death in 1983.

Perkins: "So what did you decide to do?" He adjusted his tie.

Houston: "I decided to probate the estate under the will with the thought that this might turn up John's separate property."

Rock scribbled out a note, then snapped his fingers to get Scott's attention. Scott reached back for it to read: *"How would the will cause any separate property to turn up?"*

Scott only nodded. Rock's attention shifted back to Houston, who said it made no difference whether he proceeded under the will or under the community property agreement.

Rock felt Houston knew it made a difference as to whether they proceeded under a will or community property agreement. Houston finally admitted they proceeded under the 1952 will only after he had Nell repudiate the community property agreement.

So it made a difference. Otherwise, Houston wouldn't have had Nell repudiate the agreement. If all John's property were community, they wouldn't have to repudiate it. All property would automatically go to Nell. As these thoughts passed through his head, Rock wondered if the judge was focused on this. Maybe if the judge looked more closely at the wording in the documents, things would become clear.

When Perkins handed Houston the repudiation of community property agreement, entered as an exhibit, Judge Dodson wouldn't allow any questions to be asked. Instead, Dodson leaned forward on his elbows: "The exhibit is self explanatory."

Sheryl whispered to Rock. "Is it self explanatory?" She quirked her eyebrows questioningly.

Rock was on the edge of his seat. "Hell yes. That document contains facts screaming for an egg-planation. Well, you know what I'm saying. Facts damning to Houston and Nell." A hypothetical thought crossed Rock's mind in trying to figure out what was going on here. Judge Dodson's denial of questions on the repudiation document was like helping his opposition to work in fallacies to fit their theories and disregard the facts that revealed the truth. And, there was something in the way Judge Dodson acted that didn't set well with Rock.

Perkins switched to another topic: "Rock said he told you during probate that there was a later will. That is, a will dated later than the 1952 will."

Houston: "No way. I had no knowledge of another will."

"Damn you Houston, you knew. There's no end to your lies." Rock exhaled the words under his breath, recollecting Houston's 1989 deposition, admitting he and Rock discussed whether he and Nell would proceed under the community property or under the '67 will. Rock leaned toward Scott. "Get his deposition out."

If Scott was listening, he gave no indication, other than make a tipi with his fingers.

Rock drew in a deep breath to control himself. Too many puzzles were piling skyward. He fought dizziness, because if he dwelt on himself, he'd miss what was coming next.

Houston shifted his heavy torso, then explained that if Rock had given him a valid original will while they were still in probate, he would have stopped everything.

Sheryl scooted closer to Rock. "In a bird's beak. That's a safe statement fer Houston ta make since Nell and 'e were the only ones with legal access ta the deposit box where the original was stored."

Rock stared at the American flag. Stumped by legal procedures and justice, his mind drifted to the Lincoln-Douglas debates of 1858. In history class, he memorized what Douglas said:

"In my opinion this government of ours is founded on the white basis. It was made by the white man, for the benefit of the white man, to be administered by white men."

Much of what he learned in that class was focused on Whiteman's accomplishments, and how subcultures were beholden. How appropriate Douglas' words were today, more than one hundred and thirty years later with Rock as a witness.

Of course, it was possible this trial was a figment of his imagination. Oh how he wished it were so. However, he believed his mind was still intact. He had to think positive. He had to know there were more good people than bad. Houston was a bad man. Rock had to rely on Scott to reveal Houston for what he was by blowing his testimony apart. There was no one else who could do it. Would Scott do it now?

* * *

Scott strolled up to the witness box, then stood with his feet slightly apart. The tough look, with locked knees. Rock figured the firecracker in Scott would surface here. Having been the butt end of his temper the past few days, Rock knew a fire was there.

Scott stretched his chin high: "With reference to the 1952 will, are you telling me you knew that there was a will in an envelope, is that what you're saying?"

Sheryl squeezed Rock's arm like she had high aspirations.

Houston: "Oh yez. There was an envelope on which were the names, John and Nell."

"Now he's only admitting he found an envelope. But, Scott's doing fine."

Scott leaned against the defendant's table: "Mr. Houston, as I understand it, you recollect some contact with Rock early on in the probate proceedings in your office?"

Houston: "I think so." He clasped his hands together.

Turning to Sheryl, Rock released five fingers downward, meaning 'shit'. "He thinks so. Hell, he knows so."

"He has an air o' weariness a'boot him. A part o' his strategy, I'm thinkin'." She pointed to her head, meaning 'thinking'.

Rock nodded and paused to inhale. Deep breathing was the only way to clear his head. Only this time, he discovered he was breathing in Sheryl's perfume. It certainly added a refreshing quality to the dusty courtroom and its mustard-colored law books.

His attention was soon drawn back to Houston, who related that he definitely had conversations with Rock about the community property agreement and had determined fairly soon in probate that all John's property was community: "I couldn't find any interest, any separate interest, in John's property at all. It was all community."

Excitement welled inside Rock. His scarred hands were clammy. His heart pounded in anticipation, waiting for someone to enter the mansion deed. He thought for certain that Scott was working up to this. The wall clock read

11:10 o'clock, so there was still time before lunch. Soon, however, Rock noticed that Scott changed the subject.

Scott: "I understand you weren't well acquainted with John. You never did legal work for John before his death."

Houston: "Right. I don't think I had."

"That damn quahog is lyin', if he cannae give a definite answer." Sheryl fumed quietly, sliding two fingers across her lips from right to left, meaning 'lying'. "He who has specialized in estate plannin' fer years appears ta be well primed fer this trial."

"I told you he had a brain." To indicate this, Rock held two fingers to his forehead. "And we don't know that he did legal work for John." Rock grunted and fidgeted for comfort: an impossibility sitting on unpadded wood with straight backs.

Scott changed the subject: "The community property agreement is a standard, preprinted form relating to community property?"

Houston: "Oh yez."

Listening to this was difficult for Rock. He whispered to Sheryl. "Like hell it is. It's not a standard form, because it relates only to the Carper Cannery. It didn't make the Carper mansion and John's other separate assets community property. Scott's an attorney. He knows this." Sheryl nodded.

Scott shifted his weight: "It was recorded at the request of the new owners of the Quamas Cannery?"

Houston: "Oh yez sir."

Scott: "How can that be?" He stood with a hand knuckled on a hip.

Houston: "Oh, I suppose they persuaded John to sign and get it recorded."

"Who's the they?" Sheryl spoke quietly to Rock.

Rock whispered. "Maybe the bank. Maybe the new cannery owners. I don't know."

Scott: "You know the '52 will came from the deposit box?"

Houston: "That's true."

Scott: "Did the state inventory list a will?"

Houston: "No."

Rock turned to Sheryl and snickered. "Geez. Then how did Houston know there was any will in the envelope?" Sheryl only shook her head, puzzled.

Scott: "Does your 1989 deposition represent your best memory with regard to John's 1952 will?"

Perkins lunged upward from his chair: "I object, Your Honor. If he has any questions about Houston's deposition, he can show him the deposition."

Judge Dodson, appearing caught in a moment of tedium, widened his eyes and promptly sat erect: "If someone can give me a summary of what the deposition says, I assume it's intended to be used for impeachment, but I would rather that we read from the deposition. Let's give Mr. Houston his copy to examine."

Rock sat up straight too, trying to grasp the goings-on of this judicial system. Rather than Scott guiding his own cross-examination, Perkins took over with dictatorial authority, suggesting they turn to page fifteen of Houston's deposition.

Judge Dodson: "I'm at page fifteen right now." He held the deposition open. Houston was looking at his copy.

Scott regained command, calling Houston's attention to line six wherein he admitted he could only recall an envelope in the safe deposit box. No recollection of a will. Being caught in a minor lie, Houston conceded. This was a small revelation. Rock was hoping Scott would also reveal Houston's lie at trial in '84 versus his admittance since then, concerning Rock's visit in his office.

Rock leaned toward Sheryl. "The first day I met Scott in his office, Scott said he was dynamic in the courtroom and he would reveal Houston if he did anything wrong."

"Why isnae 'e doin' it?" Sheryl mumbled her complaints.

"Sheryl, it isn't in Houston's nature to tell the truth if there's a way out. And Scott's being too easy on him."

"Impeachment isnae on the minds o' the attorneys, unless Scott publishes Houston's deposition with the court like was done with George Arnold's."

Rock realized she was right. So he waited for Scott to file Houston's deposition with the court clerk. Scott didn't. Rock didn't know what to do, so he did nothing, at least for now. Besides, Scott was out of reach.

*   *   *

Before Rock had a chance to react to Scott's deplorable behavior, Perkins forged ahead interrogating Houston: "Did you get the impression when you opened the safe deposit box that anybody had been in there before you?"

While Ralph Houston appeared stunned at the question, Rock thought the question should have been asked by Scott.

Houston stammered, like he had a burr in his throat: "I . . ." Then he slouched back slightly in his chair. Scott jumped up like he'd just risen from the dead: "I object."

Judge Dodson scowled: "Sustained."

Three outbursts in unison, shooting off in differing directions, but stuck to the same branch. Rock groaned, seeing absolutely no reason for Scott's objection. Rock wanted to hear Houston's answer. At least, now, he knew Scott was alert, only to whose benefit was highly questionable.

Eating another antacid was like putting a small twig on a broken leg. Rock was lost in a sea of legal antics beyond his control. In trying to understand Scott, Rock felt a heavy weight pressing on him, until he could hardly breathe. He felt the need to take another prescription pill, but lost track of when he last swallowed a half. Keeping a clear head was imperative. Staying calm was equally important. He saw no reason for not taking a quarter tablet. So that's what he did.

Chapter Thirty-Four

Growls of hunger rumbled in Rock's stomach. Yet Scott's tactics were killing his appetite. During a brief interlude, Scott said he objected to Perkins' question of someone entering the deposit box before Houston because it was asking for an opinion and opinions don't hold much weight.

Thinking of this now made Rock crave Mother Earth's breath against his face. To hear the lulling splash of the Sound would help him forget this stuffy chamber. Instead, Rock stared at motes dancing in the sunlight spotlighting the room. Houston sat behind the American flag with his hands folded in his lap, waiting for Scott's next question.

Scott: "You indicated in a letter to an accountant that most of the stocks were held in John's name alone?"

Houston: "Oh yez. Most of John's stocks were in his name alone."

Scott: "Isn't it true that stocks held solely in the name of one spouse could be an indication of their separate property status?"

Houston: "Could be."

Rock watched Scott hold the letter in his hands. It was a letter Houston had written to the accountant. Houston's letter listed hundreds of shares in companies like Consolidated Edison, Ford Motor Company, American Telephone and Telegraph, Lucky Stores, Standard Oil of New Jersey, Fundamental Investors Inc. and Massachusetts Investors. This letter was attached to Houston's deposition, wherein Houston admitted stating that all of the above-mentioned shares were issued in John's name alone. To Rock, the letter was important to prove without doubt that Uncle John held separate property.

Scott: "Isn't it also possible that these could be community property and be held as such?"

To Rock this question seem patronizing, like Scott was favoring Houston.

Houston: "Depends as to when they were purchased, whose funds were used for the purchase of the stock."

Rock knew that Scott knew the funds came from the Carper Legacy, spelled out in the 1942 trust agreement executed by the Carper brothers, Jack and John, and witnessed by Nell. He waited for Scott to quibble.

Scott: "So the name is just an indicator?"

Houston: "It doesn't make too much difference if it is taken in the husband's name or the wife's name."

Rock was dismayed. Scott's line of questioning was more to the advantage of the adverse party. He munched antacid tablets, waiting for Scott to enter proof of John's mansion ownership to disprove Houston's testimony.

Scott: "I am handing you the Leucojum documents. Did you receive copies of these documents from Cod Fulbright, or have any contact from him about these after John's death."

Houston refused to receive or look at them: "None whatsoever."

160

Rock shook his head. Of course not. No one in town knew whom Nell's attorney was. Houston didn't file a document showing he was the attorney of record for nine months after John's death. Rock remembered telling this to Scott early on in the trial. And Scott said he would ask Houston. So why isn't he asking?

Scott held the documents: "Among these Leucojum documents is the 1942 trust agreement. Up at the top we see your deceased partner Fred Adams Sr.'s logo with name and address. Would you agree this appears to be from your office?"

Houston seemed to turn a shifty eye at Scott: "I don't recall."

"Ohhhh. Boy." Rock jabbed the palm of his left hand with the right index finger, then thrust the index finger down toward the floor, meaning 'can't'. "Houston can't recall what his deceased partner used, even though he inherited his files, but he can recall an envelope. I can't believe this." Rock slumped forward.

Scott: "One more thing. I know you testified that everything in John's estate was community property. Are you familiar with the Carper mansion?"

Houston: "I certainly know it." He wheezed through his mouth.

Scott: "Did you do any kind of title search, tracing title back on this house?"

"At last. Here it comes." Rock reached over to squeeze Sheryl's hand in happy anticipation.

Houston: "Oh yez. I think it was when the deed was issued, at the time they purchased that property, when it was issued to John and Nell Carper, husband and wife. This is one of the things that made me believe that it was community property."

Rock froze, waiting for Scott to file the Carper house deed. Proof of John's separate ownership to the mansion. Proof that the house was never issued to both John and Nell.

Scott rested.

With gut clenched, Rock wasted no time scribbling and slipping Scott a note asking about the deed.

Scott spoke over his shoulder. "We'll get to that."

This made Rock feel stupid. Indicative that he really didn't know what he was doing. Or, he was irrational. It was 11:45. Perkins asked Houston to identify another exhibit, Nell's petition for the probate of John's estate. Houston identified it. This was an important exhibit. Contained therein were Nell's statements of John's net worth and that he held separate property. Scott stayed clear of these issues.

Waiting for facts of record to come out, Rock checked his frustration, trying to convince himself to rely on professional ethics. He had to. He was butting against a panoply of very intelligent men.

Noon finally arrived. Judge Dodson slid back the left sleeve of his robe to check his watch, then looked at the wall clock: "We'll all meet back here at 1:30." Houston was dismissed.

Scott made fast footwork toward the exit with Rock close behind. Putting a hand on Scott's shoulder, Rock reminded him of his expectations in his slow, deep emphatic voice. "I don't know what your game plan is, but you're reputed to be a good attorney. I'm depending on you to tie loose ends together and enter all evidence necessary to prove my case."

In the hall, Scott smiled at people, strangers to Rock, and disappeared seeming agreeable to the conversation.

*   *   *

A stroll in the crisp cold air and winter sunshine was a welcome relief on his way to the little coffee shop near the courthouse. Fortunately, the smell of the sea in the air stimulated Rock's ailing appetite. Sheryl accompanied him. They hurried through the cafeteria line, selecting vegetable soup, turkey sandwiches and coffee and carried their tray to a corner table.

"In the Clamton County Theater, did ye notice Perkins handin' Houston one exhibit efter another ta identify without askin' questions a'boot content?" Sheryl draped a napkin over her lap, while sitting across from Rock.

"Tell me about it. He strutted up to the clerk's desk like he had crap in his crotch, sliding in evidence without delving into content, without revealing Houston's misconduct." Rock rubbed his throbbing temples. "Scott wasn't any better. Sheryl. What am I going to do? Scott has a way of putting me off whenever he can. I don't like what's going on. Am I supposed to jump up and object?"

"Nae. Ye hired Scott ta do that."

Rock bit into his sandwich relieved at her answer. He thought a client and an attorney wanted the same things. That an attorney represented his client. Being treated like an outcast was bad enough, but not knowing what to do about it was overwhelming. All that happened thus far was too much for Rock to comprehend. Yet, all he had were impressions. There was always an offbeat chance that his impressions were wrong.

"I donnae know. Houston's protectin' Houston."

Rock swallowed. "Everyone is protecting Houston."

"Ay. I cannae figure oot Scott holdin' the stock letter in his hands and no enterin' it inta evidence." Sheryl stirred her soup.

Noises like metal against ceramic came from the direction of the kitchen. Rock leaned forward to better hear and talk. "I noticed that. Scott never demanded proof, some investigative authentic proof as to whose funds were used, or that those shares were community property. I'm upset over the legal procedures."

Sheryl frowned. "Somethin' else. Neither attorney put Houston through the paces they put ye n' George through. I suppose 'cause George came in jeans and 'is job is below that o' an attorney, this gave the attorneys the right ta run him doon."

The ringing of a cash register in the background temporarily distracted Rock. He looked around, noticing more customers going through the line. "Right. When Houston didn't remember, no one pounced on him like George."

"They shaved I. Q. points off the noggin's o' ye n' George. They 'ave a different set o' standards fer their own kind, as if a man's dress and station in life determine his intelligence n' honesty. Do ye suppose this goes on in other courtrooms?"

"I hope not. I'd love to see an attorney question Houston the same way they did George and me. Doesn't look as if it will happen here. Somehow I've got to get inside Scott's head." Rock poked around in his food and sighed. "I can't finish this food."

Sheryl wiped her mouth and hands with a napkin. "Then let's get oot o' 'ere. I'm upset too."

"Thanks Sheryl." At the moment, she seemed like the only friend he had in the world.

*　　*　　*

After lunch, Rock watched Nell's niece Beatrice Benson move into the witness box and smooth her brown-and-white checkered dress with white collar and cuffs. Her hair puffed neatly around her small artfully rouged face. She raised her brows and closed her eyes momentarily to put on glasses, while appearing to listen intently to Perkins' easy questions on her profession.

Beatrice related being a retired nurse. Then they moved on to Nell's auto injuries from the accident that led to Uncle John's demise. Beatrice described them as a fractured pelvis and contusions on the legs. She crossed one arm over her chest to support the other, which was bent upward. Her fingers played with a clip-on earring.

Rock listened to Beatrice recall retrieving Nell from the Nevada hospital and driving her to Seattle one month following the accident.

Beatrice: "My aunt was too weak and wobbly to return to Quamas until July 1st. Until then, she stayed with us in Seattle."

Perkins questioned her as to how long she stayed with Nell once they returned to Quamas. But, Beatrice wasn't one to be pinned down and would only admit to " . . . staying for a while and leaving for a while".

Perkins: "For June and July of 1972, you drove her to the bank?" He spoke softly.

Beatrice: "No, except the end of July. I went with her to attend the opening of the safe deposit box. The state tax examiner and Houston were there to take the state inventory of the box." She led the courtroom audience to believe she didn't leave Nell alone, unattended, right through the end of July.

As she made this claim, Rock visualized her deposition, wherein she admitted to leaving Nell unattended for one full week before the state inventory was held at the end of July. This point was crucial, because of the time element. It allowed Nell time to get into the deposit box and destroy the will before the state inventory. Since Perkins didn't bring out this point, Rock hoped Scott would, as they discussed it several times.

Scott was now walking toward Beatrice. "Do you recall what Mr. Houston and the state tax examiner found in that box?"

Beatrice: "The will. They gave the will to Mr. Houston."

Sheryl scribbled out a note and elbowed Rock to read it: *"Who's telling the truth? And isn't a safe deposit box sealed at death until an official inventory?"*

Rock winced his face because he was in wonder too. Houston said he only knew of an envelope. And, now Beatrice talked about there being a will. And, the inventory listed no will. "Scott told me a bank employee will testify that the box was sealed at John's death, but Nell could enter it to remove insurance policies and wills.

"Nae, really? What a stupid practice." Sheryl exhaled in a whisper. "The safe should 'ave been sealed ta everybody."

"I agree." Rock watched Scott slide a hand in a pocket, while standing behind the lectern. Then Scott changed the subject by asking one question after another about John's heart condition. Six questions total. It was as if Scott's plan to question these relatives about Nell's ability to get into the safe deposit box was forgotten. And, he seemed to be more absorbed with the witness.

Scott's inertia for obtaining some substance, some relevancy, was infuriating. But then, Rock figured, or hoped, that Scott was working on a strategy, going for the obvious in an oddball way. However, when Scott rested without asking anything tangible about when Nell was left alone and the mystery of one will, Rock gripped the bench in irritation. It was Scott's idea to have Beatrice on the stand to determine Nell's condition to get to the bank. So why didn't he pin down these issues?

During a break in proceedings, Rock drew Scott's attention. "We should enter a doctor's report."

"Why?" Scott raised his eyebrows.

"To disprove their contentions on Nell's condition. The report says she was physically able to get into the deposit box before the end of July. You know. Before the state inventory."

Scott frowned negatively. Rock tried again. "Remember Beatrice's statement in her deposition about leaving Nell alone one full week before the state inventory."

Scott acted dumb. When that didn't work, Rock tried again. "Beatrice's memory today is way out of wack with her memory in her deposition."

"Nitpicking."

"What about her statement of one will?"

Scott huffed. "Your pretrial motion asked the court to use prior proceedings as testimony. The judge will read it." He turned his back on Rock.

"Well, sucker." Sheryl sputtered softly, moments later to Rock. "Scott just padded his wallet. He isnae gettin' ta the substance o' anythin'. I'm seein' fish-bait politics at its worst, using marshmallows."

"Sheryl. Behave." Rock sighed wearily. "Okay, you're right. What's a trial without nitpicking?"

"Scott dinnae bother ta ask the niece if she was a major beneficiary o' Nell's '79 will ta show she has a lot ta gain here."

"Scott said the judge will read it." Even so, Rock leaned toward Scott. "What about asking the niece if she was a major beneficiary of Nell's '79 will?"

Scott turned to Rock. "Listen. If I get anywhere near personal interest, the judge will sustain it. He isn't interested in diddly-shit, if it doesn't prove she destroyed John's '67 will."

"Then, why did Perkins spend considerable time trying to prove Sheryl had a personal interest when she wasn't a beneficiary to any will? Justice should work both ways. The niece, whose motive is suspect at best, is a major beneficiary of Nell's 1979 will: $2,200,000 to Beatrice; $2,214,000 in Marvin's name; not to mention the money listed to friends, the Bensons and the church."

"You let me take care of it." Scott's voice was authoritative.

Rock raised his hands in surrender. He felt utterly useless, being excluded from the decision-making process, as if it were none of his business. He searched in his shirt pocket for the other quarter tablet of prescription medicine and quickly swallowed without any concern that he might be taking too much.

Chapter Thirty-Five

Perkins called another witness to the stand, a former teller, who worked at the Quamas bank during the 1970's. She was retired, had gray hair with wrinkled creases around the eyes and mouth and a broad toothy smile. "This is Marvin's witness." Rock related what he knew about her to Sheryl. This witness was a surprise to him although he knew she had presented an affidavit in this case. "Her testimony is about John and Nell's deposit box being sealed at John's death, meaning no one could remove anything, other than wills and insurance policies." Rock stopped whispering to listen further.

Perkins: "After John died did Nell get access to that safe deposit box?"

Teller: "Yes, I remember the day she came in. She had driven in. It was about the middle of July."

"Amen." Rock leaned toward Sheryl.

Sheryl turned toward Rock. "What ya elated a'boot?"

"Oh sweet spirit is shining upon us. Don't you see? Her testimony just made it feasible for Nell to destroy the 1967 will, thanks to Perkins." Rock couldn't believe this break in his favor. He leaned closer to Sheryl to explain. "The teller put Nell in the safe deposit box two weeks before the state inventory. At last, this shoots down the niece and Houston, who claim Nell was too incapacitated." Rock's smile widened, watching Scott move forward for his turn at questioning.

Scott: "How many tellers were working at the bank in 1972?"

"Ahhh. Who cares?" Rock grumbled, thrusting fingers from a balled fist, not bothering to listen to her answer. Scott rested.

Rock complained to Sheryl. "He had the trial drawn out at $1,000 a day for this?" He shook his head at Sheryl. "I can't believe this."

*   *   *

Marvin limped down the center aisle, past Rock to be sworn in. His barrel chest made him look broad and strong. He cleared his throat. Twitched his mustache. Said he was married to Nell's niece Beatrice. That he was the executor of Nell's '79 will and possessed all business and financial records to the Carper estates.

Perkins was gentle in his questioning: "And you made them available to both parties, including all expert witnesses?"

Marvin: "Yes."

Rock shut his eyes and snickered, knowing this was a damn lie. Marvin's answers were made with surly indifference. His answers were rehearsed and too short. Scott's idea of putting Marvin on the stand to prove Nell's ability to access the deposit box was becoming flimsy.

Finally Scott moved forward, scratching his chin: "You became a joint signatory with Nell on her bank accounts?"

Marvin: "I don't remember whether I was a joint signatory." Marvin's voice was gruff, raspy and irritable. He leaned his chin on first one hand and then another.

Rock flashed back to Benson's '84 deposition taken by his attorney, the one who took up mining, establishing that Houston suggested and prepared Marvin with a power of attorney over Nell's affairs during the signing of her 1979 will. Rock remembered chuckling to himself at that deposition, because after Marvin established the year of receiving the power of attorney and the signing of Nell's '79 will, he said he and Beatrice didn't discuss the power of attorney with Houston prior to 1980. Marvin also said he sold Nell's stocks and bonds, inherited from John, in 1980 and 1981 and placed them in CDs and money market certificates in Nell's name. Marvin neglected to tell the attorney he used his power of attorney in 1983, seven months before Nell died of Alzheimer's disease, to transfer Nell's accounts into new accounts for he and Beatrice. Scott knew. But, would Scott bring this out? Rock had reservations.

Scott: "I am handing you Nell's 1983 estate tax return. Specifically, I want to direct your attention to paragraph six under general information. Do you see your name listed there?"

Marvin looked mean. "Yeah." He spoke curtly.

Scott: "Does that mean you are a beneficiary of this estate?"

Marvin: "No. I was co-owner of that amount with Nell."

Scott: "Notice under the column labeled 'amount,' there is a sum there in excess of $2,214,000."

Marvin: "Yes, Nell and I owned those CDs in that amount." He stared angrily at Scott.

Rock enjoyed Marvin being trapped as a joint signatory with Nell. He bared teeth at Marvin and waited for Scott to expose how Marvin became an owner of the CDs. This would show personal interest. Scott rested instead. During a delay in proceedings, Scott reasoned to Rock with a new excuse. "It's irrelevant."

While rolling his eyes to the ceiling, Rock stifled comment.

"Settle down Rock. Now, I know what I'm doing. Please hang in there with me." Scott had a smooth way of settling Rock by switching his attention to the new order of business. "Addressing proper execution of John's 1967 will is next on the agenda. According to law, two witnesses are required to sign a testator's will, attesting to his signature and it must be done in the presence of one another. I'll read statements of one attesting witness, Henry Stoner, from the 1984 record."

"Whatever." Rock shook his head. Internally he was still pissed off and Scott knew, but acted like he didn't care.

Scott made it look like anything Rock wanted was irrelevant and nitpicking. He honestly didn't know what to make of this. The temptation to walk out was strong, like he did to Judge Randell in '84. But, he couldn't see playing the humiliating role of the betrayed client again. Besides, the medication was calming him from that kind of behavior.

"Who's Henry Stoner?" Sheryl squinted her eyes.

"Henry Stoner is the Quamas banker who befriended John and signed as one witness on John's will." By this stage in the trial, Rock was relieved to have more witness testimony read into the record. It was easier than listening to Scott and Perkins fire sickening questions to confuse a witness. Yes, by using this reading method, not much could go wrong. Or, could it?

Scott was sworn in as Henry Stoner and read what Rock surmised as about two pages of Stoner's testimony. Then the judge called for recess. Scott disappeared. Rock shrugged his shoulders, rose and suggested to Sheryl they go stand on the courthouse steps for privacy. Not that he had anything important to say. He was developing a complex of paranoia. At the moment, his thoughts and words seemed to evaporate into nothing.

*   *   *

Recesses and lunch breaks meant fresh air. A time for Rock to inhale. And, a time for Sheryl to exhale. At least that's the way it seemed to him, because she did most of the talking out in front of the courthouse.

"I donnae believe what's goin' on taday. Does Scott ask the niece if she's a beneficiary? Nae. But 'e asked Marvin."

Rock watched pigeons on the walk in front of the steps.

"Ferget the pigeons and listen ta me while I'm talkin' ta ye."

He hoisted a pant leg, putting his left foot one step up from where he was standing. He said nothing. His brain felt like a tangled mess. Besides she could read his mind.

"Then Scott failed ta ask Marvin 'ow 'e became a co-owner with Nell on those CDs. Money Nell illegally inherited from John's estate. Proof was in 'er '79 tax return, showin' she paid estate tax on bonds she inherited through fraud."

Rock knew Sheryl was recanting what Nell's accountant wrote on her tax return: "That Nell inherited the Series E Bonds from John's estate, made possible only after she and Houston repudiated the community property agreement."

Sheryl continued: "And Marvin and Houston are tryin' ta make everyone think John 'eld only community property." Sheryl sat on a step between the towering columns.

Rock looked out into space. A few puffy clouds scudded across the sky. Cars whizzed by. People walked past them, going in and out of the courthouse. "Don't forget Marvin used his power-of-attorney prepared by Houston."

"Ay. And, Scott dinnae ask Marvin when 'e entered himself as a joint signatory with Nell, which was in 1983."

"When she was well into Alzheimer's. Scott knows this."

"But, the judge donnae know it."

Squaring his shoulders, he moved toward the door. "Scott says the judge will read it in the record. My pretrial motion. Remember? Come on. You'll get cold out here."

Sheryl followed, still sputtering in sarcastic tones. "Beatrice and Marvin's testimony will be fergotten. Ye'll see. Scott's no doin' ye any good."

Rock was sure Scott would do something with the teller's testimony. She proved Nell entered the deposit box. And, although the judge came across as a little dense, Rock didn't believe him stupid. He'd see through their antics. Wouldn't he?

*   *   *

Following recess, Scott stood behind the lectern drawing the court's attention to the affidavit of the other attesting witness, Russell Fulton, another longtime attorney friend of John Carper's, who was now deceased. Rock wondered why Scott jumped to Fulton. He couldn't have finished with Stoner. Rock closed his eyes and strained to recollect the '84 record of Henry Stoner's testimony. Surely there was more than what Scott read before recess, like nine pages or more. All of Stoner's testimony was absolutely essential to prove proper execution of John's will. But, Rock couldn't remember for sure. His memory on this was like an ocean wave breaking on shore, only to slip away.

If Rock questioned Scott, he'd get the same pat answers: The judge will read it in the pretrial motion. Don't nitpick. Hang in there. Trust. He tried to trust, because his judicial knowledge could be carved on the eye of an eagle.

Meanwhile, Scott stood behind the lectern directing attention to Russell Fulton: "I ask the court to take note of this affidavit from Mr. Fulton's son."

Judge Dodson: "It is being offered to do what?" He shifted his glasses to his forehead and squinted down at Scott.

Scott: "It has been offered as the closest thing we have to prove the signature of one of the attesting witnesses who is deceased."

Judge Dodson: "I understand. Where do we go beyond that? You're saying, if I accept this Fulton affidavit, then the '67 will is established and proved? What's the bottom line?"

Scott: "Oh, I think that is the bottom line, but the statute on lost wills requires . . ."

Judge Dodson cut him off. "I understand that."

Scott: "I'm offering to prove due execution of the 1967 will."

Judge Dodson: "That's what I wanted to know. I'll take note of the Fulton affidavit in proving his signature as an attesting witness to the 1967 will." He dismissed court until tomorrow.

Rock rose, stood in the aisle and waited. As Scott approached, Rock accosted him. "Are things going right?"

"As right as possible." Scott's brow shot up. "Why?"

"Things aren't right. Maybe we should cancel this trial."

Scott leaned on one hip. "Look. There has already been trial delays. Judge Dodson won't grant anymore. No one knows that things aren't right at this stage. We won't know the outcome until the last day when Dodson makes some kind of determination."

Rock had to agree, he couldn't second guess Judge Dodson. Obviously in a hurry, Scott made a run for the exit, after quickly explaining over a shoulder that he had an appointment.

With no one of legal authority to talk to any further, Rock ambled slowly out of the room uncertain of his legal position.

*   *   *

Sheryl followed Rock down the courthouse steps. "Scott, who assured ye that all previous trial testimony, depositions and probate documents would be used, made no attempt ta use 'em in searchin' fer the truth."

"Take a breath Sheryl."

"Well, so many questions were left unasked. I thought ye said Scott was a firecracker. Or, did ye say dynamite? What's 'e waitin' fer? I'm waitin' fer him ta take up knittin'."

"Okay, okay. I agree."

"He looks like a damned Kewpie doll with freckles. The wimp: chargin' ye $1,000 a day. That cock-o'-the-south Perkins paces so much the carpet is wearin' thin. He's the only one in the room gettin' exercise. And, Scott's cross-examination o' Nell's relatives was more befittin' ta job interviews, where the interviewer asks a'boot hobbies, fergettin' the job skills."

"Knock it off." Rock spouted in anger. "Breathe, Sheryl." Silently, he agreed. Scott asked some innocuous questions.

"Eatin' too many antacids must be affectin' ye. Cannae ye see things arenae right?" She extended two fingers from her eyes.

"Look, I'm not angry with you. Maybe we're overreacting. Think about it. Scott came highly recommended by Jasper. Scott's an attorney. Attorneys are governed by ethics. The guy has to abide by professional ethics. I'll hold him to that. Believe me. Besides, we don't understand his intellectual posturing." Even though Rock agreed with Sheryl's words, he was frustrated, unable to entirely convince himself of his own words. Yet, he didn't need Sheryl nagging him. "Scott hasn't fired his fuse yet. That's all."

"Blarney. Ye're off the reservation and greener than the spit of a leprechaun." She hugged her arms as if cold and stormed off, mumbling something to the effect that he didn't understand her. She was taking medicine and felt differently about things, including her feelings for him.

At first, her accusations caused disgust to well inside him. He really did appreciate her support. But as soon as they left the courtroom, while he yearned for some ray of hope, her support came across as blame. Like it was his fault when things went wrong. Or, maybe it was her way of making him face reality and he resented it. Maybe this was what Scott was trying to make him do – face reality. He quickly shed the notion. But, Sheryl's parting remarks stopped him cold. Taking medicine? Her feelings for him? Was she changing her mind about their divorce?

He watched Sheryl purse her lips and strut away with an air of conceit. She put distance between them. This was one of those times when he wondered what he ever saw in her. "Don't come back tomorrow." With other people laughing and talking between them, he didn't know if she heard him.

He continued down the stairs. For sure, he was off the reservation and green, maybe not in the ways she meant. He knew he couldn't tolerate her gripes and these attorneys much longer. The case was making his nature explosive. A realization he couldn't get a handle on without his prescription pill and antacids.

More immediate, a big question crept into his head. What if he lost this case because of slick attorneys? Rock needed help. Advice from someone he trusted. Maybe Jasper Fulbright.

Chapter Thirty-Six

Court was in session for the fifth day with no relief in sight. Even so, Rock rubbed his fingers over his good-luck lapel pin. He needed justice, truth and honor coming his way more now than ever, because attempts to contact Jasper Fulbright before today failed. Jasper was on vacation and not expected home until January. Rock's luck was running amuck.

Now, here they were in Courtroom Two, the usual audience, including persistent Sheryl, with the addition of two new witnesses: Marvin's ink expert and his document expert.

Despite Rock's prior offer to accept the written reports of Marvin's ink expert, Richard Green was nevertheless flown in from Florida to the Coast. Green, appearing in his fifties, was tall, slim and immaculately dressed. He was rather homely with a crew cut, eyes set close together and a pointed chin. Rock tilted his head and listened to Green give an impressive chemistry background.

During Perkins' direct examination, Green recited his pretrial written reports verbatim, identifying two types of blue ink in John's handwritten initials on the Leucojum documents. Type A and Type B. Both inks were available in the '70's. This information wasn't harmful to Rock's documents.

At one point, Green's testimony brought amusement to Rock because he tripped himself by leaving a preposterous five-year gap between discontinuance of type A blue ink and the introduction of type B blue ink. Green admitted both types contained an important ingredient: Iron galactonate. Then, he added a new element at trial. That blue ink containing iron should have turned black over a twenty-year period.

"Lordie. He's entering new testimony. That ink with iron identified on the Leucojum documents should turn black with age."

"News to me." Rock fidgeted around on the bench. Sheryl smelled and looked so good, it was difficult to concentrate. And, he was determined to find out about what medicine she was taking, but so far hadn't had an opportunity. Maybe he didn't want to take the opportunity. He felt as depressed as yesterday, waiting for proof that never came.

Finally Rock returned his focus on Perkins, who asked Green about inked notes written by Leucojum on an envelope to Houston concerning an unrelated legal matter. Another surprise not discussed during the discovery process. The envelope was entered as an exhibit.

Even Scott stopped his infernal habit of tapping a pen against his teeth to admit his surprise: "Your Honor, I have not received a report of this exhibit."

Judge Dodson, seeming to ponder the fate of nations, looked at each of the attorneys and volunteered no comment.

Perkins rebutted, pragmatically: "If Scott didn't get it, I apologize."

Scott appeared to be concentrating. He fingered his pen end over end, then raised his hands in resignation: "No objections."

Judge Dodson: "If Mr. Scott has no objections, proceed."

"Geez. I mind." Rock exhaled. Well, if the judge didn't object and Scott didn't, then this must be legal. He convinced himself that Green said nothing significant about the ink on the envelope anyway. And, Rock was feeling worn out complaining to Scott, whose pat answers sounded like a tape recording. He fumbled around for an antacid as Perkins continued. Fortunately, Green had nothing further on this issue.

Scott appeared stiff moving to the lectern for cross-examination of Green. Rock called it a waddle with fat buns from inactivity. Scott soon developed the premise that Green made his living as a for-hire witness working from his own business, Green Forensic Laboratories. This was the expert's nineteenth experience in court. His fee could conceivably be as high as $8,000 for pretrial work, but settled on $3,000 for his trips to Seattle.

Scott: "I assume, from your area of expertise, you know that there are lots of folks in this country who just never would accept the ball point pen?"

Green: "There are a few diehards who wouldn't accept the ball point pen, preferring fountain pens, yes. Matter of fact, there are a lot of the fountain-pen products on the market today. They are making a very strong comeback right now. I just bought a set of fountain pens."

Green was well spoken but didn't make much sense to Rock. The words 'a few diehards' wouldn't be enough to support a market flooded with a lot of pen products. Wasn't this simple economics? So, Rock could have cared less about the popularity of fountain pens in Florida, Quamas or nationwide.

Scott: "The fact that the Leucojum documents were signed in two kinds of ink, it's possible John signed a document, went to lunch and picked up a different pen when he returned?"

Green: "I wouldn't do it, but anything is possible."

Scott: "John could have run out of ink and had to open another bottle?" Scott leaned against the defendant's table.

Green: "Yes, could happen."

Scott: "If the Leucojum documents were stored in a closed container for a long time, would that account for the blue ink?"

Green: "If the documents have been stored in that dark and closed-in container for twenty years that accounts for the blue ink."

Tribal drums beat in Rock's head; a moment of jubilation. In essence, Marvin's own expert authenticated the Leucojum documents due to storage conditions. Unbelievable.

Judge Dodson lauded Green before dismissing him: "I want to say that being from a small town, it's an honor and a pleasure to have a person with your talents and expertise in my courtroom."

Rock noticed that Perkins' demeanor exuded such pride over this remark, that he might as well have hugged himself. Rock could have hugged him too.

*   *   *

Marvin's forensic document expert, Ben Anderson, neatly attired in a brown suit, moved to the stand. He was about sixty, medium height and build, pale, thin sandy-colored hair and stubby nose. Perkins directed easy questions to reveal Anderson's fine background and residence in Washington, formerly from a New Jersey police department division. He was now semi retired.

Rock wasn't concerned about Anderson's testimony, as it was already on record that he found nothing adverse to the Leucojum documents. And, Rock believed his own expert's report of record would be entered into evidence, authenticating these documents.

Anderson implanted the idea that he originally determined John's writings to be fluent, which didn't mean much since there were inadequate specimens of John's writings. Thus, based on this same information today, Anderson was now, suddenly changing his original testimony: "I revised my original examination on specimens of John's inked initials taken from each page of the Leucojum documents."

Anderson cleared his throat. "In otherwords, I made an exemplar by cutting copies of the initials JFC 5/9/72 from each page of the Leucojum documents and pasting them on a single sheet of paper for my revised analysis." Anderson left the stand to display and explain his exemplar, using a large screen and projector and pointing with a long stick.

"That isn't anythin' new." Sheryl whispered. "The Leucojum documents and those initials 'ave been around since ye found them in 1985. Ye were put off fer years fer this?"

Rock had to admit, with disgust, this is exactly what happened. And, Anderson's exemplar of specimens, not entered into evidence, was used only to nitpick over the size of the writings. Anderson speculated that John initialed his documents at one sitting, therefore all should be the same size, without offering any authenticated writings known to be John Carper's.

Anderson returned to the witness stand.

Perkins: "With respect to the initials 'JFC 5/9/72' on each page of the Leucojum documents, you are saying that they were probably not authored by John?" Perkins paced energetically, like he had a good night's sleep, which was more than Rock could say.

Anderson: "That's correct." He put a hand to his mouth to cover a sneeze.

Perkins: "Each entry of 'JFC 5/9/72', there are so many differences between the two, that they're probably not all written at the same time?"

Anderson: "They were not written all at the same time and could be an explanation for the differences. Or maybe one person did the initials and someone else did the dates." Anderson pulled out a hanky and blew his nose.

"Maybe." Rock mimicked Anderson's answer and snickered over his speculation, which Scott appeared oblivious to. Judge Dodson appeared non-committal. Thus, Rock remained unruffled.

*　*　*

"He's daffy, that Anderson, contradictin' himself that a'way. What's 'e sayin', anyhow?" Sheryl complained to Rock in a café during lunch. She squeezed lemon into her cup of tea.

"Damned if I know. Truth from his lips was a double-edged scalpel. Scott allows speculation. Guess it doesn't matter. Scott says Ben Anderson can't talk with knowledge anyway." Rock chewed on his cheese and ham sandwich, while looking around at the other diners, then reported to Sheryl through clenched teeth. "My opposition is over by the window." They saw the Bensons, Perkins, Adams and Anderson. "Cozy like a bundle of crooked arrows in a quiver."

"There's room fer all o' us. Ferget ye saw 'em. As ye were sayin'?"

"Anderson hasn't any samples of John's writings beyond the Leucojum documents. Scott said Judge Dodson will see right through him."

"I donnae know. Opinions, I admit, donnae make facts, that's fer sure. The judge'll see through opinions, we 'ave ta bank on that. Judges are extremely intelligent and wise. Lordie, just think o' the mess our country'd be in withoot wise judges. Sooo, we 'ave ta bank on Dodson's smarts. He'll form his decisions on the real facts o' record. But, I'm feelin' ye need yer expert 'ere. I'll pay his fee. Ye ask Scott what 'e thinks."

"Thanks Sheryl, I will." Rock was overwhelmed by her offer. "What do you know about the judge?" He rubbed his sore neck.

"Nothin'. I havena lived here long enough ta find oot. Mum and Dad donnae know anythin' either. None o' us 'ave anythin' ta do with legal folks around 'ere. We're learnin' from yer diggin's. The judge looks honest. He sustained us a lot. Donnae look now, but 'e just walked in the door."

Rock couldn't help turn around and watch the display of cordiality. Before long, Judge Dodson, in a tan business suit, looking smaller without his robe, moved on to visit with folks sitting at other tables, working his way toward Rock and Sheryl's table. However, he never approached them, as if they didn't exist.

Finally, Rock suggested they leave to stretch their stiff muscles before returning to court. Anderson hadn't been released from trial yet. His testimony could make or break Rock's case.

Sheryl clutched his arm as they walked. "Thanks fer stickin' up fer me the other day."

"No problem." She seemed inordinately friendly; much to his enjoyment. In fact, other than feeling rather giddy, he was amazingly relaxed.

"Let's drive ta the beach."

Apparently, she wanted to reminisce. "Arrow Head Point? You're kidding." He stretched his arm to shorten the sleeve of his coat and looked at the time. "We've got an hour." The weather was cold and overcast, but no rain or snow threatened. "Well, okay." He wanted to talk to her anyway.

*   *   *

Rock drove them to a stretch of beach not far from the ferry landing. Watching passengers and cars load off and on the ferry was a reprieve, even from a distance. And, working against the sting of a biting wind, they walked and talked on the way to the huge rocks, high above the splash zone.

A scene of natural beauty abounded: The rise and fall of the lapping sea on the sand below. There were sun-bleached log snarls piled like pick-up sticks. Sea algae tinged the rocks at water's edge. Madronas leaned over the banks. In the summer, those trees shaded the sandy flats. The beach was strewn with stones, sea moss and seaweed. There were many bits of marine shells in a small midden. Kelp beds abounded. Up above, the sky was limitless; serene.

This place brought a private moment to Rock. He recalled silently that they used to picnic near here. He wondered if Sheryl remembered. Why would she? She didn't love him anymore. It was over, so why did he let her talk him into coming here? A diversion from court perhaps. Hell, the way things were going, he needed a diversion from life.

Sheryl picked up a short stick, called smoke wood. "We used ta light these and pretend we were smokin' cigars." She held it like a cigar for a while before flicking it over the bank.

Rock inhaled wind-sent whiffs of seaweed, fish and salt. "Oh. I love the smell. Like home sweet home."

"We used to 'ave crab races in the sand. Remember?"

"Ummm hmmm." At least she was remembering some things of the past. "We put the crabs into the center of a circle. Whose ever crab left the circle first was the winner. What a crazy game." He laughed. This place carried him away to other memories too. Of Sheryl and him building bonfires from driftwood, of them raking steamer clams and tossing them into a bucket, of them riding bicycles into the water and falling in, bikes and all. Her hair hung limp like seaweed. Her makeup had washed away, her clothes clung and she attracted him as no other woman could.

"Ye kissed me waaaay over there in yer car." She pointed. "We were hidden in the trees."

His eyes followed Maidenhead ferns, flanking a grove of pines, up to the tops of the tall stately timbers that endure all seasons. His strength used to flourish by them. Now, he rarely came here. But, this wasn't what Sheryl had in mind. He remained standing beside her, finally turning to meet her stare. She was still a beauty. Their eyes seemed to search in each other's: a time for shared memories.

As he listened to the splash of water lick the beach, Rock placed his hands on her shoulders and held her firm. "Do you remember the night I asked you to marry me; to be my friend for all seasons?"

She stared up at him, seeming sad. "Ay. I vowed, we'd be tagether always."

"What happened to us?"

"My hormones quit on me. But . . ." Her voice trailed.

She was about to tell him something, when the ferry whistled departure time. Rock checked his watch. "Geez. We'd better go too." If late to court, he doubted anyone would miss him, but he had to hear what more Anderson had to say. They ran for the car. In the excitement, he could only focus on one thing. The trial.

Chapter Thirty-Seven

"John wrote the initials on the Leucojum documents." Anderson concluded to Scott during the afternoon session, after admitting having received one example of John's initials during the lunch break, which wasn't entered into evidence. Yet, Rock wasn't about to complain over good news.

During an analysis of the signature "John" on the May cover letter, Anderson hemmed and hawed around in identifying an exception in the letter "n" which he said didn't look like John's writing. This didn't help Rock any, and he noticed the opposition still hadn't provided any external samples of John's signatures and ignored those on all the other Leucojum documents.

Scott repeated his question, sounding more emphatic: "Well, did John sign the May 9th letter or not?"

Anderson: "Outside of his normal variations as John signs his name, I really couldn't put too much significance on the indications, or that he probably didn't sign."

Using sign for 'What's he meaning?' Sheryl cupped a hand to her heart, then made compression movements with her palms, before rolling her eyes.

Rock returned in sign. "Geezus. I can't understand this bull. Take your pick. Yes, no, sure, maybe, or whatever."

"I'm wonderin' if the judge'll take it ta mean no."

Rock looked at Judge Dodson, who leaned back in his chair, while seeming to fight drowsiness, sucking on another lozenge and fingering his pen. A derogatory snicker was about the extent of Rock's gut reaction, since Anderson couldn't come up with a definitive answer.

When Scott rested and returned to the table, Rock reasoned with him very softly. "Ask him about the 'J' in "John" in John's 1952 will where that 'J' is way out of whack. That's the fly in the ointment of whomever created it."

"Shhhh. That's nitpicking. The judge doesn't want nitpicking. Besides, the '52 will isn't in question here. The '67 will is. I don't want to tick him off."

"What'd 'e say?" Sheryl leaned forward.

"Mustn't tick off the judge." Rock knew Scott was right, but Rock also believed he had a good point for argument. If Anderson authenticated the "J" in "John" in the cover letter, then the "J" in the 1952 will Nell probated under, was a forgery. Rock would have liked that. What's a trial without nitpicking? Yet, who was he to say, suggest or criticize with so little experience in all this legal stuff. He hated this feeling of being tied and gagged, putting his stomach in turmoil.

Sheryl scowled, making signs for a canoe and paddle and shaking her head. "He's paddlin' upstream in a leaky canoe an' no paddle, or maybe we are."

Perkins stepped forward: "Hokay. I'd like to enter a letter Rock wrote; a companion letter to Sheryl's; a 'To whom it may concern' letter."

This grabbed Rock's attention away from Sheryl. He knew exactly what Perkins was going for. It wasn't the typed contents of the letter that concerned

Rock, but rather his handwritten notes in the margins written in confidence to his former attorney, the one who took up mining, that bothered him. He leaned toward Sheryl. "No one told me my handwriting was an issue."

"Oou, an idiot knows yer chicken-scratch squiggles couldna be called hand writin'." Sheryl snapped, at odds with Perkins' purpose. "Are ye goin' ta sit there and let them use that? He's makin' ye look bad and muddyin' the waters. Ye cannae be lettin' them use that ta conclude ye forged John's fluent writin's on the Leucojum documents. Get Scott off 'is kidney stones."

Rock propelled himself into action like his strings snapped. He had taken enough. No more excuses from Scott would suffice. "Hey, nobody ever asked me to have my handwriting analyzed. A trial isn't the place to conduct an investigation. Besides, you should be objecting on grounds of attorney-client privilege, shouldn't you? You can see for yourself that my writing on that 'To whom it may concern" letter isn't like John's writing."

Scott didn't react to Rock's question about the attorney-client privilege, but it prompted him into immediate action, getting the letter withdrawn as an exhibit. Rock settled down.

The clock ticked by as Anderson testified, offering no authenticated exhibits to prove his opinions. Rock felt he answered questions cautiously, as if to not overcommit himself, while favoring those who paid him.

Scott now questioned Anderson about John's cover letter: "Don't you suppose John signed off "Fraternally" was because he and Cod Fulbright were Mason's; members in the same group?"

Anderson: "Maybe, but that wasn't John's usual pattern."

Rock snickered, wondering how anyone would know for certain without proof, of which Anderson had none.

Scott sat as Perkins sashayed forward.

Perkins: "I'd like to publish these John Carper letters."

Scott stood: "What does publish mean?"

This put Rock on edge again. He didn't know what letters they were discussing.

Perkins: "I want to show these letters to the judge."

Scott glanced around from side wall to side wall; taking his time; thinking. Then he looked at Perkins and shrugged his shoulders: "Oh. Well, okay. I've no objection."

Emotions inside Rock went berserk, now watching Judge Dodson sift through several dozen letters, none of which were ever shown to Rock. The two days he and Sheryl spent at Perkins' law firm came to mind. They saw no letters from Uncle John.

Judge Dodson: "Why, that's enough to boggle my mind." The judge looked down at Rock. Rock felt like the judge was viewing him as an ugly slug.

Only antacids were holding him together. Of all things, his prescription medicine was at the Leucojum house. He was certain his inadvertence was due to parts of the trial being incomprehensible, leaving him breathless. There was never time to catch up to the goings on, to fully understand things. And, he suddenly realized he had developed a fear of the legal power before him. Like the judge, Rock's mind was boggled too, knowing John Carper signed none of those letters. Otherwise, Marvin would have entered them into evidence.

Yet, Scott's complacency prompted Rock into more action. "What kind of a massacre is this? What does he mean, publish?" With narrowed eyes, Rock joggled Scott to listen.

"Shut up; calm down." Scott's jaw jetted out. His ire was visible in stiff lips. "The letters weren't proven to belong to John."

Surprised by Scott's rude abruptness, Rock gazed at the floor. He detested the tension going on between them. Being raised as an only child, he wasn't used to this. The push-pull electricity of conflict was awful. Nevertheless, he held firm. "Then why show them to anyone; especially the judge?"

"We just have a different way of doing things here."

Rock chuckled, derogatorily. At least he let Scott know he wasn't a pushover. Little good that was doing.

*   *   *

Scott moved forward: "Part of the Leucojum documents are John and Jack's trust agreement, which has a blue covering with Fred Adams Sr.'s logo, brass riveted to the two-page document."

Rock knew, of course, that Adams Sr. died long ago, leaving his son Adams Jr. to carry on. Too bad he was left to partner with Houston. Rock felt Houston was turning Jr. into a crook.

Scott: "You would have me believe Rock broke into Houston's office to steal the old brass rivets and blue paper?"

Anderson nodded: "I presume so."

Sheryl gnashed her teeth. "Scott's got rats in 'is cellar."

Rock grinned. "No, I understand what Scott's doing. He's showing how ridiculous this is; me breaking into their office."

Before long Perkins entered another exhibit prepared by Anderson, poor facsimiles of the Leucojum documents. It was apparent to Rock that this was to sway the judge that the Leucojum documents could have been created in 1984. Rock had not been provided with this surprise evidence before trial.

Scott soon revealed his knowledge of this exhibit: "I believe your fake documents prepared to look like the Leucojum documents were just typed?"

Anderson: "Yes."

Perkins sprung into action: "Objection."

The attorneys argued. Nothing was solved. Judge Dodson looked confused.

Perkins took over: "Your Honor, it's Mr. Scott's turn."

Scott looked at his notes; then continued with Anderson: "In creating your fake documents like the Leucojum documents, where did you get the date stamp?"

Anderson: "From another attorney in Quamas, a friend of Mr. Houston's."

Scott: "Where did you get the thermofax machine?"

Anderson: "Actually Ralph Houston found it."

Sheryl whispered. "Dinnae Uncle John 'ave a thermofax?"

"Yes, but he sold it with the fish business."

Scott pressed on: "And the typewriter?"

Anderson: "Adams Jr. and Marvin Benson got the old Underwood typewriter and xerox machine. They did the typing and I went to Midget Incorporated to do some thermofax testing."

Midget Incorporated didn't ring a bell with Rock. He never knew until now that his opposition had been doing experiments. And, he suddenly realized it was a team effort that enabled them to fabricate documents somewhat like the Leucojum documents. And, this enabled them to slip in more surprise evidence, that the date stamp and notary seal would not show up on thermofaxed copy, that the thickness of the 1942 trust agreement, the two pages brass-riveted to a cover paper, would not fit into a thermofax machine.

Rock's head felt like it was about to explode. His knuckles throbbed from clenching his fists. Restraint was difficult to check. All these surprises were making it definitely a tough day.

Perkins elicited more testimony from Anderson about thermofaxing, until Scott objected and Judge Dodson said he heard nothing from Anderson that qualified him as a thermofax expert, which greatly pleased Rock. However, the ruling soon appeared short lived, as Perkins continued quizzing Anderson during redirect examination: "Was the ink on your documents visible when you thermofaxed?"

Anderson: "No."

The pressure in Rock had built up again, pushing to explode through his fingers. All patience was gone. He moved boldly up to the counsel table to sit beside Scott and slammed a fist on the table. Narrowed his eyes. Frowned. "Ask Anderson about the thermofaxing effect of ink containing iron." Rock emphasized the word "iron". Scott returned his usual dumb stare, like his cylinders were still on autopilot. "If you don't ask him, I will." Again, Rock beat a fist on the table. He intended for his voice to be threatening. He no longer cared if Judge Dodson witnessed their hushed bantering, indignant faces and nodding heads. So be it, if Dodson considered Rock savage.

* * *

Finally, Scott relented to Rock's demand on recross-examination of Anderson. He stood with bent posture behind the counsel table: "You told Mr. Perkins that ink won't thermofax. So, is it your testimony that no ink signature will copy on thermofax?"

Anderson: "To my knowledge, liquid ink will not process."

Scott: "That depends on the contents of the ink, as to whether or not it has iron in it?"

Anderson: "Certainly. That's what reproduces."

"Yesssss." This was a big break. Rock clenched his fists in elation. Anderson's answer erased all Anderson's prior testimony in Rock's mind. That's because the Florida ink expert previously identified iron in the two types of ink on the Leucojum documents.

But, while settling back in the chair, Rock couldn't feel total relief, not after what he'd just gone through with his own attorney. Having to force Scott to ferret pertinent testimony made it apparent that Scott's actions weren't in sync with the original intentions for which he was hired. Rock wondered if the judge heard any of this. The great tyee was leaning back in his chair studying the ceiling. Rock looked upward, seeing florescent lighting. This had nothing to do with his case.

Scott lowered himself into his chair in a huff, grumbling. "You don't understand what's going on. Shut up now. I'm running things." Scott emitted a mean expression like Rock was a stupid agitation in his cultivated life.

Geez. The firecracker surfaced. Scott finally shook off his lazy lassitude like a fish out of water. He came alive. Red-faced, unglued, exploding at the wrong person. His client. Revulsion jarred Rock's mind. "What the hell is going on?" Rock demanded undeterred, looking Scott straight in the eyes. If anything, Anderson's testimony was the arrow to bring down the elk. "The guy just perjured himself in our favor. You just bagged him."

While Scott wiped a hand over his mouth and mumbled, Rock wrote him a note: *"Sheryl is willing to pay to have Woods come to trial and testify."*

Scott vehemently rejected the idea; still acting resentful of being told by his client what to do.

So Rock accosted Scott. "Things aren't going right."

"You don't know that."

"I smell the tide. Do something. Cancel this trial."

"Look. We've been over trial delays before. No one knows that things aren't right. No one knows the outcome until Dodson gives his oral opinion. For chrissake, this thing is going to be won or lost on closing arguments. So don't jump to conclusions."

Rock backed off, believing Scott would tie together all loose ends in his golden words. Closing arguments. Whatever that meant, Rock wasn't sure. It sounded impressive. Scott must be working on a plan. Saving the best for last.

* * *

Rock and Sheryl left the courthouse passing Perkins, Marvin and their experts huddled off to one side; conversing.

"Somethin's wrong with Perkins. He 'as a wild look on 'is face and in 'is eyes."

"He's an attorney. I've been getting those looks all week."

"Nae, look. He's smokin'. I dinnae know Perkins smoked."

"He doesn't." Rock glanced at the huddle. They looked like a tight group having an energetic debate.

"Weeel, look at him. Smokin' and lookin' foolish ta boot."

Sure enough, as they neared the knot of men, Perkins, red-faced, was smoking with a shaky hand, his magic aura gone. "I'll be damned. He's ticked off over something." Rock was too tired to care. He bid Sheryl a good day, with intentions of heading for the ferry and Seattle. He had work to catch up on, bills to pay and mail to answer before trial on Monday. And, his plans were to phone Unali and Efrem over the weekend. He needed their advice.

"Rock. Wait."

He turned around to Sheryl.

"I'm sorry. I need a ride home. A taxi brought me 'ere this mornin'. I was afraid it might snow. Can ye take me 'ome?" Her dark blue eyes and smile pleaded up at him.

"No problem." It was the least he could do, since she had been his moral support.

Chapter Thirty-Eight

"Ummmm. Smells good." Rock inhaled the fine aromas associated with homemade stew the moment he walked through Sheryl's front door.

"I had the crock pot simmerin' all day. Beef stew the way ye like it. Take yer wraps off and go wash. I'll 'ave fixin's on the dinin' table in a jif."

Rock did as instructed. No question, he was hungry and needed a solid meal. A steady diet of cold sandwiches all week hadn't helped his stomach. Finally, he returned to the dining area and leaned in the archway facing the kitchen. Sheryl was spooning stew into large soup bowls. "Thanks for inviting me to dinner."

"Knowin' ye, ye'd skip dinner or eat junk food on the ferry back ta Seattle. Ye're no takin' care o' yerself like ye should."

Before long, they were seated at the dining room table, laughing about old times. It felt good to relax, laugh and eat in Sheryl's company, away from the pressures of the trial. For too long, his emotions and nerves had been in high gear. Starting his weekend break like this was more than welcome.

After finishing their stew, Rock assisted in clearing the table. They moved onto the sofa in the living area and drank wine under one dim light. Sheryl turned on the stereo and disappeared for a short while. Soft music played in the background. He pushed off his shoes and crossed his feet over a corner of the coffee table.

Sheryl came in wearing a fancy robe cut low in front. Her heeled slippers were gold. Rock's eyes widened. He felt uncomfortable.

"Have some more wine." She poured.

Rock looked at his watch. "I best beat it if I want to arrive in Seattle tonight." He downed the wine, set his wine flute on the coffee table and pushed it toward the center to emphasize his intentions.

Sheryl moved closer to him. "Stay 'ere tanight."

Their eyes met for what seemed like four moons. Rock leaned back against the corner of the sofa, one arm across the backrest. "What are you suggesting by 'stay here'?" The wine, the music, Sheryl's outfit, her plump cleavage, her proposal. He knew what she was up to, but needed time to think. This was not like her. For years, he did the chasing, until he finally quit.

Admittedly it was due to her medical condition. Anhedonia. He remembered the doctor telling him this was a mental disorder caused genetically and by a chemical imbalance in a region of the brain. Those afflicted with anhedonia function normally, but lack the ability to be happy. This explained why Sheryl found no enjoyment in many things important to married couples, including love and a pleasant sunny day.

"Give me a chance? Please?" She placed a hand high up on his thigh.

Rock jumped off the sofa and raised his hands. "Whoa. This is too sudden. You've taken me completely by surprise Sheryl."

"Nothin' should be surprisin'." She rose to face him.

"But, we're strangers now." The situation was a challenge.

"Are we? I've stood by ye. Ye're losin' and I still stand by ye." She wouldn't back off.

"You kicked me out. Have you forgotten?"

"Even so, I've still stood by ye."

"That's because you're a valuable witness. Why are you doing this now? What has changed your mind? I'm still the same person I was before. I'm still part Indian, which you tried to stifle all our winters together. Why?" Confused, Rock backed away from her and stumbled down into the sofa. "You have no interest in me, in love . . ."

Sheryl cuddled near him. "Efter movin' back to Quamas, I missed ye terribly. And, I'm takin' medicine fer my problem."

Rock thought about her condition. This must have been what she was talking about during the heat of a recent argument and he was too thick skulled to inquire. Always thinking about the trial. He raised an eyebrow. "And you want to use me to see if the medicine works?"

"Well, ye donnae 'ave ta put it that a'way."

"Then let me ask, do you think you're cured?" He felt he had to do something in a hurry. His amorous feelings were overpowering. She had his interest going in circles.

"Nae. But I'm hopin'."

Rock sat up straight and clasped her hands in his, forming a double tipi, one stacked over the other. "Our hands together resemble what was once our world. We were one. You weren't greater or lesser, richer or poorer, or better than me. Then, when love was lost and I couldn't depend on you, things changed. Our world changed. I felt like you took the sun from me. Things happened between us. And, not for the better."

"Rock, give me a another chance?"

He watched her lean forward in an attempt to be closer, exposing her lovely breasts. More excitement welled inside him, but he held their position. "Our world broke into pieces, Sheryl. We became two islands, separate one from another." He pulled their hands apart in demonstration.

"Please Rock. Not everyone thinks the same way. So it isnae easy ta live in harmony all the time."

"But, what's important to me is to form one life so at least I can live in harmony. When two people obey the laws of respect, or of caring, it's easier to live in harmony. We lost that long ago."

"No matter the things I said ta ye, even a'fore the trial, I felt my feelin's fer ye changed 'cause ye changed. Love will hold us tagether, now that I'm on medicine. I know ye 'ave feelin' fer me. Ye put yer arms around me when I tried ta run away from court earlier this week. And, ye stuck up fer me like ye care."

"Of course I care. I'll always care." Rock sighed and rested back again. His life had become complicated like navigating in rough waters. For some odd, unexplainable reason, he felt the Nativeness in him wanted to run away. The Caucasian half that Sheryl appealed to in the past, wanted to rush in her arms.

Sheryl moved away, turned off the lamp, fell back in the opposite corner of the sofa and silently wept.

Lamplight from the street shone through the window illuminated her slender limbs and auburn hair. She crossed her wrists over her chest, indicating love, while rocking herself from side to side. An unruly curl fell over one eye.

Understanding the sign language prompted him to reach and pull her over. "Don't cry." He held her against his chest, inhaling perfume. There was no denying she was a helpmate who got him through the drudgery of the past week. And, learning she was taking medicine put a different aura on matters.

"Have ye taken yer bonnie ta bed? Is that why ye donnae need my lovin'?"

"No. I haven't taken her to bed." Rock figured her curiosity was why she changed. Apparently she couldn't stand the thought of him finding another woman. He started to move off the sofa. His need to get away became urgent before his urges took over.

Sheryl pushed her weight over him. "Then be with me tonight. Ye must be starvin' fer love."

Rock held her head close to his lips and sighed. Internally, he was trembling. It had been a long time since he had made love to her. He couldn't remember Sheryl feeling this soft and so desiring of his love, nor he of hers. A restlessness, a longing and loneliness, overtook him. A wave of exhilaration. He wanted to shout. In his internal yearning, the words slipped out of his mouth in a deep breathy whisper. "I'm starving." Their breathing quickened, exciting him further. He buried his face in her hair.

"I'm no askin' fer a commitment. Come tamorrow, ye can leave. It's no like we're breakin' any laws. We're still married. I know yer sufferin'. And, it's all my fault."

His fingers stroked through her hair. He felt dizzy with passion. Their lips brushed, ending in a long fervent kiss. The strength to stop the inevitable was gone. Court room decorum, conniving attorneys and law books faded.

* * *

In the morning, he woke in a daze, still holding Sheryl in his arms. Her robe covered them. She opened her eyes and smiled. "Will ye take me ta Seattle with ye?"

He sat up feeling like he'd been swallowed. "Gosh Sheryl. I have work to catch up on, bills to pay and mail to answer before trial on Monday."

"I wonnae be any bother. I'll phone my girlfriend in the Magnolia neighborhood. She can drive me a'boot; take me back ta the ferry. I'll spend tanight with 'er and I'll havenae trouble gettin' home on Sunday."

He gave her a hug. "Okay. You spend time with your girlfriend. But, I'll bring you back Sunday evening since I have to be in court Monday."

She was delighted and rushed away to pack.

His hesitation in not wanting her underfoot was also because he had matters to discuss with Unali and Efrem, and he needed to check on the old man, the family friend. Take him a birthday card. He just turned 91 years old. And, after what happened last night, he had some serious thinking to do. Either it was meant to be and would continue, or it was a form of withdrawal that would never happen again. In any event, he needed to question his actions, determine where this was taking them and what he had done to his friendship with Unali.

Chapter Thirty-Nine

Monday morning Rock and Sheryl were sitting in their usual places in Courtroom Two, after having arrived from a ferry ride through cold air and fog. They sipped coffee from styrofoam cups Sheryl brought in from a coffee machine. Surprisingly, Joseph Scott bounded up front with a broad grin and a quiet voice. "You'll never guess what happened after court Friday."

Rock nearly choked on his coffee. He knew what happened to him Friday night and hoped Scott was none the wiser. "What happened?"

"Marvin's fit of temper got him into trouble."

"Oh, what about?" Rock glanced down at a shiny baldhead and face full of freckles, smiling avidly, standing with his feet slightly apart, knees locked, appearing jovial and refreshed. Sheryl leaned forward to better hear.

"Marvin was pissed off when his document expert testified that ink containing iron would thermofax. He and Beatrice left the parking lot in their fancy Mercedes. Backed out of the parking lot, running into another parked car. Then, after shifting, ran forward into another car. Then they left the scene."

"I'm lovin' it." Sheryl laughed, along with Rock.

"A witness identified him. He's charged with hit and run."

"Hell, I figure Marvin will find a way to worm his way out." Rock shrugged, laughing. "Perkins will find a way to get him off."

While Scott tended to business at the counsel table, Rock became serious. He had other things on his mind, like looking forward to today. Not moneywise, but otherwise. This was the day he expected to see Scott's aggressive tactics impeach Houston, by revealing his misconduct in John's probate and misrepresenting John's property as all community. Today, proof of John's ownership of the Carper mansion would be entered, along with Rock's expert's report, authenticating the Leucojum documents.

Unable to reach Unali and Efrem by phone over the weekend, Rock knew he was on his own like an orphaned wolf. He was tired of being treated like his case was none of his damn business. And, based on what happened last week, he also knew he was no match to the legal maneuvers going on about him.

Nevertheless, without invitation, Rock edged up to the front counsel table to sit alongside Scott. Scott needed controlling, even if he was an experienced probate attorney. Staring at the enlarged cover letter of Uncle John's that Perkins had set up on an easel, Rock wondered how this would be used.

Judge Dodson entered. The audience who stood was small. The Bensons, the Carpers and the attorneys. "Good morning. Please be seated ladies; gentlemen." He smiled cordially. "Counsel. We will proceed with closing arguments. Mr. Scott, the law requires you go first."

A facetious thought drummed through Rock's mind. *"Ah. We're following the law."* Admittedly, he didn't know much law, but what he had witnessed didn't seem lawful. Nevertheless, feeling quite relaxed, Rock inhaled deeply and patted his lapel pin out of habit. Maybe it would bring him good luck today.

Dressed in a navy suit, Scott reclaimed his favorite fence post, or lectern. His legs locked like they'd never straddled a saddle. He reiterated the death of John Carper who left a 1967 will, which was described and identified by Rock's witnesses last week.

Crossing one foot over the other, Scott wove in facts about John's other documents, starting with the May cover letter being an original ink-signed letter addressed to John's Masonic friend Cod, signed 'Fraternally, John'. "The letter shows John is acting on Cod Fulbright's advice. Cod date stamped the letter and envelope the same date John died in Nevada. No witnesses are alive to tell us when Cod Fulbright learned of John's death. Jasper Fulbright didn't learn about it until later. There are no witnesses alive to tell us that Cod didn't put John's papers with Leucojum's. There are no witnesses alive to say the date stamp wasn't used at the Fulbright Firm. Jasper Fulbright said the date stamp may have been used."

After sipping water, Scott recapped further, promising to conclude shortly. "Rock relied on his former attorney Ralph Houston's advice that John's estate was being handled under terms of the community property agreement. Therefore, no will mattered. Nevertheless, Rock found new evidence in 1984 and '85. The envelopes were sealed and opened for the first time in the offices of his attorneys. One may say that Rock's discoveries of the documents contained inside the envelopes are stranger than fiction; therefore, must be true. Truth has its quirks. Fiction is well planned."

Responding to this, Rock leaned back in his chair, lowered his head and rested his arms on the table. Either Scott's last statement was ingenious or destructive. Far be it for Rock to know what was on the minds of these educated men and what they determined to be facts. He noticed Perkins rise and walk forward, setting several pages of notes on the lectern.

* * *

Perkins was decked out in a three-piece charcoal gray suit and shiny shoes. His kinky blond hair and pointed beard were neatly trimmed. With script in hand, he paced. "Now your Honor, I don't submit that Rock Carper is an expert in document forgeries. But, he created a few documents and made a few mistakes. The kind of mistakes you would make and I might make."

"Aren't you going to object?" Elbowing Scott, Rock desperately wanted to stop Perkins' biting sarcasm. "His insults are fictitious."

Scott barely flinched. "Nope. We don't interrupt in closing arguments."

Listening to Perkins thunder in loud oration crucifying his life, Rock could only wonder: *"How can they create such fiction?"*

Perkins had taken on the aura of an evil spirit filling the room. "There's no evidence whatsoever that anyone else could have typed the cover letter except John. Or, we suggest somebody else. Rock had everything he needed to create the Leucojum documents. He had collected copies of documents from state offices for names. He said so on the stand. Each and every one of the signatures in the state documents is contained in these copies. Rock had the materials for cut and paste. He had a xerox machine. Thermofax machines are readily available."

These accusations struck a sour chord in Rock's head.

"They dinnae prove the likes o' that." Sheryl gasped.

Sheryl was accurate on the materials for cut and paste and the xerox and thermofax machines. Rock had none of it. True, he did admit to gathering copies of state documents, but that was only for names of people to contact. He never thought for one minute that any of the signatures were the same as those on the Leucojum documents because he didn't look. Why didn't these attorneys ask him to provide the state documents to see if the signatures matched? Why hadn't this come up before now?

Rock turned around to see Sheryl leaning toward him with narrowed eyes, but his jaw felt too tight, too paralyzed to respond, realizing he was on trial, a victim of a cruel and deliberate hoax. His nerves were coming apart like an arrow out of control. The uneasiness of the '84 trial surfaced, especially when he walked out on the judge. Today, he was determined not to repeat the renewed temptation. If only Unali could see Perkins grandstanding to the advantage of his clients. Thus far, it made Scott's closing sound like a cradlesong.

Perkins paced. "Like little steps, Rock slid from belief to obsession, from one piece of evidence to another piece of evidence, to the Leucojum documents."

It was difficult to sit and take this verbal beating. Rock couldn't recall any physical beating worse. Perkins' opinions spread with unrivaled speed like hot thunderbolts. The back of Rock's neck broke out in a cold sweat, while watching Perkins work his beady eyes, fingers and arm movements for emphasis. His voice undulated and dripped in venom. Judge Dodson leaned over the bench top. He appeared to be taking notes.

"When you read that cover letter and you listen to the experts and you listen to how the Leucojum documents were discovered, the timing of their discovery and the place of their discovery, the overwhelming conclusion is that these documents were not created by John Carper. They were created by Rock, for whatever he thought were honorable reasons. But they were wrong. It's a fraud on the court. A crime."

Perkins, appearing intoxicated by his choice of words, came across as gruff and ornery. "Our expert Ben Anderson, tried four times to create the Leucojum documents and provided the court with a very good facsimile. Now, Anderson said he tried to age them and he didn't have the right paper. There were various kinds of papers, but he could never quite get the color exactly right. And, Anderson is trying to copy what we say is a forgery, which is much harder. Now, Anderson says that the signatures won't copy on a thermofax machine, the blue-black ink will not copy on a thermofax machine. Anderson said this notary seal on the trust agreement won't show up."

Theatrically and with such grace, Perkins moved to the side of the room and lifted one of the enlarged posters for all to view. It was an enlargement of Jack and John's trust agreement. He held it high like a billboard of the latest hit movie. "Anderson couldn't feed the trust agreement through the thermofax machine because it wouldn't fit."

His last statement cut Rock to the core. Anderson, a non-thermofax expert, whose thermofaxing testimony was concluded hearsay by the judge, was now being rehashed.

Rock noticed that the American flag made an interesting backdrop for Perkins, depending on where one sat. The flag brought to mind *The Star Spangled Banner*. Francis Scott Key, an attorney, wrote words to that song in the 1800's. Now, more than a century later, Perkins walked in front of the flag as an attorney, promoting lies, offering misrepresentations. Rock stifled a raging urge to rip off his lapel pin of the flag.

After setting the poster down, Perkins moved to the middle of the room. "Of the date stamp. Not used in the Fulbright office, but readily available in any stationery store here in Clamton County, because our expert managed to find one when he recreated his version of the Leucojum documents."

Approaching his counsel table, Perkins scooped up the journal and opened it. "Hokay. Rock said this envelope was found in this journal. Now, as Your Honor notices the first time around, the envelope sticks out both ends and it has a bright red return address up on the top from the Safeco Insurance office."

Rushing down the aisle with fiery eloquence to the back of the room, Perkins waved these exhibits overhead, like emphasizing his scathing account in exclamation points. The room was his stage. "Your Honor, you can see the envelope from back here. At this space in the courtroom, it's impossible to miss. How anyone could miss not seeing this envelope sticking out of this journal for four years is beyond reason."

Turning to watch, Rock felt so browbeaten and thrown off guard at this trial, that even he wondered how he could have missed it. Even Sheryl appeared puzzled. And, he couldn't help but marvel at the energy with which Perkins delved into the minutiae of his demonstration, before returning to his seat.

Following Scott's short rebuttal, which Rock was too numb to comprehend, the judge called for a two-hour lunch recess. Scott quickly disappeared.

Rock departed from the courthouse, feeling like he was an insignificant speck of dirt in a dark rain cloud. He was aware, however, that Sheryl was chasing after him.

*   *   *

They walked down a side street toward Rock's car. The daylight sky was darkish. A few pigeons scattered away from their feet. Thoughts depressed him. "Sheryl, Scott's closing was little defense and offered me little hope. Much of the trial was senseless because no one proved the envelopes, containing the Leucojum documents, were not sealed when I found them. Jasper Fulbright and Mrs. Willard said they were sealed. Therefore, the remainder of trial was a waste of time."

Sheryl slipped a hand behind his arm. "Long-winded tautology, it was."

While fawning the morning's events over in his head, he deliberated his mother's decision to merge into the American bourgeois aristocracy. Based on his experience, Leucojum's decision was influenced by the love for one special man. Look where it had taken Rock. To these marbled steps, columns, hallways and rooms of justice.

Christmas trappings of fir, holly, jingle bells, gay lights and music were everywhere. He could smell pine in the air. An occasional boat whistle came from the distant waters. Heavy hearted, he wanted to visit Scott at his office just a block away and tell the sonofabitch what a lousy job he had done. But, he decided otherwise. Complaining to Scott had become a futile exercise. The guy was a first-class jerk.

"Donnae worry. The judge'll see through all this. We've got ta believe."

"I'd like to believe in the judge." Her comment made him feel better, even if the air and wind made his face, hands and feet cold. He looked high to the west and detected it would definitely snow before evening.

Rock opened the passenger door for Sheryl. "Do you have any more of that stew left?"

"Ye ate it fer breakfast."

He had forgotten that they headed for her house from the ferry this morning so she could change clothes, while he ate stew reheated in the microwave. He hadn't felt the same since. Spaced out, in a cloud. And now Sheryl's perfume was stimulating his senses. Dressed in an ivory suit and heels in the dead of winter made her the most stunning creature around. Rock fingered a lock of her auburn hair. He wanted to touch more.

"It's no stew ye're needing." She turned to look at him and put a hand on his chest.

He stretched his arms between the top of the car and door, making a vee, hemming her in. His eyes were reaching out to her. "My spirit is really down."

She reached for his wrist, pulled it to her lips and kissed his watch. "We 'ave time."

He put his arms around her. "Oh Sheryl, I want you to be mine for all seasons. The way it used to be. Over the weekend, I thought that maybe we were undergoing withdrawal. But, I don't want to believe that."

"I love ye too and I donnae want this ta end." They stood there for a while holding each other, while planting respectable kisses on cheeks, necks, chins.

After Sheryl climbed into the car and Rock closed the door, he walked around to his side. It gave him time to think about his actions. He wouldn't have fallen out of love with Sheryl if only medicine had been available to her years ago. Over the weekend, he saw the change in her.

It seemed logical that if withdrawal was their problem, it would have surfaced before now, at least for most couples in their predicament, since they had been living apart for nearly two winters. Of course, Rock considered he and Sheryl were different from most couples. It was a long shot, but if they were experiencing withdrawal, it would show in time. And, since they were already married, this seemed the right way to feel.

As he sped off to her house, he glanced over at Sheryl, who leaned her head against the headrest with closed eyes and held onto his right hand, playing with his wedding ring of polished turquoise stones and a large diamond set in a gold band. She bought it from his boss Atsidi years ago to replace the original banded one. It was because of this purchase that Rock eventually met Atsidi and went to work for him. Rock took to the job at Turquoise Wholesalers like deer to a meadow.

"Rock. Yer ring is on the wrong 'and."

"Geezus, I forgot. Habits die hard." This happened after his shower Sunday morning. Stopping at a red light, he switched the ring to the left. Sheryl smiled in understanding.

Arriving at her house, he parked in back near the kitchen door. They were silent while going inside. Even on the way to the bedroom, there was no talk. Their kisses grew stronger with each step, him moving forward, her backward. Their caresses lead to pulling off each other's clothes.

"Oh Rock. Do ye really love me?"

"I really love you." The words came easily and with sincerity. Their desires sought to please and comfort. The rhythmic melody of flutes whirled in his head like someone was twirling a rope in the air. His momentum seemed to delight her through fulfillment. Even afterwards, they lingered a while like rocks to a sandy beach. "Your medicine is a miracle for us."

"Ay." She sighed in contentment. "Will ye be comin' back ta stay the night? It might snow."

"I'll stay if it snows."

"Rock. If ya donnae win, I'm pleadin' ye give up the litigation."

He rolled away, irritated. "No promises on that issue." It would have been so easy to promise her anything. But promise he would not. "I honestly can't make a decision until it's over. It's up to the judge." He kissed her on the hand. "Come on. We'll talk later. Let's attend the great council fire and find out what kind of a judge I drew in the Quamas lottery."

Rock chuckled, but he was disappointed she would make this request. At the moment, it seemed more appropriate to be talking about her moving to Seattle. And, he needed to think about his explanation to Unali.

Chapter Forty

Back in court. Judge Dodson sat up particularly straight to begin his oral opinion, by first praising the attorneys for a job well done. "As to the history and basic facts, I am not going to detail them. If the drafter of the findings needs further assistance, I would refer you to Judge Randell's recital of them. I thought he did a rather masterful job. There were portions of it, I think, in the respondent Marvin Benson's brief."

Rock knew nothing about the reference to Marvin's brief.

The judge continued. "Anyway, Judge Randell, I thought, recited the facts fairly well and fairly completely in the 1984 trial transcript. Of course, another good source for some of the facts is the court of appeal's decision and that recites the heart of this case to a great extent."

Reference to the appellate decision was good to hear, Rock decided, indicative that Judge Dodson read the prior record as requested in his pretrial motion. He wondered when the judge would rule on his pretrial motion. Maybe he did and Rock missed it. In any event, he was gladdened.

Next, Dodson referred to the enlarged cover letter on the easel, starting at the top gesturing with his head. "I find that the May letter is consistent with the plan that Rock had."

Sitting at the counsel table next to Scott, Rock was aghast. He had no plan. Other than Sheryl's statements in the 1984 trial transcript, the cover letter was the best proof he had of John's testamentary intentions at death.

Judge Dodson: "Rock had to have established a box at the bank, so he starts to set it up by making reference in that cover letter. And, yet Rock either forgot, or lost track of his plan because, well, when the deposit box was entered, the originals of the Leucojum documents weren't in there, which is surprising."

Sheryl, behind Rock, poked him in the back. "The judge's memory is shorter than a whore's skirt. John 'ad a safe deposit box and Nell 'ad the key."

Rock managed to nod, then returned his attention to the plan accusation. Surprising was hardly the word. Nell wanted it all. The Leucojum documents should have proven as much.

He listened to Judge Dodson proceed, dogmatically, sinking his legal teeth and official power into him by continuing to rip apart statements in John's cover letter relative to pulling hairs off Rock's chest.

"The only place I see a reference to separate property is the cover letter that Rock produced." Dodson looked over at the enlarged letter propped up on the easel. "Now that's interesting in that the letter in the last sentence: 'I have always held the above-mentioned assets as separate and personal property and they do pass completely in their entirety by my last will and testament of August 18, 1967 and my second codicil of May 8, 1972 to Dorian Barnes Carper, as his legacy and birthright'."

Dodson looked down at his small audience. "I accept Ralph Houston's testimony and the probate file which I guess I can take notice of. I can note that all assets were community property. The reference to separate property has been manufactured, I think, by Rock. The letter and the copies of wills, codicils and what have you, just don't mesh with common experience."

Mustardy brown law books loomed before Rock's eyes as he looked around, stirring uncomfortably. Thousands of cases. None could be like this. The room took on a solemnity. No rays of sun shone in through the windows and into his heart. He wanted to know what meshed with common experience in the judge's mind.

"I have trouble thinking that John, a couple of days, if not the day before, was going to leave on a trip, sits down and initials all of these copies. That's not very probable. And, I could probably take judicial knowledge that banks don't have any kind of safe keeping service referenced in John's May letter, other than deposit boxes. I see no other way, other than a safe deposit box."

Judge Dodson read other parts of the cover letter aloud, to bolster his opinion. "Now that's setting up a plan, that eventually is Rock's scheme. You have to conclude that, otherwise it doesn't make any sense to me. There isn't any question in my mind, but that John wouldn't have suggested that his papers be put in with Leucojum Carper's. That's strange, really strange. Stretches my credulity. It's setting up a plan."

Rock found the words offensive, insulting, jabbing. Judge Dodson didn't know this family and had no right to opinionate judgment over such matters. Rock slid down in the slatted chair to stretch his legs and cross his feet. Scott was sitting sideways with his back to him.

Judge Dodson looked at Rock, then back to his notes. "The date stamp, which purports to show it was received in Cod Fulbright's office on May 14, 1972, is inconsistent with the uncontroverted testimony that no date stamp was used in the Fulbright office." He nodded affirmatively, adjusting his glasses further down his nose, looking over the rims at the two attorneys, giving them an enigmatic smile.

It was disgusting to Rock, watching the heads of Scott and Perkins nod agreeably in carbon-copy servitude, two humble disciples before their God. Kissing ass.

"It's improbable that John would send the Leucojum documents to Cod Fulbright, who had never done legal work for him."

"That question wasnae asked." Sheryl gasped from behind. He could hear her breaking into tears.

Rock shook his head, giving her a signal to hold together. Dodson's summation was called an oral opinion. That's exactly what it was. A spiel dripping in personal opinions. Opinions don't make fact, do they? Common sense told Rock personal opinions don't count, but in this courtroom, maybe common sense didn't belong. There was no way to key off the '84 trial since it was not like this trial.

Dodson: "It's improbable that Cod, a friend of John's, if he had received the Leucojum documents the same day that John died, would have done nothing with them. He didn't give them to Ralph Houston."

Clasping his hands tightly together on the table, Rock realized that Scott never did bring out Houston's nine-month delay in announcing his legal representation in the probate of John's estate. The only explanation that popped into Rock's head at this moment was to protect Houston, a fellow attorney. Rock recalled listening to an expose on TV once about cops protecting each other. So it was now logical this would carry over into other professions. Scott protecting Houston.

"On Houston's advice to avoid stock transfer costs, Nell abrogated the community property agreement and John's property passed to her instead under the 1952 will. I don't find any evidence at all that Nell, or anyone for her, committed fraud. There's no evidence to contradict Mr. Houston's conclusion that all of John's property was community. There would be no reason for Houston to mislead Rock because all of John's property was community, so the 1942 trust agreement is probably a forgery designed to support Rock's claim that John had substantial separate property."

His opinions caused pressure to build in Rock's gut, as Dodson droned on in monotones. "There may once have been a 1967 will of John Carper, which left all of his separate property and half of his community to Rock and made him the executor of John's estate, but the contents and proper execution weren't proved."

Geezus. Rock's mind was doing flip-flops, whispering to Scott's backside. "The sonofabitch just contradicted himself. First he says Uncle John had only community property, now he had separate and community."

Scott remained silent; unmoved. Rock straightened up and rubbed his eyes. Once again, the urge to walk out hit him. But, the last time he did this to Judge Randell, he sworn he'd never do it again. What would people think? His desire to yell out was strong too, but the numbness in his head forced him to remain silent and stay put. It was like being engulfed in a fire, where someone yells to get out. But, Rock couldn't move. The flames licked him. He simply didn't know how to handle this. One minute he felt sane; the next he felt crazy.

"And, I don't understand why Rock didn't contact Mr. Houston about the later will. He had no good reason for waiting until most of the witnesses had died to file his petition to reopen probate."

Once again, history was repeating itself on this same issue. Rock warned Scott. To think, he was paying Scott $1,000 a day for this. What a stupid waste.

Dodson paused to sip water. "The community property agreement was stamped with some verbiage. Something about passing the title to new cannery owners to clear title to buy the property. I don't follow that. Anyway, Nell probably didn't know about the safe deposit box until Houston discovered it. She was disabled for several months after John's death and there is no evidence that she went to the bank before the deposit box was opened by Houston."

Rock stared at his scarred hands. None of what Dodson said so far came from an educated man who had attended this trial. How can Dodson's spin on testimony and exhibits be so wrong?

The judge flipped to another page of notes. "The testimony of ink expert Richard Green determined the Leucojum documents signed with two inks, which should have oxidized from blue to black if written in 1972, were created shortly before their discovery in 1984." Rock couldn't fathom such contrary facts being uttered by the judge.

"The testimony of document examiner Ben Anderson proves that John didn't type the cover letter, nor initial and date the Leucojum documents. The fact that the envelopes were all neatly sealed and addressed to Rock and placed by him in the journal and Leucojum's lockbox where they were found; the fact that he took them to a lawyer to be opened. These facts add to the conclusion that the documents were created by Rock after he filed his petition in 1984."

Rock resisted the temptation to slide down in his chair. These statements were nothing more than speculation. The opposition created documents, not Rock. With no escape from this verbal punishment, Rock exhaled heavily. The options in answer to these accusations were all negatives. No witness. No time. And no money to prove otherwise. Scott appeared unmoved or in a trance. The one man, who could have turned this around the first day, but didn't.

Rock looked up at the high windows. Tufts of snow kissed the windowpanes, turning to streamlets of water against the heat of the glass. He shivered even though the room was comfortable. Judge Dodson's words brought him back. Something about signing an order, rejecting his pretrial motion to submit prior reports of record. The meaning was slow to register. He glanced back at Sheryl. She wiped her tears with a kerchief. Scott remained silent.

Judge Dodson held his glasses between a thumb and forefinger and made a final acknowledgment to Fred Adams Jr., Ralph Houston's partner and Marvin Benson's co-attorney with Perkins: "Mr. Adams, I noticed you attended trial everyday, and, although you've said little, I'm certain you contributed mightily to Mr. Benson's case."

Fred Adams Jr., sitting at his counsel table, smiled, nodded his redheaded mane, jiggled his Adam's apple and mouthed a humble "Thank you".

Dodson bade all a good day, while looking up at the windows. "Have a safe trip home. It's snowing out."

Rock gritted his teeth so hard in anger that his body shook. Nothing had gone right in his litigation.

*   *   *

Once again events were happening so quickly, they eluded Rock. While forcing himself to calm down, he finally turned to Scott. "Aren't you going to enter proof of John's ownership of the Carper mansion?"

"Well." Scott looked baffled by the suggestion. "You just heard Dodson. His order rejected your pretrial petition."

"What about impeaching Houston for lying to the 1984 trial court? He caused my delay." Rock's mind refused to grasp the outcome. He just didn't comprehend that it was over.

"What about the appellate remand to address Nell and Houston's fraud in John's probate? What about Judge Randell's order to consider all evidence of record, which included the remaining transcript not read into the record? And, what about Sheryl's '84 testimony, concerning her knowledge of Uncle John's testamentary intentions?"

"I can't enter anything now." Scott shook his head to each suggestion.

"Not even my document specialist's report? My reason for this trial?"

"Dodson's order eliminated consideration of all records, depositions and affidavits."

Rock narrowed his eyes, questioningly. "Can't you object to Dodson's decision?"

"Oh, that won't help now. Only tick him off. The trial's over." The two of them looked awkwardly at one another. Scott smoothed a hand over his baldhead.

"How convenient." Rock's voice was heavy with sarcasm, his lips a tight, thin line. Scott's attitude was like whale water under the bridge. In Native language that meant whale piss. Smelly. He returned to sit by Sheryl, who was digging in her purse for tissues. Scott looked at them and then left, leaving his impressive display of legal paraphernalia on the counsel table.

"I overheard ye two talkin'. Lightning has struck twice on the same Rock." Sheryl, pale and saddened, blew her nose with one of numerous tissues in her lap. "Deja vu. This place is a hostile environment."

"I could have fared better as a peak sitter." He responded numbly, swearing under his breath and lowering his head.

"Rock, ye suuuure got mixed up with a bad bunch. Scott's assurances and yer blind faith that everythin' would come oot at trial evaporated."

"Discharged in my face. Dodson isn't even going to take notice of perjured lies by my opposition. I can't believe it." To emphasize this, Rock jabbed the palm of his left hand with the right index finger, then thrust the index finger down toward the floor. Discouraged, he slumped forward over his knees on the bench. "My blind obedience, their legal maneuvering and Scott's stalling worked against me the last day at the twelfth hour when they knew I couldn't make other arrangements to bring my specialist here."

He paused, still looking down. "I never suspected attorneys capable of descending to such malicious injustice in such a small pond. All along, I've picked attorneys who came highly-recommended by either a referral service or reliable recommendations. I relied on all the attorneys to enter all relevant evidence to promote justice. What more could I do?"

"Ay, tis a bit o' an abominable blow. Ye dinnae know these attorneys would skirl inta yer life like poisonous mushrooms." She rubbed a hand across the back of his shoulders in sympathy.

"I swear this entire trial was staged."

"We're frontier green in the eyes o' the attorneys. They're assumin' correctly that our knowledge o' the law is feeble. These fellas know the law, so they can defeat it." Sheryl patronized him in a consoling tone. Tears streamed down her cheeks. "Old Houston is an officer o' the court. The judge is goin' ta believe him over ye." She sighed. "Jurisprudence is dead."

Rock closed his eyes. The cumulative effect of Dodson's accusations left him feeling used, stupid and roiling in hate. He could hear Marvin's bunch moving from the room in stages of celebration. "Come on, I'll drive you home." They moved to the doorway. Sheryl excused herself to depart to the ladies room.

Rock lingered at the entrance. The room stood empty. Silent. Dark. Haunted. Only ghosts remained. A crime scene flooded in the room, with educated vultures speaking in split tongues, plundering the innocent to feather their nests; their careers. He looked down at the floor, wondering what happened to friendhood, honor, truth. If a spirit had come and told him that these events were destined to take place, he wouldn't have believed it. Strength in numbers meant nothing when not of one honest mind. Taking one last look at the American flag, Rock decided it didn't belong here. In humiliation, he fought against the tears welling in his eyes. "Hell, Cherokees don't cry."

Defeat and humiliation sank into his existence. As he backed away, he wondered if it were ever again possible to walk across a field, down a mountain path or through a forest holding his head high. He left, forgetting Sheryl.

Chapter Forty-One

Rock trudged down the indoor stairs alone, then shoved out the door and stood a minute or two on the courthouse landing. His misery coagulated in his mind; his soul. Suddenly Scott rushed out the lobby door, a briefcase in one hand. "Rock, why did you hold back on me?"

Flabbergasted, Rock extended his chest. "Ooooh, no. Quite the contrary." He swore angrily. "You rested on your kinky laurels and allowed Perkins to destroy me. And, you let the judge think I had a plan. You let the judge act as a witness against me on the cover letter. You know, I held nothing back. Stuff it in your weird conscience, if you have one." Rock balled his fists and moved sideways down a step. "You took away my legacy."

"Rock." Scott expelled a breath. "We have to stick together."

"Shit. We?" Rock laughed, angrily; thinking it'd be a cold day in hell. Rock moved down two more steps. He didn't want Scott close to him for fear of what he might do. Having spent six trial days unsuccessfully pleading for Scott's ear was enough to make Rock's nerves snap.

"Yes. Perkins just filed a motion for a hearing, scheduled for next week." Scott stayed on the landing and set his briefcase down, while shivering and hugging his jacketed arms. Snowflakes began covering his jacket like dandruff.

"A hearing? What for?" Rock jammed his fists in his pockets and held his position with legs and feet spaced apart.

"He's asking for sanctions against us for a frivolous action."

"Oh, it was frivolous all right. But I have neither the money nor the time for another hearing. So, what are we going to do about it?" Rock didn't know what sanctions meant and didn't ask because presently he didn't give a damn.

"Give me a chance to turn things around. I'll do it for free."

"Whatever. You go without me."

"If you have no intentions of attending the upcoming hearing, you'd better sign a note to that effect." Scott opened his briefcase, pulled out a paper and wrote some words on it, using a bent knee and the briefcase as a makeshift desk. "Here. Sign your name." He extended these out to Rock.

Grumbling, Rock grabbed the case and paper. "Got a pen?"

Scott tossed his pen.

While signing, Rock grumbled further. "I've had my fill of hearings and trials in this shit-mucking hellhole of a courthouse. I'm talking about the judge and you attorneys, how you work justice. You men aren't honest. You ruin lives." He handed the paper and pen up to Scott.

Backing down the remaining steps, Rock moved away not wanting to hear Scott's voice, his alibis and stupid wisdom. He turned his watery eyes upward toward the thick veil of snow. At one time, he'd have thought it beautiful, but not now.

*　　*　　*

In spite of Rock signing a paper forfeiting his right to the judgment hearing, Sheryl convinced him to attend anyway. So the following week, Scott, Rock and Sheryl were back in court. It took one afternoon session to have sanctions placed on Rock to the tune of $60,000 plus twelve percent interest for bringing a frivolous action and committing fraud on the court.

Rock stormed out of the courtroom with Scott in close pursuit. Outside, Rock tarried a moment, then removed the pin of the American flag, a pin he wore so proudly since the first day of trial. Turning, he flung it up the steps near a pillar and at Scott's feet. "That's what I think of your justice."

The muscles in Scott's cheeks twitched. He shrugged and disappeared back into the courthouse with his briefcase.

Disillusioned by justice, Rock walked across the sidewalk backwards. He was extremely fatigued, but evinced enough energy to mumble hysterically. "Oh Great Spirit, where are you?" He shouted heavenward, while roaming in crazy circles. "Why haven't you given me a sign, spiritual guidance, a song to assist me in making decisions on this earthwalk?" Maybe he was being punished for violating Unali's trust and for weakening to the powers of others.

"Oh Great Spirit, why do you punish me so harshly?" He extended his arms and hands skyward, with palms open for his God to see. "If I am guilty, take me for I have shamed the blood and bones of the Carper name." Totally discouraged, he became unaware of the surroundings.

A moment later, sounds filled the air. Honking horns, screeching brakes and human screams. Rock felt hit by something hard making him numb, limp and blurry-eyed, but focused enough to see metal giants all around; towering. It was like lying at the feet of the Seattle Art Museum's "Hammering Man".

He singled out one voice. Sheryl's voice, screaming his name many times. If only he could call to her, but no voice came. Only thoughts: *Dear sweet Sheryl. My first love. She doesn't deserve the pain I've caused her. The pain. Oh God, he was in pain.*

One last look upward. A whirling mass of white flakes. *Why does snow have to be white?* Almost like watching his burial. *Skee-nah*, the evil spirit had come for him. Then there was darkness.

Chapter Forty-Two

"Where am I?" Rock looked at his stark surroundings -- a room with two beds, light-colored walls, a husky woman in a white uniform and cap towering over him. He wasn't in a straight jacket, so he knew he hadn't gone crazy.

"You are in the Quamas Hospital, Mr. Carper." The husky woman's voice was deep. She was straightening his bedding like he wasn't in it.

"What am I doing here? I'll lose my job."

"Ye'll be losin' nothin' but yer head, if ye donnae lie still." Sheryl whispered, moving out of a chair to stand by the nurse.

"You stay still, Mr. Carper. You have a mild concussion." She turned to Sheryl. "I'll leave you two alone for a while." The nurse left, closing the door.

While sliding the bedding down a little, Rock noticed he wore a thin pale blue gown. "What did she say?"

"Ye're comin' oot o' a mild concussion."

"What do you mean by mild? My head's killing me." He reached up and touched bandages.

"Nothin' serious, if ye take care o' yerself. I cannae imagine black and blue eyes, a bump and a shave on the noggin' will stop ye fer long."

He noticed the other bed was empty. "I'll take care." He tried to raise himself and fell back on a pillow. Even with health insurance, he didn't relish being in a hospital.

"If ye donnae take care, the doctor said ye could 'ave other problems. Dizziness, sleep disturbances, anxiety, irritability, headache, depression and . . ."

Rock interrupted her. "Geez. Sheryl, I had those before I got here. So what else is new?"

"Cognitive difficulties."

"What kind of difficulties?"

"Cognitive. Refers to concentration, short-term memory and thinkin'."

"That's all I need." He looked beyond the foot of the bed and noticed a window. There was a tree out there with frozen snow on the limbs.

"It's not permanent, mate. And ye're lucky fer no worse, backin' inta the street like ye did. O' course, the snow dinnae help any. What were ye thinkin' to be takin' off withoot lookin'?"

"Everything was fuzz before my eyes, the headlights, Scott, the bear fat." He was recalling a Cherokee expression.

"Bear fat?"

"You know. Snow." Rock felt dizzy.

"Stop yer tribal jibber jabber." Instead, Sheryl prattled on about the display of flowers on the dresser coming from his boss Atsidi, his landlord Bud, Efrem, even Scott.

"Where's mom? Leucojum should be here."

"Oh Rock." Sheryl held his hand. "She's livin' in the Quamas Cemetery. Ye donnae remember?" Sheryl explained.

He turned away in silence.

"Donnae strain yer thinkin' now. Ye need rest."

Groaning, Rock wondered why he could remember bear fat and not Leucojum's demise. He held his head again. "How long have I been like this?"

"Over a week. I've been comin' in daily. We've been talkin'."

"Shhhhhit. Did we attend a trial or was it a dream?"

"No dream, lad. We attended a judgment hearin'. Ye likely donnae remember? The hearin' dinnae take long, maybe two hours. Ye'll be learnin' the hard way, nothin' comes free. The hearin' was another farce. Marvin asked fer attorneys' fees and sanctions against ye and Scott."

"My life is a farce, Sheryl." His voice faltered as he closed his eyes to the explosive pain. "In the name of humanity, I don't know what I did to deserve legal trouble."

"Donnae blame yerself. Scott offered ta represent ye fer free 'cause he was in a bit o' a bind. So 'e puffed off his intentions in representin' ye ta save 'is own hide. Had ta, 'cause Marvin was askin' fer $30,000, contendin' that ye and Scott brought forth a frivolous action."

Rock could recall something about a frivolous action "On what grounds?"

"On grounds that ye and Scott violated Civil Rule Eleven fer signin' discovery documents."

"Civil Rule Eleven? Discovery documents?" He tried to reach for the water glass.

Sheryl held the glass to his lips. "Ay. The farce is that Civil Rule Eleven, I found oot later, doesnae pertain ta discovery documents. It pertains only ta pleadin's, motions and memorandums. Judge Dodson said there wasnae evidence o' Scott signin' discovery documents. Therefore Scott dinnae violate Civil Rule Eleven." She set the glass aside on a table.

Resting on the pillow, he closed his eyes and used sign language for her to turn off the overhead light; the brightness hurt. Enough daylight came in through the window. He watched Sheryl comply. "I don't know if Scott signed anything."

"I checked. He signed yer pretrial motion and one other important document." In trying to remember, she snapped her fingers.

Rock groped for her to stop snapping.

"It was yer trial memorandum. But, Scott dinnae fess up. Anyway, Judge Dodson dropped charges against Scott. Once Scott was oot o' the picture, Marvin upped the ante."

Rock mumbled expletives.

"Ay. Sanctions against ye are fer $60,000 fer bringin' a frivolous action ta court, intimatin' ye committed fraud. Some $50,000 is fer attorneys' fees and $10,000 is fer costs incurred by Marvin. Oh, and they get twelve percent interest 'til ye pay. At least yer no goin' ta the poky. Ye can count yer blessin's fer that."

Rock's hands clenched into the top blanket. "I don't mind giving things away. On my terms; not the court's. They should have checked my assets first. When they find out I'm broke, I'll probably end up in the poky." Rock could hardly breathe the words. He stared at a water stain on the ceiling. At times he thought it was fuzzy, then clear.

"Nae, Marvin and his cohorts will look inta yer assets afore that happens, accordin' to Scott. I think I've given it ta ye straight. Scott gave the appearance o' representin' ye. The legal brethren used yer inheritance ta beat ye. And, now ye're expected ta pay a meager pledge fer their research."

"Meager. I financed Marvin and his whacko squatters with my legacy so they could screw me." Rock tried to sit up again.

"Royally." Sheryl shoved him flat, like a little of the big nurse had rubbed off. "Now settle doon. Perkins tried ta include me in the sanctions, but the judge said the rulin' was only on yer separate property. Not our community property, no my separate property, thank goodness fer that."

"I wonder why they didn't include you?"

"Oh, it has somethin' ta do with a Carper inheritance being separate property to ye . . . it's in the law somewhere. But I'm thinkin' ye're caught in somethin' way over yer head."

"The wind shifts in that direction, all right. Shit hit the rock." He moaned and rubbed his chin. He was growing a beard.

"Another thing. Mr. Scott is filin' his withdrawal from the case. What in the world will ye do?"

"Don't know." Rock thought for an instant.

Sheryl broke into his thoughts. "Scott says ye need ta focus."

Rock chuckled, sarcastically. "Because he didn't. Well, hell. Guess I'll file for an appeal and fight them myself. I no longer trust these men. Will you loan me your computer? Mine is broken."

"Oou. Ye really 'ave booped yer head ta be thinkin' ye can get away with representin' yerself." She grimaced. "But, since I'm not usin' my computer and printer, I suppose ye can."

"Thanks." He strained his eyes at her. "You're looking beautiful. Smell good too. Oh, Sheryl. You're too good to be wasting time around me." He turned away. "I let you down. I'm a disgrace." His shook his head sadly. Sheryl put a hand on his arm. Her hand felt warm and soft.

"I donnae believe that fer a minute. Ye tried. It was the system that let us doon, I say."

Rock remained quiet for a while. His mind was working like a computer, searching for details of the past two weeks. The ending of the trial came to him. "Scott sure had me buffaloed. He really turned out to be a derelict."

"A money-leechin' bilge rat is more befittin'."

"Sheryl, who are you associating with to come out with such foul slang." Rock exuded a pained smile. "I thought I was the foul-mouthed member in the family."

"Yer scholarly attorneys. The elite gentry o' the law. I'm thinkin' ye brought the lowest class in society inta our lives." She hardly sounded enthralled. "It bothers me so much, I'm thinkin' we should move ta Scotland."

"You're joking." He didn't know why she said 'we'.

"Nae. I'm serious."

"Sheryl, I believe you've got some gypsy under that Scottish-Irish skin of yours."

"Nae, there are other reasons. I miss my home country, and I received a letter from our son. He told me ta tell ye 'e's plannin' on movin' there efter he leaves the Army. He has fallen in love with a Scottish lass. Ye know 'e 'as no interest in the Carper legacy."

"Someday he may change his mind." Rock knew his son wasn't interested in fighting for the Carper legacy because of the reputation of the legal system. Yet, he knew that his son and he held a common thread. His son believed in the importance of values, especially to see that unborn generations have a better world. "He's got a lot of me in him. The feather didn't fall too far from the eagle."

"Ay. Testin' 'is wings, 'e is. Like father, like son."

Rock nodded a little. "Whatever you two decide is fine. But don't tell our son about this. It'll only worry him. Do you realize I'll have no relatives in this town?" Rock was drifting off to sleep.

"Ye best be gettin' some rest so I can take ye home in a few days. I've a feelin' ye'll be needin' it. Yer injury's no as bad as we first thought. But, ye've got ta take care, mind. And, donnae worry, yer boss knows what happened. Ye wonnae lose yer job."

"Sheryl." He extended an arm in her direction. "Why did you say 'we'?"

Sheryl bent over him. "Ye donnae remember what happened atween us at my place?"

"No. What happened?"

Her voice creaked. "Oh. We ate beef stew. Nothin' important." She left.

Rock brushed a hand across his hairy face. It was the hand Sheryl was holding just before she departed. It felt damp, like tears. But, drowsiness and fragmented thoughts clouded his mind. He couldn't remember the entire trial. His head rolled to the side and he faded off to the sound of the high-pitched flutes of his ancestors. A voice came through with one word: patience.

Chapter Forty-Three

It had been a while since Sheryl left him in his apartment to fend for himself. She said his recovery was progressing, but idleness irritated him, which made it difficult on her. Sitting cross-legged on the floor by the sofa, he watched the noon news on TV with disinterest. He cracked and munched on salted peanuts, while scolding himself to get organized.

Finally switching off the TV, he leaned his head against the sofa picturing Sheryl. She had been most kind in helping him in this unwanted predicament. He recalled that day she brought him back to his apartment. It was a challenge with him having dizzy spells. And, before departing, she fixed him a plate of food. At first he was too weak for his stomach to hold food. Spots blurred his vision from deciphering what was on the plate. After a bit, he became stronger and ate the food cold. Then, in paying his monthly bills, Sheryl wrote checks for him to sign and then offered to mail them on her way home.

He picked up the sack of remaining peanuts and secured the top with a rubber band, then rose to carry the sack and bowl of empty shells into the kitchen.

The doctor said he shouldn't experience anything more serious than an occasional headache. Working on the totem pole would have to wait a while. But, it was time to put his life back into some semblance of order. Fortunately, his boss gave him a few more days to regain his strength.

Not being able to make up his mind on what to do next, he returned to the living room and spotted Sheryl's computer-printer on a table in one corner. They had to ask Rock's landlord, Bud, to help bring in the equipment. He sat up to the computer and stared into the dark screen. Where to start?

Phone calls required attention. Acting like an animal pacing his cage, he roamed back to the kitchen for the phone. His priority was to contact Unali. Wish her a belated happy Hanukkah or something like that. He dialed but there was no answer, so he left a message on her answering machine, letting her know he'd try again one of these days. He related a little about the litigation and his accident. He didn't want her to freak out when she saw his bandaged head.

Finally, he sorted through more mail Sheryl left on the counter, finding a large envelope from Scott. Ripping into this, Rock read Scott's expressed sorrow over his mishap. Scott enclosed copies of three unsigned letters purported to be John's. This was all the adverse party had provided, Scott alibied. Then, there were copies of the transcripts of closing arguments and Judge Dodson's oral opinion.

Although Sheryl coached Rock in bringing back some of his memory, there were many things he still couldn't remember. So, reading the closing arguments and oral opinion would help him to further piece things together.

He curled on the sofa. The wall clock tick away as he read the pages. Unfortunately, the reading served as a pry bar, which made him moody. The transcript made him look like a wimp. His resolution was to strike back. Returning to the computer, he typed a letter to Scott, printed it and sat on the sofa to read:

"The buck became first place and the lack of fulfillment of duty prevailed. I was told at a certain point that I didn't understand what was going on. Oh, but I do now. Damn little was going on in my behalf. I work hard and with honesty for my money. I am thankful for the teachings of my forefathers. I was brought up in an environment where honesty, integrity, sincerity, completion of tasks and concern for the feelings of others prevailed. You led me to believe that you were a FIGHTER. The only fight I saw was to SAVE someone else's ASS. Now I know your heart. Have a nice day, Scott. You have stripped me of the Carper Legacy."

He'd mail this in a day or so, when feeling stronger.

Meanwhile, Rock, in realizing his spirits vacillated from low to bitter, decided to phone Efrem at his office. "Thanks for the flowers Efrem." Rock tried to sound cheerful.

"Man, you're lucky to be alive."

"Yeah, maybe. I'd save everyone a lot of misery if I were dead." Rock sat up to the kitchen table and propped his crossed legs over the other chair.

"Hell, knock that off." Efrem coughed. "Excuse me. Choked on the caffeine grog. Well, tell me briefly what happened."

"That spineless deadhead Scott tossed me to the wolves. In deciding whom to be loyal to, he picked Houston and my opposition over me."

"What do you mean?"

"I mean, according to Sheryl, Scott asked unrelated softball questions, avoiding anything that might hurt Houston, Marvin and his witnesses. With my witnesses, windbag Perkins went for the jugular. Shot lies from the lip. Perkins said nothing with such greatness. And, Judge Dodson sucked sweets and . . ."

Efrem chuckled, interrupting. "You've told me nothing new."

Rock interrupted, feeling terse, while trying to unwind the phone cord. "Damn it. I'm just getting warmed up. Sheryl said Dodson annihilated my pretrial motion the last day of trial, erased my very reason for going to trial. Bad spirit medicine. And, when one opinion pointed to guilt and one fact pointed to innocent, which would the judge pick?"

"Guilt."

"Relished the word like an aardvark takes to ants. I'm in his black book, buddy."

"So you're not the darling of Judge Dodson's eye?"

"Well, I'm not his pet rock. Sheryl said, quoting Socrates, a judge is responsible for four attributes: 'To hear courteously, to answer wisely, to consider soberly and to decide impartially.' I guess Dodson forgot to read Socrates."

"Interesting. Well, tell me more, as if I could stop you."

Rock could hear Efrem's chair squeak. "Okay, but I'm basing this partly on Sheryl's sayso. Houston's operation was slick, definitely well financed and merciless, turning situations to Marvin's advantage. Their ideology was, when things didn't happen the way they wanted, they changed it."

"You mean their strategies varied depending on what they perceived to be in their best interests?"

"Yep. Left out facts inconvenient for their purposes. No one entered a title report proving Uncle John's ownership of the Carper mansion. They didn't even file the new depositions of Jasper Fulbright, Mrs. Willard, Ben Anderson and mine as a part of the record. Scott and the judge looked the other way, I swear. Then they shackled me with $60,000 in sanctions."

"Hell no. $60,000? I don't believe it."

"Bull-ieve it. And that doesn't include interest." Rock grouched, drumming his fingers on the table. "The wheels of justice got caught up in neutral. I was run over by unverifiable conjecture. I do believe that Perkins is a sociopath, guilty of gross overkill and sabotage. That man regurgitated the wrong information enough times to convince the judge it was fact. Do you think they'd use facts from documents of known reliability? No, not in this lifetime. Self-serving bullshit. There should be a law against men like these."

Rock picked up speed from his usual slow pace of talking, excited that details were surfacing. "Judge Dodson's favorite word from the legal dictionary was 'sustained'. Anything favorable to me he sustained. My witnesses and I were big zeros."

"Hell. Sounds like Murphy's Law won again. Whoever has the gold makes the rules."

"It was a cerebral event that had me confused." Without thinking, Rock ran his hand along the back of his head. The soreness brought tears to his eyes. "The accident didn't help any."

"How will you pay $60,000?"

"Can't. My assets are already in legal pockets. They screwed me royally. But, I'm going to fight them. This isn't over."

Efrem belly laughed. "Hmmm. By the sound of things, my guess is you still need time to recover and think about where you go from here. If you get stuck, give me a call. I'm good for advice, beer and camaraderie."

"Will do." Mentally exhausted, Rock hung up the phone. But he knew he'd probably need Efrem's help. Because his head was hurting, he took pain medication, stretched out on the sofa, slept intermittently and dreamt that Leucojum was speaking, warning him about evil men: *"A warrior must learn to distinguish evil men, even in the brightness of daylight."* It was a little late for this.

Chapter Forty-Four

Ever since Gena pinned a '91 calendar on the office wall two weeks ago, she thought about her new year's resolution. Tell Rock her identity. After inserting a new tape in the recorder, she carried it to the living room coffee table. Rock was expected to arrive shortly. She gazed out the bay window overlooking Lake Washington. The water was calm. There were still signs of frost in an otherwise clear day. Seagulls flew overhead. She moved over to the stereo and flipped on classical music when his knock came. Her heart jumped on the way to the door.

"Hi stranger." While escorting him inside, Gena took his jacket and the documents he brought. Although thinner, he was still handsome and alluring. But, it was the turquoise scarf covering his head that drew most of her attention. The scarf was tied in a knot at the nape of his neck. Some of the bandages showed.

Rock followed her into the living room and sat on the sofa beside her. He explained the accident again and finished off with a wisecrack. "I was gored by bulls." His face turned downcast.

While listening and watching him, she remembered the rumors through her inquiry in court circles. He had reason to be weighed with legal woes. But, these thoughts and his head injury caused her to rethink the New Year's resolution. The timing was wrong. Not wanting to add to his problems, she didn't have the courage to tell him yet about her past. Gena's contemplation was interrupted when Rock slipped an arm around her waist. His warm lips and smoothly shaved chin brushed her forehead.

"Sorry, life has been rough, with the trial and all."

She accepted his hug, smiled and scooted forward toward the coffee table. "Tell me. May I tape this?"

He exhaled heavily. "Unali. That was no ticker-tape parade I attended. Even though I brought you documents, you must realize it was a trial I lost. Why would you want to write about me now? I'm a failure. A disgrace. Cut from my roots. When you read the closing arguments and the judge's oral opinion, you'll find out. That's what I brought with me." He sighed. "Do you know what it's like being a speck of dust squeezed from a raindrop? I do. Let me tell you."

"Stop it." Gena raised her voice. They stared at each other. She knew he had been through an ordeal. And, his confidence had been shaken. But, to let him run himself down, infuriated her. She lowered her voice. "Forgive me. Please. Let me be my own judge of your character. I've been around you long enough to know you're a good, honorable man. And, I'm so sorry about what has happened." Reaching over to hold his hand, she cleared her throat. "Rock. Your story is more important now than it ever was before. We need your story."

"Who's we?"

"Ahhhh." Her heart fluttered while her brain searched for an answer. "Society. Everyone in society must know what the attorneys did to you. The judicial system needs to clean house. What better way than through your story. So, may I record what you have to say? I don't mean all of it today. Just a little here. A little there." She watched his face broaden into an expansive grin; his eyetooth glistened in gold.

"That's what you're going to get. My memory works a little here and a little there." His posture straightened. "Okay." He rose and strolled to the window with his hands in his pockets.

Gena flipped on the recorder. "Okay. Talk to me."

He turned around slowly, stared pensively at her, then the recorder. "My heart is on the ground. I'm confused." He moved a right fist in a small circle on his forehead.

Gena chuckled. "Rock. I know that." She reset the recorder.

"I'd like to muzzle Perkins' loader. Or load his muzzle." He raised his arms upward and outward. "Well. Did you ever stop to think that maybe I don't know what I think I know? Or, I think I know what I really don't know? I don't know who or what to believe, being deceived by those who administer justice."

She rolled her eyes and tried to check her grin. This wasn't going to be easy. He was obviously on pain meds, but she decided to tape him anyway. Mona could straighten out his contentions later. "Say whatever comes to mind. I won't pressure you."

"I've been told the judge ignored Sheryl's testimony entirely, even though Perkins admitted she adequately remembered the contents of John's will. No one paid any attention to the bank teller's testimony. The teller said Nell drove to the bank two weeks before the state inventory to get into the deposit box. Her testimony vanished into thin air. Ffffft.

"Then I read in the printout of the judge's oral opinion that he determined Nell was a little old housewife who let hubby handle everything. Guess I don't understand the inner workings of the judicial system." Rock retucked his shirt into his pants.

Gena leaned against the sofa and crossed her legs. "Well, you tell me more. Talking helps." Music in the background was a soothing influence.

"Talking helps. I think you said that on the plane coming home from Dallas. This is more complicated." Rock joined her on the sofa. "I was made out as a shady character, D. B. Cooper, to intimate that I designed an escape hatch for crooked purposes."

"Which attorney did that?"

"Perkins."

"That's character assassination." She blurted out the words.

"Sheryl said Perkins sprayed fiction from an aerosol can." Rock's deep voice penetrated the room. "Yep, word by word, Perkins disposed of my life as I once knew it. Hardly impartial, sweet lady. Have you heard enough?"

She smiled. "No. But first, let's have coffee."

"Please." He adjusted his bandanna.

She switched off the recorder, left the room and quickly returned with a tray of coffee and small platter of peanut butter cookies. "Don't eat too many cookies. I have a nice dinner planned for us later."

Rock looked up from a travel magazine in his hands. "Ummm. Thank you. I need a good home-cooked meal. Should I go to Lake City for a bottle of wine?"

"No wine today." Gena nodded and laughed. "Now. Where were we?"

She flipped on the recorder again.

Rock swallowed coffee. "I gather that the fraud issue was switched from Nell and Houston in the '70's to me in the '80's. I didn't know I was on trial until the end. They accused me of creating John's documents in the 1980's without one shred of proof. Geez." He chuckled disgustedly. "My opposition proved they had all the equipment and admitted they created documents, but couldn't age them." Rock shrugged, leaning toward her.

"So help me, Unali, they proved I didn't commit fraud with their own evidence. But, from their accusations, the judge thought I, the least educated witness of the bunch, was the genius who could accomplish what the adverse party couldn't."

Gena munched on a cookie, watching Rock wad up his napkin. "Hmmm. That's not right." She found him quite uptight and nervous as he talked.

"And, the attorneys withheld evidence from me."

Her worse fears had been realized. "When a party holds back evidence for whatever reason, then it seems appropriate for a judge to shed the mantle of a detached bystander, enter the proceedings and develop facts not previously unearthed."

"Not in my case." He devoured a cookie in one bite.

"A judge owes it to the system of justice and to the country. A judge may question witnesses whether called for by itself or by a party. There's a wise precept that a fair trial and judicial objectivity don't require a judge to be inert." Gena sipped coffee to slow down and give Rock a chance to think about this.

"The judge was stuck in 'inert', but how do you know so much?" Rock appeared curious, as he finished his coffee.

Gena was prepared to answer. Her eyes lit on the small stack of magazines on the table. She knew there was a book under the stack, written by a famous judge. It would provide a quick recovery for her slip. She reached for it. "According to this, a judge should charge only what the record proves."

Rock took the book and leafed through the pages.

"Where do you go from here? Drop the case or continue?"

"Dropping the case is out of the question. I have to clear my name. Right now I'm searching for answers on how to go about it. I'd like to read this."

Gena nodded approval.

Rock set the book aside and sunk down into the sofa. "Ouch." He grabbed the back of his head.

"You're still tender." She winced as though she could feel his pain. The desire to slide down next to him crossed her mind. Seeing him again made her want his nearness.

"If I close my eyes momentarily and breathe in your flowery scent, maybe my hostilities and pain will vanish. You and the music will carry me far away to a better world." He grinned with his eyes closed. "Wake me up. Tell me I'm dreaming."

Gena giggled. "Oh, I wish I could, but you are awake." Her heart ached to soften his misery.

Rock opened his eyes and reached for another cookie. "Those damned attorneys were out to ruin me. I found out the costly way that legal representation doesn't guarantee fairness. You should write a book on the dangers of trusting attorneys. I would have thought that only a novelist could create an unbelievable story like this." Sadly, he walked over to the bay window and pivoted in her direction. "You see, if I violate my ethics, my spirit will assist the enemy. Maybe that's why it all happened. Beats me."

"The incredible is often the real explanation." She went to the kitchen for the coffeepot and returned to pour refills and set the pot on the coffee table. Rock gobbled another cookie and continued relaying events.

"You really trusted the attorneys, especially Scott, didn't you?" Gena returned to the sofa.

"Like a bow has an arrow with feathers, but I didn't at the end. Scott, in particular, had the most convincing way. Putting his hand on my shoulder, looking me square in the eyes and telling me he knew what he was doing. You know, I felt good after hiring Scott. It was like turning my problems over to a responsible, caring attorney. Like some people turn their problems over to their psychiatrist. Man, was I in a fog. Oh, there were numerous times when I knew things weren't right. I wasn't really prepared for it. I don't mean to place blame elsewhere but, Scott rendered me helpless to do anything about it." Rock returned to the sofa.

"Human nature hasn't changed over the history of man." Gena sipped her coffee and listened, thinking life was odd.

Rock nodded his head in agreement. "I blame myself too. I believe I demonstrated poor personal judgment in picking Scott. But, Scott impressed me as intelligent and well-bred, not the sort of fellow who would work against his own client." Acting helpless, Rock changed the subject. "I missed my little tenderfoot." He reached over, ruffled her hair and smiled flaccidly.

"I missed my brave." Saying it, looking into Rock's dark eyes, made her shyness come through. She groped for words, wanting to say the right things, wanting to help as he talked on, having difficulty remembering. "I wish I could have been there."

"Me too. I wish Uncle John could have been there. The judge and the attorneys speculated that John wouldn't do this or do that. Judge Dodson's opinions came through his own blood, his own gut, not Uncle John's. Hell they don't know him and his ways. Ignorance doesn't solve a case." He paused, looking at her. "You wish you were there? Mona, I mean Unali, it would have been good for your novel."

There was the name Mona again. Like a hammer. Guilt crept in, but not enough to right the misconception. The music had stopped. Feeling edgy, she moved over to the window. A small plane buzzed overhead. "Please, call me Unali."

"Okay. Sorry, I forgot. The facts of this case are in court documents. You'll discover how facts were kept out, altered, missed or ignored. Good, simple honest truth was the enemy of justice. What the judge and attorneys couldn't misconstrue away on speculation, they justified through the fact that the voices of long ago are now hushed."

She faced him. "The death of witnesses doesn't render you powerless. Especially if they left behind their knowledge in court documents signed under oath. In that respect, dead men do tell tales." Gena's voice grew louder, fired with determination. "That applies to live men, too. They tell tales through their words and actions in papers of record." She remembered the advice originally coming from her folks. She helped them in their office, their detective business, and they shared casework with her.

"Sounds logical." He rested a foot across the corner of the coffee table.

Gena paced, holding her elbows, her head lowered. "You could use that to your advantage. Maybe you could find an attorney who is willing to go after those attorneys for what they did to you."

"What do you mean?"

"Withholding and altering evidence, the judge not following the appellate remand, the clerk's office destroying evidence." She focused on examples from his conversations. "Those actions are extrinsic actions now of record, all of which prevented you from revealing the intrinsic actions, or misconduct of Nell and Houston. That's pretty serious misconduct." Gena paused to think, and returned to the sofa. "As I said, just because some witnesses are dead doesn't mean records can't speak for them. Dead men do tell tales. And live men tell tales through their words of record." She was adamant.

"Unali, you're incredible. Not just beautiful, but incredible. Maybe I could find a Seattle attorney willing to work on a contingency basis. I'll give it some serious thought."

"Good. Now that that's settled, what would you like to do?"

"You sound devilish."

It was apparent his statement and his eyes made her squirm. "Please, I misspoke." A part of her wanted to rush ahead. Another part slammed the door. There were no answers to the strange, wonderful feelings she held for this man. Having Rock here today made her realize how much she missed him. Gena reached over to stop the recorder and set it on rewind.

Swallowing the last of her lukewarm coffee, she rose. "Do you know how to play solitaire?"

"Yes."

"Then I'll teach you a game for two."

"Cards will be fine."

Gena walked ahead of him into the dining room, deciding he needed a diversion as much as she did. The guilt feelings of not revealing her true identity were temporarily pushed out of her mind. On the whole, she thought Rock did fairly well remembering things, probably since his case was so strongly implanted in his brain. She also felt he needed more time and lots of encouragement. "Shuffle, Rock."

Chapter Forty-Five

Before work, Rock sat on the sofa and flipped through pages of the telephone directory. He circled names of attorneys, then picked up the phone and began dialing. "I'm Rock Carper. I lost a trial in Clamton County that engaged in speculation and now I have a judgment against me because all the attorneys conspired and . . ."

"Mr. Carper, that's what all losers say." The attorney interrupted.

"No. I actually have proof in the record." Rock edged forward on the cushion, wondering how to best explain. He couldn't make his mind work in a logical order this morning. And, he didn't know what this attorney considered important.

"Who's the judge in this case?"

"Judge Dodson." Rock was pleased he could answer this question.

"Hell. He's a judicial ass. Nice guy streetwise."

Rock agreed. He slumped back to relax, explaining who the attorneys were and a little of what each did to him. "Can you help me? I don't have any money. Your representation would have to be on a contingency basis. We could spend time looking at exhibits and documents I have on hand."

"Where's the smoking gun?"

"Smoking gun?" Rock didn't know what was meant by a smoking gun.

"For me to help you, there has to be a smoking gun. Something outstanding withheld that would make a difference in the outcome. Something you couldn't have known about before the trial."

"Ah, they withheld surprise new evidence from their document specialist and mine. Er, the judge acted as a witness against me on my uncle's cover letter." Rock removed his bandanna to better talk. "Look, I've never claimed justice was mine to do with it as I please. But, the attorneys in my case sure as hell did. My attorney didn't represent me as originally intended. Ahhhh, I can't answer you in twenty words or less over the phone. Can't we meet?" Rock knew he wasn't expressing himself clearly.

"From what you described, I haven't heard anything to make it worth my time, Mr. Carper."

And, so it went. One call after another. Rock felt he was beating his head against deadheads. None were interested in a case that had run on so long. Legal misconduct didn't matter. Since he came up with zilch, he put the directory away and racked his brain for another possibility.

While stowing documents, he decided to arrange a visit with Efrem this week and let him ruminate over this. Suddenly, the phone rang. Rock wheeled around to answer. It was the 91-year-old gentleman, wondering why he hadn't been over to visit. Rock felt terrible, being neglectful. He promised to visit soon.

*   *   *

Rock made a quick visit with his elderly friend who wanted to know the reason for the bandanna. Not wanting to tell him personal problems, he said it was to cover a bad haircut and left it at that. They had an enjoyable visit. The cook had purchased some crab legs, so Rock cracked the legs for the old man to eat. Rock enjoyed eating the meat too.

Next he drove to Efrem's office in the Magnolia district, not far from Ballard. Efrem said he and his staff were working late.

"I knew things were tough, but I didn't expect you to get scalped." Efrem responded to the bandanna on Rock's head.

"Well, at least the bandages are off." Rock laughed, sizing up Efrem's lanky torso firmly planted in his office chair with his feet hoisted across a corner of the desk. "Man. They scalped me in more ways than this. At least, the stitches are out. My hair is returning. I hardly look romantic, huh?" Rock leaned against the front of the desk, hands in his pockets.

Efrem laughed. "Foxy. That's what the ladies around here are saying. Maybe I should trade in my western hat for a bandanna."

"I'll trade my life for yours." They laughed again. "So this is your new office. One of the secretaries said you moved up one floor when I couldn't find you." Rock looked around.

"Closer to God."

"Hehehehe." Rock loved their kidding around. He noticed Efrem's chair and desk flanked the south wall. There were built-in bookshelves on the wall behind him, where law books and miniature replicas of sea-going vessels were kept. And half a bookshelf ran under the high rectangular window with a northern exposure for slatted sunlight. Efrem had a knack for squeezing his collections into small places.

"I've never seen anyone use space the way you do." Rock sat in the only client's chair in front of the desk. He loosened his silver bola and undid the neck of his black shirt. Staring into the soles of Efrem's boots, he chuckled. "You look mighty relaxed in faded denims and holey sweatshirt."

"This is a non-court day, pal." Efrem leaned back; the florescent lighting highlighted his unshaven chin. "So, you're in a helluva pickle, my man." He nodded his head in rhythm to the slight rocking of his squeaky chair. "How are you coping?"

"I'm not. That's why I'm here." He related his trip through the telephone directory and what the attorneys had to say. "I filed for an appeal. Had to because the law puts a deadline on the filing of appeals. It gives me more time to decide what steps should come next. And since I can't get an attorney, which I can't afford anyway, I have to represent myself pro se."

"Nononono." Efrem accentuated, shaking his head. "I'm not impressed by your Geronimoan determination. When I told you to taste life I expected you to excite your red corpuscles in gentler pursuits. You're way off course."

"A fish doesn't get through life without swimming upstream." Rock defended, crossing one leg over the other.

"Hell. You're undertaking a voyage without fins. You've got no knowledge."

Rock really chuckled over this. "The judicial Mafia educated me enough to go out and get some book learning. Geez. I'm nearly forty-one and still able to learn. I don't shrink from difficulties."

Efrem laughed, heartily: "You sure don't. All the same, I don't like it.

You know what they say? An attorney who represents himself has a fool for a client. Pro-se attorneys are no different."

"I've heard that." Rock reiterated his worthless trip through the telephone directory. "Look Efrem, I'm learning the hard way. Just because some of your kind dress in pinstripes and talk fancy in a courtroom, doesn't mean ethics are adhered to."

"Got your message. Just because we swim like a shark, shrill like a shark and shit like a shark, doesn't mean we're sharks."

Rock laughed. "Oh, yeah, you're still sharks." Then he became serious. "I really can't risk trust in another attorney, unless he's willing to work on a contingency basis. Fat chance at this point. I can't afford one otherwise, and I will not drop this case. I want your advice." Rock shrugged, trying to sound upbeat. He felt weak, having not yet eaten enough dinner.

"Ssssssss." Efrem exhaled. "What to do? What to do? It'll still cost something because you'll have to order the daily record of proceedings. A six-day trial? You're looking at a fin plus two zeroes, at least."

"Five hundred. I'll pick up a part-time job, if I have to." Rock nodded, knowing this was likely. "Whatever happened to the fountain of justice I've heard about? Is it a rainbow, untouchable?"

"No, it's out there." Efrem motioned his head toward the sky beyond the window.

"Yeah, how far out?" Joking with Efrem was a challenge.

"Come on. You have to expect a few bad pennies in the fountain." He defended his profession, while clearing his throat, seeming sympathetic to Rock's late arrival to reality.

"So you admit it?"

"I'm not admitting anything. I certainly don't travel in the pack that surrounds you." Efrem nearly came out of his chair. "I don't like what goes on any better than you. I don't have much to do with other attorneys for that reason. I keep to myself." Efrem cradled his head back in his hands and studied the ceiling. "Weeell, let's think on this. You've got no funds, you don't trust attorneys, you have to represent yourself and you're on the war path."

"I wish you would represent me."

"Rock, you know I'm into maritime law. That's another ocean. And, I don't do appellate work. I'll help with what I can on the side. Have you read the rules of appellate procedure?"

"No."

"Well, for chrissake." Efrem riveted in his chair, plopping his feet on the floor. "How'd you know to file an appeal then?"

"I followed Nelson Anders' appeal procedures. I have copies of all the work he did for me. It's still applicable."

"Even so, for a man unschooled in law, well, you can't represent yourself pro se at the appellate level without following the rule book. The latest rule book. Not last year's. I urge you to buy the book." Efrem beat the desk with a stiff finger for emphasis.

"Ask my secretary for the particulars. When the book arrives, you sit and read appellate procedures all the way through, at least three times. Maybe eight. Oh, and you'd better pick up some books from the law library on how to represent yourself. I think the bar association put one out, too. Another point. You don't go marlin fishing without a pole. So, chart your course."

"Chart?"

"A daily plan. Organize your life according to a schedule. You're a hunter and know you never depart from a set plan. Keep track of due dates for filing documents along with your out-of-town work assignments. Are you with me?"

"Yeah." Rock smiled, appreciative of the advice. He stretched out his arms in preparation to stand and leave.

"All right then. I won't have to repeat myself." Efrem returned his feet to the desk corner. "So much for pro-se law 101. Now, have you taken your long overdue vacation?"

"The trial was my vacation." Rock grunted. "I found out you don't vacation in court."

"Hardly a trip to paradise, eh?"

"Hey, it was more like a preview of hell."

"How's Sheryl?" Efrem chuckled, changing the subject.

Rock flipped a hand back and forth. "So, so. Disappointed. We're still getting divorced." Rock rose to remove a pill bottle from his jacket pocket.

"What's that you're taking?" Efrem stopped rocking.

"Smart pills." He crunched an antacid.

"You'd better take the whole bottle. There's more to this than putting together an opus. When are you going to start?"

"Tomorrow."

Efrem pulled open a desk drawer. "Here, take this." He tossed a key across the desk.

Rock caught it. "What's this?"

"Key to my office. You can use my library and xerox machine whenever you need. You buy your own paper."

"Thanks, Efrem." Rock was deeply touched by this offer.

"I hope your undertaking becomes good therapy. Better that you drop it, though."

"Can't." They shook hands. Rock acted confident. He was determined to fight for his rights.

However, Rock left feeling dizzy and headachy. He passed it off as hunger, admitting quietly he wasn't certain he could represent himself. His determination and knowledge were worlds apart.

* * *

Rock slid under the blankets and turned off the lamplight. He wondered if this was going to be another night of fitful sleep and dream voices.

Recalling one dream, he woke before dawn, walked into the living room and pulled open the drapes to stare at a frozen blue-gray sky in a cold sweat because, of all things, he was dreaming of Sheryl. He didn't know why. Admittedly, he cared for her. Appreciated all she did for him. It used to be the other way around. He was always doing for her until they couldn't agree anymore.

But, tonight was different. He rolled over in bed and brought his hands to his face. The odor of Irish Spring from his shower wasn't enough to stop the ugly thoughts needling him again tonight. Because, this time, he was stone sober.

There were other nights of recent when he drowned out crazy thoughts by satiating his brain with painkillers and beer chasers. Nothing took away the hurt of his past. Haley. Anders. Scott. The trial. Sheryl. His experiences had become so unfriendly, that one late evening, he nearly took measures to end all this. The pill bottle was in his hands; the beer on the nightstand. It would have been so easy. Suicide from drug overdose and alcohol. The feelings of depression and hopelessness were almost overpowering, until an inner voice made him face the reality that he didn't want to be among the many Indian victims who solve their personal problems and disastrous life changes through suicide. Instead, he solemnly vowed to fight the legal system as he had experienced it. No one should be treated with such unfairness as he.

He flipped over to his other side and closed his eyes tightly. The past was over, at least where Sheryl was concerned. And, that's as far as his thinking would allow.

Traffic noises could be heard in the distance as Rock lay there recalling some of his other dreams. One night, mounting frustration returned and caused him to sit up with tears in his eyes. He spoke aloud. *"Oh mom Leucojum. My life is a mess. Everything has turned to mud. But, it'll get better. You'll see."*

Another night he dreamt about a mass of barnacles clinging to pilings at the ferry landing in Quamas. They opened their shells. Faces appeared from the shells: Judge Dodson, Judge Randell, Haley, Anders, the detective, Perkins, Adams Jr., Houston, Scott. All of them were waving their feathery arms and legs in search for plankton. Then Rock, a part of the plankton, swam in too close and their collective arms nabbed him. Fighting to free himself, he woke in a tangle of bedding. *"Shit. This can't be my special song."*

Finally, Rock grew weary, rolled over again and fell asleep. Before long a nagging spirit lifted him back to the trial. His words were no good. The proceedings went on without him. He was going no place in a hurry. Then, he saw Perkins looming forth, rushing down the aisle, chanting:

"The envelope sticks out both ends. It has a bright red return address up on the top from Safeco. You can see it from back here. It's impossible to miss. How anyone could miss not seeing this for four years is beyond reason."

With a fish gaff in hand, Rock was hacking at Perkins. Perkins was floundering on the *Lyda* deck like a salmon, when the dream jolted him awake. Something had surfaced. The envelope. Sitting up in the dark, he stared at the digital clock, three a. m. Then he burst out with an expletive. "Shiiiit." It wasn't just the time. Rock was almost certain that Perkins earned his spurs through deception on that envelope sticking out of the logbook.

Kicking free of bedding, he turned on the lamplight. An idea told him to rush to the closet. He tied on his robe, then rummaged around the closet floor, fumbling through boxes, finding nothing. He crawled on hands and knees to the bed, and began pulling out boxes from underneath. One box was labeled: Court Exhibits. He removed the lid and leafed through the exhibits, finding what he wanted. Sure enough, a copy of the correct envelope was smaller, contained no sticker and no Safeco Insurance company name and address. It contained John's plain Carper Cannery printed address. This confirmed his dream.

Then he remembered Perkins' closing remark about him gathering signatures in the state documents to use in cut and paste. He decided to check his copies, see if the signatures on the state documents were identical to those in the

Leucojum documents. That took a good forty minutes. Several names in the state documents were on the Leucojum documents, but none of the signatures matched up, like cut and paste as Perkins claimed.

A realization surfaced. Perkins couldn't let matters alone. He talked on and on and tampered with evidence, demeaning truth. Not in a sentence, but in many sentences. Paragraphs. Theatrics. Yes, Perkins was an animal groomed to chew the facts. The courtroom was his playpen. Rock's throat tightened. He plopped back in bed and closed his eyes. Maybe if he set his neurons in motion, he could make sense of courtroom procedures.

And now, another voice in his fully awake mind was telling him to go to the Clamton County Clerk's Office to look up Fred Adams Sr.'s estate. He didn't know why. He had to think why the attorneys went out on such a limb, altering evidence, withholding evidence, delaying trial. Too many things didn't make sense.

Unable to sleep, he spent considerable time in the shower, while trying to decide what he should do. The steam felt soothing.

After a breakfast of bacon and fried noodles, he dunked a doughnut in his coffee, munched and stared out the kitchen window. There was just enough daylight creeping across the treetops to notice a heavy snowfall blanketing the ground and leafless trees. He decided to dress in thermal underwear, wool socks, denims, plaid shirt and greased boots.

Not for a minute did he believe these dreams were special, yet, he felt compelled to act upon them. Instead of going to work, he needed to do some investigating. Rock would phone his boss to ask for the day off, knowing he wouldn't be worth much today anyway. He could make it up on the weekend. He knew his boss would agree to it since January was a slow month for business.

Chapter Forty-Six

Acting on a hunch and nervous energy, Rock drove over well-sanded roads to Midget Incorporated, the thermofax firm unexpectedly mentioned by Marvin's document expert Ben Anderson. It was the firm where Anderson conducted tests to presumably determine the Leucojum documents were forged.

A middle-aged, stocky manager at Midget took one look at the Leucojum documents. His round face smiled like a detective who discovered a new clue. "These aren't forgeries. I can tell at a glance. The 1942 trust agreement and the 1967 will are thermofaxed copies of originals."

"How can you tell by looking at copies?" Rock looked around the large room filled with copy equipment, desks and chairs. Most of the employees were away from their desks, perhaps to attend a meeting. The room smelled of ink and toner.

"By the typed print in these copies. Look at the typed print. I don't need originals to see pick-off"

"What's pick-off?" Rock peered over the manager's hands.

"These light and dark areas caused by heat during the peel-off process. And, look at the typed letters and signature lines." He underlined the areas with an index finger. "They have cancer."

"Cancer? I thought only people got cancer."

"No. Over many years of aging, thermofaxed documents develop what is called cancer. See those hollow spaces, or widening out of typed letters?"

"Yes. I see. I see." Rock's eyes widened in amazement, causing him to whistle through his teeth. "Even the signature lines look like hollow pipes rather than thin typed lines."

"That's cancer."

The manager also proved that his thermofax machine could be adjusted to take a ten-page document through the machine. John's 1942 trust agreement was only two pages with a backing. So, Rock learned that Ben Anderson lied at trial by saying the thermofax machine wouldn't take more than two thicknesses of paper without a backing. Rock left Midget in high spirits.

*   *   *

Motoring to a U. S. Bank, formerly People's Bank, was next on the agenda. Rock needed to inquire about a special service for will safekeeping other than a safe deposit box that would have existed back in the 1970's. This was mentioned in John's cover letter.

A manager was informative. "We do currently provide a special service of will safekeeping and have for some time. I can tell you, I recently forwarded a will to a customer that we were holding in safekeeping. It was dated January

18, 1951." The manager promised to mail Rock an affidavit to this effect.

* * *

At noon, a bright sun shone over the city, turning the snow to slush. Rock's progress encouraged him to head for another firm, the Statler Company, also mentioned in passing at the trial by Marvin's document expert.

A firmly spoken silver-haired manager nearing retirement, having thirty-two years of experience with both xerox and thermofax machines, also authenticated the Leucojum documents as thermofaxed copies of originals. He explained that no one could forge 1972-thermofaxed documents in the 1980's because of the discontinuance of type-11 paper. "Even if you found old type-11 paper, it would crumble under the thermofax heat in the 1980's."

Rock thanked him after receiving the manager's assurance he'd write an affidavit of his findings.

* * *

Back at the apartment that evening, Rock felt intoxicated. His progress was so enlightening that guitars joined the flutes and drums in his soul. He phoned Unali to tell her all his news.

"Rock. Nice to hear from you. What's up?" Her voice was buoyant.

"Trying to uproot information like a boar rooting for food." He joined in her laughter, then got down to business of reporting the latest. "And, managers of the Midget, U. S. Bank and Statler Companies are providing affidavits of their findings."

"That's great information for my book, especially the part about pick-off and cancer. Did any of them say anything about fountain-pen ink thermofaxing?"

"Yep, fountain-pen ink containing iron will copy on thermofax. Even notary seals are picked up by thermofax, but will have a ripple effect due to ridges and valleys of the embossment, creating hot and cold air pockets."

"That manager sounds quite knowledgeable."

"He has thirty-two winters of skill in the thermofaxing and xeroxing fields. He said there's no possible way to artificially age a thermofax of a xeroxed-copied original. There's no way to make it resemble, or even duplicate a thermofaxed document that was originally produced in the '70's."

"Hmmm. Listen Rock, I have tomorrow off. Why don't we go to Clamton County, kick our heels around in some offices and see what else we can find?"

"Really? You'd do that for me?" He was enthralled.

"Sure. "But, you'll have to come get me. I warn you, the hill out here is slippery. Wear chains."

"No problem. I have stud tires. Dress in your warmest feathers. I'll swing by at nine tomorrow."

Immediately upon hanging up the receiver, he phoned his boss and made arrangements. Then, he carried the phone back to the kitchen like a happy Native, dancing and singing.

* * *

The next morning, Rock showered, shaved and scented himself, all the while listening to blaring western music from the bedroom radio. He had picked up phrases and added his own embellishment. "Two young lovers. Yo hey ho hey. See you in the shadows." This kept Rock's mind joyfully occupied. He brushed his teeth and laughed at his hairstyle. A good old crew cut. He'd still wear the bandanna a while longer.

Yesterday's snow signified that he should dress in thermal underwear, denims or jeans and wool shirt. Even if snowfall wasn't expected today, the trip to Quamas would be bone cold.

"Love has wings, ya ye yo." While nodding his head to more lyrics, he sat on the bed to pull on his shiny boots. "Fly into my life." He inserted his leather belt with a silver and gold eagle buckle through the loops around the waist of his denims. "You make the ground shake, Yeeee waaaaah."

After turning off the radio, he slipped into a warm car coat, grabbed his keys, a jug of coffee, two mugs, his briefcase, and headed out the door for Unali's.

* * *

Rock watched Unali run out to his car. She was dressed warm from head to toe, including earmuffs, fur-edged boots and gloves. Her braid was hanging over one shoulder. He pushed the passenger door open for her.

"Hi, I hope you haven't eaten breakfast. I brought cinnamon rolls." She smiled cheerfully, holding up a cookie tin.

"And I brought coffee." He pointed to the jug.

"We're all set then. Let's head for the ferry." He made a run for the hill, fishtailing somewhat without letting up on the throttle and nearly lost momentum, but hit a big enough patch of sand to keep going.

On the way to the ferry, they ate and enjoyed each other's company.

Within the hour, Rock had them on the *Palouse* and standing on the top deck. Before going inside, he wanted her to enjoy the view -- Mount Rainier to the south, Mount Baker to the north and the Olympic mountain range to the west. The air was singed with salt. There was the sibilant whisper of waves against the ferry. He watched her lean on the railing and shade her eyes from the bright wintry glare with a gloved hand.

"I haven't been on a ferry in a long while." She shouted over the engine noises, as the waves slapped the hull. A brisk breeze gushed at them. There were other boats chugging along too.

"I thought you were a traveler." Rock embraced her sideways in friendliness. Unali didn't answer, just smiled and tilted her head against his shoulder. They watched a few seagulls.

"Ever been to Quamas on Chenowah Island?"

"I don't believe I have."

"Quamas is so small, a local resident can practically tell the season of year just by the howling of the wind, the blare of horns and whistles coming from the ferry and fishing boats, the rolling of squeaky awnings and the whir of motor bikes dancing around the dunes. Being a travel writer, you might be interested to know Chenowah Island is one of a chain of islands between Puget Sound and the Straight of Juan de Fuca. The population in Quamas is somewhere around seven thousand and growing. A windy place. Its predictability is that the wind knows no season."

They looked at each other. He felt his bandanna flapping and checked to be sure that it wouldn't blow away. "Its unpredictability is its fishing seasons. And screwy courthouse decisions."

Unali elbowed him in the ribs for that remark.

"Seriously, Chenowah Island used to thrive on its fishing, farming and timber industries. Bottom fishing for flounder and sole, and shell fishing were discouraged for a while because of contaminants from a pulp mill, a sewage-treatment plant and factories. Now these businesses are dying. No future there. In the past though, my family lived in close proximity to the Chenowahs. We became friendly and worked together. Like me, however, the younger generation tends to leave. Funny, the Native Americans on the Island are doing very well now. The Chenowahs were able to maintain their individuality as a tribe and increase their numbers by banding together with other kindred tribes. They still call themselves the Chenowahs, all beneficiaries of a federal court ruling, granting half the annual local salmon catch to them."

"That doesn't seem fair." She inhaled the fresh air.

"Yes. It's fair and in good time too. Government restrictions on hunting and fishing posed a problem, destructive to their physical and cultural survival. The federal decision, in realizing this, reaffirmed Native rights guaranteed in an 1855 treaty in trade for Native lands." Rock squinted at an eagle soaring overhead.

"Tell me about the Chenowahs."

"Years ago soldiers drove the Chenowah ancestors to reservations in order to take away their fertile land and fresh spring water. The soldiers put to death those who refused to move. Others escaped to Canada. Those married to Whitemates survived. Many have returned, because by the 1980's it was okay to be 'Indian', but not called as such due to past civil rights unrest."

"I've wondered about that. Why?"

"Someone decided it was insulting to be called 'Indian', a name given by Christopher Columbus. Although, I'm not offended being called 'Indian'. I read where the larger Pacific Coast tribes in Canada like to be called 'First Nations people'. Down here in the states we're called 'Native American'. I prefer 'Amerindian'."

"So, who would want to live there besides the Chenowahs?"

"The Seattle weary and rich Californian retirees." He explained. "Quamas is a fairly flat land with a few vistas of buttes and ridges where the rich and famous perch."

"How do the rest survive?"

"Scratch each other's backs. Serve each other in a variety of businesses. You know, providing the essentials. There are cottage businesses in many a house. Pottery, painting, jewelry, basket makers who weave with local grasses, bark and seaweeds and makers of masks, totems and dugout canoes. We even have bed-and-breakfasts in old restored houses like Uncle John's. Sad, though."

"Why sad?"

"Chenowah Island and Quamas in particular -- both are losing the rurality posture. Farms and orchards are disappearing. Only a few farms and forests remain." Rock looked out, noticing they still had a ways to go. "Come on, let's warm up inside. Brrrr. I don't have earmuffs." Rock felt this day was starting out like a vacation.

Chapter Forty-Seven

While in the Clamton County Clerk's Office, Rock and Unali hung their jackets on chair backs in the outer office where they would be spending time. The sun barreled in the room from a window. The room was small with only two chairs, some reference books and equipment for xeroxing and viewing microfilm. Rock stood at the chest-high counter and asked a young lady clerk for the Carper Estate files.

The lady wheeled out a cart loaded with documents. Unali laughed. "Where to start?"

"Yeah. Well, since I'm familiar with most of this, I'll help you find things. What are we looking for?"

"I don't know."

He leaned over her shoulder and watched her thumb through page after page, not minding because she smelled delicious. After a half-hour, she whispered. "Rock, were you aware of this motion?"

Rock pulled a chair over to sit and study its pages. It was Marvin's motion, filed with the court on the last Friday before the '90 trial. It counter attacked Rock's pretrial motion. And it informed the court that Benson would be addressing fraudulent conduct in the 1980's, accusing Rock of creating the Leucojum documents. "Hell no. My attorney didn't inform me of this. Maybe he didn't know."

"He knew, as did all the attorneys. Perkins had to provide Scott with a copy on the same day he filed this with the court."

"Then, maybe Scott passed it off because it was filed too late?" Rock was angry, but didn't want to believe Scott would purposely withhold Marvin's motion.

"Don't alibi for him. He had more than a week to tell you about it, during the trial, before the judge got around to signing an order against your timely-filed pretrial motion. Face up to what happened. Had Scott been upfront with you, you two would have brought your document expert Neil Woods to court."

"I needed Woods' report to be part of the record to cut costs."

"Something should have been worked out to pay him for a live appearance, anyway." They stared at each other in silence. "You had absolutely no warning?"

"Well, I received a threatening letter that Perkins would accuse someone of creating documents."

"I remember you telling me about that. But, that's not the same as formally charging you in a court document such as this."

"What happened to this court system, that a man is innocent until proven guilty? Marvin's gang didn't prove me guilty. No wonder I was so confused at trial." Rock handed her the papers. "Those fu..." He stopped his pungent vocabulary.

She put a hand on his arm and spoke softly. "Shhhhh. Now, calm down. We have work to do. You can vent your feelings later."

Suddenly a flash came to him. He returned to the counter and asked the clerk how to go about finding the estate file on Ralph Houston's deceased partner Fred Adams Sr. He was directed to a reference book on a shelf below the window, where the names of deceased were listed in alphabetical order. Rock located the estate file number. After providing this number to the clerk, he was in turn given a tape to view through a Microfiche screen. Rock went through frame after frame.

This time Unali looked over his shoulder. From the microfilm, they learned that Houston had hired Uncle John to be one of three appraisers of Fred Adams Sr.'s estate. "Sonofagun." Rock whistled. "Houston claimed he barely knew John."

"As an appraiser, hired by Houston, John signed his name three times on two pages of the four-page Inventory and Appraisement of Fred Adams Sr.'s estate papers, all on the same date and very likely signed at one sitting." Unali studied the papers further. "Look Rock, not one signature is the same. Even Ralph Houston's signatures vary. This proves that a person's signature at one sitting can vary."

"I'll get copies." Rock trucked up to the counter again and requested certified copies. The clerk took care of this, since the copies came from microfilm. Meanwhile, Unali continued looking through files from the cart.

Eventually, she picked up Houston's deposition to thumb through. "The last page references attachments. Where are they?"

Rock looked. "Weird. I remember Nelson Anders gave me a copy just like this one with no attachments. And, I was out of town on business during Houston's deposition, so I know nothing about the attachments."

"Your copy to me didn't have attachments either." Unali went to the counter and flagged another clerk for assistance. "Please locate the attachments that belong to this deposition?"

"Sure."

Before long, Rock and Unali were going through all the attachments and found a copy of an insurance policy Ralph Houston prepared for John, with an attached letter, signed "Ralph".

Unali looked at him. "Rather chummy for someone he didn't know. And, rather curious that we had to ask for the attachments. Obviously, they store them separately for no good reason to you. I'm guessing Houston realized his mistake about including these attachments, but didn't know who had copies. So, the attachments couldn't be destroyed. But, they could be stored separately."

Rock sighed, bitterly. "None of my attorneys showed me these attachments. Obviously, Nelson Anders, Ginger Haley and Scott weren't representing me. In his deposition, in his affidavit and at trial, Houston said he did no legal work for Uncle John."

"Here's proof he did. Scott could have impeached him on this one."

Rock adjusted his bandanna. "Scott said he read this deposition. Come to think of it, he had one of these attachments in his hands at trial and didn't even enter this into evidence. I feel so dense. Gullible." Rock stared at her. "I was stupid to work and gad fly about the country, while depending on my attorneys."

"I've got an idea. Let's go over to the auditor's office."

"Follow me." They grabbed their wraps and waved to the clerk on the way out the door.

"Don't forget your xeroxing." One of the clerks spoke up.

"Oh. Thanks. How much?"

"Seven dollars."

Rock paid the clerk, collected the copies and a receipt and led the way out the door. They walked to a building across a cobblestone courtyard, banked at the edges with shoveled snow. At that office Unali had them going through a similar process of searching files, until they stumbled onto another recorded mortgage Houston had prepared for John and Nell.

Eventually, they discovered Ralph Houston had done legal work for both John and Nell over an eleven-year period before John's death. "That damn liar. Witness survival in the courtroom is a moral test. So why aren't attorneys, the stalwart officers of the law, put to the moral test?" Rock was disgusted.

Unali shrugged her shoulders. "Beats me."

Rock received certified copies of everything.

"My dear Sherlock, where to next?"

"How about food for the ribs? There's a restaurant, the Chowder Grove, or, do you want Chinese food, with forks?"

"Love Chinese food."

So did Rock. He always felt full when he left a Chinese restaurant. And, his appetite was back to normal.

*   *   *

Sitting next to each other in a booth at Shi Lin Gardens, a slim, short Oriental-appearing waitress, dressed in a kimono-style uniform, brought them two red and gold dragon-decorated menus and a pot of Oolong tea. "One menu is fine, thank you." Rock wanted Unali sitting close.

They put their heads together, scanning dinner choices until settling on won ton soup, deluxe fried rice, crispy spring rolls, Tai-Chien chicken and hot mustard.

When conversation grew silent, music of foreign clinks and clangs filled the airwaves. Rock wondered what to talk about. He couldn't talk incessantly about his case. It was easy to think of things to talk about while apart, but which evaporated in her presence. Even when he closed his eyes, her sweet smell was larger than life, always playing crazy tricks on his emotions. At least, his legal problems weren't so monumental when she was near.

Simultaneously, they began to talk and then stopped. "You go first." Unali laughed.

"No, no. You go first." Rock insisted, putting an arm across her back.

"So, this is Chinatown."

"As close at it gets." He grinned, looking down at her.

She raised a thimble of tea to her lips. "Very nice." Her eyes rolled around. "Paper lanterns, streamers, a scene of a bygone dynasty surrounded by bonsai trees. I see Chinese motifs: Azaleas, camellias, hydrangeas, asters, lilies, roses, pheasants, peacocks and dragons."

"Very good. Get a load of these place mats. The Chinese zodiac."

Unali studied hers. "It says here that many Chinese believe the year of a person's birth is the primary factor in determining that person's personality traits. What year were you born?"

"1950."

"Okay, You're in the year of the tiger. Tiger people are aggressive, courageous, candid and sensitive."

"I should be in the year of the bat. I'm as blind as one."

"Now, quit running yourself down. It says here, you may look to the horse for happiness."

"Read the horse to me."

"Horse. You're attractive to the opposite sex, often ostentatious and impatient. You need people. Oh, it says you can marry someone born in the year of the dog, but never a rat."

"Rat, huh. Why?"

"Rats spend freely and seldom make lasting friendships."

"We know who rats are. They fit in somewhere between two-legged land sharks and ludicrous turds from Quamas and California." He winked at her.

"Rock, behave." She laughed.

"So, I may marry someone born in the year of the dog?"

"Yes, the dog is loyal, honest, works well with others, is generous yet stubborn and sometimes selfish."

"What does it say about you?"

"Says I'm a dog." She blushed a salmon color.

"Hmmm. A dog with a rosy face. So we're suited to one another." He grinned, pinching the back of her neck. "I like that one. Read on."

"It says we have to watch for dragons. Passionate people."

Rock cleared his throat. "Most people are passionate when given the chance." He noticed Unali had placed a hand around her throat. Her hand wasn't big enough to hide the red blotches.

The waitress brought their food. They ate quietly. Rock broke the silence. "So, how was your trip to Oregon? Something going on in Lake Oswego?"

Unali swallowed a bite of egg roll. "I'll let you read the article when it comes out." She choked, sipped water and changed the subject. "The lady in the clerk's office was most polite to you."

"Just an act." Rock poured more tea. "The Quamas clerks think I've got jerky between my ears. But, they know they're asking for trouble if they aren't polite. Raising a ruckus is about all I can do in this town." He chuckled. "Would you like a tour?"

"On, yes, I'd love nothing better."

There was plenty of time left before returning to Seattle. Rock decided to show her the Carper real estate.

*   *   *

"This is it." Rock pointed to the ornate mansion painted white with maroon trim. They moved out of the car. The only noise came from their boots crunching on snow. They stopped a few feet in front of the car. Unali stood in front of him, while hugging her gloved hands. Her cheeks were pink from the cold crisp air.

"Wow. It takes my breath away. So Victorian."

They stood at the edge of the property like strangers looking to buy a house. "Takes up half a block. Mighty fine tipi."

She elbowed him and giggled. "Hardly. It's a masterpiece. Turrets, leaded-glass, gingerbread trim. Oh, what must be inside."

Rock's attention was temporarily drawn to the smell of wood burning and saw smoke curling from chimneys up and down the street, then he pointed. "The fourth-floor up there is a sleeping loft. I used to stand at the round window, which we can't see from here, to look out through those dogwoods, alders and birch across the street and watch the fishing boats come into Squawk Bay."

"Hmmm. Where's the kitchen?"

"Aaaah, yes. Women are interested in kitchens. It's at the back end. There's an authentic butler off the kitchen and a parlor off the front entrance. Grandma Carper's Victorian antiques were throughout the house. Can you imagine me around Victorian finery?"

She laughed. "Well, why not?"

"After my grandparents died, Nell and John reaped the benefits of Grandma Carper's fine china. Lenox, Wedgwood and old Spode. A chest of sterling pieces for tea and coffee, sugar and cream, salt and pepper and silverware wrapped in felt, including an old set with a C engraving." He turned to Unali. "I'll bet you're surprised that I'd know about such things"

Unali smiled. "I'm more impressed than surprised." Her breath turned to vapor in the chilly air.

"There were linen table clothes and napkins and silver napkin rings and crystal. Glass goblets and tumblers etched with flowers. Carved chests were in there to store all the finer things. My dad's old rolltop desk was in the basement. I only tell you this because Marvin said he junked it all."

"Everything? All the Carper antiques?"

Rock nodded. "I guess so. Marvin isn't a Carper."

"Oh. I loath Marvin the more I hear about him. He's vindictive. He could have given them to you."

"I'm not his kind. Are you getting cold?" He put a hand on Unali's shoulder.

"No, I'm fine."

"The dining room is in back of the house. It was decorated in green and white wallpaper with ruffled green curtains in its two windows. Reminded me of fancy petticoats. One of the big open fireplaces is in the dining room too. That's the room where Uncle John used to lounge, off in one corner by one of the windows, near the old-fashion, cast-iron heater. He looked like a banker, always dressed in a business suit. Anyway, he sat there to eat lunch, read the paper, suck his pipe, nap. And, that was the same room where Aunt Nell gave me the three boxes of memorabilia in 1980."

Unali turned toward him. "Where the logbook or journal was?"

"Yep. My life hasn't been the same since."

"Tell me more."

"In the spring and summer this place blooms with camellias, roses, salvia, lobelia, marigolds and snapdragons in shades of red, white, cream and lavender. The trellises against the house hold purple wisteria."

She nodded her head.

"And, see those trees out back. Those are Bing cherry trees. I remember picking some for Grandpapa Carper when he was bedridden in his final days." He chuckled, allowing himself to reminisce. "I climbed up on his bed with a basketful of cherries. He popped a few fat Bings in his mouth and laughed when I told him 'Grandpapa, be sure to pit out the pits'."

"This house has much meaning to you, doesn't it?"

"Yes. When mom and dad traveled out of town on business, I spent nights here with Uncle John and Nell. I snuggled under the quilts between them. That is, when they were getting along. Nell eventually kicked him out of her bed and into another bedroom down the hall."

"Did you like Nell?"

"Yes, until I learned about her conniving ways. But, even then, I offered to help her. The Bensons crowded me out."

A car screeched around the corner causing Rock to look north down the street toward the Kiwi Channel and Squawk Bay. "The cannery is down there. Uncle John, dad and I made many trips there in John's old Chev. We'd climb aboard the *Lyda*, one of their fleet of cannery tenders, and they let me sit on a high stool in the pilothouse. They eventually taught me to steer and navigate in all kinds of weather."

Rock sighed, thinking those were the days when a man's word went with a firm handshake. When a smile was sincere. His dad used to say folks didn't have to be unfair, unless they wanted to be. "I worked as a boat engineer on the *Lyda* after dad died." Talking about it, Rock could almost taste seawater on his tongue and see gill-netters pitching silvers, sockeye and humpbacks into the hull of the *Lyda*.

"Do you want to go down there?"

"No. There isn't any activity going on now. It may not even be a cannery anymore. Doesn't matter. We can breathe in the fresh air from here." He put his arms around her middle and hugged.

"The air here is clean." She inhaled. "If the cannery is no longer in the Carper name, why is the Carper legacy so important, aside from this mansion?"

"My dad and uncle prepared the trust agreement giving their fish cannery and the Carper house to whomever survived, to be continued to the eldest son of kindred blood. However, the trust agreement set out arrangements to use assets for other moneymaking businesses. So it didn't have to always be a cannery or connected with the seafood business."

"Ah, you could develop your own business."

"Yes." Rock wondered if it were possible to recover anything left of the Carper Legacy. "This place would make a nice museum for Native American art. I would turn the basement into a workshop."

"Rock. A museum in a Victorian house?"

"Call it a romantic whim. I don't want to become a lost face in a tribe. Spring and summer, this community is an intriguing artist colony. That's why it probably would have succeeded. A tourist attraction full of Native art from tribes along the coast." He held up a hand to demonstrate. "The walls would be covered in murals of powwows. I'd add a gift shop. There would be a small entrance fee to all but the Natives; my way to pay back the Natives who have helped me."

Unali smiled. "Doesn't look like anyone's home."

"You know it has changed hands four times, even though it is still in John's name." He assisted her into the car. "Too bad I brought you to this town in the dead of winter. Every weekend, April to October, artisans display their works. Well, we'll go to the Leucojum house."

Seeing the mansion again and talking like this, it wasn't so depressing with Unali at his side. It boosted his sense of direction, at least for a while.

Chapter Forty-Eight

As they approached a wood-frame house at the end of a horseshoe-shaped street, Rock could feel Unali's excitement at the sight of the two totem poles on the front lawn. She oooed and ahhhed as he pulled up to the curb and turned off the motor. She flew out the door ahead of him, ran over to one of the poles and gazed up. "Marvelous. Absolutely marvelous."

He laughed and crunched across the snow-covered walkway to the verandah. He searched for the house key on his key ring and proceeded to open the door, when a fat crusty snowball splattered against his back. He spoke over a shoulder, warning her not to egg him into a snowball fight because he was bigger and would win. "Come up here." He pushed open the dark oak door.

She came up the few steps to join him. "So this is the Leucojum house." Unali stepped inside behind him and removed her shoes as did he.

Rock raised a shade in one large window. "Conveniences here aren't modern. I had the electricity shut off recently, but there's running water." To take the chill off the big living room, he bent down in front of the fireplace to prepare a fire. Since Leucojum's death, he stacked quick burning pine, cedar and spruce firewood in a nearby corner.

Unali stood behind him, hugging her arms, appearing eager to soak in the heat. "Is that beachrock from around here?"

"Yep. This is a main feature of the house." He looked up at the floor-to-ceiling fireplace made of rock. "My dad did this to please Leucojum."

"Oh. It makes me feel so welcome."

Soon the fire took hold. "When wood in the fire pings, a spirit is speaking. The spirit enters the room and our minds."

"Everything has a spirit to Native Americans."

"Yes, spirit is everywhere." Rock figured she didn't believe him, but gave her time to think about it and to gaze around. She became speechless and motionless for a period of time.

"Spirituality is a part of everyday life." He tossed her his book of matches. "Here, light that candle over there."

Unali caught the matches and looked at the tall oak table with a stout, green candle. Removing her gloves, she did as instructed and then stepped back. "Suppose you expect me to wait for a genie?" Her chin jetted out, comically.

"I detect a little mischievous defiance. Breathe in the aroma and hold a hand high over the candle to feel the warmth." He huddled near the fire and blew into his hands, while watching her. She appeared trusting and eager to please.

Unali breathed deeply. "Ummm, nice. Earthy aroma of herbs and spices." She then held a hand high over the flame. "Warm."

"You see. The genie spirit entered you through sensations. There's a cosmic unity between objects and us. The candle for instance, enhances sensation, enlarges our consciousness. Such objects shape us within."

"Interesting." She walked over to the small statute carvings flanking each side of the mantle, then to the room-size totem poles in the corners behind furniture. "Who? What? How?" She looked up at the high-beamed ceilings and milk glass light fixtures hanging from brass chains.

After stoking the burning logs on bent knee, Rock rose with a smile. "Like?"

"Love. Are these your carvings?"

"Once were. Not now. Crafting totem poles used to bring me more money in three months than what I made as a fisherman in a year." He bellied up to the fire again, talking over a shoulder. "Oh, I carved them on consignment for Sheryl's folks. They fell in love with Native American art. As their collection grew, they gifted some to Sheryl. Sheryl lets me enjoy these. Technically, all the furnishings now belong to my son. I stay in practice, working on one in the basement of my apartment. I'll pick up the tools big time after the litigation is over." He removed the plastic sheeting between the living and dining rooms.

"I hope so." Her eyes moved about the dark-paneled room. "I like the wood pillars between this room and the dining room. You carved these crests in the pillars?"

Rock looked at the three-by-four-by-nine-foot tall pillars stemming down from the high ceiling, common in old houses. "Yeah. Rugged versions of frog, bear, beaver, raven, eagle. Technically, they aren't crests, but designs of spirits."

"I notice you used the raven and eagle motifs more than the others." She rubbed her hands together for warmth.

"Yep, you've got a sharp eye. The raven is one of my favorites. I identify with him. A part of Haida mythology."

"Haida?"

"People from Haida Gwai in the Queen Charlotte Islands. No relations. While visiting them, I took an interest in their ways. Actually, the raven is also of interest to the Tsimshians and other Pacific Northwest tribes."

"Okay. Go on."

"In Haida mythology, the raven is a cultural hero. He changes things so the environment doesn't settle to a boring routine. He's a trickster who makes people laugh and cry at themselves. He can transform himself at will to better suit his plot in order to show people how their greatness is overlaid by vanity."

"That should keep him busy." She kidded. "And why is the eagle a favorite?"

"Hmmm. The eagle. Like me, he doesn't fly with the flock. And, some believe that after death we come back to earth as living creatures. I have chosen the eagle, because he soars high in the sky, rides the wind, enjoys the sights of snow on the mountain tops, flowers in the meadows, bushes with berries and slats of sun through the trees of a forest."

Unali shook and hugged herself. "That's so beautiful it sends shivers through me."

As yellow flames curled over the logs, Rock removed his wraps and sat in one corner of the brown velvet sofa with his feet on the leather hassock. "Look through the rest of the house if you like. The shades in this house are thin. Enough daylight seeps through." He watched Unali's lovely presence disappear from sight. In a heartbeat, he'd kiss her, given the chance.

*   *   *

In the dining room, enough natural light came through the sides of the shades enabling Gena to see rose-print wallpaper, a compelling contrast to the dark paneling throughout the lower half of its walls. A few flat baskets decorated the walls. Worn carpets obscured the random-width floorboards. The round oak table, chairs and buffets carried simplistic lines. Patchwork quilts and Indian blankets were draped over the furniture – a rocker, two stuffed chairs and another sofa.

"You have two sofas in this house." She hollered to Rock.

"Yep."

Two large oval wall hangings drew her attention, each containing an eagle at different angles on tree branches, interspersed with tree blossoms and smaller birds made of abalone and other shells mounted on some kind of material, maybe slate.

"Mind if I use the bathroom when I find it?" She shouted again.

"Go ahead. It's down the hall past the oil furnace."

The smell of oil hit her nostrils. A layer of dust coated surfaces. A cold draft surrounded her with no heat at this end of the house. She walked past the small oil furnace and into the bathroom. The claw-foot tub butted against a sidewall of bumpy beach pebbles. A small window, positioned high in the outer wall, allowed in light. All wood trims were hand painted with red, black, yellow and blue-green motifs gleaned from nature.

After using the facilities, she returned to the dining area and veered right to the kitchen, where again there were painted motifs on wood trims rimming glass cupboards. Above the cupboards was a display of baskets. She saw an old electric stove, refrigerator and faded calico curtains. While peeking through a windowed door to the utility room, she saw an old wringer washing machine.

Thoughts of returning to Rock crossed her mind. Instead her attention was drawn to a room entryway, draped with a beaded curtain, to the left of the oil furnace. Figuring it was Leucojum's room, she quietly parted the beads enough to enter. There was still enough daylight filtering in through the sides of the window shades to see clearly. Eagle feathers, hung low inside the arched entryway, brushed against her forehead. Suddenly the beads behind her swayed and jingled, like a draft entering the room. Nevertheless, she moved deeper into the room. It gave her an eerie feeling, like she was invading Leucojum's privacy.

"Eagle feathers are signs of good deeds and good luck." Rock came up behind her.

Gena jumped. "Oh, Rock. Don't scare me like that." She caught her breath.

"Sorry."

"I came in here wanting to understand this woman who mingled the past with the present." After settling down, Gena pointed to objects woven in with the beads. "What are those?"

"Those are deer toes, symbolic of Native American beliefs. Before we hunt, we pray to the Great Spirit that it's for a good cause, that it's only for food and nothing goes to waste.

Satisfied, she walked over to the bureau, noticing an absence of cosmetics, cologne and jewelry cases. But, she admired a few feathered fans and baskets. "Did Leucojum make these baskets?"

"No. Her mother did."

"There's nothing inside."

"No need. The outside told Leucojum enough. She looked upon these as poems from a strong heart."

"Oh, what a lovely thought. It is a form of poetry." Gena smiled and moved on. There was a quilted satin organizer and a hatbox. She lifted the lid to see dried corsages. Then she moved on to a small snapshot tucked into the edge of the dresser mirror.

"That's Sheryl, Leucojum, my son and me." He took the picture in his hands.

Gena admired them all, but Sheryl drew her immediate attention. She was beautiful. Gena felt envy.

"Leucojum didn't appreciate Sheryl partly because she was a foreigner."

"Too bad. One citizen has no more rights than another, technically speaking. America is a tapestry of human experience. Rich and diverse."

"I reminded Leucojum of our diverse heritage."

"What did she say?"

"That she'd forgotten. She wasn't well. I didn't realize the seriousness of her chest pain, sapping her strength. Leucojum took great pride in not being a bother to anyone, even me."

Gena's eyes settled on a framed picture of a Native American on the wall. "Relative?"

"No. Sequoyah. The original hangs in the Oklahoma state capital. Sequoyah was famous for creating a syllabary, a writing system for the Cherokees. There's a copy of the Cherokee alphabet on the back." Rock removed the hanging to show her. He explained how some letters form words. "NME means 'enemy'. EZ means 'easy'. MT means 'empty'. Now you tell me what this means." He pointed to 'UOK'.

"You okay?" She grinned up at him.

"Now, you're a Cherokee." He kidded, with a grin.

"That's absolutely marvelous, because it's so 'EZ'." Gena took it in her hands. "Say something to me in Cherokee."

"AH-quah-NEE-TAH. It means 'I know.'"

She tried to copy him, but had difficulty. "Your enunciation flows like the wind. I'll work on it. So Sequoyah was a Cherokee?"

"The same." Rock propped the picture against the dresser mirror. "This house is a variation of Sequoyah's house, now preserved in Sallisaw, Oklahoma."

"Fascinating." Suddenly Gena realized she was alone in a strange bedroom with a man. Yet, she felt safe with Rock. That he wouldn't try anything she didn't want. She hadn't felt this close to a man since her husband's disappearance. The noise of the crackling fire from the living room broke the silence.

"Do you think we are different?" He hesitated. "I suspect you are Jewish."

"By my nose?" She laughed. "Yes. My mother was an Ashkenazic Jew, my father Caucasian and Protestant. Both are living in California now. They taught me the best from each of their worlds. Let me pick my own path. Really, Rock, our differences don't matter to me. People shouldn't let their differences escape self-control. Otherwise, how much longer will it take this country of ours to be united?" She patted his hand. "That's what you really want to know, isn't it?"

"Yes." He bent down and lightly kissed her forehead. "I was hoping for just such an answer." His voice trailed off. "I don't know what it will take to unite this country. Especially, when the phrase justice will be served, depends on the justice of a few power figures -- at least where I am concerned." He smiled.

Trying to act unflustered by the kiss, Gena nudged his shoulder. "I understand." She started to follow him to the living room, when a thought crossed her mind. "Where's your room?"

Rock smiled and led her to the back of the house. The bare floorboards creaked under their weight. The room was dampish, musty smelling. His room was just big enough for a single bed and one dresser with a large oval mirror. The wall paint had peeled in places. Thumb-tacked to the wall were several snapshots of him on his horse. Rock called him "Gitchee". The corners of the pictures had curled from moisture. Deer antlers decorated the wall above the bed. "Christmas balls on antlers?"

"That display hung over the fireplace for my Christmas, yes." He chuckled.

He led her to another small room, equally chilly with peeling paint from a lack of heat. It was accessible only through Rock's room. He opened a cabinet door to reveal a treadle sewing machine. And, from a curtained closet he brought forth a boot-size metal box. "This is where Leucojum stored important documents, including the Leucojum Carper documents, my evidence at the '90 trial." He opened it. "Not much in it now."

Gena peaked in, seeing well-preserved snapshots of Rock in his youth, old letters from Oklahoma and newspaper clippings.

"Once beyond the large living room, this house is very small." She guesstimated a thousand square feet of total living space. "Why, when other Carpers had big houses?"

"This was intended as a first house. It became so unique, Leucojum couldn't think of living anywhere else."

"I see." As they returned to the heat of the fire, she was nevertheless amazed at what inanimate objects in this house told her. Like feeling the heartbeat of a great and varied culture -- Rock's heartbeat. She had grown very fond of him.

*　　*　　*

Rock hunched down on the hearth to slide another split log into the fireplace. It sent sparks spiraling upward. His cheeks felt hot, sensing that Leucojum was in the middle of the fire talking to him. He rose, walked over to the picture window and gazed out at the gray sky of early dusk. The fire reflected off the pane. He could see Unali's reflection and wanted to take her in his arms. Instead, he jammed his hands in his pockets, while trying to understand where his was and what he was in life.

"How did Leucojum raise you?" She moved to the hearth.

He turned to face her and quietly explained his upbringing.

"Have you visited the Cherokees in Oklahoma?"

"Yes. I've been to Leucojum's hometown near the Trail of Tears. The trail refers to the killing journey following President Jackson's signing the Indian Removal Act of 1830." He raised his voice: "Twelve to fourteen thousand Cherokee were forced out of their homeland in North Carolina. Get out Indian.

Get off your land. Make room for the settlers. That's what the signing meant. And what happened. Most were sent to live in Northeastern Oklahoma. A six-month trek, mostly on foot during the cold months. Thousands upon thousands died on the trail." His gaze returned to the fire. "From that era to this, it's a wonder there's any spirit left among us. Some were my ancestors. Ancestors matter. They are a part of my roots."

"I'm so sorry." Unali sighed. "Another holocaust."

"I remember visiting my uncle, Leucojum's only brother. We called him Nighthawk. He was at the Stomp Grounds about forty miles south of Tahlequah in the hills between the Arkansas River and Sallisaw Creek. Only about six acres of land, in a grove of shady oaks set back off the country road."

"Did he have children?" Unali moved to the sofa.

"Yes. Nighthawk and his second wife, a Caucasian, had two sons. I have two cousins. I'm close to one. His name is Blue Thunder. My age. One summer, he and I attended the Institute for Cherokee Literacy to learn to read and write the language, using Sequoyah's alphabet. I met students from numerous tribes, including Choctaw, Chickasaw, Ponca, Kiowa and Creek. I not only learned about many different tribes in the area of the country, but I familiarized myself with regional differences and similarities. Now, I think I'm a sponge." He paused a while. "And, I learned there are many Natives who did marvelous things before they passed on, like Sequoyah. You should be writing about Sequoyah or some other famous Native American."

Unali made no attempt to comment, so he continued. "Anyway, at the Stomp Grounds my uncle took us fishing in the creek. We ate potatoes and onions cooked over the fire. It was a time in my life to daydream, hide in a secret place and listen to him tell wonderful stories." Standing statuesquely with one hand held high in the air, he quoted his uncle: "We are descendants of the First Americans with a rich culture."

Rock returned to sit by Unali and put an arm over the back of the sofa. "Then we returned to the main camp. In the center was a clearing with a mound of gray ash, accumulated from many religious fires at night." He talked gently.

"I remember four large logs in the fire were pointed in each of the cardinal directions. All of us gathered around in a wide circle. Under a dark sky and full moon, the fires burned high, sending sparks into the night. Then, we danced."

She appeared mesmerized. "Their way of holding onto a heritage and bringing on a sense of renewal and hope?"

"Yes. Each of us made a promise to try harder next year. To be honorable. Live in harmony with others."

"Jews celebrate the days of awe ending with Yom Kipper for the same reason." She paused. "Do you feel lost, losing contact with your people?"

"Yes. You see, technically, there are no special laws for half or mixed breeds. I can conform to the habits of Native Americans in their country, and to the Whites when out of Native American country. Fortunately though, it was the practice of the Cherokees for Nighthawk to teach me to be a man and do the things men do. Oh he taught me much, but then he died.

"Up to now, I've had insufficient orientation with my own kind, and much orientation to coastal tribes. But here in Quamas, the senior Natives taught me like an orphan to hunt and fish with bow, arrow and gun, to whistle, warble and sing sounds of the earth. And, I learned to carve small objects, which grew into these carvings. A coastal craft." Rock swooped a hand in the air, then moved over to a cupboard, reached for a bottle of brandy, poured two glasses, and gave one to Unali. "A toast to my Jewish princess." They clicked glasses and drank in silence.

After stoking the fire again, Rock backed away, bumping his heels against an old carved chest. Bending, he rubbed a hand across its surface. He knew what was inside. Uniforms, awards, achievements and Native memorabilia. He lifted the lid and allowed it to rest against a windowsill. He could tell the sky outside was almost dark. Their main source of light now came from the fire and the candle.

Unali joined him. "Scouting?"

"Scouting. I started in Indian Scouts, learning four qualifications: bravery, good sense, truthfulness and knowledge of the countryside, meaning to see and not be seen. But Leucojum eventually took me out. Put me in Cub Scouts." Talking about all this made his heart long for the earlier days of his youth, romping with his Indian friends.

"But why?"

"Leucojum believed the move would be a good process of assimilation into the main environment. You see, when I was young, times were changing rapidly. Leucojum said there was the threat of total termination spreading through Indian communities all over the country. She believed assimilation was inevitable."

"One of the first things the White masters taught me was to sit cross-legged, or Indian-style, like an unsprouted seed resting on the soil waiting to be nurtured into a tall, straight plant. Hell, my character was already formed by the time they got me." He laughed and peeked under things in the trunk. "Anyway, they taught me to be trustworthy, loyal, helpful, friendly, courteous, kind, obedient, cheerful, thrifty, brave, clean and reverent."

"You sound like a tape recording." She laughed.

He joined in with her laughter. "A looooong list I can still recite from memory." He then recited the oath of a scout, while unfolding a deerskin, revealing his awards.

"And, in the process you earned all these?" She brushed a hand over his ribboned medals.

"Yes. These are the Eagle Scout Awards from the Boy Scouts of America. Also, these are my Silver Awards earned from the Senior Egg-plorer Scouting Program." Rock apologized for his difficulty pronouncing 'Explorer', but continued with his train of thought. "I guess you could look at these as the end result of my growing from a seedling into a plant. At first we scouts were a motley bunch, tramping off to the woods. We learned to adapt to bush life, camp in tents, sleep in bags, fetch water from a stream, wash our own clothes and make our own music." Music reminded him of his double-holed whistle he made from a heron's leg bone. It produced a loon sound.

"Anyway, at night we staked nets with strings of clam shells to deter bears. The rattling noise scared them off. We got the idea from reading old tales of Native ancestors placing shell rattles at fish traps for the same reason. At daybreak after breakfast over a camp fire, we went in search for stones, shells and bones to use in making tools to survive." Stones fascinated him. Especially the nephrite stone, an imitation of jade or jadeite. The stone was ideal for adze and chisel blades, as it was hard and took a sharp edge.

"There are many puzzles in nephrite, like enigmas that scorn the imagination and leave gaps in our understanding that can't be bridged." Not one to seek a doctrine embedded in stones, he chuckled at the statement. Because, Sheryl's moods fit this description. She was an enigma that scorned his imagination, but he wouldn't verbalize it.

"And, meanwhile, the masters continued to encourage my carving talents as a way of keeping in touch with a cultural heritage, whether or not Cherokee."

"Amazing." She whispered, while sipping her brandy.

Rock's hand bumped into his .357 magnum in the old carved chest. He raised it to check the chamber. Empty. "Well, I'm taking this little hummer back to Seattle with us." He slid it over by the front door, along with a box of shells.

"Why do you have a gun?"

"For protection and hunting. All that's left of my gun collection. I don't hunt anymore, but still love to go out into the forest to hunt for peace and solitude."

"I've never heard of anyone hunting for peace and solitude."

"Why not? Hunters are the first poets who discovered the beauty of nature, the feel of the wind, the grace of a covey of quail fleeing the brush . . ."

"I know and the music of howling wolves." Gena laughed. "You have me thinking like you."

Rock chuckled with delight. "Anyway, I reached a point where I couldn't kill birds and wild animals anymore. That's why I gave my other guns to my son. I don't know what he did with them since he joined the Army. Probably in storage."

"Hey, what's this?" She got down on her knees and picked up a collage of framed writings.

"Some of Leucojum's favorite clippings." As he left her momentarily to pour more brandy, Unali scooted closer to the fire with a clipping.

She read it aloud. "Life is like climbing a giant Sequoyah. Many careful shimmies up, only one reckless one down."

"Obviously, I shimmy down rather than up."

"Rock. Stop it." She stared at him a moment, sitting back on the heels of her feet and finally broke into a smile. "You're a Cherokee cosmopolite."

"Is that some famous coinage?" He laughed moving down beside her with their refilled wineglasses.

She sipped. "Yes. By me. Cosmopolite is a cosmopolitan person who is sophisticated in the ways of many tribes. Because of your rare experience, you have so much to be thankful for. And, don't lose sight of the fact that no one can steal the Cherokee blood in your veins. Not even a Cherokee. You can take a Cherokee out of the tribe, but you can't take the Cherokee out of your blood. And, no one can steal your values. That's what counts. Build from there." She returned the clippings to the chest.

"No one has talked to me like this before. I'm touched." Rock downed his drink feeling relaxed and set her empty wineglass on the carpet with his. Then he reached for her hand, raised it to his lips and stared at her. He saw a face full of reflective thoughts. Their silence was stirred by noises from the fire. He pressed her head to his chest and wrapped his arms around her. The room's spicy aroma overtook him. He eased her back on the rug.

She panted his name. "Rock." Flames emanated from her eyes.

Rock needed passion in his life. Something Sheryl couldn't give him.

Unable to stop himself, he lightly moved his lips on hers, then pressed into a kiss. "Oh Unali. I want you. I need you." There was immediacy in his voice. He stroked strands of hair off her face and kissed her again. Brushing his lips against hers, an inner desire was overtaking him as quickly as fire consuming cedar.

Echoes of church bells rang from a distance. Unali responded warmly to his kisses. She encouraged his advance. Her braid came loose. They were slipping gracefully into enchantment as if seized by mysticism.

Rock moved a hand over a breast while her fingers tangled in his bandanna. Her breath sounded against his ear. He kissed her again. A kiss surged with desire. She squirmed and gasped, yielding and not yielding.

Then she tugged at his collar. "Rock."

Her sudden hesitation was puzzling. "My princess, are you okay?"

"I am so sorry, but I must insist we leave now."

He nodded, although saddened to have offended her like this. She was right, of course.

While dousing the fire and leaving the house as they found it, his unspoken thoughts were in trying to figure out this lovely woman. She was married. Now divorced. He knew there was passion behind those turquoise eyes. Glancing her way, he noticed her neck was blotchy. A few teardrops streamed from her eyes.

"Unali I apologize for rushing you like this."

"Rock, don't apologize. Let's forget it happened. I have had a wonderful time and appreciate all that you have shared with me."

"No hard feelings?"

"None."

Chapter Forty-Nine

Under a silvery moon in a cloud-hazed evening sky, Gena and Rock headed back to Seattle on the *Palouse* ferry. They watched bobbing lights of fishing boats in the distance. Rock said the boats were gill netters tide drifting.

It was a long day. Gena was emotionally exhausted, riddled with guilt for nearly violating her ethics, silently thanking God that she stopped things in time. The incident made her realize how serious things were becoming.

In the Leucojum house, Rock's Native presence surrounded everything. His cologne, deep voice, his weight on top of her awakening dormant urges. He held her gaze with his fire-reflective eyes that were practically luminous in the dim room.

There was no denying, in Rock's company it was easy to forget her missing husband and their marriage. She would have to be strong and focus on procuring Rock's story for Mona's novel in busier surroundings.

Yet, in spite of what happened, the Leucojum house told her more about Rock than any court document she had read. In fact the entire day was so unique because Rock was unique. She learned things about him that she had never read in a book and she was an avid reader. There was a story here and it had to be told to others.

Rock was sitting across from her. He was staring out the window into the outer darkness. "A feather for your thoughts."

"Hey. That's my line." He looked her way with a faint smile. "Unali. I appreciate all your help."

"And I appreciate yours." She talked softly so other passengers couldn't hear. "I especially enjoyed learning about you and where you are coming from. Your totem carvings are truly a labor of love."

"Fodder for your book?" He raised a brow.

"I'd hardly call it fodder." She frowned.

"You're stalling. There's something in that pretty head bothering you."

She thought a minute on how best to answer him. His eyes appeared almost black to her. "I saw bitterness and anger that you need to recognize in order to continue your litigation, more importantly your life."

"Humph. Learning about my ancestors was like putting gunpowder in my veins. Carrying it around is frightening." He wagged a finger at her. "I understand now why a person of another race goes bonkers when a Whiteman treats him unfairly."

"Rock. Shed the Trail of Tears. It won't help you in society nor in the litigation." A boat whistle blaring in the background seemed to punctuate her last statement. "I'm no psychologist, but talking helps one heal the pain."

"Fire away. Read my leaf. I don't want history repeating itself." He held out a hand.

Gena obliged, taking his hand in hers. Smoke from the fireplace had lingered on his clothing, a reminder of his warm caresses. Her body felt weak and shaky all over again. But, since she accomplished an important hurdle in her defenses, she would remain strong.

"Matter of fact, I'll make a stab at it." She knew nothing about palm reading, but could rough it. His hand was submissive. With a finger, she traced the lines of his palm, ignoring several scars. "This major line here represents your formative years. This small line branching away represents your vulnerability. Your naiveté."

"Not naïve in love." He grinned seductively

"Noooo. A naïve respect for authority in all walks of life, so much so that you became especially deferential and vulnerable to your associations in the judicial system."

"And, how did you arrive at this conclusion?" His demeanor stiffened in explaining that he had witnessed the darker side of justice. "Marvin's witnesses brought dishonor to the system. Judge Dodson wouldn't allow truth in the courtroom. I couldn't act responsibly with all the other surprises and peculiar ways the attorneys entered evidence. Are you blaming this on scouting?"

"Well, you learned submissiveness to it in scouting. In becoming trustworthy, obedient and reverent. Just because you learned and practiced these attributes doesn't mean that others do." Voices of other passengers penetrated their conversation.

Rock looked around, then returned his attention to her. "I learned those values while growing up. Listen, I know there are good and bad in every culture. It would be nice if all of mankind honored these attributes, but my point here is that I especially relied on the attorneys to honor them."

"Exactly. In short, you were too trusting, which cost you monetarily, emotionally and mentally."

He stared into their hands, while appearing to carefully formulate his thoughts into words. "I see your point and never connected it to scouting. Relying on others for what I didn't know made me vulnerable to their evil ways." He shook his head in dismay, ignoring the noise around them, and stared out into the night.

"As the trial progressed, I knew evil was coming at me and still let it happen. My eyes were blind. I was too trusting to spend $100,000 in legal costs. I was passed off as a no-account client. Framed as a liar, a forger and now I'm faced with a $60,000 judgment."

Gena's eyes followed his, which seemed to stare at the deck lights of other boats splaying the waves.

"Oh Great Spirit. I was so wrong and so wronged. But . . ."

She felt his fingers go tense in her hand. "But what?"

"You think I walk around with my thumb up my . . ." Rock stopped.

Reaching to squeeze his shoulder, Gena blurted out with a thought that suddenly popped into her head. "You think truth springs from the earth?"

His eyes darted at hers. "I'll say this much. The wicked sprouted as the weeds. My shield is a wing of feathers, brightened by the sun. Leucojum often said to me, 'Rocky my son, happiness comes to those who walk upright under the Great Spirit's wing.'"

"Oh Rock. That's fine, but you have to help things along."

"Well. I suppose I should have stood up and hollered at the trial." The thought appeared to gag him.

"I know you don't take life lightly. And, I shouldn't rush to judgment. Yet, when faced with a crisis situation, you should have yelled when Scott didn't."

"I would have been fined in contempt or imprisoned."

"Either one is better than the judgment sanctions."

Rock sighed. "I feel gutless for lacking the nerve to fully question Scott's ways. I see that now. Leucojum used to tell me to walk among strangers as a sleeping arrow."

She was puzzled. "What does that mean?"

"To be silent. Sealed lips are the foundation of character. Good character. For me not to actively oppose, or yell, I encouraged their misdeeds. Sure, I felt numb and dumb more times than I could count." The muscles in his temples twitched.

"Still, I'd like to believe I wasn't as naive as you think. My six-day trial and those unplanned surprises for example." Rock lowered his head as he snickered. "Understand, through both types of scouting, I learned to conduct my own affairs on a higher plane than my ancestors. I was lifted from barbarism only to face barbaric tricks of the attorneys. Hell, I was overwhelmed. To tell it or write about it is one thing. To live it is different."

His forlorn facial expression and the tone of his voice came from his soul. It touched her. "The Jews in the Holocaust lived it. All because they were naïve, passive and trusting. You aren't alone." From what she had learned so far, it was apparent that it wouldn't have mattered what Rock did at trial. Justice was against him before the first day.

"Believe me. I was capable of some independent judgment. But, my judgment, my instincts served little useful purpose when Scott continued to put me off. Sometimes I felt unable to think clearly like my brain chemistry was out of wack. Anyway, I wasn't thinking of consequences so much as procedures because I didn't and still don't fully understand the law. What law Scott defined to me got worked over, screwed around and adjusted to judicial whim. I was a sleeping arrow to give in to abuse for fear of having no peace at all. Peace at any price is valuable to the likes of me. Unfortunately, it no longer flows in my veins like a river."

Rock shrugged his shoulders. "So, I didn't know what else to do other than complain to Scott. When that didn't work, I fell on the idea that attorneys and clients work together for a common goal. When that fell apart, I hoped for judicial ethics to kick in."

Becoming irritable and snappish, Rock laughed as if the preposterous suggestion of ethics was incomprehensible. "Not many clients could keep up with the legal tricks used against me. Most of it happened at the end, but I see now that the fire was lit long before trial. And, how was I to know Judge Dodson would hear only what he wanted to hear. I didn't know. In the end, I didn't know how to deal with super-civilized attorneys. I did what I was taught. To grimace and take my licks."

She stared at passengers standing in the cafeteria line, while thinking of how to respond. "I suppose you're right. It appears so simple after all is said and done. I don't mean to insult you. Only in the judicial system do you look through rose-colored glasses. And we probably don't know all the tricks they used. At least, not yet." She used 'we' to let him know she believed in him. "Meanwhile, trust no one."

Rock stared at her a long moment, appearing to cogitate her words. "Including you?"

"Even me." Her words left a heavy feeling in her chest.

"Did Perkins hire you to spy on me?"

"Now you're getting the idea. No. He didn't hire me. Even so, you have to make me, and others earn your trust. Think about your past associations with attorneys. The attorneys you hired. We now have a blueprint of their moral code. What we learned today, plus what you learned yesterday, proves they weren't representing your best interests. They weren't even representing your uncle's interests. A testator's intent should be protected by all."

She studied his hand again. "I see another telltale line branching over here. You are observant of nature. So, learn from nature. Remember, the strong pick on the weak."

"Bringing nature into this is interesting. All along, the outdoors has been my university. Yet, you're leading up to the fact that I wasn't able to apply those experiences to the courtroom. Is this what you're unveiling? You're saying I'm weak?"

"From a litigation standpoint, you are."

"Well, now. You are amazing. Remember thought, even in nature there are no absolute rules. But, I guess I put on a blanket of black feathers and flew along, doing whatever Scott wanted. When you feel people are kicking you to the ground as I did, you don't have a clear perspective of things." He stared out the window for a moment. "My opposition thinks I fell in sucker river."

"Touche. Let them continue to think it. That could be your best defense. But, change yourself so history doesn't repeat itself. Recognize that your shortcomings will strengthen your future. This isn't to say you'll win what you go after. However, you will be a changed person. For the better."

"I feel like such a failure. I don't know what happened to my instincts when I needed them most." He pulled his hand back. "On second thought, maybe my instincts did work. I backed off. Let the attorneys show their colors."

"That's a good start, because we learn best through analyzing ourselves." She smiled and patted his hand. "Rock, have you decided what you're going after in your litigation?"

"I've always been after the Carper mansion. Trouble is, that may mean unmasking Houston, and now other attorneys for violating oaths. I hate the thought of having to take this albatross to the State Supreme Court. But, I may have to. I don't like the idea of those guys getting away with my inheritance. I hate people who connive their way through life, twisting the law to their advantage. They wanted rope. Well, my naiveté gave them rope. Now, I'm hanging onto that rope, pursuing justice like I've never done before."

He held up a palm before she could interrupt. "Wait. Give me an ear. Don't think I consider myself a saint. I'm a sinner. I have flaws. I make mistakes. I ask for one thing in life." He paused for emphasis. "Man be honest."

Gena realized for now. Rock was aware of his shortcomings. Where it would lead him only time would tell. Squaring herself in his bottom line was troubling. His smile was full of trust in her. Feeling nauseated, she shoved her hands into the pockets of her jacket and excused herself for the ladies room. There was no easy way to tell Rock her problems. Weighing their problems, she felt hers seemed insignificant in comparison, even knowing how dishonesty backfires.

Chapter Fifty

Gena gazed at the fat clouds designing the daytime sky from the kitchen window, while Mona retrieved the morning newspaper from the front porch. It was her habit, her privilege, when not traipsing about the country. Mona then returned to the kitchen and headed for the coffee pot. She tossed the paper. "Here. You read the paper first. My eyes aren't open yet."

Gena sat at the table and unfolded the paper. "We're into February 1991. Saturday, Ground-Hog Day." She brushed it aside and picked over her deck of cards.

"Are you suggesting we celebrate?"

"No, just commenting." Gena could feel Mona's penetrating eyes on her as she shuffled the cards.

"Tell me about your travels in Quamas."

"I did last night. Isn't Rock's upbringing fascinating?" Last week Gena even recaptured the latest events by typing notes into Mona's computer for her.

"Yes, he is one big blast of cultures."

"I know. Unfortunately, it's part of his undoing in the court system. He misunderstood the upper crust of the race with whom he was forced to live."

"What else?" Mona rolled up the sleeves of her robe.

Gena's insides jumped. Telling Mona she nearly violated her ethics was the last thing she wanted to do. She hadn't heard from Rock since it happened, so she was trying to forget that part; just move on like nothing happened. For the most part, this worked with Shumway's disappearance.

"Mona, you've got everything you need for the novel, at least for now." She reshuffled the cards noisily. She didn't want to talk.

"Not everything, judging by your obsession with those cards. Tell me the parts you don't want put in the novel. All of it. I know when you're hiding something. You're not recapturing everything. Something happened between you and Rock, didn't it?" Mona nudged her.

Gena brushed the cards aside and stared at the sunlight coming in through the window. "Sheryl is a knockout. I saw a picture of her. Pretty red hair, little nose. I don't know what Rock sees in me."

"You have a lovely nose."

Gena snickered. "I'd expect you to say that."

"Okay, what else is bothering you?"

"Mona." Gena slammed down the cards and hid her face behind her hands, with elbows on the table. She never could keep things secret for very long. Through spread fingers, she saw that Mona's face was stern. There would be no letting up. "Okay. If you must know, I almost crumbled."

"How?" Mona scooted closer, as if everything in the kitchen had ears.

Gena closed her eyes and took a deep breath. "In the Leucojum house, I was pleasantly suffocated by supernatural powers. I swear spirits took over. Rock spun a web of love around us. I wanted to lose control. To be possessed by him. He has magnetism I can't resist. That's what's bothering me." She looked searchingly into Mona's eyes.

"You're too sensible, too solid and staid."

Gena knew ethics were important to Mona. "Not too staid for this man. Sometimes I think he weakens me with his eyes. His voice. His differences. I don't know."

Mona sighed. "Oh, honey. To think I told you to get a life." Mona rearranged the salt-and-pepper shakers on the table, then moved over to the counter to put English muffin halves in the toaster. "You still need a life. You and Rock both do. If you two are that serious, he'd better speed up his divorce. You too. And you must tell him about hubby Shumway and us, knowing how important honesty is to him." Mona buttered the toasted muffins.

"But, telling Rock about us and that I'm married and don't know the whereabouts of my husband is placing an awful load on Rock that he doesn't need right now. He doesn't have much faith in attorneys. Now you want me to destroy his faith and trust in women, too?" She became dewy-eyed. And she felt she should have leveled with Rock from the very start. Yes, this predicament was her fault.

Mona returned to the table with their muffins. "Inactivity doesn't solve problems. Go back to your attorney in Wenatchee. Tell him you want a divorce. Shumway disappeared, what, four going on five years ago?"

"About that." Gena bit into her muffin. She felt 90 percent sure that Shumway's disappearance was due to some bad accident. So there was no point in waiting any longer.

"My attorney says I can file for divorce now. I told our Rabbi about this. He interprets Jewish law as meaning I should wait seven years at which time a missing person is considered legally dead. That's compatible with Washington law. But, he says divorce will shorten the wait and that it's up to my convictions. I was hoping he would make up my mind for me. I procrastinated not knowing I'd fall in love. At least, I think it's love. I want to find out without making a complete fool of myself."

Not once did either she or Rock say they loved each other. And she recalled a time or two in Rock's arms of having a few feelings for Shumway that surfaced to disorient her.

Mona reached over to rest a hand on Gena's shoulder. "You're treading into a lurid adventure, spending so much time alone with Rock. I think you do care for him more than you are admitting to me. You're wearing your emotions around your neck. A red flag of blotches."

"I know." She held silent for a while. "What are you doing?" Gena watched Mona reach for papers on the counter.

"Going over some notes I want to discuss with you. Sis, did you know there are two community property agreements?"

Gena stared at her twin. "What?"

"I accidentally ran into these while going through the copies of trial exhibits. Here, I'll show you." Mona held up the two community property agreements. "This is a copy of the original, recorded 1971 community property agreement drawn up specific only to the Quamas Cannery. And, this one is a copy Houston typed, excluding this specificity. He submitted this altered copy with Nell's petition to probate John's estate rather than the original, signed one."

Gena grabbed the two agreements. "I see. I see. Houston used this altered copy misrepresenting John and Nell's original agreement, which vested only the cannery as community property. Rock might not be aware of this altered copy because it's unrecorded. Hot damn. Why you're a regular detective. I'm going to buy you a trench coat." Gena hugged a smiling Mona.

"Oh, I wouldn't turn that down, but please forget the pipe and spy glasses."

"You're thinking of Sherlock Holmes. Get your sleuths straight."

"Speaking of sleuths. In Agatha Christie novels, the villain is the one who tries to change his/her social class. You don't think Rock is trying to change his social class?"

"Are you kidding?" Gena waved the documents in the air. "The attorneys upped theirs and reduced Rock's. You are kidding, aren't you? The Leucojum documents have cancer, remember."

"Yes." Mona nodded. "It was something that had to be said, ridiculous as it sounds."

"I'm absolutely convinced Rock is innocent."

"But, how can you be so sure?" Mona was challenging her.

"I know the signs of lying on the witness stand. A series of little shrugs in the shoulders. Twitch of the lip. Slow blinking eyelids. Half smiles. Narrow eyes. He doesn't flinch away on anything when he talks about the Leucojum documents and what the attorneys did to him. I'm telling you, what attorneys do with their power is frightening. Besides, a decent person just doesn't approach forty years of age, then go out and commit fraud. The evidence used against him was based on a trumped up, phony hypothesis. This entire scenario simply doesn't mirror his life. Had Rock committed fraud, he would have planned it better."

"I agree. I just wanted to hear you say these things."

"Fraud isn't in him. Blind trust is. Rock is paying for the crime of others all because he was so trusting of attorneys. Scott's poor cross-examination of witnesses helped frame an innocent man. The law can be unyielding to serve a few. I don't know how Rock is going to continue his litigation. If he represents himself pro se, it will be an uphill fight. Pro-se attorneys are looked down on as neophytes."

"Neophytes?"

"Newcomers. Their paperwork is buried at the bottom of the pile. Clerk's read pro-se work, then slip it under the noses of proper authorities to sign. You know, I remember dad saying, trust everyone, but shuffle the cards." Gena shuffled.

"Dad was right. Rock needs a card trick too. One with five aces."

"Or a Mordecai miracle, as mom would say. I think he's relying on his ancestral spirits to aid him in his struggle. Think I'll phone Rock to see if he knows about these two agreements." Gena wanted to see Rock again anyway. Yet, if she couldn't see him, she could at least hear his voice. And this latest news gave her a chance to find out what he was doing.

*   *   *

"Unali." Rock expressed pleasure hearing from her, even if he did start the week in an ugly mood with work responsibilities during the daytime and legal pressures after dinnertimes. The pressures the past few days were enough to make him feel like a lost soul because of rules and regulations he must follow in filing documents in the legal system. Yet, hearing from Unali calmed him immediately. He really missed her. "How are you? I was about to phone you. What's up?"

"This may sound a bit unusual, but I would like your answering machine tapes, primarily to hear conversations between you and Scott. Do you mind? It will flavor the novel."

"Oh? Well no, I don't mind, if you don't mind hearing my conversations with others besides Scott. I'll mail you what I can since I have to go to the post office. How's that sound?"

"Great."

They visited a while about all the things he had yet to do. "I've got news. I met with a new document specialist recommended by Efrem. She took a lengthy analysis of my handwriting and determined that my writing is nowhere near the style of John's. She also authenticated the Leucojum documents. And, she compared the typing of the three unsigned letters Scott sent me, alongside other documents and exhibits from the Houston Law Firm. She noticed the rhythm of typing was similar, all prepared by the same typist, including John's earlier 1952 will. She mailed me a full report. Oh, and my appeal has been granted. But, Efrem told me to put the appeal on hold." Rock set the empty mug on the kitchen table and sat down in a chair.

"Why?"

"It's the law. My latest new evidence has to go through the superior court, under Judge Dodson's nose, as a motion for reconsideration. If the judge is convinced of my new evidence, I could win and won't have to appeal."

"Oh, let's hope he changes his mind. Sounds as if you have found an attorney."

"'Fraid not. You're associating with Dorian Barnes Rock Carper, pro-se attorney." He spoke stoutly, while looking out his window. The sun seemed to melt away all traces of frost, evident on buildings and foliage earlier.

"You're definitely representing yourself?"

"Don't sound so concerned. I have no alternative. And, don't tell me an attorney who represents himself has a fool for a client. I've already been warned. Hell. You know my record. I hire an attorney and he works for my opposition. I don't want to end up in jail for the rest of my life."

She laughed. "Well, you've got chutzpah, daring to trifle with such an undertaking."

"Agreed. But, I'm yelling, legally. Defending my credibility. And I'm following instructions in *Washington Court Rules*, a book Efrem's secretary ordered."

"Sounds like you're really getting into it the right way."

"Yes, the book finally arrived. In reading it, along with case law at Efrem's library, I've come to realize that in the eyes of the law, I'm an American first. Justice shouldn't be a racial issue."

"That's right, Rock. Justice, in America, is for all of us. Are you using our research in Quamas and your research with the various companies?"

"Most definitely. Now I'm preparing to file the affidavits on cancer, pick-off, the special service for will safekeeping and the handwriting analysis." He leaned back in his chair. "Are you snickering?"

"Yes, a little bit. I'm still thinking about your feelings on the racial issue.

For some reason, I see you as Native American first; American second."

"I didn't know I was so transparent." He wasn't sure he wanted to go into this with being so pressured for time. His patience was running thin like a thread ready to snap. "Did you phone to argue?"

"No. Oh no. But, you reversed those roles after you lost the '90 trial."

"Well, I'm trying to keep a strong sense of self and seeking my own solutions to my own problems."

"So I've noticed. Look, I phoned because what I have to tell you might help in solving some problems. Did you know that two community property agreement's were entered into evidence by your opposition at trial?"

"Errrr, not sure." He calmed down, reminding himself she was trying to help. "I know about the recorded agreement. How did a second one get into the woodpile?"

"Take a look at your copy of the exhibit titled *Petition For Probate*. The altered copy is buried in back, at page four."

"Geeeezus. I'll call you back as soon as I find it." He hung up and went in search for the petition. There were files on a table, some on shelves, on the floor, in and under boxes in the living room, kitchen and bedroom. He knew his filing system wouldn't measure up to Efrem's standards. How do attorneys keep track of all the paperwork? A daily plan wasn't working too well either.

After effort, and leaving a bigger mess in the bedroom, he returned to the kitchen and flipped through documents until he found a typewritten copy prepared in Houston's office and signed by Nell. Excited over this discovery, he returned to the kitchen to phone Unali.

* * *

Gena stretched in the swivel chair in Mona's office, while waiting for Rock to return her phone call. Her thoughts were disturbing. Rock offered no words of interest in her. All he could think about was his litigation. Yet, she realized he had to forge ahead for his own peace of mind. And what did she want from him? Sure, a story for Mona's book.

Did she love him and want him to love her? After what almost happened in the Leucojum house, she wasn't sure what she wanted. Maybe that incident was wrought out of loneliness where both were concerned. One thing she could affirmatively admit to: she loved his company. The ringing of the phone made her jump. "Hello?"

"I see what you mean. Houston didn't submit the original to the probate court during John's probate. The original is for a specific purpose, at the request of the Quamas Cannery, just like John described in his April codicil."

"You bet. Houston abused the power of his office by altering the agreement. He went out of his way to type a copy and exclude that verbiage." Gena straightened papers on Mona's desk.

"But why would Houston do this?"

"It was probably the only way Houston could represent that all John's stocks and bonds were community to all the companies John did business with. The motive was money. More money for Houston. For Nell it meant more property and money. She didn't have Alzheimer's Disease back then."

"Oh, yeah, she was clear-headed back then. But I'm not completely following you on the agreement."

241

"You see, the main thrust of the agreement was to make the cannery property, and any property purchased after 1971, as community to surviving spouse." Gena emphasized the word 'after.' "John's separate stocks and bonds were acquired before the signing of this agreement, not after." She cradled the phone on a shoulder, then uncapped the nail polish and stirred it with the brush. The polish had a pleasing smell.

"Well that info has been kicking around all along."

"Sure, and the right people ignored it. Rock, you had to lose. It shows Houston's misconduct. All the attorneys chipped in and helped mask Houston's misconduct in the probate of your Uncle John's estate. No doubt, Houston transferred assets without court permission. So the court must be protected also." Gena felt it best to blame all the attorneys involved, rather than just Scott. Scott should have revealed this. All attorneys hired by Rock should have revealed this.

"Hmmmmm. That's their motive. Money. Protect the system. And, I'm the one who catches the shit." Rock sighed. "Forgive my bad language. Well, thanks. I'll emphasize that information in the motion I'm working on now."

"How's it coming?"

"Okay. I've got a million thoughts on my mind, including you. Us. I don't know what else to say. My schedule is so full I don't know when I can see you again."

"We need to talk, but it sounds like you're too busy for me."

"Oh yes, I am in deep. I miss you greatly. And if you were over here right now, I'd prove it."

"What 's in mind?"

"Nice thoughts."

"If only we were free. Really free." She sounded pleading.

"Unali, we'll be free soon. I'll work hard to make it happen."

"Yessssssssssssss, I hope so."

"We'll talk. Later then."

*   *   *

After exchanging smooches, he heard the click of the receiver. He felt badly that he couldn't give her more time. Yet, hearing from her gave him renewed energy and determination to finish his motion for reconsideration before the next weekend.

He moved over to the computer, pulled up his motion and entered the discrepancy between the two community property agreements. Then he'd check his list to make certain he didn't leave out anything pertinent.

He mumbled: '*I've covered newly-discovered evidence, fraud committed by the adverse party, legal reps switching the fraud issue against the appellate remand, Scott's ineptness, Perkins' closing statements, withheld evidence, destruction of evidence by the clerk's office, Judge Dodson's errs in his oral opinion and Dodson's late order against the pretrial motion.*'

He would xerox exhibits at Efrem's office at night during non-business hours. Then he'd be ready for a final printout of several copies. On Monday he could drop off a few copies at a printing company for binding. So when would he have time for Unali? It had to be soon.

Chapter Fifty-One

Gazing out the window of the Chowder Grove, Rock noticed signs of ice breaking, tree branches sprouting new growth and plants turning green in sidewalk planters. Promises of Springtime put him into an especially good mood. He had made prior arrangements to pick up Sheryl and bring her here for a late lunch, since he had to file a bound copy of his motion at the Clamton County Courthouse. Also, he needed to bring her up to date and again give thanks for the use of her computer equipment.

And, he needed to approach her on a most delicate matter. "I hate to impose on your generosity, but we should delay the divorce a while longer. For appearance sake while I'm fighting my case in this county."

"Until efter Judge Dodson reconsiders yer motion?" She sat across from him.

"Yes."

"I can wait that long."

Rock couldn't believe her willingness. She almost seemed relieved. He was speechless.

"What else is goin' on?"

"The court clerk isn't happy with me. I wasn't supposed to have the motion bound in book form. I was just trying to be helpful. The clerk has to take all three volumes apart. And, he said my motion is one of the longest pro-se motions to be filed in the history of the Clamton Clerk's Office." He took a sip of ice water.

"Three volumes, ye say." She seemed surprised.

"Yeah. Actually, the first volume is the motion." He noticed how nice Sheryl looked in her navy suit. He was in a navy suit too. "The other two volumes are copies of exhibits of record proving my contentions in the motion. They labeled it 'Rock's stuff'. Can you believe that?"

"Ay." Sheryl giggled, while unbuttoning her suit jacket.

The front of her ivory blouse was quite tailored, nevertheless revealing the hint of a lace slip he knew was underneath. She smelled good too. He took a deep breath to concentrate. "You see, the actual motion consists of one-hundred-and-fifty-pages. The three volumes together total about four hundred pages. Efrem said I wasn't capable of preparing an opus. Hell, I did a mega opus."

"No one is goin' ta give a toss ta a motion that long."

"Lest I die, the story, in the words of the attorneys and witnesses, is all in there as an epitaph to justice in Clamton County. Or, should I say lies? Do you realize we witnessed more lies from power figures in that courtroom than we've heard in our entire lives?"

"Do ya 'ave extra copies fer me ta read?"

"Oh Sheryl, I'd appreciate it if you'd read my work." A feeling of great delight came over him.

"I will." She unfolded a cloth napkin in her lap.

Rock sat cross-wise in his chair and fiddled with the silverware on his right. "If it does no good in Judge Dodson's eyes, then maybe it'll help me in the appellate court. But, for now, I believe many will be closet reading to see what I said about them."

Finally, Rock picked up a menu. "No doubt, the chief clerk will check for his name. I wrote him a while back, demanding a clarification for the missing evidence. He wrote back stating that the brass staples and paperclip were removed from the Leucojum documents for photocopying and got thrown away. That's admittance to destroying valuable evidence before conclusion of the case. It's an issue in my motion."

"Good." Sheryl quickly scanned her menu. "Now, I want ta order sautéed oysters, steamed broccoli, cornbread and a baked potato smothered in sour cream with chives."

"And, I'll have the same." The dark-haired waitress took their orders and poured coffee.

"I wonder if the clerk's office employees and local attorneys are greeting Scott as firecracker or dynamo Scott? I put that information in my motion too."

Sheryl groaned above the din, while crossing her eyes and picking up the *Quamas Daily* newspaper she brought along. "There's an item in 'ere ta tell ye a'boot." She opened it. "Ye've come a long way."

"What do you mean?"

"Ye might be history in the makin'." She answered from behind the pages of the paper. "At least, someday ye might. It says 'ere on page two: 'The Clamton frontier was a curious mixture o' honesty and dishonesty'. They're speakin' o' the early 1900's. It says 'ere that homegrown crimes in the county varied from rank amateur ta semiprofessional. That white-collar crime was practically nonexistent."

Rock's eyes bugged. "That true?"

"Well, I cannae produce an affidavit as ta the veracity o' the yarn. But it's in the paper."

"Shit." Rock released five fingers downward from a balled fist. "It took this county ninety winters to become infested with sharks to my detriment?"

"Ay." She laughed, refolding the paper, setting it down. "I'm sayin', what they did ta ye is a white-collar crime. And I'm findin' it hard ta believe the stiff-necked highbrows in this town 'ave been goody-two shoes all those years. That's a crock."

"Humpf." Rock shifted around and rested his left elbow on the corner of the cloth-covered table. His eyes focused on Sheryl.

"Ye no need ta look at me that a'way. I dinnae do anythin' wrong. I'm on yer side, ye know. I'm sayin' lawyerin' in this town needs a'shuckin' inta."

He didn't mean to stare. It was like one of Efrem's beer bubbles trying to surface. Something lost in his memory. But, whatever tried to surface escaped him. He leaned back in his chair and unfolded a napkin across his lap. "The big clams around here float around free. Scott free. That's spelled S-c-o-t-t, like in attorney Scott." Rock heard noises and glanced around. Another couple walked in the door; otherwise they were alone.

"I'm hearin' ye." Sheryl laughed, blinking her eyes.

The waitress brought their orders, an earthy mosaic of fried oysters shot through with parsley and spices. "Enjoy your meal." The waitress left.

Sheryl chortled again. "A clamgate scandal."

"More like one big whorehouse of injustice."

"Well, I donnae know a'boot that, but I'd like nothin' better than ta be around when someone fries 'em."

Rock raised his head in laughter. He meticulously fingered the foil around his baked potato, spread open the potato skin, then forked the potato into quarters, releasing steam, mashing in the butter, sour cream and chives.

"I'm bettin' that's one clambake ye'd attend." She cut an oyster in half. "Ye'd skip weddin' bells fer that shindig." She quietly chewed on an oyster half, eyeing him. "Are ye goin' ta buckle doon, marry yer colleen efter our divorce?"

"Mona is her name." Under these circumstances, around Sheryl, Rock felt it best to refer to her real name, rather than as Unali. He devoured a bite of buttered cornbread, considering Sheryl's remark. At one time, he believed that if he recovered the mansion, Sheryl would want him back. That, with or without the mansion, she thought there wasn't much chance that anyone would want a halfbreed with his problems. Today, he wasn't quite sure what to think about Sheryl.

His mind wandered to times when they argued and she wouldn't speak to him for days. And then there were the times he needed a warm body next to his, but she shunned his advances. Listening to Sheryl now, he couldn't respond like he wanted. To tell her all about Mona, or Unali. And, now, especially, it was still imperative to maintain a good platonic relationship with Sheryl. So, the less she knew about his relationship with Mona, the better.

"I don't know what my plans are. Too wrapped up in the litigation. It wouldn't be right to put another wife through my problems. We've become close friends, because she's writing about my case."

Sheryl watched him closely. "Is this Mona writing about me in her novel?"

"Do you want her to?" Rock wiped his mouth with a napkin.

Her face brightened. "If I'm no painted as an ogre."

Rock knew she loved the limelight, so long as it was on her terms. "Don't worry. I won't tell her you have anhedonia. Provided you don't change your mind about the divorce. Just because I'm asking for a delay, doesn't mean I don't want the divorce." He chuckled in a teasing manner, as more customers came in.

"That's blackmail." She dropped her fork on the table.

"No. I don't see it that way."

"Ye donnae remember me telling ye I'm takin' medicine?"

"No. Since my head injury, some things have come back slowly. I probably wouldn't remember details of the trial if it hadn't been for the good coaching from you." Unali had also been helpful, but he didn't want to bring her into this. "And, studying what transcript I have has helped. My concern is organization. Things get jumbled in my head."

"Maybe there're memories ye donnae want ta remember."

He stopped eating for a moment. "Is there something I've forgotten that I should know about?"

She turned away with a frown that was next to a cry.

"Sheryl. Tell me what I need to know." He reached over to console her.

"I just did. I'm takin' medicine." She looked at him sternly.

He stared at her, puzzled. "What's this medicine supposed to do for you?"

"Makes me more lov . . ." She stopped in the middle of a word and covered her mouth with a napkin. "It helps me enjoy a sunny day."

Rock nodded. "Well good." He decided to change the subject. "Do you ever run into Scott?"

Sheryl looked down to smooth the napkin in her lap. "I'm gettin' a'boot a bit. I've seen 'im a few times." She picked around in her food. "I donnae think 'e has seen me though. His maze is a straight line a'tween the courthouse and 'is office, and a'tween 'is office and 'is fancy cottage."

Rock sprinkled pepper on his food. He noticed her brogue was getting thick, which meant she was fuming internally.

"I drove through the highlands. Judge Dodson and Scott's neighborhood. They're livin' high on the sunrise. Not like yer one-bedroom. Ye could live like a king if ye were like them."

"You know the saying, the meek shall inherit the earth."

"Ay, ye're eatin' it, laddie. That's what I put it all down ta."

Rock grinned from ear to ear with his lips pursed tightly closed, trying to swallow. He finally covered his mouth with his napkin. It was difficult to eat around Sheryl. He never knew what she was going to say.

"I donnae see any humor in it." Her face turned red, her voice harsh. "I donnae see 'ow ye could ferget the thin's we did and said durin' the trial."

Now Rock was getting overly heated. "I asked you what I'm supposed to remember."

"Well, I can say this much. Yer were quite taken with my body." She leaned closer, but spoke loudly, quite riled. "Of all thin's not ta remember."

"Sheryl, keep your voice down. There are a few others in here besides us." Rock pushed back his chair. It was time to leave. He flagged the waitress for attention, wanting the bill.

Sheryl threw her napkin in her food. "Ye've got numb nuts and scrambled brains." She grabbed her things and stormed out.

The waitress approached Rock. "Did I give her the wrong order?"

"Yes, she wanted fried brains. Mine." Rock gave her more than enough money to cover the food and tip. He was in a hurry to find Sheryl.

By the time Rock reached the sidewalk, she was gone. "That damn woman. I'll be damned if I'll chase after her." There was no pleasing a Scottish-Irish spitfire. He walked to his car and headed for Houston's law firm.

* * *

The Houston, Adams & Adams Law Firm in Quamas was an impressive two-story building, since undergoing complete modernization. Rock approached the entrance, flanked by tall shrubs. He was convinced the firm should be renamed Deception, Incorporated. Stepping indoors, he noticed plain, simple lines in leather and chrome furniture and indoor plants. An attractive lady at the receptionist desk broke his distraction. "May I help you?"

"Yes. I'm Rock Carper, here to deliver these three volumes to Mr. Fred Adams Jr."

"Certainly." She smiled and pushed an inner-house button on her desk phone, then disappeared.

Rock milled around to admire a few watercolor hangings of fishing boats on Puget Sound. Within minutes, Adams approached, offering no handshake.

"Here's a migraine delivery. My motion on file at the courthouse. Enjoy."

Redhead Adams took the documents. His eyes narrowed in on the thickness of the motion, and no doubt sizing them as equivalent to three Seattle telephone directories. He glanced at Rock with a gelid smile.

"You can share my motion with Perkins." Retracing his steps without further comment, Rock proceeded to the door. Based on the past, he knew Adams rarely attempted to hold a conversation with him, not since the beginning of this litigation. A forced up-and-down nod of Adams' head meant hello, hi or yes. Sometimes, Adams vocalized an entire thought to Rock like "I object."

Today, Adams got quite verbal as Rock held onto the knob. "I'm damn tired of this case; wished it'd go away."

Rock looked over his shoulder. Adams' Adam's apple stuck out. Rock chuckled, simultaneously wondering how Adams would deliver this motion to Perkins in Tacoma. By car? By mail? Perkins had to write the response, because he was the lead attorney. No matter. Rock opened the door, hesitated and let out one big fart. He could get quite crude around people he didn't like. Then, he let the door slam shut, leaving with solace, having dumped his legal headache and feelings of having argued with Sheryl into the laps of those so deserving.

Chapter Fifty-Two

It had been a while since Rock filed his three-volume motion. Today after work and a short visit with his 91-year-old friend, Rock returned to his apartment to check the mailbox. There was a letter from Leland Perkins. Contained inside was Marvin's reply to Rock's motion for reconsideration. Perkins titled it *"Executor's Reply to Petitioner's Motion for Reconsideration"*. The word describing Marvin as the executor of Nell's estate was disgusting.

He carried his mail into the kitchen, kicked off his shoes, loosened his tie and began reading orally Perkins' beginning words: "Where to start?" Rock sat in a chair and chuckled over this beginning, as the same words Unali uttered when she saw all the Carper files in the clerk's office. Reading further, Rock felt Perkins' outrage. Perkins' words were accusatory of him attempting to retry his case on fifty-six issues, ten new facts and more new evidence. Rock read further:

"His motion is couched as one for relief while dumping nonsense on the court. Rock even accused Judge Dodson of having a plan and being a part of this conspiracy. Rock's most ridiculous allegation of all is that I switched envelopes when cross-examining him about the journal discovery."

"I'll be damn, the prestigious turd is ticked off." Rock lifted an eyebrow, while talking to a sparrow perched on the ledge outside the kitchen window. He read the attached affidavits of Perkins and Adams Jr., who unwittingly revealed they withheld two boxes of John's documents from Rock: *"We provided Rock with seven boxes of documents for John Carper's estate."*

"Seven boxes." He and Sheryl had seen only five boxes, mostly Nell's papers, proof of which was contained in their letter written to Ginger Haley during her brief reign. It was coming back to him now. Sheryl typed the letter, then they both signed at the bottom.

Tasting his own rage, he busied himself, first informing Unali by phone of this latest and inviting her over with the premise that he would behave himself.

Next, he set the computer to prepare his reply, titled, *"Petitioner's Reply to Executor's Reply to Petitioner's Motion for Reconsideration, AMEN."*

Three hours later, a knock interrupted his mad frenzy. "Come in. Door's unlocked." He rushed to greet Unali, who had her hand on the outer knob. "Forgive my rudeness. I was in the middle of ordering a printout."

She smiled up at him. "Hi stranger."

"I know, rub it in." He took her wrap and purse, and set them on the sofa. She looked nice in denims and v-neck sweater. "Come into the kitchen. You can read my talking papers."

She sat at the table and picked up his reply. "AMEN?" She underscored the word with an index finger. "This is certainly a new use of the word amen, especially in the heading of a court document."

"Yeah? Really? You know this?" Rock scooted his chair closer, while watching her expression.

"Just guessing." Unali laughed, blinking innocently.

"It stays." He slapped the table for emphasis. "It was appropriate to me at the time I typed it, because the title is so damn long." Rock chuckled. "Besides, I think it might remind the judge and the attorneys of ethics."

"It could. So leave the amen in the heading."

"Also, it impacts another message. When you turn over this rock, you don't know what you're going to find." Rock pointed to his chest, then rolled up his shirtsleeves.

Unali's grin caused dimples to form in her cheeks. "Bugs. You'll find bugs."

He made a weak attempt to push Unali off her chair. "Yo hoh, a tease."

"Rock, you're a devil." She screwed up her nose and squealed in response. "I think the raven in you is surfacing. How can I concentrate?" She raised the papers to cover her face a moment. Then she refocused on the reply. "I notice you attached a copy of your Ginger Haley letter, complaining about only seeing five boxes. And, you've addressed the misconduct exercised against you in a court of law."

Rock blew in her ear. "Love your perfume. Damn I've missed you."

Unali pushed him away like a pesky fly. Her blonde braid fell over a shoulder. "I've missed you too. Now, be serious." She returned to the papers. "I'm pleased you wrote in the third person. More professional that way."

She read his words aloud: "Perkins finally admits that there's a conspiracy going on. And, all along Rock thought it was an ambush. Well, Mr. Perkins is an attorney, he should know. Rock will concede, the trial was a conspiracy." Wide-eyed, she looked up from the reply. "Did he really admit to a conspiracy?"

"He did. The more he talks, the more he jams his foot in his mouth. He's a balloon full of hot air. And, he does it with such arrogance. When I say arrogance, I mean a-i-r-o-g-a-n-c-e." Rock spelled the word to emphasize "air". "And, the judge sucked it aaaaall in like one long string of spaghetti."

Unali mused with a smile and continued reading his words: "Rock Carper has not dumped anything on the court other than factual, truthful evidence most of which is neatly tucked away in the Clamton County Courthouse's tin box of records, for which all counsel were aware of before trial. Leland Perkins so stated in his reply, 'Rock's lawyer ignored a ton of evidence.'"

"Hmmm." Unali turned a page to continue reading. "Rock wants Judge Dodson to know he is considered a fine, honorable judge with a professional benchside manner, even though Rock doesn't agree with his opinions. The judge's opinions that Rock had 'a plan' are accurately referenced in his motion for reconsideration. Judge Dodson's opinions were based on misrepresented, twisted evidence seriously limited in scope."

She set the pages down. "Well, the judge surely won't take offense to this. That's good. You're learning to play politics."

"I had to put that in there. Perkins was trying to make me look bad in the judge's eyes. Perkins has done enough of that already." Rock raised his mug and engulfed some cold coffee. Then he nodded his head for Unali to continue reading.

Unali read Rock's complaint of withheld evidence: "Two boxes of John's records have been withheld, which Rock didn't learn about until after trial. Mr. Adams' affidavit identified one of the boxes as a banker's box and I quote him: 'The banker's box contained check registers, a file folder full of exemplars of business correspondence, deeds and other legal documents bearing John Carper's initials.' That's plural Your Honor, 'initials' is plural. Ben Anderson said he had no initials until one set at trial recess. So Leland Perkins, Fred Adams Jr. and the executor Marvin Benson withheld evidence from all document specialists and Rock."

Unali again put down the pages. "Withholding of evidence should go hard on them, I think. And, it mentions deeds, probably one to the Carper mansion?"

"Right. Now read this part, about discovery rules."

She followed his finger and continued reading: "Rock was never shown original copies of all those letters published at trial to boggle Your Honor's mind. According to the civil rules, the person producing the materials may substitute copies to be marked for identification, if the person affords to all parties a fair opportunity to verify the copies by comparison with the originals. This wasn't complied with before nor during trial."

"I wonder what their religion is?"

"You file this immediately and we'll find out. I compliment you my dear friend. This is well organized and direct." Unali tossed the reply papers on a corner of the table. "What does Sheryl think about your motion for reconsideration? It takes you back to Quamas."

"I'm glad you asked. Surprisingly, she's not upset. Even when I asked her to delay our divorce, she didn't argue."

"You what?" Unali's body stiffened.

"I asked her to delay the divorce until after I present my motion to Judge Dodson. It's only for appearance. The divorce is imminent."

As Unali pushed away from the table, his papers fell to the floor. "I wonder what your religion is?" She quickly headed toward the bathroom.

Rock felt helpless, while watching her disappear. He knew he said something to offend. An old saying crossed his mind: It's not always wise to tell a friend everything. He placed his head in his hands and groaned for having stuck his foot in his mouth.

*   *   *

While lingering in the bathroom, Gena noticed Rock's hair brush on the tile counter. The light blue handle was of a nude lady with big breasts. This sight confirmed in her mind that men are so predictable, no matter the tribe. At least, the oddity made her get ahold of herself.

She didn't know what possessed her to responded like this, except that she thought there was a chance for her and Rock. Therefore, his announcement was devastating. Enough to make her blurt out the question about his religion. It didn't seem right to be hanging onto two women and that's exactly what was happening.

She looked in the mirror and decided she didn't look too frightful. Now, the need for her to talk became a priority.

Suddenly a piece of notepaper slid under the door. She waited a moment, then stooped to retrieve it. The note read:

"UOK? You'll find me on the front porch."

Wrestling with her emotions, she settled down at the sight of the letters UOK, remembering them from Sequoyah's alphabet. The note had a calming effect. This didn't alter the fact of needing more time to get used to his news and of talking to him. While being so absorbed in reading his papers and gathering information for Mona's novel, she misjudged him. Gathering information for a novel was one thing. Information that concerned her life was another. Rock was no more to blame for his messed up life than she was hers. Yet, a man just doesn't postpone a divorce for the sake of appearances.

Gena went in search for Rock. She found him sitting on the porch steps.

"Rock. Please forgive me for acting so school girlish." She sat down beside him.

"Hmmmm." He smiled rather sadly, while pulling a nail clipper from a side pocket. "I'm searching my soul for an answer to your religion question. Until now, religion has been mostly a private matter to me." He looked skyward, sighed, then turned toward her. "Other than praying for a better tomorrow, being human, standing proud and being a trustee of strong values, I don't know what my religion is anymore."

He paused for a while, still clipping his nails. "In my youth, a doctrine was pumped into my thick skull. I accepted it on faith. Now you're looking at a skeptic."

"Good. That means you're thinking and questioning. The best way to come to workable solutions."

"Don't you ever have doubts about life? I do. Like why am I here? Why am I in this mess? What's the reason for these gross experiences? What is justice?"

"Yes, I have doubts too. My folks say life doesn't have an exact meaning."

"For instance?" He resumed cutting his nails.

"An hour means one thing to someone on death row, another thing to a child at a birthday party, and quite another to you and me. I suppose life could be compared to an ocean wave. It washes ashore, then out again, never to return quite the same. So we have to go on and on seeking new experiences like new waves washing in. But Rock, we don't recognize new experiences as opportunities when we hang on to old ones." The advice pouring out impressed even her. That she should be listening to herself.

"I know, hanging onto Sheryl."

"And your hatred for anyone who crosses you."

"Huh. You want me to forgive and forget. Rotate the tipi." He shoved the nail clipper back into a side pocket.

"That would be better than letting your feelings consume you. I've been told that by forgiving others, you gain greater insight into yourself. And, by understanding others, well, it frees you to move on."

"Hohoho. It would take a lot of understanding why those bastards crossed me. I feel hopeless, insignificant and bored with life. I, I hoped you'd understand and . . . oh never mind."

"I'm sorry. I don't mean to pin you to the wall."

"You are. I feel like religion is a hoax, a lie like everything else in my life. I used to believe that if I lived an honest, decent life that somehow, I'd be rewarded in other walks in my life. Huh. It doesn't work that way."

This talk wasn't making Gena feel any better.

"I remember Leucojum joined an Indian Church. They read the Bible and sang hymns to organ music."

"That was nice."

"Not for me. I reminded her that our ancestral traditions are our religion. I teased her for trying to be something we aren't. That we didn't come from Adam and Eve."

"Rock, you didn't." Her voice sounded demeaning, while watching a crow land on a bush and peck at purple berries.

"Yep. I think there's only one God. One Great Spirit. They're the same. It's the actors I'm not convinced of. The church that counts is inside me." Rock pointed to his chest. "Oh, Leucojum didn't take offense."

He folded his hands together and stared at them. "My religion is a partnership between guardian spirits and me. Oh, I still believe everyone should be equal. I respect my elders, even aunts and uncles. Their decisions were usually right. You didn't joke around with them. That was low-class behavior. Sooo, I put the elderly and persons of high positions on a pedestal." He turned to face her. "You're on a pedestal in my mind. Unali, we must try to understand each other."

"Thank you." Trouble was, Rock didn't know her situation. He was so wrapped up in his own life, he never really asked, like he didn't really care.

She noticed worry lines creased at the outer edges of his eyes. "My dad told me if things don't work out you pack your bags and move on in life. I thought that was your intent and that I fit into your life . . ." She hesitated, then continued. "To delay a divorce for appearance reasons seems so base. So frivolous. Maybe even possessive. Like you don't want to let go."

"I suppose I deserve that cut. Well, Jasper Fulbright originally suggested that a married man appears stronger in the Clamton County Court system. It made sense at the time. It still makes sense to me."

"But, it did you absolutely no good at the trial."

It didn't take long for this comment to register. "You are absolutely right. No good. Makes me want to question Jasper's influence. It was his persuasion that made me stop divorce action." Rock thought a while longer. "Ohhh, I could never prove that Jasper had bad motives."

"And there is more. Like what happened between you and Sheryl?"

He lifted his arms over his head to stretch. "That's personal."

"Please, I must know." She looked away in embarrassment. "I can't put my own affairs in order without knowing your true intentions."

He lowered his arms, rose, stepped down and stood in front of her. "If you mean what broke us up, nothing truly satisfies Sheryl. She's rich, spoiled and needs no one but herself. Oh, she cares for me in an odd way. Making me miserable gives her a sense of satisfaction. Our differences got in the way. We spoke a different language, had different habits and customs . . ."

Gena guffawed at this as preposterous. "Rock, You two stayed together too long for language, habits and customs to get in the way. And, she's going along with whatever you want. Sounds like she is being nicer to you since the separation. Perhaps she falls apart when you're out of her sight for very long. You know the saying, 'Absence makes the heart grow fonder.' Anyway, I fail to see how all this makes you miserable." If anything, it was making Gena miserable.

"You do have a point." He put one foot a step up and leaned on his knee. "Lately she has changed and been nice. But, it hasn't always been like this. I remember the years of misery. The times Sheryl forgot what counts to me. A man needs a woman's love. I have a heart. I feel. I have the need to love and be loved, Unali." He shoved his hands in his pockets and stepped down on the walkway. "I'm talking too personal and you'll scoff at me."

She glanced around. Kids were playing across the street. "No I won't. Love is important to me too." The afternoon air was crisp. No sun. A layer of clouds. Barbecue smoke from the area filled the air, making her hungry. There was time to talk further. Gena felt she'd stay until dark if necessary, wanting to understand Rock's actions. "What does love do for you?"

He hemmed around, before speaking. "Love does for me what the tides do for the seashore and seasons do for the weather."

"Rock, talk straight." Gena was growing impatient.

"Okay. Love renews me, gives me a new face, a new song." He inhaled deeply. "Sheryl and I used to have love until she came down with a condition interfering with her ability to enjoy life and love. Then, one day I needed her to be my witness. At first, Sheryl went along because her main concern was what she might get from this, if I win. She likes to own everything. But, the litigation made her so moody I couldn't live with her anymore. Our relationship ruptured about two winters ago. Some of it is my fault. I spent too much money on legal fees."

"I appreciate your explanation. But, do you think it's okay for a married man to seek love with another woman?" Gena felt her neck turn blotchy, having blurted out such cutting commentary.

He squinted at her. "I should ask why you divorced."

"You're avoiding my question with another question." Gena's heart quickened, knowing he was talking about Mona's divorce. "Let's return to Sheryl. You admit she has changed?"

"Well, something happened between us. And, I don't know what it is. My memory is blocked. Sheryl says I don't want to remember. That my smoke signals are haywire."

"Sounds like amnesia." Still sitting on a step, Gena hugged her knees and thought about her missing husband. Was he carrying on like this with some woman?

"My doctor said that memory loss from a head injury depends on a variety of factors. The severity of the blow, what part of the brain was injured and so on. He predicted I'd recover ninety percent, if not all, in time. I'm doing my best."

Gena thought about this. His memory block weighed on her mind. "I wonder what it is that you can't remember?"

"It has something to do with her taking medicine." He stepped up to sit by her and sighed.

"Obviously it's serious to Sheryl."

"There are times when it's best to keep feelings hidden under the deep water like seaweed. I deep-sixed it real good, huh?" He stretched his legs down two steps.

"It couldn't be anything against the law. With your kind of luck, we'd know by now. It has to be something that happened between you and Sheryl. Perhaps personal."

"What if I . . ." He stopped himself. "Never mind. My notion is ridiculous."

"You think you made love to her?" She stared at him intently.

"I fear the unknown. That I could have done something like that, yes. I'm telling you this because our friendship is important to me. I admit I've dreamed about it lately and don't know the significance." He looked straight into her eyes. "If I did that, then I violated your trust in our friendship."

"No you haven't." The idea did cut into her heart and she turned away. "You're afraid of being less than perfect. You're still married. Rock. I can't interfere with a marriage. Your marriage. Call it God's justice. Our values must lean toward the marriage first, the friendship second." Gena was talking to herself with equal force, although she hated what she was saying.

Rock slapped his knees and raised his voice. "How can I get it through that lovely head of yours that Sheryl and I want the divorce? Huh? You, of all people, know I'm being pulled in all directions with my case. I'm only one person, trying to be four or five. There are times when I feel like half a person, especially when my mind tries to remember things. Geezus." Rock stretched upward, hobbled down the steps in a huff and paced the grass.

"And I'm only adding to your problems." Gena followed him, feeling squeamish, pressing him like this. "My dad also used to say that we create new problems when we don't face the ones we have." Admittedly, she was no better than Rock in this respect and was finally ready, yes finally ready to elaborate, tell him about her dishonesty.

Rock swung around and held up a palm. "Enough. I didn't invite you over here to argue about my wife and our divorce." His eyes were angry. "I don't lie. My marriage is over. That will never change. The divorce has been filed by Sheryl's divorce attorney, but held open pending closure of this case."

Two men were coming out of the building. Rock pulled her around the corner of the apartment and grasped her braid in his hand, forcing her chin up, as if to emphasize a point. "You have taken my heart prisoner, yet you shun me and my ways? You're the only woman in my life, Unali."

"Am I? Your wedding ring is on the left hand this time." She watched him quickly check his hands.

"Only because I was in Quamas recently. I told you I don't want my opposition to know about my private affairs. This ring has monetary value. Nothing more." He moved the ring to his right hand. "Is that better?"

While pushing away, she snapped at him. "Sometimes I think you grew up believing everything in life should come your way in a neat package with a bow and arrow, a free ride and truth to guide you."

His dark eyes bored into hers. Scolding. He stepped back and hooked his thumbs inside his belt, while pumping out his thick chest. "What's with your religion, anyway? Has it given you a sudden case of celibacy?"

"Sudden? How dare you." He touched a raw nerve. "Rock, the Ten Commandments were originally intended for Jews. It's only right that I should obey them."

He hemmed around for a while. "There are too many translations to the Bible to confuse me. Obviously you and I don't think alike. I think you'd better leave."

"Oh, Rock. Don't say that. The basic principles in religions aren't so different. Only in man's attitude." Pausing, she glanced at the clouds in disarray, like them.

"Please don't." He held up his hands. "My mind is on overload. I need to enjoy and cherish our moments together."

"Why?" Exasperated, Gena leaned against the apartment wall. So far, nothing they said brought them to any meaningful understanding, like treading water.

Rock placed his hands on her shoulders. "Gv ge yu a."

"What does that mean?"

"I love you."

This was the first time he told her this. She clasped her hands over his. His scarred hands were big, strong, yet so gentle. She bushed her cheek against his warm fingers. "Oh Rock, I feel the same way." Squeezing his hands tightly, she squinted up at him. "That's why our situation is so difficult. That's why I'm upset that you asked Sheryl to delay the divorce. You gave me the distinct impression that the marriage was kaput. And, you've made it quite clear that you want sex with me."

"Not sex. Love." He slid his hands around her neck. "I want to love you simply for the pleasure of loving."

"Oh, Rock. Don't make this difficult."

"Say it. For Chrissake, you would enjoy it too."

She felt her lower jaw drop. "How can I after your announcement? Hanging onto Sheryl. What happened to your Scout Oath of being morally straight?" Her words and her own guilt almost put her in tears.

"My God, maybe my case has derailed my thinking, my indifference to your religion, but we don't have to live by one interpretation of morality. You're divorced. Despite what you might think, I consider myself legally separated." He pulled her toward him and kissed her passionately.

Gena could feel him pressing against her. His breath smelled of coffee. His arms swelled over her like an eagle's wing caressing it's young. She was craving him again.

Finally he released her and asked: "Is that wrong?"

"Yes. Yes. It's wrong. I'm human and you're playing with my emotions." Her hands trembled in trying to remain strong.

He stepped away. "I respect your wishes. Since you need space when we're together, I'll back off."

"I'd like that." She hesitated. "I mean, that's not what I want. It's what has to be. "Rock I have something to . . . ."

"Hope I'm wrong, but you're coming across as a moody, cold fish, woman." Now he was leaning against the building with a mocking expression. His unkind words came barely above a whisper.

Gena stared down at her sandals and fought to keep from crying. "Rock I have something to say." It was now or never to tell him about Shumway.

"What?" He slid his hands in his pockets and stood at attention. A wisp of wind blew at his hair.

"If I was married, wouldn't you feel the same way?"

"Putting it that way, yes. What else?"

"I." She coughed in hesitation. The slight breeze swayed the leaves in the maples across the yard. "I . . ." This became one of her most cautious moments. Standing there so close to him, she wished things could be different. Rock had become a lonely, almost desperate man. His memory and marriage were troubling. Gena's head was swirling with guilt. She wanted to tell him she wasn't free, but could be. If she revealed her dishonesty, it might drive him right back into Sheryl's arms for good. What a web of deceit she had woven. These thoughts were ugly and the words wouldn't pass her lips. Wringing her hands didn't help. "I don't feel very well."

Rock looked at his watch, appearing agitated. "We should call it a day. Think I'll work on my totem pole and cool off. The only safe thing I can do." Taking on an air of indifference, he walked backward putting distance between them.

She started to follow. "What are you going to do?"

He picked up a stone lodged in his path and threw it fiercely across the lawn. "I need to screw the pole to a sturdy, flat base. Then, rasp the pole to a rustic finish and brush on two heavy coats of wood preservative. It'll last a century against weather and chewing bugs."

"*Chewing bugs.*" The words stopped her cold. This was a lousy way to end their discussion. Gena took his sudden change as a means of punishing her for not seeing things his way. He had learned to fight back like an attorney. It was also a hint that she should leave. "I'll go home." She really didn't feel well. Him hanging onto Sheryl for any reason was too much. "We'll talk another time, after we've both had a chance to think about this."

"Suit yourself." Rock headed for the basement.

She ran to her car feeling abandoned.

Chapter Fifty-Three

Gena lingered in her car in front of Rock's apartment. Their discussion caused her to re-examine her life. She was going no where and she hated it. She hated herself for not telling Rock her circumstances; that obtaining information for Mona's book was no longer her sole purpose for being around Rock.

Jealousy over his delayed divorce had settled in, leaving questions of 'what if' these delays sent him back to Sheryl. Yet, another part of her scolded for her own delays concerning Shumway. Frustration had set in with a vengeance. Her stomach cramped. Her hands and feet became cold and numb. She beat on the steering wheel. Feeling nearly paralyzed, she slumped across the seat and cried.

* * *

From the dining room window, Rock stared at the view of flowering fruit trees highlighted by pole lights across the street. Poles fascinated him. He'd look at street poles as potential totems. What would society do if he started carving figures in poles like kids do with graffiti? He chuckled at the thought.

He flexed his fingers. His fingers were sore from working on his latest totem pole. At least it gave him time to think about Unali's remark of him not wanting to let go of Sheryl. He passed it off as preposterous. Nevertheless, their entire conversation seemed to set them backwards, yet he still believed Unali had feelings for him. Or she was overly determined to get a book from him.

Suddenly, his gazing out the window caused him to spot Unali's car still parked out front. He thought she had left two hours ago.

He ran out of his apartment and opened her car door. She was slumped in the seat, quietly sobbing like a worn-out recording. He soon had her in his arms and carried her back to his apartment, while talking softly, telling her everything was going to be okay.

He knew she was delirious and needed a bathroom, but didn't understand the jabber about losing Shumway and now him.

* * *

In no time, Rock had Unali sitting on the sofa. He spoke softly in trying to calm her.

"I feel like I'm dying and you want me to keep my head in this sack?" Unali's voice was weak. Her eyes were swollen and her hands shook while holding onto the large brown shopping bag.

"That's right." Rock believed she was having an anxiety attack, because he had been through this with Sheryl years ago. "Now keep your paleface in there. Breathe. It'll stop you from hyperventilating any further." Unali obeyed.

Rock draped the Navajo blanket, which had been folded over an arm of the sofa, around her. A table lamp provided lighting. He gently rubbed her arms and legs and continued talking in soothing tones for a while, then became bossy again. "You're not leaving until I hear what's troubling you."

He left for the kitchen to fix her hot coffee diluted with hot tap water. He could hear her breathing becoming more stable, but the crying started again.

He returned to her side. "Here. Sip this." She sat up, squinted her swollen eyes at him and finally sipped, which halted the crying.

"Ahhh. This tastes good." She stared at him for a while, as if to see him differently. "Why are you doing this? I'm not worth it."

"Friends help each other." He sat back in the opposite corner of the sofa and crossed one leg over the other. "Come on princess. Tell me what's really wrong. What's causing this?"

"I deceived you."

"Do you think you've done something so terrible that revealing the truth might destroy our friendship?"

"Well, in blocking the truth, I hurt terribly, afraid it might destroy us . . . our friendship. I have so much on my mind, I don't know where to start." After setting the mug on the coffee table, she leaned back and stared up at the ceiling. "I'm married."

Her words dissolved into a chilling silence. "Married?" He jumped off the sofa. His adrenaline and strength were charged; then his knees felt weak, so he paced the carpet and rubbed a hand across his forehead.

"Unali. Why don't you hit me on the head? I've been screwed by the judicial system. I've had more misfortune in my life than most men, trying to keep the wolf from the door, but this tops them all. Why didn't you tell me before now? Geeezes. All I need is to have a husband running after me." His voice grated.

"I'm almost divorced." Her face and voice trembled.

"Almost?" He raised a questioning eyebrow. "Where's your husband?" Rock couldn't believe what he was hearing. Being jerked around by attorneys and Sheryl, and now this news left him cold.

"Five years ago, my husband Shumway Cox, a Native American like you, and I were living and working in Wenatchee. Then, one day while on a fishing trip or some vision quest, Shumway and two friends in Shumway's floatplane disappeared. They were heading for the Siskiyou Mountains, Klamath Falls area, when last seen." Her words poured out as part sobs, part words.

"That was the last stop they made to refuel. Following a futile search, they were presumed dead resulting from a plane crash. After a couple of years and no word, I changed back to my maiden name, Bradley, and moved to Seattle to start a new life."

"You never had any children?"

She shook her head. "No. A bad case of the mumps made Shumway sterile." She paused a moment. "It's only since meeting you that I decided not to wait the seven years, so I filed for a divorce. But, I'm not sure what stage my divorce is in. My attorney in Wenatchee is working on an inquiry."

With this Rock calmed down, even started to laugh. "We're both kind of in the same boat." He returned to sit next to her.

"Not quite. There's more. I'm not Mona Bradley. I'm a court reporter. My name is Gena Bradley."

"Then who's Mona?" His postured stiffened.

"My twin sister. A travel writer. She's writing the novel."

"Who have I been budding with all this time?"

"Me. Only me, ever since that first day you met Mona on the plane."

"Why in the blazes did Mona send you into my life?"

"Because she saw a story. But, she was too busy traveling. So, she wanted me to get your perceptions. Your experiences. Your world of sounds, sights, smells, sensations. Your emotions. Because my background was more conducive to getting all this, I entered into your life. Besides, Mona thought I would take to someone like you."

"And did you?"

"Yes. I filed for divorce because of you." She put the sack up to her face and took a few deep breaths before continuing. "You hurt my feelings by delaying your divorce again. Your announcement today made me feel rejected all over again -- first by Shumway's disappearance, then you."

This made him uncomfortable. Like she was trying to put him on a guilt trip, but said nothing.

"When you and I were in the Leucojum house, you attempted to make love to me. I insisted we leave, if you'll remember. I held back from you because my best friend loved a married man. Desperately." Unali's voice quivered. "She and I were roommates together in college for two years. After the married man got what he wanted, he left her for someone else."

"Gena." He said the name for the first time. It sounded strange to him. "I'm offended you'd think I'd do that to you. Geezzus. You think all married men are snakes?" He drew away.

Shrugging her shoulders, she wiped away the tears with the sack. "My friend committed suicide."

"Oh, I'm so sorry." Rock's expression and voice softened.

Her face darted into the sack.

He resumed pacing around with his head down. "If only you had told me all this before now."

"I got pretty good putting all my energy into deception. Now, I don't know what's real anymore. Guess I was afraid of telling you for fear of rejection; of losing a part of myself . . ."

He wasn't certain where they were going with this. She always seemed so 'together'; so strong. Now she was fragile. Under any other circumstance he'd have been furious. But he could see the pain she was going through, like him with his case. Rock returned to her side, sighed and held her close. "We're both vulnerable to hurt."

"I allowed you to become too close without being honest upfront about my loss of Shumway. Not knowing whether he's dead or alive took away any finality. I haven't been able to put his disappearance to rest. I'm angry with him because he left and I wasn't able to say a final goodbye, that I loved him, that I'm sorry for any unresolved arguments."

"I felt that way when mom died. The pain deepens for a while until one day you finally let go."

"I'm not there yet. Lately, I've been pretending that Shumway is alive. I guess it's because of being around you that I really need someone. By keeping my problems secret, I thought I was protecting you from any hurt. And, while learning your story, I started looking upon you as mystic and your beliefs as magic for me. In gathering information for Mona's book, I tried to help you . . . until you said you delayed . . . well, you know."

"Gena." The name was foreign. "Oh shoot, I'm going to call you Unali. Forget about me for the moment. Since Shumway is gone, you must learn to live with that incomplete feeling. There will always be some sadness surrounding it. Accept that he is gone. It's futile to be angry at him, yourself, me."

"Suppose you're right. Otherwise I'm setting myself up for more hurt. Are you angry at my deception? I know how important honesty is to you."

"Yes, I'd be lying if I said this didn't bother me." He released his hold on her and rested back, while rubbing her neck. She crunched the sack in her lap. "A court reporter? No wonder you knew so much. Well hell."

Neither spoke for a while. Finally, Rock asked: "What do you think?"

"I. Ah. We both have to get our lives squared away."

Rock flashed a sympathetic smile. "Then your healing process has begun. Come on, I'll drive you home and take a taxi back here." He couldn't hold a grudge against her, not after seeing what self-inflicted punished had done.

Chapter Fifty-Four

Days later, Rock was on the sofa after work watching TV and thinking about Unali. He had talked with her by phone. She was putting her life in order. Most of all she appreciated him getting her through the anxiety attack. She said she had to make decisions without his influence. He admitted to doing the same.

The conversation made him realize how easily a life full of expectations can lead to disappointments. She also offered to make arrangements for him to meet Mona, but he politely declined at this time. Making room for a twin in his thoughts would be adding too much to his confused life. And, under the circumstances, a platonic friendship was best.

The phone rang. He went to the kitchen to answer. "Hello?"

"Will ya ever fergive me fer walkin' oot on ye?" Sheryl's voice was raspy and pleading.

Forgiving seemed to be all he was doing these days, at least to his loved ones. "It's all behind us. Entirely forgotten." Besides, he told himself, he couldn't shake this woman out of his life. He was teetering on a fence that leaned toward Sheryl.

He strolled in the living room with phone in hand, turned off the TV and sat on the edge of the sofa. Nervously, he fingered the fringe on his moccasins. By this time he had a strong hunch they did something together that he should be remembering, but wasn't ready to face. Yet, he had to face it sooner or later out of fairness to all concerned.

She giggled in higher spirits. "But, ye must be knowin' ye have a reputation."

He didn't know what she was talking about, but played along. "Damn right. Perkins put me on the swindler's list."

"That's no exactly what I was tryin' ta tell ye."

"Then what do you mean, I have a reputation?"

"I'll spell it oot fer ye, then. A wind o' rumors is spreadin'. I swear on the Quamas sod. Everyone connected with the Clamton County Superior Court knows Rock Carper by sight an' name. Yer reputation is that o' bein' outspoken and fer writin' lengthy tomes in the pursuit o' justice. I ran inta some of the court folks. They know me as 'Rock's wife'. What do ye think o' that?"

Feeling thirsty, he returned to the kitchen. "I'll be damned." Stepping around the phone cord, he opened the fridge for a beer. "Society taught me to take charge of my life, be a good citizen, then they label me. They're the eccentric ones."

"Ay. I'm thinkin' that everytime a document o' yers arrives on either Perkins' or Adams' desk, it stirs up immediate headaches n' indigestion. What must irk 'em the most is that ye, bein' the petitioner, always get the last word. Old Houston probably doesnae much care anymore, knowin' 'e wonnae outlive the case. Little time ta enjoy the fruit off the vine, I say. Now Fred Adams must be figurin' if 'e remains quiet, 'e'll slip through the cracks. Perkins can always move back ta California. But, I'm bettin' they all prefer ye were fishin' rather than filin' briefs."

"My lengthy motion must have ruffled a few turkeys. The Clamton Clerk set May 13th for oral argument. I'll be in town then. There's no backing out of this step, albeit being on display as a pro-se attorney scares the hell out of me." He cradled the phone between his ear and shoulder to pop open the beer, making a fffffft sound.

While putting his mouth over the foam, he heard Sheryl cackle. "There's no end ta yer determination. Ye're like Shakespeare's valiant flea that dared ta dine on the lip o' a lion. Well, why donnae ye come ta my house the evenin' afore? Ye can eat dinner and practice yer speech in the livin' room."

This offer was too good to be true. Law was the epitome of intelligence for which he personally had neither the utmost confidence nor knowledge, even though he was learning. Worried that he might still be relying on fair play in the judicial system, he was grateful for Sheryl's offer.

"Thanks. I accept. Meanwhile, I'll keep polishing my speech." He knew he was slow. Although, the speech was nearly completed. His papers were on the floor in disarray. The only way he could compete in the judicial system was to have things written out and held in front of him. The rule book said he shouldn't read his oral argument, so he'd try to memorize some of it.

He swilled the beer and hung up. Before letting go of the receiver, he thought about phoning Unali, then decided to send her a post card instead. He'd inform her of his scheduled oral argument. Their friendship had taken a beating. He still cared for her, but she needed space to put her own house in order.

Chapter Fifty-Five

Early Sunday evening Rock ferried over choppy waters, landed and sped over the road, cleaving the countryside to Quamas. Outside, the north wind whined and blew steadily against the Firebird. By judging from an occasional glance in the rearview mirror, his speed created a trail of powdery dust. Entrapped debris mingled with bits of grass and dried leaves created swirling eddies alongside the two-lane road.

Before long, sheets of rain splashed against the windshield. Finally, Rock turned on the wipers and listened to them swishing rhythmically. The noise mingled with western music coming from the radio.

Rock was on the way to Sheryl's house. But, his mood and thoughts were on Unali. He held the steering wheel tightly for fear he might lose his grip entirely, like it was Unali slipping away. That's what was happening. He wasn't doing anything to stop it.

His mind phased in and out, while catching hold of lyrics from the car radio towing in his mixed-up feelings like a surf lapping a sandy beach: "I need you near me. The world's too much to face without you. Remember, I'll always be there so long as I breathe. I'm yours."

Some lyrics bothered him because of Unali having let him down: "I'll give you harder times than you thought you'd go through. I'll give you a promise tonight that I can't keep." These lyrics seemed to pertain to both of them.

He pondered whether it was fate or destiny meeting Unali at a time when he really didn't need the emotions that come with falling in love, not at this time in his life. Yet he pursued her. Maybe it was her nearness, her opinions, her warmth and delicious perfumed presence that attracted him, increasing his desire to possess her again and again.

True, he asked for her friendship. Friendships are important. Everyone needs a friend. But some spirit within told him this friendship had nearly crossed the line into paradise, especially that evening in front of the warm fire in Leucojum's house. Unali's rejection gave him a special kind of hope. That is, until their last meeting. The conclusion of that meeting left him uncertain. It was true, Sheryl had been nicer to him since their separation. But, this didn't mean he was going to run back to her. Great Spirit, this was confusing.

What if he and Unali could eventually return to the level they were before learning of her deceit? All that Rock had to offer Unali was his love. That being the case, she surely wouldn't accept his other emotions. Not for long. Particularly those attached to a constantly changing lifestyle unfamiliar even to him. The intangibles. The judgment sanctions, delayed divorce, untrustworthy attorneys, an oral speech to deliver. These were insolubles that gnawed at his guts, nerves and pocketbook. His relationship with Sheryl was proof of this.

Finally, Rock puffed out his cheeks and exhaled in exasperation. With nothing to offer Unali, he might as well focus on the immediate, the now. Sheryl was expecting him tonight. They would work on his speech in preparation for his oral argument tomorrow.

Meanwhile, to change his thoughts, he turned off the radio, unrolled the window and, on impulse, leaned his head out just far enough to inhale the country air. The wind whined and shook the telephone wires. Raindrops against the side of his face refreshed him. Bucking the wind was an escape from courtroom walls and loose tongues. The elements of nature he understood. He howled into the air like a lone wolf.

*   *   *

Rock quickly combed his hair back into a duck's tail before entering the house. "Ummmm. Smells good and I'm hungry." He found Sheryl hovering over the stove in denims, blouse and apron.

"I've a mind ta serve yer meal on manila folders considerin' the lifestyle ye've chosen. The innards o' my cupboards are lookin' like an office with binder clips on the cereal and raisin packages."

He was pleased she had moved back to Quamas so he had someone to visit in the little town.

"And, I'm wishin' ye'd get yer legal stuff out o' my spare fridge in the garage." Sheryl looked him over with a smile. "Like yer hair. Tis back to normal."

"Maybe my hair is, but I'm not. No lectures today, Sheryl. You're talking to a man with a reputation." He squeezed her shoulders from behind. "I'm willing to devour anything in sight. What's cooking?"

"Chuck steak stewed in chunky tomato gravy with parsley potatoes, peas and scones. Ye'll be needin' yer strength come the morrow. Set yerself in the diner, dearie." She motioned with her head toward the dining room as she ladled food onto oval plates.

They laughed, while talking about old times during dinner. Later, Rock stood at the head of the dining room table silently checking over his speech notes.

Sheryl sat in an easy chair. She crossed her legs over the armrest and proceeded to munch on walnuts. "Donnae be embarrassed by my presence. Likesay, I'm insistin' ye practice yer speech afore tamorrow 'cause the judge hasna time ta read everythin' ye file. Ye cannae expect ta be makin' an impact with Dodson if ye donnae know yer speech inside oot. Ye havena been schooled in dishin' oot legal shit let alone in takin' it."

Finally settling down to business, Rock recited his speech, finding his vocal chords playing tricks in her presence.

"Rock, ye need ta speak with more force. Pound yer fist on the table. And remember, ye're unloadin' a lot o' accusations on Dodson. Ye're treadin' yer moccasins in his murky territory. Lordie, ye donnae want ta tick him off. He'll give ye the dickins. Oh well, we know the judge looks on the likes o' ye as an evil peon and doesna expect ye to confess yer sins in court."

"Hell. I'm not confessing. I'm revealing the sins of others."

"Well, judges know the gates ta bliss and blisters are open ta all mankind."

"Bliss and blisters?"

"I'm referrin' ta heaven an' hell. Now, put through yer speech again, if ye've a mind fer it." She pulled a stopwatch out of a pocket. "I'll time ye."

He did this several times and felt more at ease.

"Yer speech takes fifty minutes. Ye're allowed one hour."

He couldn't help but slump down near her. "Oh Sheryl, who are we kidding? I'm no match for those guys. I talk slow and . . ."

Sheryl reached over and ruffled his hair. "Demosthenes, the great orator, stuttered. Ye'll do fine, if ye donnae ad-lib much. Tell ye what, if yer tongue's waggin' at a snails pace or ye get off the beaten path tamorrow, I'll warn ye by coughin'."

This was a good idea since his back would be facing Sheryl in the courtroom during his delivery.

Following more practice runs, Rock left for the Leucojum house to sleep. Sheryl invited him to breakfast in the morning. Not liking her foreign coffee, he suggested they go to *Clare's* near the courthouse. Thanks to Sheryl, he was better prepared for tomorrow. Although, like life and love, there was always the unexpected in the legal system, he was learning.

Chapter Fifty-Six

Gena didn't have to work today, Friday. She rose early to the wind howling like a pack of wolves. And, the rain pelted the roof and windows like sharp needles. She was doing much better since a great pressure had been lifted. Yet, she had Rock on her mind during the night. And, she couldn't shed a nagging thought as to what kind of hold Sheryl had over him.

"Ohhhh shoot. Gena, get in here quick; listen to this." Mona, calling from another room, interrupted her concentration.

Gena was in the kitchen listening to the radio. She recognized Mona's remark coming from the office. She ran to Mona, curious. "What's wrong?"

"I'm listening to the latest tape from Rock's answering machine." She rewound a part of the tape.

Gena remembered receiving several tapes in the mail from Rock and hadn't found time to listen to them.

"It's Sheryl's voice, talking to a girlfriend, from Rock's apartment. And, Rock isn't home." Mona pushed the play button, while sitting up to the desk.

Gena listened with avidity, catching the vital part:

"Rock's a breast man. That's what turns him on. But, I dinnae rely on that. I put my medicine in his coffee several times during the trial. It worked. He made love ta me. But I donnae think he remembers 'cause o' his head injury."

"Well, what does the medicine do?"

"My doctor said it makes a person amorous. I even stirred it inta my beef stew.

"Does Rock know?"

"Nae."

"Ohhhh, no." Gena plopped down hard on the bed with her hands wound in a dishtowel. The news was shocking. She heard Sheryl sigh, contentedly. Gena wasn't ready for this. "Turn it off."

Her lower lip quivered, as she fell back on the bed. Tears filled her eyes. This was so devastating she thought she'd faint. The earth seemed to shudder and quake. "I doubt I'll ever find happiness with Rock. Our journey is over." Reality hit hard. Until this, a part of her hoped there was still a chance after their divorces were final.

Mona turned off the machine. "Sis. Rock doesn't know about this. Sheryl said so on the tape. Remember his head injury?"

"Oh. I don't agree. He has remembered about everything else. How could that big Cherokee forget making love to Sheryl, while he was drumming on my heart?"

"The litigation is foremost on his mind. And besides, you, Rock's friend

266

Efrem and Sheryl coached him and none of you, except Sheryl, knew about this." While pacing around the room, Mona mumbled obscenities. "I honestly believe Rock would have told you. He's that honest."

Gena sat up to dry her eyes with the towel. She looked into Mona's eyes. "Are you serious? That he doesn't know?"

"I couldn't be more serious. Rock couldn't bluff his way out of a paper bag. Yet, I doubt we'll ever know if the medicine was responsible. What worked for Sheryl doesn't mean it worked on Rock. All the same, Sheryl's your enemy. Not Rock."

"Sheryl's devious. Oh, I don't know why I'm so mad. I was devious too. And I more or less told Rock I needed time to understand myself." She looked at Mona.

"Calm down. You're angry because . . ."

"Because I don't need Sheryl controlling things, that's why. She's the one who kicked him out. Now she wants him back. It's so damn unfair. I'm trying to overcome guilt and rejection, and now this?"

"You hate to lose." Mona appeared dumbstruck too, or she was thinking up a new scheme.

"Mona. There's not a damn thing we can do about any of this. If he had only forgiven me, really forgiven me, I might have tried harder." She remained quiet for a minute. "I'll bet he's spending the weekend with her."

Gena knew they'd be together this Sunday, practicing his oral argument. While bent over her knees, she put her head in her hands. A lemon scent from dish soap permeated. "He'll probably sleep with her, especially if he's eating there. I can just see Sheryl fortifying the grub. Ooooh. I hate that woman." Gena flopped back on the bed again.

"Sis. I'm not happy about this either. "Let's face it. You have to play the tape for him."

There was the scheme. The tape. Leave it to Mona. "No. I'll never play that tape for him." Gena sat up blurry eyed. Her braid came undone. She felt sloppy in her sweats.

"All is fair in love and war." Mona walked over, held Gena's shoulders and shook her. "You play that tape for him and you'll get him back."

Gena raised her eyes at Mona. "For how long?" She started to laugh. "You know, this is turning into a battle between you and Sheryl."

Mona laughed. "Perish that thought."

"Mona. This is something he has to find out on his own. That's where I draw the line." She raised a hand for emphasis. "I confessed my sins. Now, she can confess her own damn sins."

Western music was echoing down the hallway from the kitchen. Rock's favorite music. Defiantly, she flipped back her hair, wanting to call Rock a dumb buck. He wasn't dumb. But, she bet her life that he'd fall for every scheme Sheryl dished out. Of late, she came to the conclusion that he moved to his own tune, while also moving to everyone else's tune, and was probably driving everyone crazy. He was driving her crazy. "One thing's for sure, none of us will forget Rock Carper."

"When it comes to scheming, we're as bad as Sheryl. It's not only in the judicial system that lying and cheating are resorted to in achieving selfish results. But, I don't think we'll forget Sheryl either and we haven't even met her."

"Yeah, only through Rock's interpretation." Gena should have recognized there could never be anything beyond gathering information for a novel the first time she heard the name *Visiting Warrior*. It was like placing a river between her and Rock.

Trying to learn about and think analogous to Rock enabled her to see him as stubborn and proud. Not one who could be subservient to anyone, except Sheryl. He and Sheryl were like two knobs on a cactus plant, like the one on the windowsill. If Gena brought this to his attention, he would turn on her. She flared at Mona. "Please leave me alone."

After Mona left, Gena flipped off her shoes and curled into a ball. "I won't cry. I won't cry." From the time she was old enough to be on her own, she felt forced to find her way in a big world she didn't know. And, she still didn't know it. Obviously, because of Shumway's disappearance, she yearned to be in Rock's arms. What right did she have to expect this when she didn't share her problems upfront?

Gena bounded up on her knees and looked in the mirror at the head of the bed. No makeup, messy hair. "Oh, darn. Am I living in hell?" Slumping down, she started to justify her dishonesty with Rock. And, that he knew his marriage bothered her. Excuses, excuses, excuses.

Then, she stopped to blow her nose to relieve the pressure in the sinuses. Reality to this situation hit even harder. Like Rock, she was experiencing the hurt. Yes, it hurt to lose on someone else's terms, but kidding herself hurt more. In facing Rock about this, there would be no tears. There couldn't be. Keeping their affair mostly platonic was where they were and there was no point going beyond what hadn't happened. No. This time she would not fall apart and hyperventilate.

Mona reappeared. "I want you to talk to mom about this. Or even dad."

"Mona. I'm in my thirties . . ."

"So, I've know women in their fifties with heartaches like this. They still talk to their parents, if they're alive. Listen, to our parents we're still kids. We'll always be kids to them."

"Maybe Shumway will return." Gena sighed.

"You're regressing again. It's okay honey." She wiped the tears with the edge of an apron. "You know the futility of that. Now stop it and phone mom." After pointing to the phone on the desk, Mona slipped out of the room.

Gena glanced at the phone. Maybe.

Chapter Fifty-Seven

"Are you goin' ta use all those documents and books taday?"

Rock was spreading organized piles across the left-side counsel table in Courtroom Two in preparation for his oral argument. "Looks impressive, like I'm armed for bear."

He grinned, while buttoning his dark blue suit jacket. "If Scott can do it, so can I." Rock aimed the thumb of his right hand directly at the center of his chest. Then he doubled his fists, held them vertically and with effort pushed both fists to the right, meaning he aimed to do his best.

Sheryl, sitting in the front row behind Rock's table, acknowledged his sign language with a nod. "But, dinnae Scott use a briefcase, instead o' a suitcase?"

"Yeah. But, I had to bring my three-volume motion along. Might need them." After emptying the suitcase, he closed the lid. Then, he turned and nodded his head for Sheryl to see Perkins, Adams and Marvin strutting up the aisle confidently, each carrying briefcases. "The con artists are here."

Marvin sat across the aisle from Sheryl and ejected his usual irritating cough. Adams assisted Perkins in spreading their copies of Rock's three-volume motion on their counsel table with a heavy thud, thud and thud. A few cuss words from Perkins accompanied each thud.

Rock and Sheryl stifled grins. No one exchanged words or glances. Rock poured himself a cup of water from a water jug on his table, sipped and set it on the corner near the lectern for later.

The room grew quiet. Rock looked around. The atmosphere was deathlike. Nothing grew here. He believed that the words tossed around in this room echoed off the paneled walls to destroy people. Not a pleasant thought. He brushed a hand across his lapel out of habit. His pin of the American flag was gone. "Sheryl, do you know what happened to my pin? I seem to have lost it."

"Nae." She shook her head. "Just think on yer speech."

"Ha. That should be easy with all the arguing I've done with you and Mo . . ."

The dimples in Sheryl's cheeks deepened. "Aaaah. So ye and yer bonnie are 'avin' a tiff?"

"Don't read anything into it." Nevertheless, he felt all the arguing with the women, whatever their names, should prepare him for something." A commotion at the side of the room drew their attention. Their eyes followed Judge Dodson's walk to the bench at ten sharp. No bailiff this time.

After formalities, Rock was invited to start. He ponied up to the lectern with his typed speech. Before starting, he inhaled and said a silent prayer, hoping to release hidden potential. *"Oh Great Spirit. I am not eloquent like these men. My tongue is slow, but be with me."* He cleared his throat and began. At first he felt on display under the florescent lights. His voice quivered a little at the thought of standing before legal representatives who knew the ropes, while weaving through points taken from his lengthy motion.

Nevertheless, he pressed onward, tempering raw nerve with prudence. Gradually, his deep voice became forceful, drumming the attorneys and Marvin's specialists as a bunch of liars, including that Houston lied about performing legal services for the Carpers before John's death. Revealing lies was distasteful, but the only way to demonstrate his values, his cultural beliefs, hoping if would make an impact on Judge Dodson's sense of fairness.

"For this reason, Marvin Benson's bunch can't win on truth." While feeling like the new kid on the block, Rock could have bolted for the door, having blurted out blatant remarks. Yet, he had accepted their misrepresentations long enough and had no reservations about dishing out their kind of shit. This was his day to yell and by God he was determined to do so. If these attorneys thought of lesser men as savage, lazy and without honest enterprise, they were going to learn otherwise. So far, no one objected. Judge Dodson appeared composed. Although, his eyes fixated on Rock.

"I did not have a fair trial. I went to trial believing it would be consistent with the appellate court's instructions to address the misconduct committed in the probate of John's estate between 1972 and 1974. And, I was relying on Judge Randell's order to consider all the evidence of record. My counsel filed my pretrial motion for this purpose and to use my specialist Neil Woods' report authenticating the Leucojum Documents. This was intended to save costs as I was running out of money."

He glanced down at his notes to cite examples of unexpected surprises sprung at trial: "Mr. Perkins misled the court using the wrong envelope in the journal . . . that it stuck out both ends. He made me out as less than honorable. And, you, Your Honor, hadn't heard of a special service of will safe keeping. And, perhaps you didn't hear document specialist Anderson contradict himself on ink. He said it wouldn't thermofax. Then said it would. Anderson said the fold lines and notary seals wouldn't thermofax. He said a thermofax wouldn't take the thickness of John's two-page 1942 trust agreement. All surprise evidence, without proof. Today, you have new affidavits refuting Anderson's findings."

He paused for effect. "And, to this day, I haven't seen two boxes of John's documents described after trial by these attorneys. They withheld evidence." He looked up and down from his notes as he spoke, finally pausing to sip water. "I've never seen the originals of the unauthenticated letters Marvin submitted at trial. Those letters are suspicious due to the rhythm of how the typist hits the keys."

A momentary glance back at Sheryl told him she was attending to her stopwatch, hidden inside the pages of a crossword puzzle book.

"My opposition withheld deposition testimony showing Nell was fully recovered one week prior to the official state inventory of the deposit box. Marvin's attorney Mr. Houston testified that Nell was informed and based upon said information, believed that the effect of the community property agreement was to simplify the transfer of properties from John to Nell. They didn't realize the complex situation, which could arise particularly in connection with the transfer of John's stocks.

"This is contrary to another exhibit wherein Nell said: 'The community property agreement didn't attempt to change the status of any separate property owned by either spouse.' And, if there was no separate property, what were Nell and Houston transferring? We know the original community agreement didn't vest all of John's property in Nell. That isn't what the original agreement says."

Judge Dodson glowered, while leafing over exhibits Rock handed him.

Rock addressed the laches issue. "The point is that many forces operated against me in this eight-year litigation, a litigation in which I was a pawn. I was delayed as a result. Mr. Houston misled me. A later will would have made a difference."

Rock cited case law. "Laches is a remedy to prevent injustice and hardship. It shouldn't be employed as a mere artificial reason for denying me that which in equity and good conscience I'm entitled to receive when the assertion of my claim, though tardy, is within the time limit by statute and the right of no persons have been prejudiced by this delay. Laches is to be applied as a means to administer justice. It isn't to be used as a barrier to defeat meritorious claims grounded upon principles of common honesty."

He paused a moment to catch his breath and shift his weight. "I had no warning that my handwriting was under scrutiny. No warning that Houston would submit my mother's confidential notes in his possession regarding another legal matter." Rock hesitated, hearing Sheryl cough. A signal to speed things along. While flipping through his notes, his hands felt sweaty. There were still two pages of notes.

Rock gripped the lectern and carved his words in presenting proof from trial exhibits that Houston and Nell misrepresented John's estate with an altered community property agreement.

"And, the *coup de grace*, Your Honor, the *coup de grace* of all statements, diluting Marvin's case to zero, came from his attorney, Perkins." It was Rock's turn to become theatrical. "Now, I quote Perkins, who stated at trial: 'I want to point out one more thing and that is something I forgot before. All wills of John and Nell Carper and the 1972 wills were found in the same envelope by Ralph Houston in the safe deposit box. It was aaaaall in there, suggesting that this was their last will and testament as of May 14, 1972.'" Rock turned toward Perkins, who was in a mad frenzy, scribbling notes. "So Your Honor, Perkins admitted the wills favoring me were there."

Rock then turned back to the bench. "My new evidence shows that the Leucojum documents have cancer, something that can't be achieved by hanging paper in a sunny window or heating in an oven, or whatever Anderson tried in his tests. His documents didn't rise to the occasion. His cake flopped flatter than a pancake because his documents don't have cancer."

He scanned the page and decided to skip ahead. "My new evidence raises substantial questions of fraud and perjury committed by Marvin's representatives. I have provided Your Honor with case law in my motion where a party's lack of diligence in obtaining new evidence isn't controlling, when new evidence raises questions of fraud and perjury."

"Have you just about concluded, Mr. Carper?" Judge Dodson's voice was stern.

"Yes, Sir, almost. Frankly, I was distraught that my counsel let me down. However, that doesn't give license for my opposition to lie. Mr. Perkins made threats to me to settle or lose everything and then carried out his threats in creating additional costs. He presented a fraudulent trial supported by twisting testimony, through perjury and by withholding evidence based on a hypothesis no more tangible than a balloon of hot air."

Rock looked over at Perkins and Adams. They were grinning at each other. The thought surfaced in his head that he wasn't litigating against Marvin at all, but rather against attorneys, especially Perkins. Rock trudged on, seeing no humor, trying to remain adamant. "I shouldn't have to pay for Adams' appearances and expenses since he's defending fraudulent behavior. The same goes for Perkins. My new evidence shows I didn't bring forth a frivolous action. The charges should be reversed because my new evidence materially affects the original grounds for the court's decision regarding John's 1967 will, confirmed in '72."

Again, he heard Sheryl cough. There simply wasn't enough time to cover all that he wanted. He had to wind down. "We must recognize the strong policies favoring fulfillment of the testator's wishes. The last will of a competent testator will be upheld and the court will not by intentional rulings of statute or other legal constructions defeat that right."

Again, Rock knew he had to end this. He looked up from the notes and added a new thought. "Now, Your Honor, today you are the law. I know you will give my oral argument careful consideration. I sincerely thank you for giving me, a non attorney, an opportunity to be heard."

"Thank you, Mr. Carper."

Rock returned to sit at the counsel table alongside Sheryl, who scooted nearer and slid him a note: "Sixty minutes on the nose. You did great."

He felt things went better than expected. But, he couldn't relax yet, not knowing what Perkins would say.

* * *

After sitting, Rock unbuttoned his jacket and rubbed his eyes to break the tension. He then turned toward Perkins, who raised slowly, scanning handwritten notes on wrinkled paper.

Judge Dodson looked down from the bench, his glasses propped low on his nose. "Mr. Perkins, are you ready to proceed?"

"Yes." Perkins' hair and beard were neatly combed. Dressed in black pants, light blue shirt and navy blazer, he slowly approached the lectern with the air of a troubled man. His papers were shaking. Silently posed and staring at his loafers a few minutes, he began by placing the notes on the lectern, like they weighed a ton.

"Your Honor, I have to admit I'm not quite sure where to begin." Pause. His hands clutched the lectern. "There have been two trials in this action. It appears that virtually everyone in the world is conspiring to deprive Rock of his rightful inheritance. He has accused Mr. Benson, Adams, his own counsel Scott and me of withholding evidence. And, he's accused Houston of perjury, withholding documents, conspiring with Nell to deprive him of his inheritance. I frankly don't know what the motivation for that is, because I'm not a psychiatrist. But I will address some of it."

Perkins inhaled, then proceeded. "Rock's attorney filed a pretrial motion to bring into evidence all of the testimony and the trial transcript of the previous trial. We opposed it and then the court denied Rock's pretrial motion. Even so, virtually all of the witnesses who testified at the first trial testified this time. Those who were unavailable, we took their testimony through the trial transcript from the previous trial. Everything that could have gone in did go in. At least everything that was offered by Scott went in. I can't recall Mr. Scott saying to the court, 'I can't get this witness testimony'. I can't recall him saying, 'Your Honor, I can't get ahold of Mr. Woods.' There was no surprise."

Sheryl slid a note to Rock: *"How could anyone suggest this when Woods' report was eliminated AFTER both sides rested?"*

Rock shrugged his shoulders, deciding Perkins' knowledge verged on the annoying.

"Secondly, Your Honor, Rock claims that he wasn't prepared for being personally accused of fabricating documents. I pointed out in a letter to Mr. Scott that we'd seek attorney fees if there was evidence of wrongdoing by Rock. Before trial, we took Mr. Anderson's deposition. He went through his entire trial testimony, comparing John Carper's prior correspondence and comparing it with the cover letter -- the letter that was supposedly signed by John, the letter attached to the Leucojum documents."

Perkins tugged at his goatee while running a finger of the other hand down his notes to find his place. "I made numerous phone calls to Scott. Told him we're developing copies of the Leucojum documents and he ought to look at them. Maybe redepose our experts Mr. Anderson and Mr. Green. He declined. Then before trial I sent a letter to Scott pertaining to what we were going to prove at trial, that the Leucojum documents aren't what they purport to be. We believed Rock's documents were a fraud on the court. He shouldn't be surprised." Pause.

It pleased Rock that Perkins made no attempt to pace today, obviously out of sorts.

"In any event, Your Honor, we produced all of the documents ever asked of us. In fact, we produced everything we had even when it wasn't asked for. We didn't dance on the niceties of a request. We said, 'You want what we have? Here it is. Look at it. Here's a copy. Here are the originals.'"

"Bull." Rock seethed in anger under his breath, releasing five fingers downward from a balled fist, while watching Perkins fidget nervously. His voice cracking occasionally, as Rock would expect of a first, second and third-degree liar.

"There's been much ado about the withholding of evidence. We gave Scott a folder full of exemplars of John Carper's files. We held nothing back, Your Honor. We provided Rock and/or Scott with all the letters we published at trial. They were there at the taking of Anderson's deposition. There must have been thirty six of those copies there. When I say copies, I mean the carbon copies that were the records themselves. They were the only things we had because they were carbon copies, tissue copies, of original correspondence that John Carper had written."

He sipped water. "In other words, Your Honor, except for the slanderous statements by Rock, there is no evidence that there was any evidence withheld whatsoever. I will concede one thing. When I wrote my affidavit, it's possible, that there may have been only eighty-five documents in my office that were the original files from John Carper. There were other boxes we kept in a separate room in our office. All the documents that I had that came from John and Nell."

Sheryl leaned over to Rock and whispered. "Well, there's admittance they withheld many o' John's documents, keepin' 'em in separate rooms." Rock nodded agreeably.

"We said, 'Hokay. Here, you can look at them.' The only documents that Mr. Adams had were exemplars that were pulled out for Anderson to examine. And, Your Honor, I resent having my integrity impugned. I'm not going to put my reputation on the line to withhold documents."

While crossing his legs, Rock controlled an urge to laugh.

"Now, no lawyer is perfect, but I didn't hear Rock stand up and say, 'My counsel is doing a bad job. I'm not getting a fair trial.' In any event, the law is that in a civil case if his lawyer didn't do a good job, made mistakes that rise to the level of malpractice, he's got a remedy. Go to another lawyer. It's not grounds for a rehearing."

Dodson rested back in his chair, nodding, taking notes.

Perkins brushed a hand over his notes. "I don't think his new evidence of cancer can come in. And, his new document expert says she looked at John's signatures on the Leucojum documents and they were found to be genuine. Of course they are. That's the whole point. Those signatures are genuine, because we claimed the documents were fabricated using cut and paste techniques. So we agree with her."

Sheryl slipped another note to Rock: *"But, cancer disproves cut and paste."* Rock only smiled.

"Now, as to the next leap of fate, we have to talk about Ralph Houston. Mr. Houston testified that Rock never told him that there was another will. So he went ahead and probated John's estate. Now, Mr. Houston's testimony on the stand at trial was that he couldn't recall doing any work for John Carper. Then Rock brings in a piece of paper, a recorded deed or something like that, showing that Mr. Houston may have done some work for John and Nell. Your Honor, how long has Mr. Houston practiced law?"

Judge Dodson remained silent.

"Fifty years." Adams volunteered, stretching his head up, revealing his protruding Adam's apple.

"Over fifty years. Possibly, he forgot that once upon a time he did something for John and Nell as opposed to just Nell."

Rock looked at Sheryl to whisper: "Once upon a time. I provided more than one deed in my motion. Ralph did eleven winters of legal work for John."

Perkins drummed on. "I want to elaborate that Mr. Scott had all the opportunity in the world to depose Mr. Anderson or find other avenues about the thermofax process. Rock finds a new thermofax expert who says he's familiar with its operation and materials used in connection with thermofax. So is Mr. Carper. So is Fred Adams. So are a lot of people, but it doesn't make them experts in this case."

Again, Rock wanted to laugh. This was all speculation. Yet, at the trial, they sure displayed him as an expert.

"Even if Rock's new expert comes to testify, what is said in the expert's affidavit isn't sufficient to overturn Your Honor's findings about the genuineness of the Leucojum documents."

Remaining calm was difficult as Rock listened to Perkins' gibberish. Rock's expert's affidavit was more than sufficient had it not been excluded after the trial. And now the new evidence attached to his motion for reconsideration was sufficient too.

"Finally Rock suggests I admitted there was a later will in the safe deposit box when it was opened. Well, Your Honor, I haven't seen the trial transcript on that, and I don't know whether I misspoke or what. It's a slip of the tongue."

"Geeze, they toss around tongue slips like Frisbees." Rock was irritated, discovering how well versed these attorneys were in alibi and abuse. Particularly since he was certain Perkins' statement in the written record consisted of more than fifty words. Hardly a slip of the tongue. Sighing, Rock was convinced they lie as water runs. It seemed that evil thrived here like a well-oiled machine. He glanced at Perkins, sizing him as the runt of the legal liter with a small head, a big mouth and tall tales.

"Now, I don't know what the court is going to do with this mess. I think it has to deny Rock's motion. Also, we have to move for sanctions because there's no remedy outside of this courtroom for Rock's defamatory statements. I'm a big boy and I've been called worse by other lawyers. I can take it. Mr. Adams is a big boy. He can take it." Perkins crossed his arms, now appearing relaxed.

By this time Rock wondered why Perkins referred to him as Rock rather than as Mr. Carper, unless it was to put him down.

"This court must tell Rock he can't call Mr. Houston a liar in open court and get away with it. The court should tell Rock he can't imply that the court participated in a plan. Rock accuses the court, lawyers, staff, everybody associated with the case, as liars and cheats except for Rock. The message is that Mr. Adams and I can care for ourselves, but Mr. Houston has been in the profession for a long time. The bulk of what Rock had to say was that Mr. Houston and Nell perjured themselves both in the probate proceedings and Mr. Houston did it again at trial. The only remedy available to cure this conduct is through sanctions by this court."

Dodson leaned forward, removing his glasses, pouting his lips. "I agree with that." His face took on a hard-boiled look. "All right. We'll take a five-minute recess. Mr. Carper, I'm going to give you seven minutes for rebuttal. Then I want to make a few brief remarks and a ruling. I have a criminal matter coming up."

After acknowledging the judge's comments, Rock gulped in air. Now he had another new problem. More sanctions.

Chapter Fifty-Eight

In the hallway, Rock spoke low to Sheryl. He was overwhelmed at the bleakness of the situation, his first shot in court as a pro-se attorney. "Sounds like I'm going to have more sanctions imposed against me."

"Bosh. I donnae give a fig." She pressed her lips together in a stubborn line. "Tell 'em ta put it on yer tab. Calm doon. They cannae get bluid from a tuber. Besides, ye 'ave ta say what ye know ta be true. They cannae sanction you fer what ye can prove from the record."

Now Rock was sarcastic. "Hell. In this court? The record means nothing. Truth is irrelevant. This damn system could add sanction after sanction if it wanted to."

While Sheryl broke away and headed for the ladies room, Rock spotted a penny on the marbled floor. He stooped to fetch it, thinking it might bring good luck, when he overheard a man about his age talking to his attorney: "The bastard had to keep lying to preserve his integrity. You gonna tell the judge?"

The attorney fingered the lapels of his jacket and hinged back on his heels. "Don't worry, I'll take care of it."

Their conversation was sickening. The same old line Scott used. Rock recalled busting his ass to afford Scott who, in the end, threw the Carper legacy's blood and guts to the wind. Rock wanted to add his two bits worth to that conversation, but checked himself, and disappeared into the men's room.

* * *

After everyone returned to the courtroom and Rock was about to present his rebuttal, Perkins hurried forward. "Your Honor, I want to comment. Rock's affidavit from his new document expert says: 'It is my opinion that the signatures J. F. Carper, John and J.F.C. were penned by John Carper.' That is an unauthenticated hearsay statement."

"Thank you. Any response, Mr. Carper?"

"What Perkins just said is untrue. It's not hearsay." Rock pounded the lectern. "Under the Revised Code of Washington 9(A), it says that if a person signs and dates his affidavit, then it's authenticated and . . ."

"Okay. Okay." Judge Dodson eased back in his chair, while attempting to cut off Rock's important statements.

Rock ignored the judge and continued, while using written material of record Sheryl had provided for him. "I also want to say that Mr. Perkins said, both here and in writing, that I set Your Honor out as less than honorable and a cohort in this operation. That the court is involved in the conspiracy stating that you falsely accused me of having a plan."

Rock paused a moment for effect, looked up at Judge Dodson, then continued. "My motion clearly states: 'I want the court to be aware that Judge Dodson is a fine judge even though Rock doesn't agree with his opinions.' Mr. Perkins enjoys misrepresenting the facts. He twists them around. Turns them into pretzels." Rock glared at Perkins.

Perkins leaned back in his chair, shaking his head in disgust.

Next, Sheryl slid his motion over, opened to a page. Rock scanned it quickly. It was right on point. Rock picked it up and read aloud: "Mr. Perkins said all kinds of documents were brought to Anderson's deposition taken by Scott. Let me quote what Perkins really said that day. I quote: 'Mr. Scott, just so you understand, these three examples here are representative of dozens of letters, using the same format which Anderson examined. But he only brought three unsigned samples here today.'"

Rock sighed. "Your Honor, this proves Anderson didn't bring in a mass of letters that Perkins claimed in his rebuttal today." Rock saw no point in belaboring this point any further, since his motion elaborated that the three letters were unsigned, unauthenticated copies. Not tissue copies.

Then, rather than sticking to notes, Rock talked on about the opposition's ink expert's speculation of the two inks used in the Leucojum documents. Sheryl coughed.

"I've got to wrap this up." Judge Dodson looked at his watch as if Sheryl's signal pertained to him.

"Then this concludes what I have to say."

"Thank you, Mr. Carper." The judge nodded.

His flamboyance in disarray, Perkins jumped up. "Your Honor, could I say something I forgot before?"

Rock nudged Sheryl. "Something I forgot before seems to be a phrase common to Perkins."

Judge Dodson nodded patiently. "You may."

"Rock said I switched envelopes. I'm at a loss as to how I could have switched anything." His eyelids twitched.

Rock knew he was referring to the journal trick mentioned in the motion. Rock jumped up alongside Perkins, whose face wore an expression of horror. Perkins ducked back beyond Rock's reach, obviously not appreciating the heat Rock was generating. Rock ignored this, and reiterated Perkins' stunt of tucking a longer envelope in the journal.

"Well, let me wrap this up quickly." Judge Dodson ignored their jawboning. "I don't think Mr. Perkins suggests, Mr. Carper, that you indicated that I wasn't fair. You said yourself in your motion. You allowed as how you didn't agree with me. I didn't expect you, the losing party, to agree with me. I'm going to deny your motion, Mr. Carper. I worked this case hard and listened to it for many days. Although, I didn't read everything in your motion."

This last admittance shocked Rock. He found it unacceptable that any judge would make decisions without reading an entire motion. Otherwise, how can a judge make objective decisions? And, it seemed stupid for Judge Dodson to admit his inattention.

"For the record, I should indicate you have about five inches of exhibits and writings. I can't find and I can't conclude that what you presented by newly discovered evidence really comes within the rule at all. Your new evidence could, with reasonable diligence, have been discovered before trial. I have no problem denying your motion based on that argument."

Rock humped over the counsel table, his face grimacing.

"I have practiced in this county for thirty years with Mr. Houston. I haven't heard one word about Mr. Houston's credibility; his honesty. I think that Mr. Perkins and Mr. Adams were forthright and upstanding in this case. I must disagree with you. I think I know you disagree with me.

"But, for the fact that you are pro se, I probably would have shut you down when you made derogatory remarks about Mr. Adams, Mr. Perkins and Mr. Houston. That isn't the way we do it in court. Although more lawyers are doing that than I would like to admit. It seems to be the latest trend. I don't like it. It's purely a conclusion for you to say they lied about this or that and the other thing. That has no bearing on my decision. If I thought you were correct in this motion, I would have ruled for you."

Judge Dodson checked his watch. "I can't touch on every point, Mr. Carper. I just don't have time. I will not accept that you weren't given critical evidence because you and your lawyers have ways of enforcing that. All the lawyers have to do is come into this court and ask the court to make them produce it. I don't recall any such request."

The judge looked down at his notes, then up again. "The reference to Mr. Perkins' comment about how the wills were in the envelope, I can't help but put it down to a slip of the tongue. I make them all the time. What Mr. Perkins said isn't evidence. What was evidence is what I heard up here out of the mouths of the witnesses and the documentary evidence."

If this were true, Rock thought, why overlook the bank employee's testimony of Nell driving to the bank two weeks before the state inventory to get to the safe deposit box? Why overlook Anderson's contradictions? Why overlook Perkins' misrepresentation of Jasper Fulbright's testimony on the date stamp? Why overlook the journal trick? Why overlook Fred Adams' admittance in his affidavit that the thirty-six letters published at trial were introduced for the first time at trial? Why overlook cancer? Why?

"Let's see, I guess there's one more thing to cover. You should have called Mr. Woods, but didn't because of the dollars. You really were penny-wise and pound-foolish. But, that was your decision."

"Pardon me, Your Honor. What about you unfairly signing an order the last day of trial, leaving out my document specialist Neil Woods' report, unfairly preventing me from making other arrangements?"

Judge Dodson creased his forehead. "You didn't know about my order until the end of trial? I don't know what that is all about."

Rock felt his nervous system crumbling. "And the ink?"

Dodson interrupted. "You haven't shown me anything meaningful about ink. I don't think there was any evidence I remember about iron oxide ink and that it would copy, or wouldn't copy. I don't remember any evidence about that."

This issue was so vital to his innocence, remembering it was the only reason Marvin ran into two parked cars while leaving the courthouse parking lot.

"The separate property thing still I'm confused about. I don't see any evidence that there was separate property." Dodson fiddled with his glasses. "These are some of the various points that I wanted to mention. That's about all I was able to get down on paper as you spoke. The only thing left is the estate's request for sanctions, but I don't think I will do that Mr. Perkins. That's all I have to say."

Shrugging his shoulders in acknowledgment, Rock felt the only momentum his speech gained inside a house of justice was in stopping Perkins' cocky pacing. However, he did accomplish an important goal of having his new evidence and documentation made a part of the official record in this litigation, all now submittable in his forthcoming appeal, if he decided to go through with the appeal.

Rock watched Perkins, Adams and Marvin leave the courtroom on the run, looking like winners of a marathon. Rock packed his documents in the suitcase, tortured by futility, muttering to Sheryl. "I know when I'm standing in crap." He dug in a pocket and pulled out his car keys.

The judge's response confirmed in Rock's mind that he was over his head in a battle against attorneys who conflicted with his standards. Watching and listening to them package lies in different ways was beyond his grasp. Earlier, Dodson said he didn't expect losers to agree with him. In Rock's estimation, losers should at least come away with respect for the judicial process.

Judge Dodson lingered, still sitting behind the bench, leaning on crossed arms, watching. "Rock, you did a fine presentation. Best oral argument I've ever heard. Second to none. And a fine job you did with your volumes of exhibits." Dodson condescended in a regretful tone.

"Thank you, Your Honor." Rock acted composed, yet felt humbled and surprised, because he was dissatisfied with the cavalier attitude afforded him by Judge Dodson. Now, he had no choice other than to acquiesce. And, up until now, Judge Dodson emitted a fearing power. But, the compliment softened Rock's hurt.

Clicking his suitcase shut, he nodded at the judge and walked down the aisle with Sheryl ahead of him. At that brief moment, he believed that Judge Dodson knew he was telling the truth.

Chapter Fifty-Nine

Going out the back exit of the courthouse to the car, Sheryl complained. "Ye best be learnin' there's no justice fer ye 'ere. Just a revolvin' door."

"Only because Judge Dodson and the attorneys aren't about to be upped by an ordinary citizen." Rock wanted to say 'Redskin" but by now he knew race had nothing to do with this case. He was disappointed but not devastated by today's outcome. At least he had his say.

"They must be hard up for bad people, so they create them." Rock unlocked and opened the passenger door for Sheryl, then stepped back to check his surroundings. Parked cars were angled-in nose first, facing a strip of lush green lawn and flowering Dogwood trees. Marvin, Perkins and Adams weren't in sight.

He admired Sheryl's pretty legs when she hiked her skirt to step into the car. There wasn't time earlier for him to notice her in a stunning ivory suit and heels. But, she always looked stunning; her perfume riling.

She slid into the car, obviously eager to chat. "And, judges donnae admit ta makin' mistakes. They make interestin' discoveries. In keepin' with that, attorneys donnae lie, they make slips o' the tongue."

Rock interrupted. "Perkins sure has a knack for revising his lies."

"Sure. He has reputations ta protect. Believe me, nothin' ye say, do or show in documents o' record means a tinker's damn. We donnae belong ta their club, mind ye. From Dodson's view, we're wimps."

Rock made no response and closed the car door. He walked around to the driver's side, noticing a dour sky. Bird chirps in the few trees in the parking strip were soon drowned out when he opened his door, hearing Sheryl still venting.

"Face it, maun. Injustices across our nation are spreadin' like cancer. Justice here has affirmed a new meanin' ta me. Justice is unjust, I say. And we're just findin' oot a'boot it, too late. Ye're a one-man conglomerate. What chance 'ave ye got? None. We're insignificant people in a pile o' legal garbage. Ye might as well drop it. I see no fat left on the pork chop."

Rock settled in behind the wheel unable to let the pork chop remark pass. "Too much fat, you mean. The attorneys larded the record with fat lies through their imagination and prejudice. Adulterated the truth. The judicial system stands between me and the truth."

"Okay. Okay. Now ye need ta get on with yer life. Life is a reality, I say."

He started the engine and sighed. "Damn, I wanted justice." He wondered if this would ever be possible. Letting go wasn't an appealing solution.

"This whole thin' with the attorneys has been a bank robbery with a pen instead o' a gun.

Rock laughed, derisively. "It appears so. The litigation has been my initiation into civilized society. I do not like what I've heard and seen. It offends my senses. I had grand delusions that Judge Dodson would reprimand them for all their misconduct." Rock cruised out the parking lot.

"Ye best be leavin' that jabber." A few tears ran down her cheeks. "There's a sayin' that liars enjoy liars."

"Yeah, bird's of a feather. Well, it's not acceptable for a chief to do evil. His right to rule depends upon his fairness." Rock looked both ways, then eased onto the main road. "I'm puzzled about the judge. Damn it, he has a likable manner despite what has happened. And, I'm not totally convinced he was aware of what was going on at trial. Perkins and Scott controlled everything that happened in court."

"Blarney. Seriously, that judge shouldnae be judgin' if he hasnae time ta read and 'ear everythin' that really counts. No one is lookin' ta impugn Scott, Perkins, Adams and Houston, except ye! Who are ye? Yer a no-account . . ." She pulled out a hanky and patted her eyes.

"Leucojum said I was a mixed blessing." Trying to lighten up Sheryl, he decided he'd had enough. She was right, but if he didn't stop her, she'd use stronger language. "Sheryl. That's enough. I'm proud of my accomplishments today and I have you to thank for your wonderful guidance."

"Well, ye donnae deserve half-assed justice, is what I'm sayin'. The scales of justice were tilted 'cause ye made the wrong decision, no bringin' yer expert Neil Woods ta trial."

"I did that on Scott's advice."

"So, now it's yer fault. That's what the judge is a'sayin'."

"Yep. That relieves the misconduct of the attorneys. Well, I'm not buying it." This issue greatly disturbed Rock for reasons he couldn't define. He aimed the car in the direction of Sheryl's house.

"I wish ye could o' seen Perkins and Adams look at one another when ye mentioned cancer. They're the ones who created documents, no doubt in my mind."

"That was admitted at trial. Their specialist Ben Anderson said Houston's and Adams' staff helped him create his fakes."

"Why? Why, oh why?" Sheryl looked so hapless, while biting her lip and wiping fresh tears.

"Efrem told me one time to think of motive. The only motive I can think of is that greed for money started this entire mess." He sounded sarcastic.

"Ay, you're right." She sighed.

"There was a lot I wasn't able to bring up today. It's not your fault." Putting on the signal lever, Rock moved to another lane to pass a car. "Say, I really do appreciate your help today."

"Ay. Are ye goin' ta appeal Judge Dodson's decision taday?"

"Maybe. I'm perturbed and desperate, but not dysfunctional, not empty of hope for justice at a higher level."

"Oou. Ye're a coyote in a chicken house." She sighed.

Rock turned from his driving a moment to glance at Sheryl and chuckle. Her eyes were round and serious.

"Since ye arenae interested in droppin' yer madness, I might as well get on with the divorce. There's no point, me kowtowin' ta a deave ear." The words trailed off when she looked out her window away from him.

"Fine. You do that. And, you're right. So far, only the Great Spirit knows what's in the record." Rock grumbled the words, as he approached Sheryl's house. "But, I agree. You have to get on with your life and me with mine."

Sheryl rushed out of the car, mumbled 'goodbye' and shut the door. She didn't glance back. So, he headed for the ferry landing. On the way, he made mental plans of visiting Efrem in a day or two before deciding where to go from here, litigation-wise. Women-wise? Well that wasn't any better.

En route, he would gloat over Dodson's complimentary words. *"Fine presentation. Best oral argument ever. Second to none. Fine job."* The words boosted Rock's morale.

At the same time, he was damn well relieved this phase of the day was over, uncertain that he wanted a repeat. And, he was disheartened that Judge Dodson didn't read all of his motion. Had Rock been a bona fide attorney, this wouldn't have happened.

Traces of Sheryl's perfume lingered. Suddenly, he clicked his fingers and hit the steering wheel. He forgot to ask Sheryl what it was he forgot to remember. Simultaneously, confused images of her in that ivory suit and heels entered his mind. The back door, the clothes. She wore that suit to court the last day of trial. Driving onward, he envisioned her bare beauty shimmering across the windshield. "Oh Holy Spirit."

In the process of slamming on the brakes to make a U-turn, he had to pull over onto the shoulder of the two-lane road to wait for a passing car. On the front seat near him was Sheryl's crossword book, creased open to the page she had been working on. The puzzle was only a third finished. But, one answer in the puzzle was heavily inked: LOVE.

What would cause her to retrace the letters in this word? Unless . . . His most inner reality was coming out in slow-motion scenes. After checking his bearing in the rear view mirror, he accelerated in the direction of Sheryl's house. He had to know if what he was thinking really happened.

*   *   *

Rock barged through Sheryl's back door, through the kitchen, the living room and finally the bedroom. He found her face down on the bed. He sat on the edge and rubbed the small of her back. "Why are you crying?" He noticed there were no lights on, but he could still see.

"It doesnae matter any ta ye. I thought ye left."

"Sheryl. I need answers. My memory is playing tricks. Please help me."

She blew her nose with a wad of tissue, then rolled over to face him. "I'm glad ta see ye. But I cannae do anythin' fer ye. I've tried."

"Tried what?"

"Ta get ye back. That's the reason fer my tears."

"Why? You're the one who kicked me out. Look. We've been through all this. And, there's more to this that I'm not understanding. The last day of my trial, we came back here after Perkins' closing arguments. Didn't we?"

"Ay."

"You were wearing this suit." He touched the sleeve. "And, we came through the back door."

"Like lovers sneakin' in 'ere ta make love." She started to roll away.

Rock held her by extending an arm on her far side. "I . . . We actually made love?"

She nodded her head up and down. "All the way. We dinnae have a stitch on. Ye asked me fer love. I knew ye needed it." She pounded the bedding with a hand. "Right 'ere in this bed."

Looking about the room, he saw pictures on the dressers of Sheryl and him. "Geeezus." Rock rubbed his chin, not knowing what to do, let alone say.

"That was the second time."

"Second time?" His stomach muscles tightened.

"The first time was on the sofa. A Friday night efter dinner. Ye were wonderful."

"I was?" Hearing this put him in a drunken daze.

"Ye had the tribe dancin' in my head."

"I wish the tribe had danced in my head."

"As yer witness, the tribe did, matey. Sorry ye donnae remember."

Actually, the more she talked, the more relieved he became, like a load of snow fell off his shoulders. Still, he rose and walked into the living room. He stared out the window. Night was settling in early. The sky was studded with dark clouds. The greenery was damp with fresh rain. He started to laugh.

Sheryl was shuffling into the room and upon hearing him, laughed too. "Are ye disappointed?"

"Just surprised." He moved over to the sofa opposite the chair Sheryl sat in. She crossed her legs and one leg bounced up and down, like she was waiting for him to say more.

"Are you pregnant?" He looked straight at her, knowing that if she were he'd never leave her. The room went silent, except for a gust of wind against the windows. The room smelled of perfume.

She dabbed her eyes. "Nae. 'We decided ta use a condom. Ye 'ad condoms in yer wallet. Probably intended fer yer bonnie. Did ye two do it?"

"Would it matter to you?"

One strong flick of her slim ankle and a shoe soared across the room. He sat there quite relaxed until it landed in his lap. He tossed the shoe aside and shifted to the edge of the cushion. "You've no right to ask."

Sheryl said nothing more. But, while studying her demeanor, he knew he still loved her. "What changed your mind about us?"

"The medicine changed me. And, efter movin' back ta Quamas, I missed ye so much. I wanted ye back in spite o' the litigation."

They stared at each other for a while, until he held out an arm and motioned for her to come." Responding quickly, she curled into his arms.

"Sheryl, Sheryl. I want to believe you." He spoke softly. "I'll never forget what a help you've been to me, knowing how much you hate the litigation." Her head rested against his chest. She slid an arm around his waist, squeezing him as other realities seeped into his mind.

"I can't imagine you moving back to Seattle. Surely, you aren't thinking of me living in this hellhole. Not after what the judicial system has done to me. I'm sure you can understand that."

"Ay. I'll accept whatever ye want."

He stared down at her. That was the most important answer he sought. Whatever happened between he and Unali didn't matter to Sheryl. It was the now. She was beautiful, even with puffy eyes and messy hair. But there were still concerns. "I don't know about this. Being separated all this time was your idea, not mine. What's to change your mind again?"

"I'll stay on the medicine." Her fingers played with his tie clasp. Her body became rigid.

"What's wrong?"

"I tricked ye inta makin' love ta me during the trial."

"Taking medicine to help you feel better isn't a trick." He found nothing wrong with this. And he was more focused on what they did together and where to go from here.

"It helped ye too. Ye loved my caresses as much as I loved yers. I think, maybe that's why ye wanted a nooner the day that Perkins blasted ye oot o' the water. I was willin', I was."

After putting a hand under her chin, he raised her face to his. "If we were to continue this marriage, I wouldn't want things as they were before. I'd want them better. We've had enough unhappiness in our lives. And, I can't make any promises where my litigation is concerned. Otherwise, we'd be right back where we started. Is that what you want?"

"Nae." She spoke softly. "Oh Rock, the physical strain and mental tension we've experienced came because we desired Uncle John's inheritance. When we dinnae get it, we suffered the lack o' it. We set our sights on what it would mean ta get it back. Ye must know my thinkin'."

"I know." Kissing her passionately told him she was being sincere now. Yet, the past still had a hold on him. "Damn. I want to believe you. But, this needs a lot more discussion. And, I have to leave town for two weeks. A buying assignment." All of this confused him. He needed to get away from everyone.

Sheryl rose and walked to the middle of the room. She seemed disappointed. "Rock, ye could spend the night. Please?"

"Now wait a minute." He waved a finger at her. "If you think a roll in the hay makes everything right, I'm sorry I misled you." Pausing, he glared at her. "Sheryl, I'd love you with every fiber of my being if I knew you loved me, me, a human being with problems, a human being some folks treat as second fiddle."

"Ay. But, ye proved yer a fighter. Even losin', ye set the record straight taday. Even losin' you won. Ye won yer reputation. Put respectability back inta the Carper name, ye did. I'm proud of ye Rock Carper." She lowered her head. "I realize there are sacrifices. Until this litigation, I did everythin' my way. And, I've never given ye a chance ta help me. I ran ta my folks. I've been like Aunt Nell. Always tryin' ta run the show."

"Thanks. I'm glad you finally see that about yourself. Your words mean much to me." Rock sighed and rose in preparation to leave. He brushed a curl off her cheek. "You've given me a lot to think about. I'm not the type to heal overnight, you know."

"I know."

"Sheryl, all I've ever wanted was a normal life. Huh. Around me, nothing is normal. Can you honestly live with that?"

Sheryl rose and to met him. "I can." Tears were forming again.

"Oh Sheryl. Don't. I'm sorry if I come across as mean." He smiled. "I don't regret making love to you. Just kicking myself for hurting you and others in ways I didn't intend." She melted into his arms and they held their embrace for a while. "We'll talk more when I return. We'll make a decision then."

Rock drove off in a downpour of rain, wondering if he messed up three lives. Having two women interested in him felt pretty damn good. But not at the expense of hurting them. Well, at least Sheryl would give him time.

Chapter Sixty

"What are judges for?" While sitting in a beanbag in Efrem's den two evenings following his oral argument, Rock had to ask this question, after explaining that he lost in the process of setting the record straight.

Efrem laughed. "Judges were invented to keep the lowlife in line because ministers couldn't."

"I should have guessed you'd give such an answer." He reached out to receive a coffee refill from Efrem.

"Well kiddo, I think you discovered that for yourself. At least you recovered your dignity, putting up a good fight."

While settling across the room, Efrem grasped a copy of Rock's oral argument he had read earlier. "Judging from this, you missed your calling. You should have been an attorney. Sounds like Dodson was impressed too." A quizzical expression spread across Efrem's face.

"Not at first. Dodson walked in with the unruffled conviction of a man with secrets stuffed under his black robe. I swear, the legal eagles are so busy recording our sins, they don't think we notice theirs. Where I'm concerned, they got the wrong sinner.

He scratched his head. "Judge Dodson's knowledge of the true facts is as flimsy as a paper house. I don't know if he's confused, ignorant or what. He admitted he didn't read and hear everything. The big question is why? He said I gave a fine presentation. Best oral argument he'd ever heard. Second to none. And, he said I did a fine job with my volumes of exhibits."

Efrem leaned back and made a triangle with his fingers.

"The compliment was like Judge Dodson throwing a hungry wolf a hunk of red meat, but at least I believe the judge knows I'm innocent. Hell, man. He could have fined me in contempt of court for my derogatory remarks against all of them."

"I wish I could have heard it." Efrem chuckled, throwing his head back. Finally, his laughter whittled down and he focused on Rock with a mischievous eye.

Rock held out his hands, a little perplexed. "How did I get involved in this in the first place?"

"It's a difference of opinion that leads to law suits, Rock. Those attorneys have only an inkling of what they're missing. You not only weathered the storm of criticism, but you're one-of-a-kind."

"You've lost me." Rock was puzzled. He never considered himself any kind of hero and being one-of-a-kind was a new wrinkle.

"That me, an attorney, has a friend like you. One who hates attorneys. Hilarious." Efrem, in tight denims, shifted his lanky frame, reached for his coffee, sipped noisily and swallowed. "Through some mysterious power, I inherited you."

"Yeah? You want *Visiting Warrior* to pack his arrows and move?"

"Nonononono. I love you, guy."

"In that case, and keeping in mind that the underlining premise here is that I lost my inheritance, what should I do? Drop it or continue? My appeal is still in the crib." Rock stretched his legs and crossed his booted feet.

After setting his cup down, Efrem drummed his fingers together, pursed his lips and paused. "Weeel. What do you think about dropping it?"

"Crimeny. We're going to play psychiatrist, answering a question with a question."

Efrem held up an outstretched arm. "Remember me telling you all is fair in life, love and litigation? By this time, I hope you've broadened your experiences in each category, especially in the litigation. And remember the old adage: 'wealth enters; poverty exits'."

It didn't take long for Rock to respond with enlarged eyes and a stomp of a boot on the carpeted floor, especially since he was feeling the effects of his bones having traveled down the long corridors of the courthouse one time too many. "Wealth enters. poverty exits. Now that should be on an engraved sign above every legal office and courthouse in America." Absurdity put him in a better mood.

Efrem grinned, leaning over his beanbag. He looked at Rock through an unruly lock of brown hair that draped his forehead. "Well think about it."

Rock knew Efrem was warming to a lecture. "You want me to drop it. I can tell by the tone of your voice. You think I can?"

"Yes, damn it. You're a lot smarter since digging around in legal books. You did your best. Sounds to me as if Dodson really does agree with you. However, he's saying you discovered your new evidence too late."

"Too late." Rock expressed shock. He could hardly believe that being late would prevent truth from winning out and told Efrem as much. So far, the experience was like talking to himself.

"The fact remains. You're back at square one and have spent more time in litigation than your ancestors did in the Civil War."

"You care to discuss treaty promises?" In thinking of the years of Native American struggles to restore prosperity and pride, Rock slapped his hands together, energetically, like he was ready for a lively powwow.

"Hell no. Forget I raised that issue. Point is, you need to take a break. Get in touch with yourself. Think about where you're going. For example, do you really want to pursue an appeal? Don't answer. Just think about it. And, think about the Carper mansion. And anything else important in your life. As far as the judgment sanctions, you can go bankrupt. Start over."

Rock hummed. "At least, no one has tried to take the Leucojum house away from me. Look Efrem. Before I leave, I want you to know something. I listen to you. And I don't hate all attorneys. A few bad attorneys don't reflect a collective image of the profession." Rock made a Native sign of shaking hands, meaning we are brothers always.

"I know." Efrem ambled upward. "Maybe Scott used bad judgment." He shrugged. "Sounds like he gave a fair closing argument. Maybe since it was short, the judge didn't buy it. Scott may not know the crooked things done by Houston and Marvin."

"What about Perkins and Adams, Jr.?"

"Maybe they were a little shady to win a case for their clients. Surely, Perkins doesn't know how crooked Marvin and Houston are."

"Awww, stop pulling my leg." Rock rose to leave.

"I'm serious. Remember, attorneys are like fraternity brothers, especially in a small town like Quamas. They aren't going to make a fellow attorney look bad for fear it may backfire on them someday. So, they give each other slack." Efrem cleared his throat and walked over to Rock.

Rock stared searchingly into Efrem's eyes.

Efrem squeezed Rock's shoulder. "If any attorney does wrong, his glory will be short lived. Trust me on that. Men destroy themselves. Usually, they don't need any help." He stepped away, crossed his arms and nodded affirmatively.

"I hear ya." Rock left in heavy thought. The message was serious and one that would linger a while in his crowded mind.

Rock hopped in the car and headed for Unali's house, while still contemplating Efrem's advice. Efrem was such an ideal counterpoint to Rock's temperament. When Rock became uptight, Efrem cranked out wisdom in wisecracks.

Funny, this life. One can look back with such insight, but see little into the future. Milling over Efrem's advice, he knew he needed to make the most of the opportunities as they presented themselves. The only way to do this was to take a break.

* * *

Rock reached Unali's porch and rang the doorbell, while wondering what he'd say to her. Was an apology in order? He wasn't sure. There was the feel of footsteps coming from the other side of the door. Were they Mona's or Gena's? He noticed the moon over his left shoulder, a moon full, bright and beautiful. It appeared to have risen from the calm, still waters of Lake Washington. Rock knew that nothing is as calm as it appears.

A twin opened the door and greeted him with a warm smile. "How did the motion go?"

"Which twin am I talking to?" He brushed slowly past her.

"Unali. Mona is out."

Rock took this on faith and walked deeper into the room. A candle flickered its spicy scent from the coffee table. "The motion was a no-go." He looked down at his feet. "Although too late, the new evidence of cancer, et cetera salvaged some of my credibility lost in the '90 trial debacle. Dodson complimented me for a good presentation, but wouldn't change his mind. Means I'm stuck with more litigation, unless I shovel the works in the fire."

"Rock, I . . ."

He raised a hand to continue. "I'm feeling a bit disillusioned. You see, I had such faith in humanity before the trial -- with my friends and those in the judicial system. Somehow, no matter which avenue I took, once I arrived, things went wrong. Without my special song, I felt my hopes disintegrating."

She stepped closer to him. "As I was about to say, you have nothing to be ashamed of. You can keep your beliefs and your perspective, knowing that there are accessible documents supporting your story. It's that simple. No other person in the litigation can say as much. I said it before and it still holds true."

This idea hadn't crossed his mind with such impact before. "You're right. I can still believe in my innocence." He paced around with his hands on his hips.

Unali remained nearby. She was wearing turquoise slacks and sweater tied with a fringed sash that matched her lovely eyes. "Aaaah. Unali. We both have some adapting to do. I'm here for another reason."

"Oh?"

"Let's sit down." They sat at opposite ends of the sofa. She glanced over at him; waiting.

"I made love to Sheryl during the trial. Due to my head injury, I didn't recall it until recently." He spilled out his uncertainties; his confusion.

Unali rose and walked toward the bay window. Her braid draped neatly in back.

Rock could see around her. The curtain was open to the evening sky. The room was too quiet. He went and stood behind her.

She spoke to his reflection. "You know why you made love to Sheryl?"

"I fell into two weak moments. Puzzling. With you I would have understood, but not with Sheryl. Not after what she and I have been through. Now, Sheryl doesn't want the divorce." The expression on Unali's face reflected in the windowpane. It wasn't congratulatory.

"So what are you going to do?"

"After thinking it over, I've decided it's best to get away for a while. I need to find out who I am, where I'm going and who's walking toward me. Call it a search for affirmation, so I can better travel my trail."

"Do you still love her?"

"I do have an affinity for Sheryl. I feel there's still love between us. We've had many seasons together. To please me, she's taking medicine to change. I can't ignore this. When I return, I should honor my marriage."

"Visiting Warrior is through with me." She pressed her forehead against the window. Her breath left fog on the pane. She appeared sad, but not hapless.

The urge to take her in his arms and tell her he still loved her too was running through him like a fast river. Yet, his sense for fairness wouldn't allow it. Instead, he stroked her braid. Her hair smelled of sweet shampoo. "Please understand." Rock whispered his words. "Don't turn around until I'm through."

He paused, choosing his words carefully, checking himself from blurting out how she inspired his heart. "Of all people, you know I don't go out of my way to hurt people. I didn't visualize the possibility of falling in love with two women in my lifetime." He let go of her braid. "Your morals made me realize the importance of marriage."

Unali remained motionless. No tears.

This time she turned around, holding her chin at a defiant angle. "My morals. I knew it. Nice girls don't have any fun. Blondes don't either."

To his surprise, she sounded more resigned than angry. "Unali, I didn't plan it this way. I'm asking for understanding. The issue isn't totally settled. Frankly, I'm confused."

While adjusting his bolo, she shrugged. "I need space too. We both have hurt feelings that keep us apart. You and Sheryl have a history that you and I don't, for which I can't compete. I know you're on your earthwalk and still haven't experienced your song."

He sighed. "Dreaming about barnacles and legal eagles may be all the Great Spirit will grant." He scratched his temple not expecting her to be so understanding. "But, I'll keep on believing there's a special dream coming."

"We can still keep in touch until the novel is completed. I've enjoyed gathering your story. You've had me seeing, hearing and feeling things through the eyes of Native Americans. If you and I could live their earthy philosophy, we'd be better off than we are right now."

Her words were a relief. "Thanks. You're so special. I should have asked you days ago where I should go to get a life repaired."

"Leave it to your Great Spirit. He has a plan when he's ready, not when you're ready." She toyed with her fringed sash.

He chuckled. "For sure. Meanwhile, it's important that you believe me."

"I believe you more than I can say. You want my honest reaction to all this, other than what I've said tonight?"

"Yes."

"I realized several days ago that it had to end this way. My purpose of being in your life was to get your story and to be a friend."

"Come on. What's your secret for taking this so well?"

She laughed. "I guess it's because I know you really have forgiven me for my dishonesty, which means a great deal to me."

"And?"

"I'm using a technique my mom reminded me of several days ago. We talked on the phone. She reminded me that problems don't inhibit life. That problems are a conductor for greater things unless one wallows in self pity. This resulted in my spending several minutes a day reveling in the good things in my life. It slows a person down. Gives peace. Like a pep talk to your inner soul."

"Does it work?"

"Yes. I see things objectively. Before long, laughable absurdities emerge." She took his hands in hers. "So, are we *Unali* friends?"

He gently squeezed her hands. "*Unali* friends." After a moment of silence, he smiled with her. "Are you sure you want to finish the novel?"

"Your story isn't over. Your earthwalk is in progress. Meanwhile, your Great Spirit is mightier than the twisted words of attorneys -- words that someday will break them into pieces. The battle belongs to your Great Spirit."

Rock left a little saddened, yet happy Unali was so understanding.

*   *   *

Closing the front door put distance between Gena and Rock. They parted in the archway saying "good night", not good bye, with their hands in a clinging grip. Their eyes held, but she didn't break down.

Now, she found herself rushing to the darkened kitchen to peek out the window from behind the curtain. It was like looking into a crystal ball. Rock was walking toward his Firebird; his raven hair smoothed back on the sides. He turned toward the lake as if to take one last look. What was he thinking, she wondered? Then he extended his right hand toward the sky, like a sign for hope.

Letting go was difficult for her. Yet she couldn't lose what she never really had. At least, she wasn't the loner she once was. Rock led her out of a cubbyhole. In fact, until meeting him, Gena saw only the obvious things. Now she was seeing the hidden things giving her a better concept of self.

Her mother and the Rabbi agreed she must move on. They were right. It was clear that Rock honored his marriage.

She watched the red Firebird disappear up the hill and into the night. "Oh Great Spirit, give him his dream. You are his conductor for greater things." Then she turned away.

Chapter Sixty-One

One last look at the lake. Everything was quiet, fresh and clean like the end of a day with the promise of a brighter tomorrow. There was the Burke Gilman trail. Memories of jogging with Unali flashed before him. His eyes watered. He reached out to grab the memories only to hold air. Rock turned away and climbed into his car.

Steering single-handedly up the hill toward Lake City, he rubbed his chin in meditation over his visit with Unali. She was a strong lady. Nothing seemed to get her down for long. Whereas, Sheryl was flighty with a bounce and an unpredictability that attracted him. He also believed Sheryl really needed him.

He must need her too, because it hadn't occurred until now how lost he'd have been during the oral argument without her. Judge Dodson only allowed him five minutes to prepare a seven-minute rebuttal. Five minutes. Then when the seven-minute rebuttal started, Perkins jumped up with all sorts of distractions.

Meanwhile, Sheryl flipped through Rock's three-volume motion to locate certain exhibits. She marked the exhibits with stickers and slipped the exhibits toward him. That's how he got through the rebuttal. Her familiarity with his motion revealed an amazing fighter, someone who deeply cared in spite of her hatred for the case. This mattered to him more than all her schemes.

Rock gripped the steering wheel at the realization that many forces in his life taught him to grow upward straight as an arrow, be strong as the wind and above all, be honest. Honest? How fragile the word. Even he couldn't comprehend what it truly meant to mankind. But, he'd still try to follow his principles, survive and start over. The entire ordeal sharpened his wits. Injustices are a part of living in and out of the courtroom. This must be what Efrem meant when he said all is fair in life, love and litigation. Thus, wallowing in a sea of self-pity was futile.

Also, while thinking back in time, his dad was right about him being rustic as winter, gullible as an autumn leaf in a strong wind and compassionate as summer. All three got him into trouble. Nevertheless, his rustic, gullible and compassionate nature also made him into sterner stuff.

And, the answer to Leucojum's warning about capturing his special song finally came to him. Only through his own dreams could he be successful. Not through the dreams of any Carpers.

From all this chaos, he had to plan for the future based on the past and present, the good and the bad. Upon entering the ramp to I-5, his stomach felt more settled than it had been in years. Grabbing the antacid bottle from the seat, he flung it over his shoulder into the back seat. "I don't need you anymore."

His heart was gladdened that Sheryl wanted him back. He never truly got over her. It was all the good years they had together. Years that couldn't be erased. She gave him a fine son. His thoughts turned to Unali and decided his love for her was an extension of his love for Sheryl. Unali and the truth had set him free. Now, he felt better prepared for the future. What was it Unali said, something about the battle belongs to his Spirit. Yes, only then could his losses become gains, open new doors to new strengths and further discoveries.

All the red taillights lining the freeway ahead of him lit the night like a Christmas tree. He pumped the brakes to slow his speed, not caring how long it might take to reach the apartment. He believed he was on the road to finding happiness not enjoyed before. It gave him the urge to sing. "Gv ge yu a, heh yu." I'm awake and on the totem pole." Being on top of the totem wasn't really all that important anymore. Rather, it was the old feelings of achievement and honor seeping into his soul.

No matter the attempt, no judicial system can alter a man's honor in the Great Spirit's eyes. He felt he proved he was the better man in the Carper litigation.

EPILOGUE

Rock Carper returns to Seattle following a work-oriented trip in Arizona and a few days visiting Cherokee relatives in Tahlequah, Oklahoma. He starts a new life with Sheryl, when legal representatives put pressure on him to pay the judgment sanctions.

Because his opposition goes after the Leucojum house, Rock is forced back into the litigation, representing himself pro-se at the trial court, appellate court, bankruptcy court and supreme court.

Read *Earthwalk Two* containing more courtroom drama, bankruptcy, romance, conflicts with attorneys and comedy. Suspense is added after Rock's life is threatened. The reader will finally meet Rock's boss and his 91-year old friend, both of whom provide unexpected surprises.